# SHIFTERS AND GLYPHS

FAIRY TALES OF THE MAGICORUM • BOOK 2

# CHRISTINA BAUER

First Published by Monster House Books, LLC in 2018
Monster House Books, LLC
34 Chandler Place Newton, MA 02464
www.monsterhousebooks.com

ISBN ePub: 9781945723124
ISBN Print: 9781945723131

# CHAPTER ONE

I'm a teenager who can wield magic, so you might think my ultimate in fun would be casting a spell.

*Not really.*

Plus, I live in Manhattan and—since my aunties no longer have me locked me up in a penthouse—you'd imagine that I love roaming the city.

*Nope.*

I'm also a werewolf, so racing under the moon could be my fave for fun.

*It's not.*

Instead, my ultimate smile comes from what's happening right now: snuggling on the couch with my boyfriend Knox. To be specific, Knox and I are wrapped in a blanket with my head resting against his right bicep.

*Perfect.*

It's almost time for dinner, but I hardly notice my stomach growl. Knox is in jeans and a T-shirt; I'm sporting what I call my unshreddable outfit: black leather pants and a cropped top that I got from the fairies. Why unshreddable, you ask? Because before I got my enchanted clothing, shifting into my were form was murder on my wardrobe.

Cute outfit? Check.

Shift to werewolf? Fine.

Return to being human? I'd be buck naked and my nice outfit would be nothing but scraps of fabric.

Now, I have my magically enhanced outfit, and it's all good. I never again have to worry about turning into a wolf and then into a very naked girl, all in the age of camera phones. And without that worry hanging over my head, I can more fully relax. Like I am now.

In fact, at this very moment, Knox and I are chilling out while watching an old movie called *The Breakfast Club*. In it, a bunch of human kids get detention at high school. For me, this particular movie is valuable life research, considering how tomorrow's my first day in a typical classroom.

That's right. My first day of school.

Ever.

On screen, most of the action takes place in a library. The place looks as large as the Metropolitan Museum of Art. I sniff. "You think our high school will be like that?"

Knox leans in to kiss the top of my head. "Like what?"

"All that space for like six people. Plus, they're in the library, right? I think there should be other kids around studying or whatever."

Not that I know these things from personal experience. Growing up, my aunties always home-schooled me. But come morning, I start senior year at West Lake Prep, a high school for other Magicorum kids like me. In other words, for shifters, fairies, and witches/warlocks. I'm unusual in that I can wield all three types of magic. Recently, I found out that makes me a kind of magic-user called a Trilorum. Go me.

"This must be one of those Hollywood schools," says Knox. "I mean, they take six bad kids and put them in a room without anyone to watch them. That's a crock."

"Right?" All of a sudden, this story seems very unfair. "They should be more careful. Maybe there are other kids out there like me, who need honest representations of high school for life research."

"There's no one like you," says Knox gently. "And I mean it in a good way."

I cuddle back onto Knox's bicep and smile. He's being sweet, but I'm not all that special. In fact, I'm pretty typical for Magicorum (well, apart from the Trilorum part of it). Why? Like all Magicorum, I live by a fairy tale life template.

Sleeping Beauty.

For starters, I look the part, what with my slim build, brown hair, and blue eyes. Plus, I've got three fae aunties as well as an odd friendship with Colonel Mallory the Magnificent, a super-powerful fairy dragon shifter who cursed me with a sleeping sickness for the first seventeen years of my life. Not that I'm complaining. The Colonel did it for my own good—his sleeping curse hid my triple-magic from people who wanted to kill me and steal my powers—but I still used to fall asleep at odd times.

School wasn't an option before.

But that's all over now. These days when I fall asleep, it's mostly at night. Sure, I take the occasional catnap during the day, but my eyes are closed like a normal person. This is a lot better than what used to happen, which involved me freezing like a statue and staring off into space like a nutjob.

Needless to say, I'm glad the curse is over.

As an extra bonus, ending the curse also released my fairy, shifter, and witch powers. The next step? Master that magic by attending West Lake Prep. As a bonus, I'll learn typical human stuff, too, like math, science, and literature.

It's all super-exciting.

And totally terrifying.

At least Knox is also attending West Lake, along with our best friends, Elle and Alec. Even so, every time I think about school, my insides knot up. So I actively avoid more thoughts of West Lake by focusing on the movie. Specifically, I've been following one of the characters, John Bender, a broody guy who reminds me of Knox. Honestly, I'm not watching the movie as much as waiting to see what Knox-Bender will say next. I drum my fingers on the comforter, ready and waiting.

Sure enough, Bender's character mouths off to the school principal. "Does Barry Manilow know that you raid his wardrobe?" True fact: my auntie Mirabelle loves the musical stylings of Barry Manilow, so I happen to know that if you adore polyester leisure suits, then Barry Manilow is your guy.

I snort-laugh. *Does Barry Manilow know that you raid his wardrobe?* Perfect.

*"That man reminds me of our mate,"* says my wolf.

*"That he does,"* I reply in my head.

Now, most shifters can only sense the moods of their inner animal, like if their wolf is happy or sad. But I have mental conversations with my animal, which requires major levels of power. With magic disappearing from the world, that's a rare skill.

I can always block my wolf out, but she likes to watch movies as much as I do. And how she just called Knox my "mate"? Even though I'm seventeen and Knox is eighteen, we're mates. To shifters, that means your soul has found its other half, which is awesome. In my case, my other half is over six feet tall with black hair, sharp bone structure, ice-blue eyes, and a protective streak a mile wide.

I'm one lucky werewolf.

Speaking of Knox, he tightens his arm around my waist. "You were laughing again."

"That bit about Barry Manilow." I bite my knuckle to stop giggling. "That's absolutely something you'd say."

"I'd say something like that? Nah."

*Wow.* I can't believe he's fighting the obvious. "Yesterday, you asked Alec if he got his clothes from Preppies R Us." As a powerful warlock, Alec also lives his life by a fairy tale life template. In Alec's case, that template is Prince Charming. Alec sure looks the part, too, what with his blond hair, blue eyes, and winning smile. And yes, Alec dresses like he fell out of the Preppy Catalog.

"Oh, that." Knox's voice is a deep rumble. "I said Alec dresses like Biff McPreppy. But that was only one time I sounded like this Bender guy. Once."

"Once? What about last week? At Lucky's, that werewolf Rich challenged you." Lucky's is a shifter bar in Brooklyn. Knox and I don't typically hang out in bars, but Lucky's is where Knox's guardian Azizi lives.

"Yeah," says Knox slowly. "I remember that were. He wanted to prove he's the best fighter. Not sure how that makes me like Bender."

I shake my head. "At Lucky's, you said another line from the movie. Remember when Bender was talking to the principal…and that guy's name happens to be Richard, too, just like the were at Lucky's?"

"Oh, I remember that part." Knox's shoulders shake with a held-in laugh. "Bender calls him a dick."

I clear my throat. "Bender says and I quote: '*Uh, DICK? Excuse me, Rich.*' You said that at Lucky's. Word for word." It was hilarious, too, since the shifter in question was being a total jerk. Knox didn't want to fight him, but the other were wouldn't back off. Dick-Rich ended up with a broken nose.

"Well," says Knox. "Rich *is* that werewolf's name."

My head is still curled into Knox's bicep, so I can't see Knox's face. There's no missing the smile in his voice, though. "You might have a point," he says. "Maybe I'm a *little* like this Bender guy."

"Nope." I look up, catch his gaze, and grin. "You're way better."

"*Correction,*" says my wolf inside my mind. "*He's the best.*"

"*I agree.*"

"You spoil me, Bry." Knox kisses the top of my head, and we go back to snuggling. Within a few minutes, the movie winds down. On screen, all the kids from detention go outside to get picked up.

The sight makes my breath hitch.

Remember how I was avoiding the fact that school starts tomorrow? All of a sudden, there's no avoiding this reality. Why? In the movie, the kids leave detention by getting into cars driven by someone else.

Their parents.

I've never met my mother and father. I don't even know their names. The closest I have to parents are my three fairy aunties, and they're pretty much evil. What else would you call people who raised me to be a zombie bride for Jules, an evil Denarii mummy-king who started off life as none other than the real Julius Caesar? The good news is that my aunties' plan flopped and all their magic got drained. Now my aunties spend their days hiding out in a fairy shantytown hidden under a boulder in Central Park.

Living under a rock. Sounds about right.

Knox inhales deeply, checking my scent. Weres can tell a lot about someone by catching their smell. "What's wrong, Bry? You thinking about those dreams of yours again?"

I've always been plagued by weird dreams. Time was, those dreams were about ancient Egypt and translating papyri. Lately, I can't remember them at all when I wake up. I'm just left with this uneasy feeling.

Honestly, I've been waking up wide-eyed, sweaty, and totally terrified.

When I open my eyes each morning, my pulse is racing. I'm shivering with fear. And I have absolutely no memory of what scared me so much.

"No," I say slowly. "It's not my dreams." *For once.*

Knox leans in to whisper softly in my ear. "What is it, Bry? You can tell me anything."

I squirm under the comforter. Not sure why the true answer is hard to share, but it is. "Everyone in the movie has someone to pick them up."

"And we don't, is that it?"

I nod, not trusting my voice to reply. All my life, I've searched for my parents. There's no trace of them. After I left my aunties, I thought it might be different. After all, Lauralei, Fanna, and Mirabelle could've been using magic to hide my family for some reason. But after lots of checking around—in other words, hacking into secret systems with Elle—I haven't been able to find out anything new.

"I get you about the family stuff," says Knox.

*And he does.*

Knox's parents were killed by the Denarii. Sure, he has Azizi, but Az isn't really a "drop you off at school" kind of guardian. Azizi was the warden of all shifter magic, meaning he used to be the most powerful shifter on the planet. Now, Knox has both the job and the power.

Thinking about Knox and his wolf puts everything in perspective. After his parents were killed, Knox spent years racing around the world, hunting down evil Denarii as a way to avenge their deaths. My poor mate.

I take in a deep breath. "You know what? Everything will be fine."

"Are you about to give a pep talk now?" asks Knox. I'm well known for my pep talks—mostly because they're either really great or totally dismal. Either way, it's always something to remember.

*That said, my next talk will be awesome. No question about it.*

"Yup," I say with confidence. "Prepare for some serious pep."

"Let's hear it."

"Well, to start with, magic is disappearing from the world. Sure, you and I have a ton of it and most Magicorum kids have next to none, but that won't be a big deal to everyone else at school. High school kids are well known for being mature."

I wince. That wasn't my best argument. Shaking my head, I keep going. *My next bit will be absolutely stunning.*

"And yes," I continue, "we've had different life experiences from most kids. I was almost force-married to a mummy-zombie king last summer. You spent most of your life hunting down Denarii, but the other kids won't care. And the whole parent thing? It definitely won't hurt like hell to see everyone else with a mom and dad all the time. Only in the beginning." By the time I finish my speech, my eyes are prickling with tears.

"Is that it?" asks Knox softly.

"Not one of my best talks, huh?"

Knox sits up and slides me onto his lap. His six-foot tall frame and heavy arms wrap around my shoulders. "Remember what Azizi always says about relatives?"

"Sure." My voice comes out all dull and lifeless. "There's your family of chance and your family of choice."

"That's right. And I choose you. We're mates. That's forever." He rubs my arm up and down in a soothing motion. Closing my eyes, I lean into our embrace. Knox's scent of sandalwood and musk surrounds me. Hugging Knox always makes the world feel safe and comforting.

I blink back my tears. "Most people never find the other half of their soul. We're lucky." Looking up, I scan the familiar features of Knox's face. Loose black hair. Scar on his brow and chin. Sharp bone structure. Ice-blue eyes.

My mate.

"We're a team." Knox's full mouth quirks with a grin. "Don't forget, Elle and Alec care about you, too. Alec's parents are putting a computer workstation into West Lake Prep for you. They even found you some new papyri. That way, you can keep translating, only now it won't just be a hobby. You'll get class credit."

"That's really nice of them."

Which is true. Setting me up with a workstation is a cool thing for Lydia and Nixon Le Charme to do. Even so, just thinking about Alec's parents makes me fidget. They are too smart, too beautiful, and too totally obsessed with me translating the papyri that make up the *Book of Isis*. In fact, Alec's parents remind me a little of the Denarii. Those zombie mummies were all killer instinct wrapped in 1950's style perfection and odd obsessions.

"But…" prompts Knox. He can always tell when I'm holding back.

"Don't get me wrong," I say. "It's really nice of Alec's parents and all. But they must have their reasons."

Knox sighs. "True."

I don't need to say anything more; Knox knows what I mean. While Knox is the warden of magic for shifters, Alec is the warden for witches and warlocks. Wardens have a responsibility to find, guard, and activate the fountain of all magic, which has been hidden for thousands of years. No one knows why. If the wardens don't take care of the fountain, then they can't marry without magic killing their spouse. It's the system's way of keeping them focused on what's important: the fountain.

8

Talk about a motivating factor.

Closing his eyes, Knox tilts his head. I've seen that move before. My mate is having an inner conversation with his own wolf. I take Knox's hand in mine. "Your wolf is talking to you, isn't he?"

Knox opens his eyes. Lines of worry tighten across his face. "More like howling. He's hurting. Says he feels like he's on fire." He scrubs his hands over his face. "My wolf is always unpredictable this time of year, but not like this."

"Why would this time of year affect him?" Knox and I have only been dating for a few months. Before that I was locked up by my aunties. Long story short, I'm constantly learning new stuff about shifter culture.

"The fall equinox is coming up," explains Knox. "It's always rough on wardens. No one knows why, though. Not even Az."

"Autumnal equinox." The words rattle around my brain. I rise and pace a line by the couch, my mind churning at double speed.

Knox has seen this routine from me before. "You getting something, Bry?" And by something, Knox means an idea on my papyri translations.

Here's what's going on. For as long as I can remember, I've had dreams of Ancient Egypt and papyri. Wardens like Knox and Alec can't get married until the fountain of magic is found. And the location of that mysterious fountain? It's listed in the *Book of Isis*, which is currently just a bunch of papyrus scraps. For some reason, I'm the only one who's had any real luck assembling them. And now, the words *autumnal equinox* are making me picture my old translations in a new way.

"I just translated something about this." Turning on my heel, I speed over to my workroom. It used to be one of Knox's extra bedrooms. That is, until he fixed it up for me with a mega-computer, monitor, and cloud storage. Now I can get at my papyri scans from anywhere. After rushing into the room, I fire up the system, grab my mouse, and start sifting through old translations. Knox moves to stand behind me, resting his hand on my shoulder.

Minutes pass. So much staring at a screen makes my inner animal restless. "*We hates computers,*" she grumbles.

For the record, when my wolf gets grouchy, she starts talking like Gollum.

*"It'll only be a minute,"* I reply in my mind.

*"But you always say that and it's a lie."*

*"Not this time."* I tap the screen with my pointer finger and look over my shoulder at Knox. "Here's the section I was looking for."

Knox leans over my shoulder. He and Alec have translated their share of papyri over the years, so it's no problem for my mate to translate these glyphs.

*Once every five thousand years, the fountain shall rise.*

Knox frowns. "But you translated that a week ago. Where's the equinox part?"

"Here." I tap on a new section and read the translation aloud.

*Look to the crossing of the sun and earth.*

"The next part is all smudged out," I continue. "However, the next glyphs clearly say something about *twice a year*. I bet they're talking about the fall and spring equinoxes."

"I think you're onto something." Knox keeps reading.

*The fountain shall be born at one crossing, and then shall begin to give its bounty at the second.*

Knox winces. "Born? That's an odd way to put it. It takes eons for fountains to form."

"Not always. Sometimes geysers erupt out of nowhere." Over the years, I've become a self-taught expert on fountains. Personally, I believe that the fountain of magic is actually a geyser. Those erupt on a schedule, and the fountain of magic only "gives its bounty" once every five thousand years.

Definitely a geyser.

"Makes sense." Now it's Knox's turn to tap the screen. "Next, it lists a bunch of numbers." Knox squints at the screen. "Those are dates."

"Yes, those are all around the time when the first pyramids in Egypt were designed."

"Or," Knox says slowly. "Those dates could refer to the equinox stuff."

I lean back in my chair. Knox's words rattle around my head. "You're right. The fountain first went off five thousand years ago." The chill on my neck creeps down my spine. Something about all this sets off my sense of danger.

"And it says the fountain activates once every five thousand years. In that case, it's due to go off again and in five days, no less. That must be why my wolf is hurting."

My insides twist with worry. Knox is supposed to find, guard, and activate that fountain. What will happen if he doesn't?

"We could be wrong, you know." I glance at Knox over my shoulder. "What about Alec? Are things worse for him this year, too?"

"Good question." Knox pulls his cell out of his pocket and makes a call. "Hey, it's me. Have your spells gone nuts with this equinox?"

In case you're wondering, most of Knox's calls to Alec begin with *hey it's me* followed by some kind of demand.

A pause follows before Knox speaks again. "Look, man. I know all magic is weird lately, but your spells always go to *extra crap* around the fall equinox. What I want to know is this—is it any worse this year compared to last year?" Another pause. "So, worse. And are you in any pain?" Knox rolls his eyes. "Nice." He hangs up.

"What did Alec say?"

"He says his spells are definitely worse this year compared to last year. But he's not in any pain. And I should stop worrying about him because I'm not his nana."

I can't help but smile. "That's so Alec." My moment of happiness soon evaporates as I think through our new discoveries. "I don't like this."

"What part? The papyri or Alec's big mouth?"

"You know what I mean. Being a warden with the fountain about to go off." I twist around in the roller chair so I can face Knox directly. "We should talk to Az."

"Yeah. I promised to stop by after school tomorrow. We'll head over together."

I rub my forehead, thinking all this through. If only we knew all the secrets from the *Book of Isis*. All of a sudden, the pressure to translate that book presses in around me, tight as a vise. I slump forward in my chair. When I speak again, my voice is a hoarse whisper. "What if I can't do it? What if I don't translate the *Book of Isis* and...everything goes to hell?"

Knox kneels before me. His ice-blue gaze turns intense. "I'm not worried about that, Bry. In thousands of years, no one came close to translating the *Book of Isis*. Until you. No question in my mind. You *will* do this."

The power of his faith in me makes my body feel boneless. Good thing I'm still sitting on a chair. "I don't know what to say."

"Say nothing. Just be you."

Little by little, Knox leans in to give me a kiss. His warm breath cascades over my lips. Our mouths are about to meet when the moment is shattered.

A police siren ringtone blares from Knox's cell phone. There's only one person who causes that particular ring: Knox's ex-girlfriend, Ty. Pronounced Tea—like the drink—and spelled Ty. She's a real piece of work.

"Damn," Knox growls. "Alec just put another blocking spell on this thing to keep her away. How'd she break through?"

Ty is not only Knox's ex, she's also a powerful sorceress. For years, Alec's spells blocked her. But now? No matter what Alec casts, Ty can eventually get her call through. It's not just Ty, though. Word is that everyone's magic has been going haywire lately.

*"Let's go find this Ty,"* grumbles my inner wolf. *"Then we bite her face off."*

*"We don't bite faces."*

*"But this is for our mate."*

12

"*Knox wants us to stay out of it. We need to respect that.*"

My wolf says something that sounds like *grumble-grumble-mate-grumble-grumble-bite-grumble-grumble-Ty*. Point taken.

For the record, my wolf and I had our differences over the summer, mostly because she was just released from a super-long sleeping curse. Since then, I've learned how to give her some structure through my inner magic. Mostly, the process involves calming her down with my shifter powers and—in case of a true emergency—putting her in a stasis. That's like sleep, only my wolf won't dream or anything. Again, that's super-rare. Most times, my wolf and I get along pretty well.

Knox pushes some buttons on his phone, but the siren's wail doesn't end. "I have to take this, Bry. It won't stop otherwise."

"That's fine. I get it."

I twist back around in my swivel chair; Knox goes to stand by the door. "What, Ty?" A short pause follows before Knox speaks again. "I don't care what magical junk you found this time. It's over between us. You get that? Over." Knox chucks his phone against the wall. It shatters into a hundred pieces. *That would be over, all right.*

When Knox turns to face me, his eyes glow with golden light. "I need a run."

And in this case, *run* doesn't mean through Central Park. Knox wants to ride his Harley, reach his land in the Adirondacks, shift into wolf form, and race through the night.

Knox rakes his hands through his loose black hair. "Want to join me?"

Inside my soul, my inner wolf lets out a yawn. "*We ran this morning,*" she says in my head. "*Let's go back to our den and rest.*" And by *den*, she means our apartment, which happens to be in this same building as Knox's, only two floors down from here.

"*Are you sure?*" I ask in my mind. "*You're always up for a run.*"

"*We'll see many fae in the morning. I need my strength so I can play with them.*"

My heart sinks. Unfortunately, my wolf sees fairies as fast-moving chew toys, which is totally dangerous. The fae are crazy.

*Ugh.* Between my wolf and the fairies, I'll have my work cut out for me tomorrow.

"Thanks for the offer," I say. "But it's a school night. I should get some sleep." *Or try to, anyway.*

A shiver of dread rolls across my shoulders. Fast as a heartbeat, Knox kneels before me. "What's wrong? I can scent your fear."

"I don't know." My voice comes out high-pitched and wispy. "Something about sleep... Dreams."

"You said you haven't gotten more night visions about papyri. Are you sure about that?"

"No, there are no papyri." Closing my eyes, I try to focus on my latest dreams. Fear ricochets through my system, making me clutch my elbows. It's those terrible nightmares. I know it. I grasp for the memories, but they stay just out of reach. What have I been seeing?

"Think hard, Bry. I know you can do it."

"There's something about shadows and..." The memory vanishes entirely. Searing bright flashes of white appear in my mind's eye. An odd chill crawls over my skin. Is magic at work and erasing my memories...or am I just stressed out about school? Why can't I remember my dreams?

"This isn't good." Knox scowls. "You're frightened and you don't know why. I'm not going for a run. Come to think of it, you should stay here at my place tonight."

Which I definitely could do, considering how Knox has a ton of bedrooms. Still, we've only been dating a few months. There's no way I'm ready for the whole sleepover thing.

"It's fine. I'll stay tonight at my place."

"Then I'm inviting myself over to sleep on your couch."

I shake my head. "Go run. That's an all-night activity, and we both know it." Knox sneaks a look at the door. His ex-girlfriend always gets his wolf up.

"You know you need to go," I add.

Knox shakes his head. "I won't leave you like this." The muscle along his jaw is positively jumping with anxiety.

I pull my cell out of my pocket. "Take this. I'll call you from Elle's phone if anything goes wrong." We've done this before. As long as Knox stays within a few miles of the phone, his wolf hearing can make out the ringtones just fine. I press the cell into his hands. "Run." When I speak again, I make sure to use a playful tone. "I can protect myself, remember? In fact, I saved your handsome butt from Jules."

*All of which is true.*

Knox stares at the phone for a long moment before slipping it into his pocket. That means one thing: he's going for a run. I exhale.

"You'll call me if anything bad happens, yeah?"

"I swear it."

"In that case, I'll go." Knox brushes a gentle kiss across my lips. The press of his mouth makes my stomach do flip-flops.

*Hmm. Maybe staying here isn't a bad idea.*

I push against his shoulder. "Get ready before I change my mind."

"As my mate demands." Knox steps around his apartment, gathering up his bike helmet, wallet, and other stuff. He'll also change his outfit to be more road compatible. The good news is that Knox's jaw isn't twitching anymore, which is a good sign. In fact, now that he's heading out for a run, Knox seems far more relaxed in general. Meanwhile, my nervous system goes haywire. The reason? What I said before.

*I swear it.*

When I make a promise, I do everything I can to keep it. Something tells that this time? That just may not be possible.

# CHAPTER TWO

Knox says he's heading out. Even so, my mate insists on walking me to my door first. *So cute.* Soon Knox and I are strolling down a long white hallway lined with silver doors. Having left Knox's place behind, we've now migrated two floors down to the twenty-seventh level of Le Charme Towers, where we pause before my door, 24-G.

On reflex, I type the first of many security codes into a small black wall panel. Alec put a ton of magical wards on our place, but I don't need to worry about those. Alec's spells only activate when they detect a stranger. If there *is* trouble, the wards then launch some pretty typical guarding spells: humans can't see our door, anyone with magic feels the need to run in terror, that kind of thing.

As I enter in my third code—did I mention that Elle and I are a little safety conscious?—Knox leans in to whisper in my ear.

"I don't have to run, you know." His voice is a low growl that I like quite a lot. "I can still sleep on the couch."

I elbow him playfully in his rock-hard stomach. "Didn't we have this conversation already?"

"Maybe." More growling. More liking.

*"Our mate needs to run,"* says my wolf inside my head. *"That Ty is bad news."*

"Agreed."

Twisting around, I give Knox a quick peck on the nose. "Get out of here."

"You'll get Elle's cell and keep it handy, yeah?"

I roll my eyes. Knox already reminded me about the phone twice in the elevator. "Yes, yes, YES. Now ride safely."

"Always." Knox saunters off down the hallway. Since he's riding his Harley, my mate's changed into his leathers, and wow, those pants fit his backside quite well. Knox gets halfway to the elevator before he stops and turns around. "You staring at my butt?"

My face burns red. "Ummm…yeah?"

"Good." After giving me a wink, Knox steps into the elevator. The doors close with a *ding*, which means that—sadly enough—what I like to think of as the Knox Show is now over. I return my attention to my front door, finish off the last security code, and pull on the handle.

The minute I step inside, I hear the familiar grunts, clicks, and overblown music that means video games are blaring in the living room. Alec and Elle are playing again. My wolf-sharp sense of smell picks up the scent of Chinese takeout from the kitchen. Yum.

With all the deliciousness, my inner wolf is no longer ready for sleep. *"Food, food, FOOOOOD!"* she cries in my mind. *"Let's eat!"*

My wolf brings up a good point. There's deliciousness in the kitchen, and Elle in the living room. Which one do I approach first?

Tough call.

Shaking my head, I head off to the living room. It's a key routine that I always check in with Elle when I first get home. This is another one of our security things. Ever notice how in horror movies, someone (let's call her BDS because she'll Be Dead Soon) gets home and starts talking to her roommate without actually making eye contact? You know those scenes. Little Miss BDS chats on for like ten minutes from the kitchen:

*"You won't believe my day."*
*"Sheesh, who dumped out all our knives?"*
*"What's all this red stuff on the kitchen floor?"*

Meanwhile, as the BDS chatters on, her roommate is dead in the bathroom or something. Worst of all, there's a big bad lurking just outside the kitchen, waiting to kill her dumb butt. Maybe Elle and I have watched too many scary films, but we've sworn that we'll never end up a BDS. We always make eye contact and say hello right after walking through the door. It may be an overly elaborate security system, but I had an evil zombie king after me. Plus, Elle is a semi-pro con artist and jewel thief. Let's just say we both have reasons to be paranoid.

All of which is why the moment I close the front door, I make a beeline for our living-room-slash-gaming-area. Like the rest of our place, the living room's modern in style with leather couches and blocky shelves. All Le Charme apartments come pre-furnished, so it's not like we picked this stuff out. Long story short, Elle and I live inside the equivalent of an Ikea catalog. No complaints though—I like Swedish design. Plus, growing up, my aunties had our penthouse done up like a psychedelic drug den from the 1960's. I'm surprised all the bright colors didn't burn out my retinas by age nine. Ikea is just fine, thank you very much.

Sure enough, once I enter the living room, I find Elle and Alec camped out on our couch, pounding away on their keyboards. The backs of their heads are silhouetted against the flickering screen.

"Hey, guys," I say.

Moving in unison, Elle and Alec hit Pause on the game, shift on the couch, and look over at me. I hate to admit it, but that move sends a little pang of jealousy through my stomach. While I've been spending more time with Knox, Elle has been doing the same with Alec. Unfortunately, Elle and Alec can only be friends. The reasons are a little sketchy, but it has something to do with keeping Elle safe from her evil stepfamily. Even so, Elle and Alec have become crazy-good buddies. I mean, Elle and I never moved in unison like that.

Hence, the jealousy.

And then, there follows boatloads of guilt over being jealous.

*Ugh.* Relationships are tough.

"Hey," says Elle. "You have a visitor in the kitchen." She bobs her eyebrows, meaning this is a visitor of the significant variety.

"I do?" My first thought goes to our supposedly perfect security system. "How did they get through the wards?"

Sadly enough, Alec's wards have been on the fritz lately. Instead of repelling humans, they've been attracting them right into the apartment. Once inside, those hapless mortals often get compelled to do weird stuff. For instance, Elle and I came home the other day to find our doorman cleaning our toilet. Not that I don't appreciate the effort but... Whoa.

Alec shoots me a winning grin. "Believe it or not, my wards actually worked today." He really does look like a surfer-dude version of Prince Charming, what with his yellow T-shirt, tanned face, and bright blue eyes. "Your guest knocked on the door, we opened it, end of story."

I scrunch up my face in confusion. "Who do I know that knocks?" Alec uses magic to transport in and out. Knox likes to lean on the intercom and growl until I open up. Elle knows all the codes. That's pretty much my entire list of friends and family there.

Elle bobs her brows some more. "Your mysterious visitor is none other than Colonel Mallory the Magnificent."

"What?" I take a half step backward. "He's here?" They both nod. "You should have texted me."

Elle shrugs. "The Colonel said not to bother you." She lowers her voice. "Plus, we ordered the *good Chinese*, and he's been chowing down in the kitchen. The guy was so happy, I didn't want to disturb him."

I'd forgotten about the food smell. *The good Chinese* means we ordered from City Lights of Beijing. They have the best food in Manhattan, but unlike every other Chinese restaurant nearby, they take forever to deliver. So we save them for special occasions. I guess the night before school starting counts.

My stomach growls. "I'll go say hi and get some dinner."

"Sounds like a plan," says Alec.

"I want details later," adds Elle.

I roll my eyes, which is my way of saying, *Of course you're getting details later.*

Moving in unison once more, Elle and Alec return their attention to their game. Time was, all of us were terrified of Colonel Mallory. And why wouldn't we be? The Colonel had placed a sleeping curse on me. But a few months back, the Colonel was a huge help in the battle against Jules and his evil undead minions, the Denarii. And since then, the Colonel's been stopping by to visit every month or so. Mostly he uses fairy magic to transport in, but if the Colonel wants to use the door, there are no complaints here.

As I step toward the kitchen, my inner wolf howls with rage. *"No, no, no, no, no, NOOOOOOOOOO! No kitchen! That evil fairy cursed us both. I was trapped in a lockbox for years."*

*"Come on,"* I reply in my mind. *"You've met Colonel Mallory before."*

My wolf lets out a series of yippy-whining noises in my head. She can be a little bit of a drama queen sometimes. *"He cursed us."*

*"What are you, Gollum? The Colonel saved our lives."* My stomach growls again. *"Let's take a little breather here."*

My wolf sniffs. *"Fine. Talk to the evil fairy, but if you end up dead, don't say I didn't warn you."*

Sometimes, having a wolf in your brain is no fun. Time for a little magic. Closing my eyes, I tap into the golden power that makes me a shifter. This is one of the many new skills I learned from Az over the summer. That guy knows every shifter trick in the book. As I take control of the magic, a flush of gold mist moves across my skin. Shifter energy. Within seconds, my wolf quiets and goes into stasis. It doesn't hurt her, and it gives us both a break. With my wolf under control, I march toward the kitchen.

A snug white space, our kitchen holds a small number of appliances in one corner and a high-top table by the entrance archway. Colonel Mallory sits at the table, an array of white takeout boxes laid out before him. As always, he reminds me of the actor Clark

Gable from the movie *Gone With The Wind*. The Colonel even wears white suits with matching wide-brimmed hats. He looks up as I step into view.

"Hey now, if it isn't Bryar Rose."

"Hello, Colonel."

His silver eyes narrow. "Something about you keeps staying the same."

"It's my outfit." I gesture across my cropped top and dark pants. "Got these from the fairies. They don't shred when I shift." I raise my pointer finger. "And they're enchanted to clean themselves, too. Super handy."

"Enchanted clothing for shifters," says the Colonel. "Wish I'd thought of that." Using his chopsticks, he points to the array of white boxes. "Grab yourself some egg rolls. I know how your wolf likes them."

I slide onto the stool across from his. "She's in stasis right now, but I like egg rolls, too."

The Colonel pauses with his chopsticks halfway to his mouth and dripping with lo mein noodles. "Is your wolf still frightened of me, sugar?"

"She's not really scared. It's more the principle of the thing."

The Colonel sighs. This conversation always upsets him. "Your animal needs to understand. I simply had to hide your powers. Very few Magicorum can wield all three kinds of magic. You're one of the Trilorum, and that's very rare. Last one was recorded ages ago. But even with your magic locked up, Jules still found you. He was waiting until your powers got to their full extent on your seventeenth birthday, so he could, you know…"

"Try to kill me and eat my brains?"

"That. Even so, if he'd known how powerful you really were, Jules would never have waited. You'd have been too tempting a meal for him." The Colonel pokes at his white box of lo mein noodles. If I didn't know better, I'd think he was acting guilty about something.

The Colonel stops poking at his food, but he doesn't look up when he speaks. "Did Jules ever…well…say *anything* about me?"

*Correction.* The Colonel is *totally* acting guilty about something. And since that something seems to be Jules, I suddenly lose my appetite.

"No, Jules never mentioned you. Mostly, he pretended to be this loser Philpot who talked about money all the time." I set down my egg roll. "What's this about, Colonel?"

"Oh, Bryar Rose." The Colonel keeps right on staring into his lo mein box. It's like he's a million miles away, even though we're at the same table. "There's no way to begin."

I slip off the stool and step closer. "Try."

All of a sudden, the cabinet under the sink starts to shimmy. The small white doors look ready to snap off their hinges. Since all we keep under there are Windex and cockroach traps, I can't imagine what's up.

I point to the rattling doors. "Did you cast a spell there?"

My words snap the Colonel back to attention. Turning around, he spies the rattling doors and frowns. "Damned pixies. Crazy as March hares."

Pixies are literally pains in the neck, considering how they love to bite. I've only seen a few of them, and that was at the parties my aunties threw. Pixies are all small, angry creatures with speedy wings, green skin, and sharp teeth. Not sure why they'd want to hang out with my Windex and dead cockroaches.

"Let me get this straight." I say. "There are pixies under my sink?"

"No, sugar. There are pixies trying to use the doors under your sink in order to transport here from Faerie Lands."

"No way. We had this place warded again last week. I can't believe they're failing this fast."

"Sugar, right now your wards are as useful as wings on a toad. No offense to that Alec boy. But everyone's magic is off these days. Did you know I couldn't transport here before? I had to knock on the door like a regular so-and-so." He raises his arms. Silver fairy dust appears around his hands. "Let's just take care of this here pixie problem."

I blink hard, trying to process this news. "Because a portal from the Faerie Lands is opening up under my sink."

"Why not? If they have enough power, the fae can turn any regular door into a portal to Faerie."

"I didn't know that." I frown. "My aunties never went to Faerie."

"Ah, your aunties never had much in the way of power. Takes some strength to open a door." He shoots me a big smile. "I do it all the time, of course." More silver dust gathers around his arms, forming clouds of gray magic.

The door under the kitchen sink shimmies so violently, I'm surprised it doesn't burst. "Should I get Elle?"

"That would be a bad idea." In Colonel Mallory-speak, a *bad idea* is another way of saying *major catastrophe*. "We can handle this."

Anxiety tightens my limbs. I've fought the fae before. Most recently, I went against Queen Nyxa in a lingerie store. Long story. But it's never an easy battle. Fae are both powerful and unpredictable. The pair of little white doors under the sink rattles more violently than ever before.

Then they burst open.

Pixies fly into the room. At first, the cloud of green bodies makes me think, *This must be what a plague of locusts looks like.* Only, locusts don't have tiny humanoid forms, forest-green skin, or round heads that are filled with needle-sharp teeth. Also, locusts aren't known for having tiny, feathered wings that flutter at hummingbird-style speeds. And they certainly don't talk. As the pixies flood into the kitchen, the horde chants, "Elle, Elle! We want Elle!"

At this point, I have two choices. First, I could keep my wolf in stasis. That would mean she'd be definitely be asleep and therefore, unable to attack pixies. But that would also mean *she'd be asleep and unable to attack pixies.* My shifter power is the only one I have any real kind of control over.

No question about it. I'm going with door number two: waking up my wolf. I stir the shifter magic inside my soul. My inner animal perks right up.

*"Pixies!"* she cries. *"They want to play! Let's go furry and tackle them all."*

I tilt my head, considering this idea. It might work. *"Let's wait and see,"* I reply.

The cloud of pixies circles the kitchen a few times before rushing toward the exit archway. My heart sinks. No doubt about it; they're heading straight for Elle and the living room.

Colonel Mallory raises his arms and addresses the pixie horde. "Oh, no you don't." There's a growl to the Colonel's voice that's distinctly dragon-like, which makes sense, considering how a large black dragon is his shifter form.

*Interesting.* The Colonel feels as protective about Elle as I do.

Instantly, silver dust flies from the Colonel's hands to coat the room in a thin metallic sheen. Hundreds of small green bodies slam into an invisible barrier, stopping any chance of leaving the kitchen. The pixies grumble and pound on the clear wall, all while making lewd hand gestures. After a few seconds, they pick themselves up and take to the air once more. The horde hovers by the kitchen ceiling while glaring at me and the Colonel. Their chanting starts up again.

"Elle! Elle! We want Elle!"

Now, I knew Elle had some fairy magic. But she never got unwanted attention from random pixies before. Magic really is going haywire.

The Colonel crooks his finger at me. "Come over here, sugar."

"Are you sure we shouldn't warn Elle?"

"Positive. My magic blocks all sound. We need to keep Elle well and truly out of this. You just saunter yourself over and stand by me. I'll leverage an eentsy beentsy piece of your fae power, and this will all be over in a heartbeat."

One look at the enraged faces of the sharp-toothed pixies and I don't saunter over.

I run.

# CHAPTER THREE

Hundreds of pixies hover by my kitchen ceiling. A sense of menace pours off them in waves as their hummingbird-style wings drive a gentle breeze through the room. Too bad it smells of bubblegum and dumpster juice. The scent makes my inner wolf go nuts.

*"Bite, bite, bite!"* she cries in my soul. *"Me want bite!"*

For the record, it's never a good sign when my inner wolf starts talking like Cookie Monster.

I stand beside the Colonel. "Do you still need power?"

"A little boost would be welcome." The Colonel gets super-polite at the oddest times. "That still fine with you?"

Instead of replying, I grasp his right palm. The moment our hands touch, the fairy energy inside my soul goes berserk. In my mind, I picture the quicksilver strands as they spin and flow about each other in an elaborate whirl. It reminds me of a ball of yarn, only alive and glowing.

"Thanks, sugar." With those words, the spool of power unwinds inside me. As each thread becomes untangled, it disappears. No question where the power is going, either. A moment ago, only a thin layer of fairy dust surrounded the Colonel's left hand. Now, that haze grows heavier. Within a few seconds, it's impossible to see the Colonel's arm at all.

"Y'all need to go home now," announces the Colonel.

"No! No! We want Elle!" chant the pixies.

*You have to give it to them. The pixies have a goal here.*

"Last warning," adds the Colonel.

The chants of "Elle, Elle, we want Elle!" now turn deafening. Wincing, I set my left ear against my shoulder—since my left hand is still clasped with the Colonel's—and press my right palm against my right ear. It helps a little, but dang, those pixies can screech.

"Buh-bye," says the Colonel. He sets loose the power from his left hand. The fairy dust congeals in midair, taking the shape of a massive net. It reminds me of the kind for catching butterflies—the net had a little round O at its opening and a super-long sack behind. The big difference here? This butterfly net is large enough to catch an adult, is made of shiny silver fairy magic, and now hovers around my kitchen ceiling.

*Welcome to my world of weird.*

The Colonel snaps his fingers. The net swoops across the ceiling, scooping up all the pixies as it goes.

The Colonel grins. "Not too bad, considering how crazy magic has been." He turns to me. "Now, see those tiny sink doors that the pixies came though?"

"Hard to miss," I reply.

"You just hold them open while I send this here net through. After that, we'll be done with this entire business." He gives my hand a squeeze. "And thanks for the extra energy."

"No problem." I release his hand and head toward the kitchen sink. I'm not two steps away from the Colonel when it happens. All the fairy mist around the Colonel vanishes.

The net falls apart.

Large swaths of silver fabric waft to the ground.

My breath catches with fear.

*Uh-oh.* The pixies are free.

Even worse, the little monsters are angrier than ever. Their round green heads splotch red with rage. The pixies chatter away, mostly about how they still want to see Elle.

"Blast it all." The Colonel wipes his forehead with a white handkerchief. "I must have needed your power more than I thought."

What happens next takes seconds, but every fraction becomes embedded in my memory. Turning on his heel, the Colonel rushes to stand beneath the exit archway. Spinning around, he presses his hands against either side of the arch. His normally calm features wince with effort. Meanwhile, the pixies race toward the exit—and the Colonel—in a great blur of motion. I don't see individual faces so much as flashes of pointed teeth and tiny claws.

On reflex, I race toward the Colonel. My heart pounds so hard, I feel my pulse in my neck. Hundreds of pixies slam into both Colonel Mallory and the barrier that's keeping those little green buggers in the kitchen. The Colonel's invisible barrier bows under the force of the pixie attack, but it still holds. After that, the pixies go after Colonel Mallory instead. They bite into his arms and scratch his face. Blood drips down the Colonel's cheeks and seeps through the fabric of his white suit. The coppery scent of blood fills the air.

Rage corkscrews through my limbs. Colonel Mallory saved me. How dare they attack him? On reflex, I call upon my inner shifter power. Threads of golden light pulse through my soul. A haze of magic surrounds me.

After that, my wolf bursts out of my skin. The motion is instant and painless.

Before I know it, I'm all white fur and red fury. All conscious thought leaves my head, save for one idea.

*Stop the pixies.*

Leaping forward, I bite into pixie after pixie, flinging them off the Colonel. At the same time, my claws skewer even more of the little creatures and toss them away. In the process, I slam into cabinets and tear through the floor. Dishes crash from their shelves. Glasses shatter everywhere.

I'm having the time of my life.

In response to my attack, the pixies come up with a new plan.

They go after me instead.

Crap.

A heartbeat later, my fur is covered in tiny green pixies as they chomp into my skin, poke at my eyes, and generally hurt me all over. This isn't working. In my mind, I picture the Colonel's last spell—the magic net worked perfectly until it fell apart. Now, great sheets of enchanted fabric rest on the kitchen floor.

That just might be something I can work with.

Sure, I have no idea how to start up a fairy spell from scratch— that's what school is for—but this particular spell has already been started. All I need to do is finish it up. Plus, it's magic that was partly formed from my own energy.

I can fix it.

Absolutely.

Possibly.

Actually, I have no idea what my powers can do, but I'm getting chomped on by hundreds of little pixies, and those green monsters want to go after my best friend. I'm giving this all I've got.

In my heart, I call out to the strands of magic.

*Reform the spell. Send the pixies back to the Faerie Lands.*

Nothing happens. Except that I keep scraping off pixies from my fur, only to have them reattach a second later. Dang, these things are persistent.

Time to try another tactic. I call out to the magic inside me once more.

*We have to do this. For Elle. These pixies want to hurt her.*

For whatever reason, using Elle's name when calling upon my fairy magic gets a big response and fast. Instantly, a thick cloud of silver fairy dust appears around my fur. The pixies that were biting into me? They all cough and sputter under the new haze. After that, the little green creeps fall to the floor, gasping for breath.

Once my fur is cleared off, the silver mist leaves my body, turning into a compact orb of fae power. That fairy energy speeds over to the broken sheets of netting that lie in a neat pile on the kitchen floor. The ball of magic slams into the broken sheets, sending a great pouf of silver rising up from the floor tile. A second later, all the useless scraps reweave together, forming the mother of all butterfly nets.

*Perfect.*

Calling to my soul, I give another order to the fairy magic.

*Round them up. Send them back.*

The magic net now moves with lightning speed, scooping up pixies as it goes. The tiny creatures howl and bite, but it's no use. Soon the entire kitchen is pixie-free again. Next, the net slams straight through the doors under the kitchen sink, shattering the wood into a hundred little pieces. There's a flash of silver light as the net-o-pixies vanishes as well. Now that's what I call good magic.

I prance across the ruined kitchen floor, feeling mighty pleased with my wolfy self.

The Colonel straightens his wide-brimmed hat. The rest of him needs a lot more work to be back to normal, though. Scratches still mar the Colonel's face. Plus, his suit is all raggedy with tiny bite marks and blood. I scan my fur. I've got my own share of marks as well, but I'm too happy to care.

"That's my first time casting a fairy spell while in my wolf form." It's always a little tougher to talk in my wolf form, what with my extra teeth and all.

"Well done," says the Colonel.

My chest swells with pride, and I celebrate by mincing about in another circle. "Thank you."

"Since you did the hard work with the pixies, how about I clean up?" The Colonel doesn't wait for my reply. Lifting his arms, he summons a fresh cloud of fairy dust to appear around his palms. While twiddling his fingers, he issues a new command: "Make this better."

In response, the fairy dust zooms out from the Colonel's hands and fills the room. For a moment, it's as if there's a silver snowfall in my kitchen. The Colonel claps his hands, and the fairy snow disappears. The cleaning-up spell is over, and it certainly worked. My kitchen looks good as new. There are no broken glasses or shattered cabinets to be seen. Plus, the Colonel has returned to his normal state as well. His white suit is pristine once more. I can't see my fur, but I certainly feel healed as well. I'm guessing whatever marks the pixies left on me have disappeared too.

My inner wolf lets out a loud yawn. *"I'm ready for a nap,"* she says.

*"That's fine,"* I reply in my mind. *"You've earned it."*

Focusing on my shifter power, I will myself to return to human shape. This time, the change takes a little longer. Turns out, there's nothing like homicidal pixies to inspire you to change forms, fast. The magic hears my call. My bones realign. Claws and fangs disappear. Skin replaces fur. Overall, the experience doesn't hurt so much as tickle. Soon I'm back to my regular human shape, including my black pants, heavy boots, and cropped T.

Love the unshreddable outfit.

The Colonel eyes me from head to toe. "I can see why you like that fairy get-up. Unshreddable. I'll have to get me a suit like that." He shakes his head. "Nothing worse than shifting into a dragon, changing back, and having all your private business out there for the world to see."

"Yes," I say. "That's exactly how I felt." Most shifters are super-comfortable with nudity. I'm glad that the Colonel and I are both firm members of Camp Clothing.

"Where did you get that outfit anyway?" asks the Colonel.

"Queen Nyxa. She runs a secret store for fairies in Manhattan."

"Nyxa, huh?" The Colonel settles himself back onto a stool by our high top. "I'll have to pay her a visit. That one owes me a favor or two."

"She does?" There's no mistaking the shock in my voice.

"Everybody owes me something, sugar. That's why I'm me." The Colonel tears into an unopened box of food and smacks his lips. "Now, do you mind if I feast on this here cashew chicken?"

"Help yourself."

Using his chopsticks, the Colonel points to the open space across from him at the table. "Why don't you come set a spell with me? We need to talk." The *set a spell* thing is Colonel Mallory talk for *please sit down.*

Now, it may be that I just fought off hundreds of evil pixies in my own kitchen, but the way the Colonel says those words—we need to talk—it makes me feel like I'm heading into battle once more.

I slide onto the stool across from the Colonel and wait. My appetite is still firmly at zero. No matter. Whatever is coming up, I have a feeling it's not dinner conversation anyway.

# CHAPTER FOUR

For a long minute, I sit quietly at the table and try to soak in everything that happened. The Colonel and I just forced hundreds of pixies out of my kitchen and back to Faerie. Now, he's sitting at my table and enjoying his meal of cashew chicken.

*Well, okay then.*

Plus, we're about to have *a talk*. Let's not forget about that.

The last time we had one of our talks, the Colonel told me I was a rare kind of Magicorum called a Trilorum, meaning that I could wield all three types of magic. So I asked why I'd never heard of Trilorum before. The Colonel informed me that all other Trilorum had been killed long ago. Surprisingly, they weren't murdered by Jules, the egomaniac who wanted my brains for dinner. Nope, all other Trilorum had been killed by enterprising—and yet incredibly evil—witches and warlocks. It seems that, combined with a spell or two, dried-out Trilorum livers fix any ailment.

*Eew.*

Needless to say, that was an un-fun conversation.

I eye the exit archway to the living room. Maybe there's some way to get out of this chat before I learn something else that's both disturbing and disgusting.

The Colonel dabs the corners of his mouth with his handkerchief. "You'll never guess who I ran into the other day."

"Queen Nyxa?"

"No, not that old hag in a ball gown. Reggie."

On reflex, I pull on my ear. I must be mishearing things. "Reggie?"

"That's what I said."

"You mean, Reggie the guy who was alive with Julius Caesar, who then got made into an evil Denarii mummy-zombie, was then captured by Knox, lived in Alec's basement, and just escaped over the summer? The last Denarii alive? That Reggie?"

"That's the one. He sends his regards."

My skin prickles over with shock. "Reggie is crazy."

"As a bedbug. But he's very concerned about the fountain of magic."

I tilt my head, considering. "That's rather sane of him."

"Folks like you and me, we aren't alive solely because of magic. But Reggie? His every breath is thanks to magical energy. He's rather concerned that it stay safe and active."

"Why, is something threatening the fountain of magic?"

"That's what I'm here to find out."

I frown. "Last time you visited, you were heading off to the Faerie Lands. I thought you were staying there for a while."

"That's true, sugar. I got a little detoured from Faerie, but don't you worry. The fae are still expecting me. Seems I'm the only one who can stop the fae from going to war."

"War?"

"Is there an echo in here?" The Colonel winks. Somehow, the guy manages to be smooth, sarcastic, and hospitable, all at the same time. "Why, yes. *War*. But after I talked to sweet Reggie, I decided to put preventing massive bloodshed on hold and stop by here to see you." He points at me with his chopsticks. "And at great time and expense, I might add."

33

"Thank you." *I think.*

"Reggie told me you recently came by some papyri that concerned the equinox and First Wardens."

Whoa, Reggie knew? *The plot thickens...* "That's true," I say slowly, still processing this whole "Reggie" thing. "In fact, I was just looking at those sheets. They say the equinox is important. This year's autumn equinox is in five days."

The Colonel's silver gaze turns intense. "And?"

"According to the papyri, the fountain of magic is supposed to give its bounty next week right on the equinox." Saying those words makes my insides quiver. Knox is in pain because that equinox is getting closer. Shaking my head, I refocus on the conversation with the Colonel. "That will be the first time the fountain has gone off in five thousand years."

"Quite right." The Colonel sets aside his box of chicken. "Have you been getting any bad dreams, sugar?"

I stare at my hands. Talking about my nightmares feels way too personal for a chat with the Colonel. "I've always had dreams of Ancient Egypt and papyri. Knox was usually in them, too."

"That's not what I mean. I'm talking nightmares." The Colonel leans forward. "You *have* been having them, haven't you?"

There's no point lying to the Colonel. He can always tell when I try. "How did you know?"

"Tell me about them." The Colonel sets his palms flat on the tabletop. Every line of his body tells me that the way I answer this question is critical. Adrenaline pumps through my bloodstream. I hate feeling like there's something going on that I don't understand...and which can also make my life hell.

Unfortunately, that feeling happens a lot when the Colonel is around.

I steel my shoulders. "When it comes to my dreams," I say slowly, "I don't remember a thing about them."

The Colonel settles back onto his seat. "That's very good." Whatever answer the old fae was looking for, it seems I gave the right one. "Very good indeed."

"No, it's pretty frightening. I hate waking up terrified without knowing why."

"And I believe you." The Colonel picks up his chopsticks once more, then circles them by his ear in the motion for *I'm nuts*. "Don't pay me no mind. You know how we fae are."

"I do." *And fae are tricky.* I drum my fingers on the tabletop. The Colonel is hiding something, I know it. My mind sifts through everything he said tonight until I hit on one particular item. "You mentioned something about First Wardens before. What did you mean? I've never heard of them."

"First Wardens?" The Colonel stuffs an enormous amount of cashew chicken in his mouth, then motions across his lips with his chopsticks. It's a signal that means *I can't talk now*.

He's stalling.

It won't work.

I fold my arms over my chest. "I can wait."

The Colonel finally swallows his mega-bite of chicken and coughs. "Can you get me a glass of water, honey?"

"If I get it for you, will you answer my question?"

The Colonel smacks his lips. "You'll never let this drop, will you? Always so willful."

"*Always* so willful? I've had less than ten conversations with you my entire life. How do you know what I am?"

"Ten conversations. Is that so?" The Colonel chuckles. "Oh, I know plenty about you. Now get me that water, and I'll tell you all about the First Wardens."

I stomp over to the sink, fill up a glass, and head back over. The stomping part is a little childish, but I'm seventeen. I figure I'm allowed.

"So." I set the glass down before him. "The First Wardens."

The Colonel takes a long sip. "Well, when magic first came into the world, it was a doggone mess. Shifter, fae, and witch power—they all got mixed up. No one knew how to do anything."

"So they were all Trilorum?"

"Yes and no. The magic inside you is still in three separate groups of threads, as it were. Back then, magic was worse than that junk drawer where you and Elle keep stuffing all them wires into."

I lift my chin. "We're hackers. You never know when something will come in handy." I slide back onto my chair. "But I get what you mean. Magic was a total mess."

"Just so. And it stayed that way until the First Wardens. They built the first tools to separate out magic. That was pyramids, you know."

"You mean the ones in Egypt?"

"No, South America." The Colonel waves his hand dismissively. "Sadly, those ancient pyramids are long gone, so don't bother looking for them on a map." He goes back to eating his dinner. I give the Colonel all of two bites before I prompt him to start back up again.

"So," I say. "The First Wardens used the pyramids to focus magic into shifter, fae, and warlock. Then what happened?"

"For thousands of years, it all worked out fine. After that, everything changed. We don't know why, but the First Wardens decided that they needed to destroy magic."

"Destroy magic? How is that possible?"

"Well, it wasn't possible as it turns out. Their plan backfired. The First Wardens only ended up blowing up the fountain and the pyramids as well."

"That's terrible." Closing my eyes, I try to picture any reason why people would want to destroy magic. Nothing comes to mind. "Why would the First Wardens want to wipe out magic?"

The Colonel shrugs. "I can't say."

"Meaning you don't know," I say slowly. "Or you *do know*…but you won't tell me?"

The Colonel gives me the side-eye. "You gonna let me finish my story here?"

Now, when the Colonel cracks out his *you gonna let me finish my story* line, then there's no point pushing him any further. He'll say what he wants and that's it.

I drum my fingers on the tabletop. "I'm listening."

"Well, there was a second set of wardens," continues the Colonel. "They called themselves the Luxalta. They designed the pyramids in Egypt and tried to revive the fountain. They were a-hoping they wouldn't have to wait five thousand years for the fountain to give its bounty. Their spells didn't work, at least not when it came to bringing back the fountain. Other things they tried were more successful, though. In fact, they cast the spells that put those glyphs on your were-boy's back."

"His name is Knox." The Colonel is forever calling my mate *your were-boy*. For some reason, the Colonel believes that there's no guy in the universe good enough for me. Forgetting Knox's name is his way of saying that. For someone who put me under a curse, the Colonel can be oddly protective.

"Knox," repeats the Colonel. "Is that his name now?"

At this point, I'd remind the Colonel that I've told him Knox's name about four hundred times. Sadly, that would just derail the Colonel away from telling me more about the Luxalta wardens.

"Let's not talk about Knox right now." I force on a smile. "I really want to hear the rest of your story."

"If you insist. Well, them Luxalta wardens tried to get the whole pyramid setup to work like it did with the First Wardens. After all, the fountain begins to give bounty every five thousand years. There was a chance it could begin again, even after that catastrophe of the First Wardens trying to destroy magic. The Luxalta wardens designed the pyramids of Egypt. Unfortunately, those pyramids never helped anyone find the old fountain, let alone activate it."

I rub my neck, my eyes lost in thought. "The old fountain, was it a geyser that appeared between the three pyramids in South America?"

"You could say that." Which is the Colonel's way of saying that I'm partially right. The fae will never lie. That said, they find a ton of loopholes to avoid the truth. For some reason, the Colonel is holding back on me with this whole wardens story.

It could be that he has an ulterior motive.

It could also be that he just likes toying with mortals.

When it comes to fairies, you never know.

I shift my weight on my seat. "Let me ask you another way. The Luxalta wardens designed the pyramids in Ancient Egypt."

"True enough."

"Were they trying to get a geyser to show up between the pyramids?"

The Colonel purses his lips. "You could say that."

"Let's get one thing straight between us." Using my pointer and middle fingers, I gesture between the Colonel's eyes and mine. "These are non-answer answers. You're holding out on me and I know it."

"Of course you know it. You're my sweet girl and you're very, very clever." He wags his chopsticks in the air. "Now, where was I?"

Once again, I'm back to the truth that the Colonel won't say anything that he doesn't want to. So I decide to simply answer his question. "You were saying that the Luxalta wardens couldn't get the pyramids in Egypt to start up or activate the old fountain."

"Yes, that was it." The Colonel stares at me for a long moment. I know this look of his as well—the Colonel's debating whether or not to tell me something else. At length, he drops his chopsticks on to the table. "And that's the end of my story. Afraid I must be going."

"You can't mean that."

"The fae are going to war. I have my duties. It'll only be a day or two until I return. You'll be fine for that long."

My jaw falls open with shock. "You always say you'll return in a few days, and it always takes you weeks or months."

"If I could stay, believe me, I would. But I've got a war to deal with. Besides, Reggie will watch over you until I'm back."

My jaw-opening routine turns absolutely fishlike. I'm not only staring at the Colonel with my mouth open, I'm also periodically gulping at air like a guppy. "Reggie. You mean that psychopathic brain-eating mummy-zombie?"

"That's the one. He's smarter than he looks. Or acts. Just trust me."

Taking in a deep breath, I get ready to explain the dozen or so reasons why the Colonel's plan to leave me with Reggie is a loser. But before I can get out a single word, the Colonel raises his arms. Instantly the kitchen fills with a thick haze of fairy dust. A moment later, the silver cloud of fae power is gone.

The Colonel has disappeared as well. *Crud.*

I cup my hand by my mouth. "Colonel, I know you can hear me. Get back to the kitchen and finish our talk. I know you're holding out on me."

Instead of a reply from the Colonel, I hear raised voices echoing in from the living room. I set my hand on my throat.

*Elle!*

In all the excitement, I'd completely forgotten about Alec and my best friend. The Colonel had cast a protection spell to keep the pixies in the kitchen, but his magic had also fallen apart. What if some of those evil green buggers broke through? Tempting as it is to keep yelling for the Colonel, I must find out if Elle's okay.

Rushing out the exit archway, I hightail it for the living room. There, I find Elle and Alec seated on the couch with their backs to me. The two are still playing their game. Things look okay, but when your life involves magic, you never really know.

"Is everything all right?" I ask.

"Absolutely not," says Elle.

My chest constricts with worry. "What's wrong?"

"This loser right here." Elle glares at Alec. "He went into battle again without taking any healing potions to recover from the last fight."

"Potions." I let out a long breath. If that what she's worried about, then everything is totally fine.

The whole potions thing is an ongoing fight between these two, by the way. Alec hoards healing potions. He has like 500 at a time, and he refuses to use any of them. I don't blame Elle for getting irritated. She has to cast healing spells on his hoarding butt.

Did I mention that it's lovely to be worrying about things like video games instead of the lying old fae who was in my kitchen? It is.

Alec shoots a quick glance my way. "How's our Knox?"

"Good," I reply. "Out for a run."

"Ah, so Ty must have called again." Alec winces while still focused on the screen. He's really into this game.

"Yeah, she called, all right," I say. "Knox chucked another phone against the wall."

"No worries," says Alec. "I'll redo the blocker spells when he gets his new cell."

At the mention of that particular item, I remember my promise to Knox. "Elle, mind if I borrow your phone?"

"Official, anonymous, or burner?" As a con artist, Elle has a variety of phones for different occasions. She does it all for a good cause, though. Elle specializes in returning stolen jewelry to its original owner… For a fee, of course.

"Your official one, please," I say. If I want to call Knox, then that's the one with my number preloaded.

"Sure, it's on the coffee table."

I scoop up the phone in question and drop it into my pocket. "I'll leave you to it, then." Their only reply is more clicking of keyboards and complaining about healing potions, so I head back to the kitchen.

After all, I never did get any dinner.

For a long time, I stuff myself with plenty of egg rolls and lo mein. Once my belly is full, I head off for bed. All the while, my mind spins through everything that happened today. Ty's call. Knox's pain. The Colonel's non-story stories. Finally, I decide to hit the mattress and at least try to snooze. I slide under the covers and text Knox with my latest super-secure chat app.

*OnlyCallMeElle: It's Bry. Hope you have a great run. See you in the morning.*

He texts back right away, which makes me smile.

*FortMe: Just arrived at the Adirondacks and about to shift. Sleep well, my mate.*

At those words, my grin grows wider. It definitely helps to know that Knox is safe and happy. Sadly, the moment my head hits the pillow, any happy thoughts of Knox get buried under an avalanche of worries. Jules. The Colonel. Elle. School. My lack of parents. It takes a while, but I eventually fall asleep.

My dreams start off as a little weird, but not especially frightening. Something in my soul tells me that won't last for long, though.

Lately, it never does.

# CHAPTER FIVE

In my dream, I stand in a snug room that seems carved out from layers of shale. A kid-size bed sits in one corner, a small sandbox in the other. Drawings made by a child decorate the walls. They seem to have been hung by a kid as well. The tops of the paper have been crammed between the stones to stay put. Someone didn't want to throw a single thing away. The thought makes me smile.

There's something safe and comforting about this place.

*I've been here before, I know it.*

White mist rolls across the floor, covering me up to my knees. Looking down, I notice that I'm wearing a gray hooded cloak, which is strange. I went to sleep wearing boyshorts and a T-shirt, like always.

*What a strange dream.*

All of a sudden, a child's laughter echoes behind me. Turning about, I try to see who's here, but I only see the flash of a small body racing around.

A girl. Perhaps six years old.

I cup my hand by my mouth. "Who's there?"

"You." She giggles. "Me. We're the same thing, silly."

My breath catches. This has never happened before.

*I'm dreaming, but not about Ancient Egypt. This is about me as a child.*

Shock and excitement zing through my nervous system. This is huge. I don't remember anything from when I was under six years old. All my memories are of my aunties, and I came to live with them at age six. I straighten my spine and ask another question.

"Are you saying that you're a version of me at six years old?"

"Yes, and we're in a dream." She's so young, that last word sounds more like *dweam*.

I spin around, searching for her in the mist. "Where are you?"

"Come and find me!"

I stumble about, searching for the child version of me. Small glimpses of her appear in the haze, and I chase after them with gusto. Still, I can't get a clear view. And no matter which direction I run, the tiny room seems to stretch on and on.

*Stupid dreams.*

Even so, a few details become clear. Child-Me wears red, silver, and gold. I race harder, but the room keeps extending. Soon I give up on having a face-to-face chat with her. Instead, I opt for more questions.

"Why don't I remember you when I'm awake?" I ask.

"Poppa had to hide our memories. They're still locked down tight."

Bands of anxiety tighten around my throat. "Poppa? Who do you mean?"

"Who do you think, silly? He's standing right here."

A dragon's tail swooshes by my feet. After that, I glimpse the curve of a massive scaled back. There's a flash of red spikes jutting out from along the spine. Dragon. And I'd know this particular combination of black scales and red spikes anywhere.

"Colonel Mallory." I take a half step backward. "You're my Poppa?"

The tail flicks once before the dragon vanishes off into the mist.

"Colonel Mallory? Are you here?"

There's no answer. And the dragon doesn't reappear, either.

My head spins through all this information. There's a six-year-old version of me locked inside my own soul. For some reason, she thinks that Colonel Mallory is her Poppa. That doesn't make any sense. Colonel Mallory is one of the best-known fairies in the world. If he had a child, it wouldn't be a secret for long. A chill crawls up my limbs.

Is that why my memories are locked down? The Colonel might have been trying to keep me hidden. My rib cage seems to swell with excitement.

*I might know who my father is.*

Scanning the mist, I look for Child-Me again. Will she look like the Colonel? I call out to her again. "Why did Poppa hide our memories of him?"

"Because of the man in the angry mask," says Child-Me. "We couldn't let him see us. Later, we couldn't remember him at all."

With that, a man appears in the corner of the small room. All of him is hidden in mist, except for his golden helmet and faceplate. What I can see of him positively screams Ancient Rome. The helm even has those tall red plumes along the top. Plus, the faceplate is shaped into the image of a man with narrowed eyes and a deep frown. Could that be Jules...or perhaps one of his minions? Back when Jules was Julius Caesar, he had a large Roman army at his call.

The Roman man disappears.

Well, if Jules or one of his minions was after me as a child, then that would explain a lot. If the Colonel hid my memories of Jules or his warriors, then it was probably to keep me safe. After all, that's why the Colonel locked up my powers—to keep them hidden from Jules. Did he hide my memories for the same reason? I shake my head. That doesn't make sense, though. If all this were true, why wouldn't the Colonel release my memories after Jules died?

I press my palms against my eyes. This is a whole lot of guessing based on some little girl's ramblings in a dream. Maybe I just want to know who my parents are, so I'm making this stuff up while I sleep.

That has to be it. Colonel Mallory is not Poppa material.

Around me, the haze lightens. My heart pounds faster. Child-Me speaks once more, only closer this time.

"Bet you can't find me," she calls.

I tilt my head. Should I chase this child?

Little girl laughter echoes again through the mist. The giggles are high-pitched and sweet, like the tinkling of tiny bells. I can't help but smile. A weight I didn't know I carried seeps off my shoulders. In my heart of hearts, I know what I need to do. There is more to this dream than conversations in the mist. I need to see this girl face-to-face.

"I'll find you."

More sweet laughter follows. "Watch where you walk!"

Mist rolls away from around my feet, revealing a sandbox. In it, Child-Me has drawn the rough image of a pyramid. I lean in for a closer look. Child-me also added the picture of an eye above the pyramid's peak. My mind churns over this image.

Pyramids and eyes. *I've seen this before. But where?*

Before I have time to think things through, Child-Me sounds behind me, closer than ever before. "Catch me! Hurry!"

A realization flows through my soul, one with all the clarity that only a dream can give. If I can just catch this girl in the mist, then I'll have what I've always wanted.

Answers.

Spinning about, I step forward. Sure there may be other obstacles hidden in the mist, but I don't care if I trip over any of them. Instead, I rush forward, blindly grasping at anything in the clouds around me. "Ready or not, here I come!"

Her laughter fades. "I have to go. The bad people are coming."

I pause.

Around me, the shale walls heave as if the room is taking in a breath. The air becomes so cold I exhale puffs of white cloud. Long shadows creep down the walls, which isn't necessarily a bad thing, except for one fact.

Nothing is causing them.

The shadows lengthen, seeping down the walls in a way that reminds me of so many drips of dark gray paint. Once the darkness reaches the floor, the shadows consolidate into a pair of humanoid shapes. These creatures are tall, slender, transparent, and gray. There's the slightest curve in one silhouette; that one might be female while the other's male. Each creature has bulging eyes that are all white and glowing.

An electric charge of awareness moves through me. For weeks, I'd been struggling to remember what happened in my dreams.

But I know these creatures.

Hazy bodies.

Many voices.

Beings made of shadow.

What are these creatures called again? *The name is so close…*

I scan the room. Around me, the mist dissolves into darkness. All signs of Colonel Mallory, Child-Me, or the mysterious Roman soldier disappear. The walls of the underground chamber melt off into utter black.

My dream is over.

And this is something else entirely.

The creatures stare at me, their bulbous eyes glowing more brightly.

"You've come to visit me."

They nod.

"This isn't the first time."

They nod again.

There is almost an audible snap as whatever held back my memories breaks in two. Once, I couldn't recall anything about my nightmares. Now, all those nightly visions return with a vengeance.

All-white eyes.

Gray limbs.

Dark intentions.

"I remember you," I say in a rush. "You're the Shadowvin. The Void is your master."

They nod one more time, and the motion sends adrenaline zooming through my bloodstream. More memories appear. The Shadowvin and Void keep visiting my dreams. Every time, they ask me to find some artifact related to the fountain.

No, they don't ask.

They insist.

Threaten.

Terrify.

I scrub my hands over my face. So why don't I remember any of this when I wake up? The answer appears in a flash. The Shadowvin's magic stops me from recalling what happened. My chest tightens with anxiety. Now, I'm back with the Shadowvin again.

Definitely time to run.

I survey my surroundings. Pitch darkness still stretches off in every direction. *Not exactly ideal conditions for an escape.* I straighten my back. *Whatever.* It's not in me to stand around while the big bads get closer.

With all my will, I try to move. It's no use. Although I twist and squirm, my feet stay rooted to the spot. Panic streams through me.

The two Shadowvin stride closer. After that, they pause. My limbs tremble with fear.

"A new world is about to dawn," says the female Shadowvin. My eyes widen as I remember her name from previous dream visits: *Tithe.* When she speaks, Tithe's voice sounds like a dozen old ladies speaking at once. "We come to offer you eternal life and youth in this upcoming era."

"You have been chosen to translate the *Book of Isis*," says the second Shadowvin. His voice sounds like a dozen old men whispering at once. I remember him now; this one's name is Slythe. "In it, there's a description of an important artifact—a device called the Codex Mechanica. Vow to find this machine and use it willingly. Then, you shall be rewarded with life eternal."

"And youth eternal," adds Tithe.

"Will you vow to help us?" asks Slythe.

On reflex, my hands cross over my throat. This is what the Shadowvin have been offering me, night after night, only the curse wipes away the memory afterward. And every time they appear, I always refuse them.

No question why I turn them down, either.

These are two creepy alien-ghost creatures who won't explain what they want with me and the Codex Mechanica. All they talk about is my vow to both find and use it. *PUH-lease.* I know how magical vows work. If these Shadowvin have enough power to wipe out my memory, then they have enough magic to hold me to my promises. And if I agree to find some weird artifact here in Dreamville? I'll be mega-compelled to do just that when I'm awake. Even worse, I'll have no idea why I'm under a compulsion.

Magically forced to help the Shadowvin? *Uh, no.*

"We've had this chat before," I say. "There's no way I'm helping you." Besides, I'm not sure where these two got the idea that being an eternal teenager is so awesome. Even so, it's what they keep offering me, over and over.

"This is your last warning," says Tithe.

Slythe's eyes narrow to glowing slits. "We've protected you by erasing your memories come morning," he growls. "A few twinges of fear, that's all you know of us."

"But that will change, unless you agree right now." Tithe's many female voices take on a menacing hiss. "You don't want to live in terror of us. It will drive you mad."

"Vow to translate the *Book of Isis*," adds Slythe. "Vow to hand over the machine and use it. Our magic will hold you to your promise."

"Let me think about that." I purse my lips in mock-consideration. Inside, my heart is pounding away, but there's no way I'll let the Shadowvin see that. "You want me to commit to you in my dreams, get stuck in some kind of magical vow, and then not remember anything in the morning. That way, I'll be forced to keep my word without ever remembering why. Plus, magical vows have other nasty side affects. I won't be able to get any aid to stop..." I wave my hands around. "Whatever all this is."

"You don't mean that," says Slythe.

"This is me, meaning every word." I fold my arms across my chest. "Like I've told you before, bring on the daytime memories. No problem. I almost had my brains eaten by a zombie version of Julius Caesar. I can handle remembering a few googly-eyed shadows." By the way, I'm really happy with how serious I come off here. I mean, I'm trapped in a bad dream with shadow baddies. By rights, I should be blubbering on the floor.

"If you don't fear remembering, then we shall be forced to call in the Void," adds Tithe.

My insides churn with worry. As names go, the Void sounds like a not-so-friendly type person. Still, I keep playing my sass card. Running away still isn't an option, so it's all I've got at the moment.

"Keep bugging me, and I'll do something you don't want, either." An idea appears. "Since translating the *Book of Isis* is so important to you, tell your master that I refuse to translate another hieroglyph." I set my fists on my hips. This is a conversation that's better had when you're in a power pose. "I'll tell you what I will do, though. I'll take every battle class at West Lake Prep. I'll learn how to use my magic, even when I'm asleep. And the next time you bother me in my dreams, I'll destroy you both."

For a long moment, the Shadowvin say nothing. My pulse speeds. Maybe I actually turned things around here.

"She isn't afraid of us," says Tithe. "Again."

"I suppose we'll have to try something different," adds Slythe.

"We could trick her into helping us," says Tithe. "You know how I love to play games."

"No, I prefer more direct ways of changing her mind."

"Agreed."

A jolt of fear moves through me. *More direct ways.* That sounds bad.

Moving in unison, Slythe and Tithe lift their transparent arms. Pain radiates through my torso. Wisps of color and power rise from my palms, all in shades of red, gold, and silver. Agony spirals down my spine as the colored threads of power float away from me…And into the outstretched arms of Slythe and Tithe. My very soul feels torn from my core. My legs buckle and I crumple onto my knees. Part of me wants to tell them this isn't so bad, but I don't trust myself to speak. If I open my mouth, I'm afraid I'll scream. There's no way I want the Shadowvin to see my weakness.

"You'll find the device and give it to us," says Slythe. "Or we'll make you comply."

"Don't forget your friends," whispers Tithe. "And your mate. We can drain them, too. Do you wish to cause them pain?"

Finally, I'm able to speak one word. "No." When I next speak, it comes out as a half-cry. "LEAVE!"

The next thing I know, I'm sitting upright in bed, my covers kicked onto the floor.

And I'm screaming. The noise awakens my wolf, who starts to whimper inside my soul.

Elle rushes into the room. "What's wrong?"

It takes me a few minutes—because that was one terrible dream—but eventually, I'm able to stop screaming. I can only echo Elle's words. "What *is* wrong?" With all my will, I try to remember, but I can't quite find the words. For a while, it's all I can do to breathe. Finally, I calm down enough that I can answer. "Maybe I was having a nightmare about school tomorrow."

"Maybe?" Elle shakes her head. "You're guessing, Bry."

My eyes sting. "I have no idea what's happening. Something is wrong."

Sitting beside me on the mattress, Elle pulls me in for a hug. "Hey, I'm here. Everything is going to be fine."

At those words, a thought appears in my mind.

Danger. Elle, Alec, and Knox…they're all at risk. I can't remember why or how, but I do know one fact from the bottom of my soul. There's only one way I can protect my friends and my mate.

"You're right, Elle. Everything will be okay."

And I know why, too. Because no matter what happens, I refuse to translate one more hieroglyph from the *Book of Isis*.

# CHAPTER SIX

The next morning, Knox and I stand on a wide stretch of sidewalk in front of a three-story brownstone. There's a short flight of steps up to the front door. A small sign sits by the door, reading *"West Lake Prep."* You'd think a big high school would be inside a huge building, but this is Manhattan. We can fit half a skyscraper's worth of stuff into a utility closet. And that's with IKEA, not magic.

I straighten the folds of my blue blazer and plaid skirt. The emblem on the pocket reads *"West Lake Prep."* It's all an illusion, though. All students receive a charm to hide their real clothes from the mortal world. If humans knew there were Magicorum kids at this school, they'd be camped outside, waiting for selfies.

In reality, I'm wearing a leather duster, cropped tank, black pants, and heavy boots. This outfit is something that Elle and I got from the fairies. It's unshreddable, so even if I shift, the outfit will be whole when I turn back into my human form.

My inner animal grumbles inside me. *"Why can't we dress like we want to? That's what Knox is doing."*

"We do dress the way we want, it's just that humans can't tell yet. It's the glamour from this charm bracelet."

*"We should never hide. Our mate isn't."*

Unlike me and every other kid waiting on the sidewalk, Knox left his charm bracelet at home. In other words, all the other boys are wearing a blue blazer and plaid pants. Not Knox.

I really don't blame him, though. Plaid pants are rough.

Instead, Knox wears his regular outfit of black pants, dark T-shirt, and a fitted leather jacket. It's all couture—werewolves have a great sense of style, after all—but it's most definitely not school standard, at least not for the street.

Inside my soul, my wolf paces in frustration. *"We shouldn't have to hide anymore. At least, we should dress like our mate."*

Now, I get where my wolf is going with this. After all, she was hidden most of her life. *"Look, this is the first day of school. Let's follow the rules for twenty-four hours and see how it goes."*

*"But Knox does what he wants to now,"* whines my wolf.

*"True. But I don't know how he always gets away with it."*

I have my suspicions, though. As the warden for all shifters, Knox is the alpha of alphas. Everyone senses it on some level.

As if on cue, a teacher steps over. She's tall and lithe with long white hair. Probably Fae. "Are you a West Lake Prep student?" she asks. Her voice has a jingle to it, which is another sign that she might be fae. "I'm Lady Pinkalicious, one of the para-enforcers here. We're here to make sure everyone follows the rules."

*Lady Pinkalicious? Oh, she's definitely fae.*

"Yeah, I'm a student," says Knox.

"Then why aren't you wearing the school uniform?" Lady Pinkalicious tilts her head in a way that says, *You need to do this.*

"Nah." Knox folds his arms over his chest. "No uniform for me." His eyes flare golden with shifter power. Alpha energy rolls off him in waves. Knox really hates the idea of plaid pants. Sure, it isn't real. But Knox says that if a human can still take a picture of him in plaid pants, then that's real enough. I get it.

Inside my soul, my wolf yips with glee. *"See? We should take off that enchanted bracelet now so we can be seen in our leathers, too."*

*"It's only for while we're outside,"* I reply. *"Once we're inside, the bracelet will deactivate."* Each school has its own dress code.

Shifters can definitely wear leather. Witches and warlocks don long robes. Fairies dress up in, well, whatever they want to. So my leather ensemble will be fine.

"That a problem?" asks Knox.

"Oh. No. You're fine." After that, Lady Pinkalicious keeps on starting at Knox. Sometimes Knox's alpha power has this kind of hypnotic effect on members of the opposite sex. Take Ty, for instance.

And now, it's affecting Lady Pinkalicious, too.

Who is a teacher.

Gross.

Knox and I ignore her. Sometimes that helps. After a minute or two, Lady Pinkalicious should come to her senses and walk away.

While we wait, I watch the other kids mill about the sidewalk. Most walked here alone or with friends, which is good. I was dreading seeing too many parents around. Scanning the faces, I try to assign kids to their Magicorum classification. The hefty linebacker types are probably shifters. The more lean and lithe could be either fae or witches. And then there are ones with no magic at all, who are still considered Magicorum. It's weird, but it happens.

Why? Magical kids get born into non-magical families all the time. Now, suppose you've got magic and your fairy tale life template is the twelve dancing princesses. Trouble is, you're an only child. In that case, you'd think you're off the hook for having eleven siblings, right?

Wrong.

When there aren't enough magical relatives to fill out your template, then magic drags your non-magical human relations into the mix, such as aunts, cousins, and so on. As a result, regular humans can get subjected to our curses, evil stepmothers, and everything else. Dead or missing parents are especially common. When that happens, an otherwise normal person becomes an official member of the Magicorum. That's why some of the kids here today are non-magical, but they're still attending West Lake. They're here to learn the ropes and build alliances. It's only fair.

Lady Pinkalicious pokes Knox in the shoulder. The dazed look in her eyes says she's still under Knox's alpha spell. "Hi. I'm still here. Lady Pinkalicious."

"Yeah, I got that." Knox loops his arm around my shoulders. "I'm Knox. This is my mate, Bry."

"Do you need help with tutoring or anything?" Lady Pinkalicious is still staring at Knox and not getting the hint. I almost feel sorry for her.

"You know what?" I ask. The rest of my words become lost. A flash of white light appears in my mind's eye. An ethereal cold crawls over my skin. Magic. A voice sounds in my head.

*"Find the device."*

On reflex, I speak back. "No, I won't translate another word." And I might say that a little too loud for the sidewalk. A bunch of people stops chatting to turn around and stare.

Lady Pinkalicious shakes her head. My outburst seems to have snapped her out of whatever spell she was under. "What did you say?"

My face burns red. *Did I just say that out loud?* "I said, I think I saw someone breaking a rule over there." I point in the general direction of the opposite area of the sidewalk.

"Um, okay." Lady Pinkalicious narrows her eyes, looking at me like I'm nuts. But after all I've been through I won't be intimidated by someone named Lady Pinkalicious. She winks at Knox. "Bye for now."

*"Let's bite her,"* says my wolf.

*"No way. We're not shifting and biting anyone."*

*"You're no fun."*

*"True, but the last thing we need is to change into wolf form on the sidewalk. There'll be a dozen humans here in heartbeat, and all of them will be asking for autographs and taking selfies. No way."*

*"It still would be worth it. Just one little nip?"*

*"Not a chance."*

My inner wolf sniffs. *"If you're going to be boring, I'll do something else for a while."*

For the record, the ability to shut each other out is a two-way street with my wolf. A heartbeat later, I can sense her going into her own version of stasis. It's her way of saying she's ticked.

Knox gives my shoulders a gentle squeeze. "Your wolf giving you trouble?"

"She's gone into stasis."

"Let me guess, she's not happy that she can't bite Lady Pinkalicious?"

"How'd you guess?"

"Because my wolf is howling about it." Knox shakes his head. "I envy you and your wolf." I know what he means. As far as I know, I'm the only werewolf who can shut out her wolf and vice-versa. Knox is stuck with his in his head 24-7.

I go on tiptoe. "Where are Elle and Alec, by the way?"

Knox is a head taller than me, so he has a better view of the crowded sidewalk. "About ten yards off, trying to get through the crowd and find us."

"Trying?"

"All the wizards and witches want to talk to Alec."

"And Elle can't get past Alec's posse?"

"Not exactly." Knox frowns. "No, Elle's surrounded by fae kids."

My protective instincts kick in. "Are the fairies hurting her?"

"No." Knox shakes his head. "They're being...nice."

"Huh. I guess the fae can be nice. I just didn't expect it." A mixture of surprise and concern battle it out inside my nervous system. Fae being nice. There just has to be a catch.

Knox turns so he's facing me nose to nose. "What was all that before with Lady Pinkalicious? What did you mean, you won't translate another word?"

I rub my temples, like the action will shove the needed thoughts back into my head. "I don't remember."

"Let me guess," says Knox. "You feel pressured to keep translating the *Book of Isis* because you feel guilty about me and Alec."

"I don't think that's it. Honestly."

Knox eyes me for a long moment. "Okay. Just do what you want to do, not for me and Alec, yeah?"

"Agreed." I go up on tiptoe again, but this time to give Knox a gentle kiss on the cheek. As I lean in I catch the barest scent from his skin.

Copper and smoke.

I know what that means.

Knox is in pain.

"What's wrong?" I ask. "You're hurting."

Knox scrubs his hands over his face. "It's been getting worse since I got to school. I think it's because the equinox is getting closer."

"But Alec said he wasn't in pain because of that, only that his magic was getting weirder."

"Alec isn't a shifter." The veins in Knox's forehead throb. "Az will know what to do, you'll see."

"That's right. We'll see him after school today." I try to slap on a smile, but the scent of Knox's pain only grows stronger. Worry tightens up my neck and shoulders. Last night, Knox said he wasn't feeling well, but I certainly didn't scent any pain. There's no avoiding it.

Knox is getting worse.

All of a sudden, it seems really selfish of me to refuse to translate any papyri. If I can translate the *Book of Isis* and help Knox find the fountain, then it might end Knox's agony. If there's even a chance I can help my mate, I should do it.

I stiffen my shoulders. "I want to help you, Knox."

"Let's focus on school first, yeah? The papyri can wait."

I press my palms against my eyes. "It's hard to focus on anything."

"It's 'cause you're worried. I am, too." He gives my shoulder a gentle squeeze. "I've got an idea. When I'd get anxious about a mission, Az would make me talk through each step on the plan."

"Doesn't that make things worse?"

"Nah. Gets you focused on what you're about to do instead of picturing everything that can go wrong. Willing to give it a try?" He leans in and runs his nose along the length of mine. It makes my knees turn to jelly. The scent of Knox's pain lessens. "Work with me here, yeah?"

For the first time in what feels like hours, I exhale with relief. Talking through school. This is something I can do, and it doesn't involve hieroglyphs. For whatever reason, that makes it a fine choice. "Sure."

"So here today, everything starts once the teachers open the front door. After that, what happens next?"

"Once the teachers open the doors, we march up the steps and go inside the school. West Lake Prep is actually three schools, each with its own principal."

"Shifters get two principals, though. Because we're the best." The vein in Knox's forehead has stopped pounding, which is another improvement.

"No question, weres are the best," I say with a wink. "Inside the school, there's the Wolf's Den for Shifters, the Silver Galleries for the fae, and the Crimson Keep for witches and wizards."

"Good. And how do you get into your school?"

"After we pass the threshold, the first stop is a reception room with three doors, one each for the Crimson Keep, Silver Galleries, and Wolf's Den."

"And that last one is the best doorway," says Knox while bobbing his brows. "In case you ever change your mind."

Since I have all three kinds of magic inside me, I could theoretically go through any of the three doors. I've already decided to go with Elle, though. "It's tempting, but you can use your alpha powers on other weres. Alec is the most powerful warlock around. But fairies are crazypants. No way am I letting Elle go in there on her own."

"Yeah, I get that." Knox kisses my temple. "You're doing the right thing."

At that moment, two of Knox's were-buddies, Abe and Hollywood, rush up to us. Abe reminds me of a younger version of Abraham Lincoln, what with his lanky form, messy black hair, and big ears. He's also terminally honest. Hollywood is tall and buff with amazing blond hair. This is a stunning genetic gift, by the way.

Normally after we shift, werewolves normally look like they have a week's worth of bedhead. Or at least, I do. Hollywood always appears camera ready.

"Good morning, alpha," gushes Abe.

Knox shakes his head. "I'm not your alpha." There's no anger in the words, though. Knox is slowly warming to the idea of Abe and Hollywood being pack.

Hollywood bows slightly to me. "Your Princessness." This summer, Abe and Hollywood decided that since I was a Bryar Rose life template—and Bryar Rose is a princess—then they would be knights in my court. I think it's their way of saying they are pack and not having Knox snarl at them.

Clever wolves.

I roll my eyes. "I am not your princess." Even so, I can't hide my grin. Abe and Hollywood are sweet.

I take a few steps away from our little not-a-pack. "I need to find Elle."

Knox gives me one of his classic chin-nods. "Find me if you need me, yeah?"

I wink. "Yeah."

A knot of kids blocks the sidewalk. Even so, I'm able to elbow my way through to Elle. I suppose in other places that would be rude. But in New York, if you can't use your elbows to get around, you'll spend your days huddled in a corner.

Stepping up to Elle, I wrap her in a huge hug. "You look gorgeous." Most people look dumpling-esque in the little blue jacket and plaid skirt, but Elle makes the ensemble seem fantastic. It's one benefit of being a Cinderella life template, I guess. The negative side is the whole evil stepfamily thing. Yipes.

Elle winks. "You, too."

"I can't wait to get inside and no longer be in the glamoured-up outfit." I lower my voice. "I can't help but worry that if I somehow lose control and shift, this school uniform won't be unshreddable, if you know what I mean."

To Elle's credit, she takes my somewhat unreasonable fear seriously. "They'll be opening the doors any second now."

The front doors swing open, and the mass of students starts to file up the stairs and into West Lake Prep. Side by side, Elle and I follow the crowd up the staircase. For years, I wanted nothing more than to walk inside this particular school. And now that the moment is here, a ton of emotions battle it out inside me.

Excitement.

Fear.

Worry.

I slap on a smile, straighten my back, and march up the steps. Elle moves along beside me. My badass werewolf boyfriend waits nearby. And most of all, I've faced much worse. Like last summer, when Queen Nyxa tried to flay me. Or before that, when I had to take down Jules, leader of the Denarii.

Whatever happens, I can handle this.

With each step closer to the school, a sinking sensation moves through my soul. Translating those papyri is a bad idea. There must be another way to help Knox. Besides, my mate would never force me to translate that book. And if someone else pressures me into assembling those dumb papyri? I'll just brush them off.

No one can force me to translate the *Book of Isis*.

But even as I make that internal vow, some deep corner of my soul whispers to my waking mind…

*Your fate has always been to translate those hieroglyphs.*

*And doing so will cost you everything.*

# CHAPTER SEVEN

Elle and I slowly march up the steps to the brownstone. A jumble of kids surrounds us, all of them flowing past us in a rush to reach class. It's like me and Elle are stones jutting out of a fast-moving river. My bestie links her elbow with mine as we close in on the front door. Bands of worry tighten around my throat.

"Remember when we built that zip line over Sixth Avenue?" asks Elle.

"How could I forget?" Some of the tension loosens from my neck. Elle and I built that thing in the middle of the night. "We got three good runs in before someone called the cops on us."

"Hey, what about the time we put hair remover in Alec's shampoo bottle?"

"We got to call him Doctor Evil for two weeks before he figured out how to magic up a new hairdo. Good times."

Elle bumps my hip with hers. "We own this town. And we'll get this high school thing down next. You'll see."

I can't help but smile. "Did you just guide us down memory lane to cheer me up?"

"I don't know. Did it work?"

"As a matter of fact, it did. Totally."

"Then yes, it was my master plan."

"And *that's* what makes you amazing."

Elle winks. "I know."

We reach the school's main door, which is heavy, wooden, and propped open. Elle and I move past the threshold and into main reception area. It's a long, oak-paneled room with three doors along the back wall: red, gold, and silver. That's for witch, were, and fairy. As kids pass through the door, there's a flash of light and their appearances change.

No more uniforms. At least, not the ones from the sidewalk.

As the other students go into their respective halls, our enchanted bracelets deactivate. The masquerade of looking like typical high school students ends. Witches and warlocks wear crimson robes. Shifters change into couture leather. The fae are dressed in pastel shades with their long silver wings on display. I only catch a glimpse of each kid as they transform. A second or two passes before the other students speed down their respective hallways and into their own learning areas.

*This is really happening.*

Anxiety cinches around my chest. Here's the moment I've been waiting for: starting a new school with actual classes, students, and teachers. The scent of sandalwood and musk washes over me. Knox stands behind me. He sets his hand on the juncture my shoulder and neck. I catch that scent of copper and smoke. Pain.

Reaching up, I grasp his hand. "How are you feeling?"

"I'll be fine." Knox leans in. "Seriously." In other words, my asking him if he's okay every two seconds isn't helping. Fair enough.

"So," I say. "What's your first class of the day?"

"History, I think."

"You think? I've got fae art."

"I'm not getting my hopes up. Az made me learn enough stuff for ten high schools." Which is true. In my case, my home-schooling was actually pretty awesome until I hit the equivalent of freshman year. After that, my aunties downscaled all my education into preparation for marrying Jules. So I started taking online classes. That way I wouldn't fall behind. Meanwhile, Az oversaw Knox's schooling, and that old were never let up on my mate for a second. When Knox wasn't killing Denarii, Az was grilling him on everything from quantum physics to how to block a roundhouse.

I rub the back of Knox's hand with my thumb. "That's not what I meant."

"I know." The scent of pain grows stronger. "Alec is magicking me up a spell for the pain. It'll all be better soon. Don't worry."

Even so, I do worry. We've covered this territory, though, and I know Knox. Talking about it right now won't help any. "Want me to walk you to your door?" I ask.

Leaning in, Knox presses a kiss to the top of my head. "Nah. I need to see you go in with Elle. My wolf won't stand for anything else."

With that, my inner animal starts chatting away inside my mind. *"I don't like leaving our mate,"* she growls. *"But I do want to scent all those delicious fairies. Let's play!"*

Here it comes. Again, my wolf sees the fae as magical chew toys. *"No, we are not playing with the fae. They are murderous and cast curses, remember?"*

My wolf sniffs. *"We'll play nicely with the yummy fairies."*

I pull at the golden shifter magic inside my soul, commanding my wolf to obey. *"No playing with the fae."*

My golden power surrounds my wolf, quieting her soul. This is a new skill, by the way. Over the summer, Az has been showing me the ropes like a pro. Long story short, shifter magic has quickly become my go-to power. I know from watching Colonel Mallory that silver fae energy is chaotic. He's warned me not to touch the stuff. And my witch magic? That's still a great mystery. But that's also why I'm here: to learn how to master all three.

Elle taps my shoulder. "Ready?" There's a nervous warble in her voice.

Turning around, I give Knox a soft kiss on his bristled cheek. He cups my face in his firm hands, pulling me in for a gentle brush of our lips. "You be safe with those fae, yeah?"

"I'll be fine. Don't let the big bad wolves get you down."

Just beyond Knox, I see Abe and Hollywood. They've positioned themselves as guards for me and Knox. Basically, they guide people toward their respective doors. Knox's alpha energy makes everyone naturally stop in their tracks.

"Move along," says Hollywood.

"Nothing to see here," adds Abe. There are a few familiar faces in the crowd. For a moment, I think I see Scarlett and Avianna, two girls from my old Magicorum Teen Therapy Group with Madame. But they're gone too quickly to be sure.

Knox runs his nose along the length of mine, breaking me out of my thoughts. Touch is very important to shifters. "My wolf says to kill anyone who's mean to you, by the way. But he's kidding. I think."

"I'll remember that." For the first time in what feels like forever, I smile. "You're the best."

"Yeah." Knox winks. "Have fun with the fae."

I roll my eyes. "I'll try." Squaring my shoulders, I turn to Elle. "Let's do this."

Walking side by side, Elle and I approach the silver door. Like the others, it's propped open to allow students to flow through. Elle marches right past the threshold. I walk forward and—SMACK—I hit an invisible barrier.

What the—?

Pulses of white light flash around me. I check the faces nearby. Is anyone else squinting in the spontaneous laser light show? Nope. This is a brightness that only I can see. My skin chills over as if I were dipped in arctic water. A rush of electricity runs through the air.

This is magic. Even worse, it feels both familiar and frightening.

A thought nags at the back of my head. *I know what this magic is and who it's from.* No matter how hard I try, though, I can't access the memory.

I shake my head. Maybe I imagined getting stopped by an invisible wall. I am pretty stressed out today. Weirder things have happened.

Reaching forward, I push my hand against what feels like a glass wall. Students stream past me as if nothing is there.

But it is.

This invisible barrier is preventing me from going into the Sliver Gallery. I'd heard that the doorways automatically blocked anyone who wasn't Magicorum, but I have fae power, right?

Moving sideways, I shove my shoulder against the invisible wall. Elle tries to help from the other side, but to her, there is no barrier. Soon, a small group of fae kids stand around me. Some are giggling. Whispers echo through the air.

"There's one every year."

"Must be human, and she thinks she's part of someone's life template."

"So sad."

My face burns about three shades of red. *Please, let me just walk through this door like a normal magicked-up teenager.*

Nope. Still not happening.

Knox steps up, grasps my hand, and guides me away. "Let's hit the Wolf's Den, yeah?"

I blink hard, trying to think through this turn of events. For some reason, I can't pass through the doorway to the Silver Gallery, which is the fae part of the school. I look to Elle. "Cool if I go with Knox?"

Elle nods. "Sure. I'll be fine." A small group of fae kids have gathered around her. Now, they pull at my bestie's wrists, encouraging her to step deeper into the galleries. The glint of fear shines in Elle's blue eyes. The fae may be acting nice now, but there's no predicting what will happen two seconds into the future. Even so, there's nothing to be done about it. I'm definitely causing a scene here, and school starts in twenty minutes. I wave a quick goodbye to Elle, and she steps off down the silver hallway. Seeing Elle walk away makes something in my chest ache. I lift my chin and regroup.

I can do this.

Taking Knox's hand in mine, we stride over to the second, golden door. All the other were-kids stand aside as we walk along, partly because of Knox's alpha power. Mostly, it's due to the fact that Abe and Hollywood are clearing a path for us by yelling, "Make way for our alpha and his mate!"

"Guys," growls Knox. "I'm not your alpha. Officially." In other words, there's a thread of pack connection between me, Knox, Abe, and Hollywood, but we haven't done the sacred rites that make us pack. Whatever those are.

Abe stretches his arms wide, preventing anyone else from approaching the opened red door on one side. Hollywood does the same move on the other side.

"Go on," says Abe. "You two can enter now."

I know they both mean well, but the way they're acting? It's making an even bigger scene than what happened at the fae door. Knox steps past the threshold. I step forward and—WHAM—I hit another invisible barrier. The same sensations roll over me.

White flashes that only I can see.

Bone-chilling cold.

Electrical energy from a foreign kind of magic.

And worst of all, that sense that part of me knows what this is. But I just can't grasp the memory for some reason. Fury zings through my bloodstream. I kick at the wall in frustration.

"What is this?" asks Knox. "I know you're a were."

Panic zings down my spine. A few minutes ago, I was nervous about making my dream of going to school a reality. Now? West Lake Prep might not be happening after all.

If the reception room were a movie, it would be like someone hit Pause. All the students have stopped to watch the drama. Elle waits along with the crowd. Acting on instinct, I rush over to the opened red door and stop before the threshold. This time, I'm cautious. I reach forward slowly.

My fingertips hit another invisible barrier. Oh, no. This time, there are only the barest flashes of white light in my vision. But there's no question that foreign magic is at work here.

Beside me, Abe and Hollywood drag out two adults from the Wolf's Den. They are a burly pair, a man and a woman. I've seen pictures of them in the West Lake Prep brochures. The entire school follows its own fairy tale life template. For West Lake Prep, that's Goldilocks and the Three Bears. The principals for the shifter schools are were-bears named Mums and Pops. In other words, the adult shifter couple standing before me has the life template of Momma Bear and Poppa Bear from the Goldilocks legend.

"Here they are." Abe gestures at me and Knox. "Our alpha and his mate. Fix what's wrong with the doors. Let our queen pass."

The woman is the first to speak. "I'm Mums." She hitches her thumb at the barrel-chested guy beside her. They're pretty much identical—burly with brown hair, eyes, and matching jean overalls. The only difference is that Mums has long hair. "This here's Pops." She focuses her big brown eyes on me. "And you're a queen?"

My face burns with the mother of all blushes. "That's just something Abe and Hollywood say. What I am is trying to get into the Wolf's Den. Or any of the three doors, really. They don't seem to work for me."

Like they're watching a tennis match, everyone switches their gazes from me to the shifter principals.

"Enough." Pops lets out a bellow of a growl. "Get back to school, you two." He points at Abe and Hollywood before gesturing to Knox. "You, too."

Knox lifts his chin. "Not until I know what you're doing with Bry."

"She can't get in any doors." Mums has a bellow of a voice, too. "So this here situation is bigger than me and Pops. We've got to take her to the office for all the principals—that means shifter, fae, and witches. Nothing bad'll happen to her."

"We get one like this every year," says Pops with a sad smile. "We know how to handle things. It's all good."

A tiny witch in flowing red robes steps across the threshold to the red door. She has big brown eyes, cocoa skin, and a gentle voice. "I'm here." I recognize her from the website, too. While Mom and Pops lead the shifter school, this is the principal for the Crimson Keep, the school for witches and warlocks. Clearly, she's the baby bear in this fairy tale template. Plus, her name is Babs, so that's a major giveaway. Principal Babs has a plump face, rounded figure, and hair that's braided into two ear-like buns atop her head.

Yes, that's baby bear, all right.

Babs scans the lobby. Somehow, past the knot of students, she's able to realize someone is missing. "Where's Goldi?"

A small fae flies out through the opened silver door. She reminds me of Cindy Lou Who from the *How the Grinch Stole Christmas*. Only this version has curly blonde hair and slaps a swirly lollipop on her palm in a movement that reminds me of a gangster movie.

"What's the problem here?" asks Goldi. Her voice is singsong sweet with an undercurrent of evil.

So. Fae.

"Problem student," explains Babs. Everyone in the lobby gasps. *Kill me now.*

Goldi smacks her lollipop against her palm. "Let's take care of this."

"Agreed." Babs lifts her hand, gemstone in her palm. "Let's go to our joint office and discuss."

Red light glows between Bab's tiny fingers, which is the sure sign a spell is about to begin. All at once, a hundred cords of red mist burst out from Bab's palm to loop around me, Babs, Mums, Pops, and Goldi. Fast as lightning, I'm surrounded in a thin layer of red cloud. The students and reception area all disappear under a haze of crimson. Only one thing from the outside world penetrates my magical cocoon: the sound of Knox's voice.

"Bry! Bry!"

There's no need for me to catch his scent; I know Knox is afraid and angry right now. With all my heart, I want to tell him I'm fine, but whenever I try to speak, the enchanted mist clogs my throat. Knox's voice becomes more faint. After that, it disappears altogether. My body gets that "going around the Ferris Wheel" feeling that means I'm being transported somewhere else by magic.

Now I know I'm a real student in one way. I'm getting sent to the principals' office...and I hate it.

# CHAPTER EIGHT

I've been moved around by transport spells before. Alec's spells are like riding a Ferris wheel; my stomach does a few flip-flops, and then it's over. But with Babs? Things may start off like a Ferris wheel ride, but they don't stay that way. Soon, it feels as if needles are pricking into every inch of my skin. Red smoke burns my eyes. I hiss in a pained breath.

A moment later, the spell is done. I'm in the principals' office. On reflex, I hug my elbows.

The office is a tall space with striped wallpaper: red, gold, and silver. The ceiling is made of pressed tin that's been painted in alternating blocks of the same three colors. A long black table lines the far wall. Three high-backed chairs stand behind it. Glancing behind me, I find there are no chairs for students. No additional furniture either. Not sure what I expected. A filing cabinet, maybe? Some shelves of books? The mostly-empty space sends a shiver up my spine.

Mums, Pops, and Babs all settle into their high-back chairs. Goldi hovers in the air above them.

A long silence follows. The quiet becomes so perfect it sets my ears ringing.

I raise my hand. "May I ask a question?"

"Not yet," says Babs in her high-pitched voice. "Goldi is deciding what to do with you."

For her part, Goldi flits back and forth over the heads of the other principals. Every few seconds, she smacks her huge lollipop against her hand. Long lines of goo stretch between her palm and the treat. It's unsettling.

My wolf rouses inside me. *"I want to shift and leave."*

*"I agree. But we can't."*

Goldi flits over to me and points the lollipop at my nose. "You." Her sweet, singsong voice makes me wince.

"What?" I ask, breathless.

"You have to go home," finishes Goldi.

A wave of shock rolls down my limbs. "What do you mean?"

"What she means," says Pops, "is that Goldi here is our expert in all types of magic, but especially doorways. If there's any way to get you into any one of our schools, then Goldi would know it."

Mums adjusts the straps of her overalls. "You sure you got magic?" For a teacher, her grammar is pretty sucktastic.

"Am I sure that I *have* magic?" I ask, subtly correcting her.

"That's what I done said," replies Mums. I glance around the other teachers. No one is correcting Mums. Instead, they're all staring at me like I have two heads.

*Well, okay then.*

"Have you heard of the Denarii leader Jules?" I ask. If anything will prove I have magic, it's how I battled that evil character. I broke through about a thousand ropes of enchanted thorns before I blasted him with so much magic, the big bad basically imploded.

Oh, I have magic all right. Not that I could do that trick again on demand.

Not yet, anyway.

"The Denarii are guardians of magic in our world," says Babs in her gentle voice. "It was such a shame when they disbanded."

Goldi sighs. "How we loved them."

Shock tingles across my skin. *Denarii love? Seriously?* I open my mouth, ready to say that the Denarii were actually evil zombie-mummies and their leader, Jules, was a two-thousand-year-old Julius Caesar and a psychopath.

All of a sudden, I notice all the other principals are nodding along with Babs while murmuring stuff like "those wonderful Denarii."

I press my lips closed. Clearly, the principals adore the Denarii. Not that I blame them. Once upon a time, I thought the Denarii were the good guys, too. That is, until their leader tried to eat my organs and turn me into his unwilling zombie bride for eternity. Talk about a bad moment.

Mums tilts her head. "What? You got somethin' to share 'bout the Denarii? Was such a shame they all got killed."

"Nothing to share, come to think of it." Unfortunately, the words come out far too bright to be believable. "Do you want to see me shift or something? I've been practicing, and I've gotten pretty good at it."

Babs sighs. "This is why we have the doors, Miss Bryar. You can have an enchantment on you that makes you think you're Magicorum, but it might all be a glamour." She glares at Goldi while she says the glamour part.

Goldi chuckles, a low-pitched sound that's oddly unsettling. "I might do that from time to time. But only on Magicorumettes." That's a not-so-sensitive name for regular humans who are related to Magicorum, but don't have any power on their own. "But certainly not on any Magicorumettes who've been invited to attend West Lake Prep." She slaps the lollipop against her palm again. "Except last year, but that was a mistake."

Babs lifts her brows. "And the year before that?"

"Another mistake," says Goldi.

Mums clears her throat. "And the year before—"

"Fine, I do it all the time," says Goldi. "But I didn't cast anything on *this* girl."

I can't believe what I'm hearing. "Are principals *supposed* to use magic that way?"

Goldi lifts her chin. "Fairy principals, sure." Her singsong voice really leans into the word *sure*. I was raised by three fairy aunties. Over the years, I've seen the nutty things that the fae can do. Giving birthday presents of shoes to make their mortal owners dance themselves to death. Paying debts with chests of gold that are actually dried leaves. Glamouring ski slopes so all the paths actually lead straight off a cliff. For the fae, making someone think they're Magicorum is actually pretty low on the cruelty scale.

*Boom...Boom...*

A thudding noise sounds from the wall behind me. I suck in a quick breath. Spinning around, there's no missing how the tri-colored door shakes on its hinges.

*Boom...Boom...*

"What's that?" asks Mums.

The faintest scent of sandalwood and musk hits my nostrils.

"That's Knox," I whisper. "He's trying to break in."

With that, my inner wolf leaps inside my soul. *"Our mate is coming! Knox is so handsome and strong! Can we howl and encourage him?"*

"No."

*"Yip maybe?"*

"Double no."

She huffs out a breath and turns away. *"You're zero fun."*

Back in the visible world, Babs waves her hand. "Let him try. I personally recast the wards on that door every day. No one is strong enough to break through them."

*BOOM!* The door splinters. Knox stands framed in the shattered remains of the doorjamb. He's all leather jacket, bulging muscles, and unbridled rage.

Inside my soul, my wolf yips with glee. *"Our mate is here! I knew he'd come. Let's play with the golden-haired fairy chew toy."*

"Let's not."

Knox stalks across the room, his boots thudding on the tiled floor. He pulls me into a deep hug. I lean in to his hold. It's been a tough morning. "You smell of fear." Knox turns to glare at the principals. "What did you do to her?"

There's a long silence where the principals stare at Knox, open mouthed. Babs is the first one to break the silence. "How did you do that? I set the wards myself."

Knows growls. His eyes flare with golden light. After that, the golden hue moves across his entire body, including his clothes. I press my hands against his jacket. He still feels like the same Knox, only every inch of him shines with golden energy. It's like dating an Oscar statue.

*Wow.* I had no idea Knox could do this.

"I'm the warden of shifter magic," says Knox.

"We didn't realize," whispers Mum.

"I don't advertise it," counters Knox. "But I am. So, whatever power you think you have, it's nothing compared to warden energy. And Bryar Rose here? She's stronger than I am. Show some respect."

The principals all share looks with raised brows. They've gone silent. Even so, there's no question what they're thinking.

*If Bryar Rose were so powerful, she'd be able to walk through a door.*

Knox exhales, and the magic fades from his body. He turns to me. "You want to go? You don't need to take this."

The question echoes through my soul. *Do I want to leave?*

Memories appear. Staring at a book for hours, trying to figure out algebra on my own. Hearing other kids play outside while I was locked in the penthouse with my sleeping curse. Rearranging kitchen chairs into a classroom and pretending other kids were there with me. My entire childhood, I wanted to be in school. Now, I'm here. I only have one more year to experience what it's like to be a student. Maybe I'll hate it, but I have to try.

I straighten my shoulders. "Thanks, but I want to stay."

"What about you?" Babs motions to Knox. "What's your fairy tale life template?"

"Yeah," grumbles Pops. "We should know that afore you get into the den."

Knox pales. I catch the barest scent of earth and rain from him. Sadness.

Now, Knox has tried to tell me his life template before, but I can tell that whatever it is a major point of shame and grief. I told him I don't care what his template is, and I don't. Stepping forward, I move to stand right between Knox and the principals. I may want to go to high school, but not enough for them to hurt my mate.

"Look here," I say. "That means you too, Principal Goldi." The fae leader keeps flitting around, so I snap my fingers at her. "I said, here."

Once I'm sure I have all their attention, I keep going. "I've read all your rules and bylaws online. There's nothing in there about knowing anyone's template. And that stuff doesn't really matter, anyway. It's who you *are* that counts, not how someone else defines you, even if that someone is magic." The principals stare at me, their eyes wide and jaws open. "You should be helping us realize our best selves, not playing into stupid stereotypes."

Pops' weathered face slumps with a look that can only be described as "guilty as hell." I scan the other faces. All the principals look regretful as all get-out, too. I lace my fingers with Knox's.

"You know what? Maybe I don't want to be here after all. Let's go."

At that moment, Elle strides through the smashed-up door. Or rather, she steps across what was left of it. "Wait there, Bry. Please."

There are very few things that would keep me in this room right now. A major gun battle in the stairway leading downstairs. A freezing spell from someone as powerful as the Colonel. Or Elle asking me to wait. It's a girl thing. I'm not leaving my bestie alone.

Babs frowns. "Who is this?"

"I'm Elle."

"She's one of mine." Goldi wrinkles her nose. "Do you have a glamour on or something? Why can't I see your wings?" She snaps her fingers. "Show them, now."

"I don't have to do that," Elle says confidently. All the same, she swishes her hair over her face. I know my best friend. She does that to hide when she's upset.

I frown. Elle has wings? I suppose it makes sense. All the other fae I've seen have wings. Somehow, I just never thought Elle would.

Elle lifts her chin. "And my wings are nobody's business anyway." There's a warble in her voice, though. This whole conversation is upsetting my bestie. I move to stand by Elle's side.

"She totally doesn't have to show her wings," I say. "I read that in your bylaws."

Goldi purses her tiny mouth. "You sure?"

"Absolutely," I say. "You guys post way too much stuff on your website." Which is true. The fact that there is a bylaw about wings is a total lie, though.

"Oh," says Goldi slowly. "In that case, it's fine."

For the record, what the fae don't know about technology is a lot.

Elle sighs with relief, and I could cheer. We so have each other's backs.

Now Alec strides into the room. He's all tanned face, bright smile, and charm, charm, charm. He walks over and shakes all the principals' hands in succession, while repeating the same phrase over and over.

"Alec Le Charme, nice to see you again."

It's interesting to see how the principals all react to Alec. Mum blushes. Pops pumps Alec's hand with fervor. Babs fans herself with her hands, like she's at a boy band concert and Alec is the lead singer. Goldi is the only one who seems immune to his charm. In fact, she makes a point to rub her lollipop across her hand before shaking his. When Goldi and Alec are finished with their greeting, long strings of lollipop goo stretch between their palms. If that grosses out Alec, he doesn't show it. Impressive.

Alec's greeting doesn't derail Goldi from her wing-thing. She's had a few minutes to think over my website comment and is ready for round two.

Goldi looks to Babs. "I can change the internets, can't I?"

"Sure thing," says Babs.

Goldi grins and rounds on Elle. "Then as of this moment, I Goldi, Principal of the Silvery Galleries, do hereby require every fae to show their wings." She flutters over to Elle. "Now, where are your wings, young lady? We don't have fake fae here."

Still grinning, Alec wraps his arm around Elle's shoulder. "Didn't I tell you? Elle here is my third cousin twice removed. Part human, part fae. All Magicorumette. And she's from *Norway*." He says that last part like it explains everything. However, when Alec starts grinning, you want to believe whatever he says.

Goldi smiles back. "Magicorumette. Why didn't you say so before? In that case, it's all fine." I don't like the evil gleam in Goldi's eyes, though. After her other story, I get the feeling that Magicorumette kids aren't safe in the Silver Gallery.

"And I'll tell you what else will be fine." Alec hitches his thumb in my direction. "Bry here. She'll be more than fine, as a matter of fact. My parents and I are confident she'll be an amazing addition to our little community."

At these words, the principals stop being dazzled by Alec and go back to considering me as some kind of menace. Mums and Pops lean back in their chair, folding their thick arms over their overalls. Babs purses her lips. Goldi narrows her overlarge eyes.

Clearly, the principals aren't convinced I should be here. With that realization , my eyes sting, which doesn't make any sense. I mean, a minute ago I was ready to walk away from this place. Why does it make a difference to walk away versus get kicked out?

Somehow, it does.

I clear my throat and try to regain my sense of righteous anger from earlier. "There's nothing to worry about. I'm leaving."

Alec steps to block my exit through the massive door hole. "My family made a big donation to build a workstation for assembling papyri. You put it in the study annex behind the building. Bry here is the only one who can use it."

Babs drums her tiny fingers on the tabletop. "Anyone can use a workstation."

"No, we've been trying for thousands of years to reassemble the *Book of Isis,* all so we can find and activate the fountain of all magic." Alec takes in a long breath. Like Knox, his skin changes. In Alec's case, he becomes solid and translucent. It's like his body was carved from a single, massive ruby gem. "Look, I didn't want to have to do this, but I'm the warden of magic for all witches and warlocks."

Babs freezes. "I didn't know that."

"Knox and I don't advertise it, but yes, we're both wardens. You know how important it is to my parents that I produce a legitimate heir. No fountain, no marriage, no family. It's critical that Bry work on the papyri."

Mums leans forward. "But Bryar Rose can do that anywhere."

Alec pinches the bridge of his nose. "What I'm saying is that my parents built a workstation *here*. It's in the lower levels, right?" All the principals nod. "So Bry can still go to school; she can just work on the papyri." Alec pulls out his cell phone and starts typing. "My parents are about to make a big donation, aren't they?"

Across the room, Mums raps the tabletop with her thick knuckles. "How big?"

Alec finishes typing and flashes the screen at the principals. "This big."

Goldi flits around at double-speed, a super-wide smile on her face. "In that case, it's so exciting to have you here, Bryar Rose. I'll ask every one of my teachers and students to work on some kind of spell to help you get through the doors to our part of the school, the Silver Gallery."

"I'll do the same," offers Babs. "No one will rest until Bry is in the Crimson Keep with the other witches and warlocks, only you must stay at West Lake and work on the papyri. Please."

Mums leans back in her chair. "Let's see if the donation comes through. Until then, she's in."

"I agree," adds Pops.

"Well then," says Babs. "It's official." She looks at me and grins. "You're accepted on a provisional basis."

Alec punches the air with his fist. "Yes."

Knox leans in to whisper in my ear. "What do you say?"

I glance at the overly hopeful faces of the principals. "I don't trust them."

Knox lowers his voice to a level only I can hear. "Neither do I. But I don't think there's any deep hidden meaning here. They want to make one of their major donors happy, that's all."

Alec raises his pointer finger at the principals. "Give us a moment, won't you?" He and Elle step over to join me and Knox.

"What do you think, Bry?" asks Elle.

I hug my elbows more tightly. "I don't know."

"The West Lake kids seem nice," says Elle. "There are even a few girls here from our Magicorum Teen Therapy Group. They were asking about you. But…" Elle sighs. "That alone isn't enough for you to stay. Whatever you choose, you know I've got your back."

Alec steps in closer. "Look, all magic is going haywire these days. If you give me some time, I'll figure out how to fix the doors." Alec looks almost desperate. "I won't lie. We need your help to translate those papyri."

Knox shakes his head. "I already told Bry. She can refuse to translate another glyph. It doesn't matter." There's that scent again, though. Copper and smoke. The veins in his neck darken. Knox hisses in a short breath.

My mate is in pain.

I press my palms over my eyes. There was a reason why I didn't want to translate papyri anymore, wasn't there? Now, I can't remember what it was. I lower my hands. Alec looks so sad. Knox grits his teeth in pain. And Elle looks close to tears.

"Well," I say slowly, "it wouldn't hurt to take a look at the work-station, would it?"

Alex exhales. "That's the spirit." He turns to face the principals. "She's on board."

"You'll just love the workstation," adds Goldi. "I'll take you there right now."

Now, I know fae enough to realize one thing. The workstation is going to be anything but lovable. But I've faced down zombie-mummies, crazy fae queens, and my evil aunties. I can handle this. Let Goldi do her worst. The bottom line stays the same. I can't stand by while Knox gets sicker. If translating those papyri can help my mate, then that's what I'll do.

Even so, as Goldi leads me and Knox away from the principals' office, some small part of me keeps screaming *danger*. I shake the feeling off and refocus. What's the problem with translating papyri? Some small voice in my head keeps whispering the same advice, over and over.

*You don't know the problem. That's the real trouble.*

# CHAPTER NINE

A few minutes later, Knox and I stand in a darkened basement filled with spiders, dust, and—I'm pretty sure about this last part—at least a dozen rats hiding in the corners. Everything is rough stone and packed dirt. A tarp covers the far wall. There are no signs of cockroaches, though. Total bright side.

Goldi flits beside my shoulder. "How do you like the basement of West Lake Prep? Not the posh accommodations you're used to, am I right?" A sly smile stretches her cherub-like face. She's totally expecting me to crumple into a pile of blubbering teenager because of some dust and rats. She's wrong.

"Looks fine to me," I answer. "Before here, I worked on my papyri in a rundown cabin."

"You did?" Goldi's plump cheeks droop into a frown. "Where's this cabin now?"

Knox raises his hand. "I burned it down."

Goldi's pointed ears twitch. "You did?"

"But only after he killed the zombie hanging out inside," I add.

"But you killed her first, Bry." Knox gently kisses my temple. "My girl is tough."

"Oh, well." Goldi flits a little farther away. She's keeping her distance now. Clever fae. "I'll leave you to it, then."

"You do that, yeah?" Knox grins. He's enjoying this. A lot.

A great poof of silver fairy dust surrounds Goldi. For a moment, she's nothing but a small gray cloud in the dark basement. After that, the haze disappears, taking Goldi with it. *Good riddance.*

Knox shakes his head. "Fae." That's all he has to say, and I know exactly what he means. Fairies are totally out there. Who thinks it's a spectator sport to lock some teenager in a basement? The fae, that's who.

I take in a deep breath. "Better see what we're dealing with." The rest of the basement is stacked with boxes and lined with shelves. Every place where something can be stacked or stored seems to overflow with scraps of paper. The place looks like a storage area. No computer workstations to be seen. Looks like I might not be translating papyri after all.

That little voice in the back of my head starts back up again....

*No papyri or translations. Danger!*

I search my soul for my wolf. She's alert and waiting inside my soul. *"Hey, do you get a bad feeling down here?"*

My wolf sniffs. *"No."*

*"Are you sure? Isn't there something telling you that we shouldn't translate papyri?"*

*"Why wouldn't we help our mate?"* My wolf gasps. *"Of course, we'll help Knox."*

*"Good."* With that, my wolf settles down, sets her chin on her paws, and closes her eyes. That's my wolf's way of saying, *'shut up and get to work already.'*

I lift my chin. *My wolf is right.* I need to help Knox. Plus, the idea that translating papyri could be dangerous? Talk about unlikely. I'm just twitchy because it's the first day of school.

And I got magically blocked from walking through any of the doors.

Then, I was sent to work a sketchy basement.

Really, who *wouldn't* be feeling a little vulnerable?

I straighten my shoulders. "Where is this workstation, anyway?"

Knox gestures across the room. "Alec and I set you up over there." At the far corner of the basement, there's a makeshift wall made from a hanging tarp. I stride over to the far wall of the room and pull back the rough fabric. The motion sets the lights flickering overhead, revealing a large space that's filled with a massive U-shaped desk, three keyboards, and twelve monitors. I suck in an excited breath.

"You like?" asks Knox.

"Yes, I do."

"Alec and I designed it. We wanted it to go into the roof annex so you'd have a view of the city while you worked, but…" He shrugs. "Hope it's okay."

Kneeling down, I scan the stacks of servers under the desk and gasp. "This is more computing power than I've ever had before."

"You're always saying how it takes forever to move the bits of papyri around. The extra server power will make your work easier, yeah?"

"That's right." Rising, I turn around to give Knox a huge hug. "Thank you so much."

Knox winds his arms around me. "Whatever makes my girl happy." He steps back, releasing me from his hold. After that, he gestures to the keyboards. "Give it a try. Hit any button on the keyboards and it'll fire up. Alec set it to magically start with your fingerprint."

Spinning back, I tap the space bar on the nearest keyboard. One by one, all the monitors flicker to life in quick succession. I can't believe what I see. New bits of papyri fill each screen. Excitement charges through my nervous system. "These are all parts of the *Book of Isis*."

A few minutes ago, I was super-worried about reassembling the papyri. Now, those worries seem like a case of first-day jitters. Some other part of me is still screaming for me to run home, but I decide that part is certifiable.

"The papyri… Are they good?" asks Knox.

"Good? These are some of the largest and cleanest fragments I've ever gotten. I can make some serious headway now."

"That's what I thought." Knox frowns.

"What has you worried?" I ask.

"It's not the papyri, it's who got them for me. Ty."

"Your ex." The words come out before I can stop them. Is it a little creepy that Knox's ex-girlfriend is hunting down papyri related to the *Book of Isis*...All so I can find the fountain of all magic, which is the key for Knox to be able to make a real commitment to someone? Ty is clearly carrying a torch of massive proportions for Knox. She's not helping me find the fountain so I can have a happily ever after with the man she sees as hers.

So, yes. The fact that Ty found these papyri is a lot creepy.

Still, in the end it doesn't matter how the papyri scraps got here. These are key pieces to the puzzle of reassembling the *Book of Isis*. I'm taking them and getting to work.

I slip into the fancy leather rolling chair. "Hey, I'm just glad to have the info, wherever it came from." I glance around. "Where's your chair?"

Knox rubs his neck. "That, well… We hadn't exactly planned out that part, I guess." He pulls off his jacket and tosses it aside. "I'm sure they've got an extra chair around here somewhere."

A red haze appears on the floor nearby. Magic. The particles of crimson light grow heavier until a person-sized cloud hovers nearby. With a burst of red brightness, the haze disappears. Alec now stands in its place. His surfer-guy smile is gone, replaced by a tight frown.

"I've been texting you, Knox," says Alec. "I need your help, man."

Knox tilts his head. "What's up?"

"Your pack members are causing trouble upstairs. No one can control them."

"You mean Abe and Hollywood?" I ask.

"The same," says Alec. "They're protesting that you and Bry have been expelled. They're staging a sit-in. Actually, they're calling it a den-in. No one will leave the main room and go to class." Alec rolls his eyes. "You've got to show your face and let them know you're okay, man. The principals are about to call in the Apex."

Now, I may be new to the shifter world, but even I've heard of the Apex Predators. They're shifter police for hire, and they aren't too nice.

"Damn," grumbles Knox. He kneels down so we're at eye level. Our gazes lock. "You'll be okay down here, yeah?"

"I'm fine." I make shoo fingers at him. "Go take care of your pack."

Knox gives me the side-eye. "They are not my pack."

I wink. "If you say so."

Knox stands and focuses on Alec. "Fine. What's the fastest way to Abe and Hollywood?"

Alec reaches into his pocket and pulls out a handful of gems. "I think you know the answer to that question already."

Alec raises his hand, magical stones held tightly in his fist. As Alec murmurs a spell. thin beams of crimson brightness leak out between his fingers, casting odd patterns around the room. A few seconds later, both Knox and Alec are surrounded in the red haze of a transport spell. For a moment, the cloud burns more brightly than ever before. Then both Alec and Knox are gone. All of a sudden, the basement seems loaded with shadows and doom. A shiver runs up my spine.

I dreamed something about shadows, didn't I? Closing my eyes, I try to picture the vision from my nightmares, but I can't quite make the connection. That's been happening a lot lately. Probably just stress.

Swiveling around in my chair, I return my focus to the keyboard, monitors, and amazing new papyri. Some small part of me screams that these scraps of the *Book of Isis* came from Ty, so I should delete them, not analyze them. Knox's ex-girlfriend is a sorceress on a mission, after all.

But my gaze catches on an image on one of the monitors. The hieroglyph for *fountain*.

This is good; I'm getting closer.

I start working on the papyri. The monitors flicker with images of glyphs. Gripping my mouse, I move the scraps of papyri into their proper places. All the world melts away until there is nothing but me and this papyri.

Drag.

Drop.

Paste.

Build.

Shadows lengthen around me, but I barely notice them. Instead, I can only focus on reassembling the puzzle before me. *The Book of Isis* becomes clearer than ever before. There's no question anymore about shadows or danger. Thousands of years have passed since anyone read this book.

I simply must know what stories are hidden inside. Yes, that small voice is still saying this is dangerous. But this is for Knox. I simply have to cowgirl up and finish the job.

Soon the images form a greater pattern. Unfortunately, it doesn't make any sense. All the glyphs describe is a bunch of nonsense. My eyes widen with a realization.

Unless you read every third glyph. Then, the meaning becomes clear.

My heart beats so hard I worry that I may crack a rib. At last, clear instructions about the fountain appear on my monitor.

*After the First Wardens*
*There came us, the Luxalta*
*We reassembled the sacred site on new land*
*The fountain remains hidden*
*But never to the sacred device,*
*The Codex Mechanica.*

For a long minute, it's all I can do to stare at the assembled papyri on the screen. The Codex Mechanica. That's the first time I've translated those particular words.

Codex Mechanica.

That term should seem new to me, but it doesn't. Instead, the name feels very familiar. I pull my keyboard closer and start typing like mad. Doctor Google should know what this thing is.

In a shocking move, Dr Google has nothing on the Codex Mechanica. It keeps bringing up searches for other stuff. Did I mean to search for these ancient codices? Or these hacking tools? Or perhaps these old steampunk books?

My jaw locks with frustration. How can the words *Codex Mechanica* be new to the universe? If only I knew what the thing looked like, then I could search that way. I decide to try some different spellings instead.

*Codex Mechanica.*

*Mechanical Codex.*

Still nothing, but making up misspellings is one of my better skills. I've barely begun typing a new list when white lights start appearing in my vision once more. Cold bites into my skin. All of a sudden, I can't keep my eyes open. My limbs feel heavy with the need to doze.

That small and worried part of me balloons into full panic. Falling asleep right now isn't normal. Magic is at work. For a moment, I worry that my old sleeping curse might be back. But this sensation is different from what I used to feel. With Colonel Mallory's curse, silver light blocked my vision. That was clearly fae magic. And I'd always sense a lockbox rattling in my soul.

But this time, there are no magical colors at all. And the lockbox is long gone.

No, this is something else entirely.

Exhaustion weighs down every cell in my body. Scrubbing my hands over my face, I do my best to stay awake. It's impossible. Instead, I slump back into my chair and collapse into a deep sleep. As my eyes flutter shut, I can't help but notice how the shadows around me lengthen and shimmy in strange ways.

Not a good sign.

If only I could remember why.

# CHAPTER TEN

The moment my eyes close, I begin to dream. White lights flash all around me. On reflex, I hop to my feet. The basement at West Lake Prep vanishes in the brightness. Blinking hard, I try to adjust my vision. A few heartbeats later, I find myself back in that snug subterranean room with the child's bed and walls dotted with child's drawings on sheets of construction paper.

Memories flood my mind. This is a dream. *My dream*. And I've had it before. Each time, my dream takes over for a short while. But in the end, it's always interrupted by someone else's magic… and that leads to a nightmare.

I step around in a slow circle, taking in my surroundings. Last time I saw this room, I was too overwhelmed to realize where I might be. But the fact that I met the child version of myself here?

This could only be one place.

It's the place where I slept as a kid.

Looking down, I find myself now wearing the same long gray robes that I did the last time I had this dream. The hood hangs loose down my back. Around me, the walls heave in and out in a steady rhythm. Just like last time, my dream makes the room seem alive. So strange.

My eye catches on the sandbox in the corner. I step over for a closer look. Inside the box, there stand model-size versions of the pyramids as well as a variety of small wooden figures painted silver, gold, and red. Only, something is different. The three main pyramids are no longer in a line, as I've seen in pictures. Instead, they've been rearranged into a triad. I could draw a perfect triangle in the sand, and the three large pyramids would mark the corners of that figure.

At the center point of this triangle, someone has placed what looks like a multicolored rock. Again, the shades of the stone are red, crimson, and silver. My gaze stays riveted on it.

I've seen this image before. It was drawn in the sandbox I saw the last time Child-Me visited my dreams.

Pyramids and eyes. It means something.

My mind races through everything I've learned about pyramids. Nothing connects. But once I start running through information on geysers, that's a different story entirely. In my research, I've seen pictures of stone formations like the tiny model in the sand before me: cones of rock that all spout water or stream on a regular schedule.

The Fly Geyser in Nevada.

The Geysers Del Tatio in Chile.

The Castle Geyser at Yellowstone.

I'd always suspected that the fountain of magic was a geyser. After all, it goes off once every five thousand years. Plus, the Colonel confirmed that the pyramids were built to harness the fountain's power. And here, in my childhood room, there's a sandbox with three pyramids positioned around a cone-shaped geyser.

All of a sudden, my fascination with Ancient Egypt takes on a new meaning. Were my parents keeping me hidden for some reason and feeding me information about the pyramids? How was Colonel Mallory involved? My Child-Self seems convinced that Colonel Mallory is her Poppa, but not every six-year-old truly understands family relationships. And my memory of that time has definitely been tampered with anyway.

Excitement speeds through my bloodstream.

Maybe I have parents. Okay, my parents seem to have let me sleep underground for some reason, but that's something I can worry about later.

Right now, I'm in my childhood room.

It's time to explore.

My legs turn rubbery beneath me as I kneel beside the sandbox and pick up the rough wooden model of the geyser. The walls of the chamber heave at a faster rate as I turn the small object over in my hands. It's a rough cone in shape with a large hole down the center.

The fountain of all magic. It has to be.

White mist rolls across the floor, obscuring the sand beneath me. I rise to stand. As before, the sound of the little girl's laughter echoes through the air.

*"Come find me!"*

It's the child version of me again.

"I'm looking for you," I call.

More images appear in the mist, the same as before. There's the tall figure in golden Roman armor, his helm covering his face. He disappears, only to be replaced by a massive black dragon that can only be Colonel Mallory. The girl's voice sounds in my head once more.

*"Is that you, Poppa?"*

Looking down at my hand, I find I still hold the tiny model in my fist. Up close, it looks like the top of a natural geyser. Rivulets of dried color stream along the body of the conical stone. The colors remind me of the remains of minerals that are left behind at a natural geyser. Only here, the red, silver, and gold don't represent minerals.

These are the remnants of magic.

I can picture it so clearly. The fountain of magic in its natural form, spouting great plumes of red, silver, and golden mist into the air, replenishing the world of power. Around me, the walls breathe even more quickly.

Another memory pushes to the forefront. Somehow, I know this is the most important one of all. I close my eyes, trying to pull the realization out of the depth of my soul. There is something I need to remember about the fountain. I picture the pyramids and how the fountain was set in the center of them. My pulse speeds at double-time. This is all part of the secret to recharging the world with magic. It's why the Luxalta wardens built the pyramids in the first place.

Something critical…

It's so close…

Suddenly, the room becomes bathed in blinding light once more, derailing all my thoughts. An arctic chill cuts through my body. With every exhale, my breath freezes into white plumes. That oddly familiar electric charge fills the air.

Foreign magic.

The brightness turns so intense, my eyes water. After that, it disappears. The snug underground room has disappeared, replaced by a yawning darkness that stretches off in every direction. Three figures now stand before me. Two are the gray forms of Slythe and Tithe, the Shadowvin. And this time, they are joined by another figure, this one all-white with a glowing body and all-black eyes.

"I am the Void," he says, and his voice is a deep rumble. "I seek the fountain. Give me the fountain." His wispy arms reach for me.

I freak the hell out.

Every bone in my body seems to melt with panic. My hands tremble uncontrollably. This isn't some snarky shadow minion trying to trick me into agreeing to give them the Codex Mechanica. This is a big bad who wants to hurt me somehow, no question about it.

The Shadowvin float-walk closer. "Will you give us the Codex Mechanica?" asks Slythe. "We know you found out about it at school. The name alone will be enough for you to find the device. Bring it to us."

A memory appears. The words of the papyri I just translated.

*After the First Wardens*
*There came us, the Luxalta*
*We reassembled the sacred site on new land*
*The fountain remains hidden*
*But never to the sacred device,*
*The Codex Mechanica.*

"I know why you want the Codex Mechanica," I say. "You can use it to find the fountain of magic. And based on the way you've been pulling in my powers, I don't think you want the fountain because you plan to share its magic."

"The fountain is ours," says Tithe.

"We own its power as well," adds Slythe. "We need the fountain's magic to take a solid form. It's only just."

My thoughts spin through this news. "So, you want to no longer be Shadowvin. That makes sense. I know some powerful warlocks and fae. They can help you change into whatever you want to be. You don't need to go after the fountain of magic alone."

The Void's body flares more brightly with white light. "The fountain." His voice is a deep rumble that I feel reverberate through my chest. "Take me to the fountain of magic."

"This is beyond you, little Trilorum," says Slythe. "You've been chosen to find the Codex Mechanica. Get it and bring it to us. You're only returning what was ours in the first place."

"My answer hasn't changed," I say. "No."

"Such a shame," says Tithe. "Perhaps we're being too kind. It may help her clarity to remind her what we do." Her eyes flare more brightly. "And you will do what we say, whether you wish to or not. You only make things harder on yourself."

"When you awaken," says Slythe, "you'll remember our visits, but no one else will. It's called the Curse of the Void. Few keep any memory of him. But you will recall everything now, especially the pain. Perhaps with time and thought, you'll come to see reason."

Both Shadowvin raise their arms. Instantly, tendrils of colored smoke wind up from my hands and pour into their bodies. As the magic is drained from me, every nerve ending in my body feels on fire.

Inside my soul, even my wolf writhes with pain. *"It hurts,"* she whimpers. *"Make it stop."*

*"I can't,"* I reply in my mind. *"I'm so sorry."*

Before me, the two Shadowvin speak in unison. "We can do this to those you love as well," they say. "And more."

After that, the Shadowvin take the forms of Elle and Knox. Yes, they're still semi-transparent, but the point is made.

My wolf's whimpering turns desperate. *"Our mate! Protect our mate!"*

More colored lines of mist float off every exposed inch of my skin. Even my face seeps out power. My eyes sting so hard, it's as if I rubbed my face with Tabasco. I force myself to speak through my gritted teeth. "Leave them alone."

Next, the False Knox turns toward the False Elle and roars. His upper torso expands, turning wolflike while his legs stay human. Knox's face elongates into a muzzle as he leaps toward the False Elle. Both sets of his claws are poised at her throat.

In my mind, I know the Shadowvin are pretending to possess my friends and force them to kill each other in front of me. It's an illusion and a threat, but that doesn't change the fact that it's terrible to see your mate try to murder your best friend. A mixture of white-hot rage and terror stream through me.

I scream, "Stop! Now!"

The pain intensifies as more wisps of colored light fly out from my body. I collapse onto my side, my body twitching with pain. The False Knox and False Elle turn to me, speaking together in voices that sound so real, my heart cracks.

"Will you give the Shadowvin the Codex Mechanica and save us?" ask the illusions of my friends. "Vow it once and that's all you have to do. Then, you'll be under a compulsion to finish the deed. And we'll be safe. You love us, don't you?"

The pain turns so intense, all rational thought leaves my brain. All I know is that the agony is overwhelming, and saying something to these creatures will end it all. "I...I…"

I close my eyes tightly against the pain. Under the roar of magical wind, a voice reverberates. The agony is too intense to open my eyes, but I lock on to that voice just the same.

"Bry!"

It's Knox. The real one.

White light flashes past my closed eyes. Cold bites into me with more force than ever before. My body feels like it's being turned inside out. Agony bursts through every inch of me.

And then, it's gone.

I open my eyes to find myself back in the rolling chair at school. I'm in the basement at my workstation, just as I'd been when I'd fallen asleep. Knox kneels before me, gripping my shoulders.

"Bry! Wake up, please."

I launch forward and wrap my arms around his neck. "Knox, it was horrible."

"Shh. It's all right now." Knox scoops me off the chair and onto his lap. The feeling of being encased in his body and arms is just what I need. "What happened?"

I shiver. "Nightmares."

"Do you remember this time?"

I close my eyes and a tear rolls down my cheek. The visions were so powerful I hadn't even noticed I'd been crying while I was asleep. "It's the Void. He's evil and works against the fountain of magic. I translated some of the papyri today. It said something about needing this device, the Codex Mechanica, in order to find the fountain. The Void wants me to find the device and give it to him."

Knox kisses my temple. "I'm going to kill this Void guy."

"He's got these transparent ghost minions called the Shadowvin."

"So, I'll kill them, too." The barest scent of burnt charcoal fills the air. *Rage.*

"We need to talk to Azizi. He tried to tell me about the Void last summer, but there's this curse about the Void. You can't remember anything about him after you hear it." I take in a shaky breath. "And there's more. If I don't do what the Void wants, he'll…" I force out the words. "He'll hurt you, Elle, and Alec. I have to stop the Void and the Shadowvin before they get anywhere near you all."

Knox hisses in a short breath. Another scent fills the air. Pain.

Leaning back, I scan the familiar lines of Knox's face. His neck is twitching again. That's not a good sign. When I speak, I take care to make my tone gentle. "It's getting worse, isn't it?"

I don't need to say what I mean by "it." We both know I'm talking about the pain Knox has been feeling lately. And it's getting worse as the autumn equinox approaches.

Only four days to go until the equinox is here.

"We should go see Azizi right now," I say. "Ask him what's going on. I think he'll know about what's hurting you as well as the Void."

"The Void…" Knox rubs his eyes for a long moment. "What were we talking about again?"

"The Void and the Shadowvin. I saw them in my dreams. They want the Codex Mechanica, or they'll hurt you, Alec, and Elle."

Knox rubs his forehead. "What?"

My shoulders slump with disappointment. "The Shadowvin told me there was a curse. For a long time, I couldn't remember anything about the Void, even if it was said a minute ago. Now, the same thing is happening to you."

Knox shakes his head. "I must be having a crazy day because I'm having brain drain. Can you go over that again?"

I debate explaining it once more, but that doesn't seem to be a good use of time. This curse will just wipe everything away as soon as I say it. "Maybe we should go see Azizi now." Now that I have my memories back, I recall Azizi saying something about the Void last summer.

Knox's ice-blue eyes narrow. "Not sure that's a good idea anymore. Az is worrying too much."

My mate is the king of understatement. If he thinks someone is worrying too much, then it's probably a huge deal that needs more focus, not less. "What is Az worried about?"

Knox sighs. "My pain is getting worse."

"But we knew that."

"It's *worse*-worse."

I grip Knox's hand in mine. He's trembling. "How bad is it?"

"Azizi called me."

My eyes widen. Azizi never uses his phone. "What did he say?"

"Az said his glyphs are coming back, so I checked mine. They're fading, Bry."

All the oxygen seems to get sucked out of my lungs. As wardens, Azizi and Knox have glyphs from the *Book of Isis* on their back. As Knox grew in power, his marks grew darker. Azizi's grew lighter. We always knew that when his marks disappeared entirely, Azizi would die.

Inside my soul, my wolf howls with fear. *"We can't lose our mate!"*

*"We aren't losing anyone,"* I reply.

I steel my shoulders. There's no way I'll be the weepy girlfriend when I ask this next question. "How long do you have?"

"I don't know. They're fading faster by the hour."

My heart pounds so hard, I feel my pulse in my throat. "Give me a timeframe. Please."

"Based on what I just saw? Days."

I slide off Knox's lap. "All the more reason for us to see Azizi together right away."

Knox slowly rises. For the first time, I get a good look at him. His skin is turning gray. Some of his muscle tone has faded. This isn't the same Knox I saw this morning.

"Good," says Knox. "We'll see Az together." He looks so open and worried, I can't even stomach the idea of leaving him alone anyway.

"Agreed."

Hand in hand, Knox and I step up the winding staircase that leads to the main reception area. Somewhere in the back of my head, I realize this is my first day at West Lake Prep, and I'm already skipping school. But honestly? I can't find it in me to care. All I can think about is seeing Azizi. That old were has been a warden for hundreds of years. He must know something that can help.

Because Knox's glyphs are fading. He's dying.

As bad as I thought things were, everything has just turned infinitely worse.

# CHAPTER ELEVEN

It's lunchtime by the time Knox and I pull into the parking garage near Lucky's. This part of Brooklyn is still pretty deserted, even during the daytime. It's all part of the wards that Alec cast over Lucky's. This bar is a werewolf hangout, and humans are most definitely *not allowed*. Even so, the protective spells have been going haywire lately. When that happens, this empty residential street gets mobbed with humans and their handhelds, all of them dying to take a selfie with a real werewolf.

With magic disappearing from the world, shifters, witches, and fairies are more sought after than Hollywood stars. Shifters have it the worst. Our *fans* call themselves howlers, and once they find a were? They're like blood-sucking ticks. Hard to get of. Plus, it's even harder to magically wipe their memories and cell phones afterward.

That's why wards are so important. Better to keep the howlers out in the first place.

Knox pauses along the sidewalk. "You should eat."

"So should you." The scent of copper and smoke has never been stronger. Knox's pain is getting worse. "Maybe you should skip this meeting at Lucky's. I can talk to Az myself."

My wolf stirs inside my soul. *"Our mate is in pain. This is a good idea. Let him rest while we talk to Azizi."*

Knox gives me the side-eye. "Your wolf talking to you again?"

Inside my head, my wolf yips for joy. *"I am! I am! Our mate is so wonderful to have guessed!!!"* Once again, my inner animal proves to be Knox's biggest fan. *"Tell him what I said."*

"Yes," I reply to Knox. "She thinks you should rest."

"She's a protective animal, which is cool, but you know I'm not leaving you to chat with Az alone. Don't get me wrong, I love the guy. But he's, you know, Az."

I know what Knox means. Az is like a werewolf version of Gandalf. Knox's guardian is forever making cryptic and dire predictions. "Az doesn't frighten me."

"Even so, my wolf still won't stand for you to be alone with him. My animal thinks the old were will upset you." Knox gives my hand a squeeze. "It won't take long, and we'll get some grub afterwards, yeah?"

The mention of food perks up my inner wolf. *"Tell him we want rabbit,"* says my wolf. *"Or some of those fae who look like sheep."*

*"That's not happening."* I reply in my mind. *"We're leaving the fae alone."*

In all honesty, the idea of food sounds unappealing. Sure, I haven't eaten all day, but Knox's glyphs are fading. There's no way I can force anything down until I get some answers. Even so, I slap on a smile. "Sounds like a plan."

We quickly reach Lucky's. It's one of those basement bars where you have to step down into the pavement to reach the door. In fact, if you looked at the place from the street, it wouldn't look like a bar so much as a nondescript brick building. Weres like their privacy.

Knox and I step down the five short stairs to reach Lucky's main door. Once inside, the place looks like it always does: dimly lit with a low ceiling, lots of small round tables, and a back wall that's lined with shelves of alcohol. About twenty shifters hang out at the tables, most of them guys. Girl weres are rare. The moment

Knox enters the room, all eyes lock onto him. Everyone's irises glow with golden light, which means their wolves are near the surface.

I hang with Knox all the time, so I'm immune to this effect, but other weres feel his presence like a lightning bolt. It's Knox's natural alpha power, which is the energy that drives him to lead a pack. Or in Knox's case, since he's warden of all shifter magic, he's built to be the alpha of alphas.

My inner wolf just loves this kind of thing. *"Our mate is supreme. All other wolves want him to lead them."*

The room falls quiet as Knox and I cross the floor. Usually, Knox asks the bartender if Az is asleep. That's not what happens this time. Instead, the moment we're within a yard of the long wooden bar, the bartender—a freckled guy about our age named Thad—nods toward the back door. "He's waiting for you."

Knox gives Thad one of his chin-nods. Together, we open the back door and make what feels like an incredibly long trek down the hallway to Az's room. As we get closer, I recognize the deep rumble of Az's voice as well as the softer tones of other female voices. My brows lift. Az has visitors. That's new.

I knock on the wooden door. "Hello, Azizi? It's Knox and Bry."

His reply echoes through the wood. "Come in."

My mind takes a snapshot of this moment. There are a number of ways my life could go, depending on what Azizi has to say next.

*Please, let the old were know some way to save Knox.*

My hand trembles as I twist the handle and push the door open. Inside, I find a scene I'd never have expected. Az is in human form, which is shocking in itself. Normally, Az stays in his wolf state, lying on the floor. Knox told me he was always worried about Azizi not lasting much longer. Plus, Knox is constantly concerned about Az refusing to change into human form. It's not healthy for shifters to stay stuck in their mortal or animal states. But now? Azizi is out of his wolf state and walking about as a man—something I've never seen before. Az also looks fit, with copper skin, a shaved head, and thick gray eyebrows. He has a round face and lean body. Today, he's wearing a traditional white linen kilt, the kind they wore in Ancient Egypt.

And he's got visitors.

In fact, the people with Azizi are none other than Scarlett and Avianna, two girls from my old Magicorum Teen Therapy Group. I scan Scarlett first. She looks just like she did in group, with her ebony-dark skin, light amber eyes, and long braids. Today, she's leaning against the wall and wearing red leathers. So badass.

Scarlett tilts her head. "I saw you at school this morning."

"And I saw you," I say.

"Crap deal about the doors," adds Scar.

For Scarlett, that's a lot of sharing. She's a werewolf who has a Red Riding Hood life template. Since her name was Scarlett, I assumed she put the *red* in Red Riding Hood. Although looking at her now? She could possibly be the wolf in that tale as well. My were senses detect something shifter about her.

Avianna steps forward. She's wearing a long black dress and has a crow perched on her shoulder. Combined with her pale skin, black hair, and pronounced eyebrows, she's working the full evil queen look. *Poor girl.* Avianna's life template is to be the evil queen from Snow White, which is a bummer. She seems like a nice girl. No one wants to end up dead in a ditch while being uglied up by their own potions.

Az focuses on me. "You've returned." Even as a human, he still has a deep voice with the staccato of an Arabic accent. "And now, you remember, don't you?"

The words are out there, but unspoken: *you remember about the Void.*

"I do."

Sure, I could say more, but I'm not quite ready. After all, Avianna and Scar are here. Anxiety bunches up my spine. Not sure how much I want to share with those two around. Don't get me wrong—they're nice girls.

But this is life, death, and magic here.

Az rounds on Knox. "And you." He eyes my mate from head to toe. "You look like camel dung I scraped off my sandal."

Knox gives him the side-eye. "Thanks."

Az gestures across the room. "I see that you already know my friends. Scarlett I've known for years. Avianna is her friend."

I give them a half wave. "Hey. Nice to see you again."

"I saw what happened with the doors at West Lake." Avianna's voice comes out as a peep. "That was rough." Her crow lets out a small caw that sounds like it sympathizes, too. "Shh, Bernard."

A crow named Bernard? Somehow with Avianna, it works.

"Yeah," says Scar. "I saw that, too. Then Az called us over. He and I go way back." Scar folds her arms over her chest, a movement that makes her leathers creak. She's so badass.

Avianna raises her hand. "I'm only here because Scar asked me. She knows Az and everything." The bird caws again. "And Bernie wants you to know that she's our best friend."

This is a lot of sharing from Avianna. I get the feeling she doesn't hang out with folks other than Bernie and Scar very much.

Az steps closer to me. He has issues with invading personal space, even in his wolf form. "You've learned something."

By the way, Az does this a lot. "*You've learned something*" is meant to be a question, but Az rarely asks questions, technically. So, I go through everything that happened. I start with school and the weird situation with the doors. After that, I tell him about assembling the new papyri and learning that we need to find the Codex Mechanica in order to locate the fountain. And finally, I share that I saw the Void.

I almost say something about Knox feeling worse, but I'm guessing that the camel dung comment means Az is on to that part already. Instead, I segue right to my big question. "You know anything about the Shadowvin?"

"Yes. I had an unfortunate encounter with them once, many years ago. One side affect is that I'm now immune to the curse about the Void. The Shadowvin and Void like to work through dreams."

"For a while, I couldn't remember when they visited."

"The Shadowvin make exceptions to the Void's curse when it suits them. And now, in your case, it seems to suit them." He gestures to Scar and Avianna. "I asked these ladies here to help Knox, but now that you know about the Void?" He rubs his chin slowly. "Perhaps the is only one way to help Knox…and that is to aid you."

Scar tilts her head. "Am I the only one who's having trouble remembering what Az says?"

"There's something going on with my memory too." Knox blinks hard, like he's trying to clear his mind. "But if it's something we need to know, then my guardian will tell us when the time is right."

Scar nods. "True that."

My brows lift. Indeed, Scar must have known Az for a long time if she's used to how he withholds information. It's yet another personality trait he shares with Gandalf. I decide to start off with a simple question. "Az, what do you know about the Void?"

"Only what I've learned from my unfortunate encounters with the Shadowvin. The Void is an evil creature that came into being when magic was created. According to the First Wardens, the Void wishes to consume the world into nothingness."

Knox turns to me. "Why didn't you say anything before?"

"I did tell you." My voice is tinged with sadness. This memory curse is terrible. I hate keeping things from Knox, even if it is beyond my control.

Az gestures around the room. "Just be patient. All will eventually be made clear to you."

Avianna and Scar share a confused look.

"Hey," grumbles Scar. "We need to…to… What were we talking about again?" She turns to Avianna. "Do you remember?"

"No idea," says Avianna.

Az grins. "We were discussing the fate of the world."

"Sure we were," says Knox. "You're doing that thing again."

"What thing?" asks Az.

Knox shakes his head. "The one where you talk in riddles."

"Ah, that. Apologies." Az chuckles, but there's no humor in it. He focuses his attention on me. "Now that you're ready, there are some things I can do to help you."

My inner wolf starts to howl. *"Help our mate! Our maaaaaate!"*

*"I completely agree,"* I say in my mind.

I hold up my hand with the palm facing Az. This is the universal symbol for *stop right there, friend.* "Before we do anything else, you need to help Knox. Why is he getting sick?" I ask.

"You wouldn't tell me on the phone," says Knox. "Is it because I need to find the fountain before the equinox? That's only four days away. Not sure that's really possible."

Az's mouth thins to a line. "I'm no wizard, but I know a few witches and witches. I've consulted a powerful witch with expertise in diagnosing magical ailments. Your sickness is not due to the fountain." He lowers his voice. "This is a personal matter that can wait until we are alone."

"No," growls Knox. "You can tell me now. I've got nothing to hide." His gaze scans Scar and Avianna. "From anyone."

Az swipes his hand over his bald head. It's the motion he does when he's about to deliver really bad news. "Magic doesn't like you two together. You're a warden. You should focus on finding the fountain of magic. No other shifter warden has found his mate before discovering the fountain. That's become a problem. You're distracted by your love for Bryar Rose."

"But Bry and I aren't married, Az." Knox's words come out as a low snarl. "Magic is supposed to leave us alone unless we try to get hitched. You said that to me." Knox pounds his leg with his fist. "Hell, you encouraged me to go after Bry. You said if you'd had a chance at love, you'd have risked everything."

"I gave the best advice I could at the time," says Az.

I pinch the bridge of my nose. This is all moving so fast. The autumn equinox is coming up and the fountain's about to rise. I hate to think this, but if magic wants Knox to find the fountain fast, maybe he does have a better chance without any romantic distractions around.

Without me.

Inside my heart, my wolf rouses. *"We're hurting our mate,"* she whimpers. *"We can't be with him."*

"*Az is wrong,*" I reply in my mind. "*There must be another explanation.*" But my words don't have a lot of force behind them. Az has never been wrong before.

Az steps up to Knox. "Magic does what it wants. There's no controlling it or predicting it." The old were places a meaty hand on Knox's shoulder. "And magic wants you to find the fountain. It sees your love for Bryar Rose as lessening your chances."

Knox keeps his gaze locked with Az. A long pause follows before my mate utters a single word: "No."

"Here is the truth of the matter," continues Az. "The more time you spend with Bryar Rose, the more ill you'll become. It has nothing to do with the equinox in four days' time. You must be apart. Spend your time searching for the fountain, but do it separately. It's the only way you'll live."

"That's a load," snarls Knox. "I know who you go to for magical advice, and my ex-girlfriend is not a great source of information."

My eyes bulge with shock. *Did Knox just say ex-girlfriend?*

I round on Az. "You know Ty?"

"For years," says Az.

"Az knows everybody," adds Knox. "Especially if they play any serious role in my life. But he can get too emotional when it comes to my safety. I've seen it before." He shoots a pointed look at his guardian. I know that expression from Knox. It says, *You're full of crap on this one.*

"How can you doubt my methods?" asks Az. "As always, I consulted many more experts than merely Ty."

"But she's on the list." Knox folds his arms over his chest. "Look, Ty is a manipulative freak. I don't trust this *or* her. I have to be apart from Bry or I fall over dead? I call bullshit."

Avianna takes a half step toward the door. "Maybe we should leave?"

"Nah," says Scar. "Things are just getting interesting."

Az steps away from Knox. "You asked for my assessment. That's what I have to tell you." This time, Knox doesn't reply. The quiet in the room turns deafening.

Inside my soul, my wolf curls up into a ball and falls silent as well. The fact that she's turned quiet means she suspects the truth the same as I do.

*I'm killing my mate, just by standing near him.*

Azizi sighs. "Now, if you don't mind. I need to help Bryar Rose travel through time."

All the air gets sucked out of my lungs. This was already a pretty surreal day. I must have misheard Az. I clear my throat. "Let me get this straight. Did you say travel through time?"

Az lifts his chin. "I did."

Inside my soul, my wolf stands at attention. *"Travel through time? Will there be fairies to chew on?"* I have enough to worry about right now, so I decide to ignore my wolf for a bit.

"Sorry," I say. "I'm still stuck on the last thing we talked about. If I'm near Knox, I kill him? I don't want to go anywhere until we figure out if that's the truth."

"I disagree," counters Az. "We must protect the fountain of magic and stop the Void at all costs. Do you understand?"

Time travel. Knox dying. And now, the fate of all magic is at stake. My brain goes into overload. My eyes well with tears. "This is too much, Az."

"Come here." Knox wraps his arms around me and pulls me against the solidity of his chest. Closing my eyes, I soak in the warmth of his touch. A long minute passes this way before I feel ready to talk once more.

"Why me?" I ask.

When Az speaks again, his voice is gentle. "I don't know. All I can say is that magic has chosen you."

"I still say the stuff from Ty is crap." Knox holds me more tightly. "Bry is my life. Being near her would don't hurt me." He glares at Az. "You made a mistake."

"Anything is possible," says Az. I've heard that phrase from him before. It's Az's way of saying, *I'm right, but I'm done fighting with you.*

There's a long moment of silence where no one's quite sure what to do next. We can't stand around like this all day, so I step away from Knox. Losing his touch hurts, but waiting around forever isn't an option. Turning, I address Scar and Avianna. "I guess you're going to take me through time, then?"

A small smile rounds Scar's mouth. "If you're up for it."

"I am. Let's do this."

And so we begin.

# CHAPTER TWELVE

"Glad you're ready for your journey," says Az. "I've asked Scar and Avianna here to take you to the past. You alone will keep the memories afterward. That's the best I can do."

I shift my weight from foot to foot. "Out of curiosity, what were you planning to do *before*?"

"Before?" Az raises his brows.

"Before I said how I remembered the Void."

"Ah," says Az slowly. "Knox told me you were accompanying him here. By that point, I had already spoken to my witch contracts. I learned that your future with Knox ends in tragedy." He shoots a pointed look at Knox. "I brought Scar and Avianna here to use magic and try to show you the truth. Bryar Rose is draining your life force. The two of you are better off apart."

"I see." The words come out as a croak.

*I'm hurting Knox. We need to be apart.*

Knox glares at his guardian. "You can't know that for sure. This is all scaring Bry for no reason."

"Now, now." Az raises his hands in a motion that says *calm down*. "In this moment, fate and magic have seen fit to give Bryar

Rose certain knowledge. We now know magic and the fountain are at risk. It is no longer the moment to prove to you the truth of your future without Bryar Rose. We must focus on the fountain." He turns to Avianna and Scar. "Let us not waste the time of our valuable allies."

I turn to Scar and Avianna as well. "How can you help?"

"I created a potion that will allow you to travel through time," says Avianna.

Before I can stop myself, my mouth falls open. "You can really do that? That's a rare skill even for a senior witch or warlock." I'm no expert in magic, and even I know that.

Avianna stares at her feet. "Thank you." Bernie caws again while puffing out his chest. That thing is growing on me.

Scar steps forward. "And I'm a shifter with an unusual gift. I'm a spirit shepherd."

I take in a shocked breath. "I thought those were myths."

Spirit shepherds help guide you in any number of ways. They can take the form of a loved one and provide advice…or they can reincarnate someone from your worst nightmares. Whatever the situation, spirit shepherds are powerful, all-purpose shapeshifters. Like me, they are super-rare. No wonder Madame had recruited Scarlett and Avianna to our little teen therapy group. Jules would have loved to consume our powers.

Scar shrugs. "There aren't many of us, but we exist. I can take any form I want, including a wolf when it suits me. And when I need to, I can guide people on the path to their future. Sometimes that's by taking a form they need to see, like a loved one. Other times, it's being a more literal guide." She turns to me. "After you take the potion from Avianna, I'll ask a question. Based on the answer, we'll both move physically to another time. Once we're there, I can take the form of a local and help explore from there."

"Will you know about the time we visit?" I ask.

"I'll ask what you need to know about the Shadowvin," says Scar. "Safe bet we're going to the past. I don't know exactly when in time we'll arrive, though."

"Isn't that dangerous?" I gesture across her red leather outfit. "Depending on when you arrive, you could not exactly fit in."

Scar shrugs. "I'm good at bluffing. Plus, my powers help us both understand what everyone is saying and be able to talk their language."

I grin. "That's great."

"Oh, this is magic." Scar chuckles. "There's a catch. We need to stay connected. As in physically. By a cord."

"Handy," says Knox.

"Good guess," adds Scar. "We have to keep our hands tied together in order the magic to work. It's a pain."

I look down at my outfit. I'm still wearing my unshreddable clothes from school: a duster, dark pants, and heavy boots. That said, I still do wear the bracelet that can glamour me into looking like I'm wearing the school's uniform. "Not sure I'm wearing the right clothes."

"We don't know where we're going, so there's no point in changing. Besides, you'll have me with you. I can look like a local like that." She snaps her fingers. "And I'm fast on my feet. We'll talk our way around it."

The world seems to pause for a moment. I'm about to take some sketchy potion and travel back in time with a girl I barely know. Words tumble from my mouth without any conscious thought from my head. "Can I trust you?"

"You've got nothing to worry about from me," says Scar. "All I know about how to control my powers, I learned from Az. If he says I'm to allow my magic to guide you to wisdom, then that's what I'll do." She nods toward Avianna. "And this one's a goodie two shoes who'll do anything for anyone." That last phrase is said with a little venom, as if this is part of an ongoing fight between these two. Bernie caws in agreement.

Avianna lifts her pale chin. "I'm doing the right thing." She could be talking about helping me, but she isn't. The way she glares at Scar, I can tell this is all part of another conversation. *Interesting.*

Scar sighs. "You're too good, Vi." After that, Scar fixes her gaze on me once more. "What do you say? Are we doing this?"

I look Az over carefully. This guy basically raised Knox. "If Az says you both can be trusted, then I'm in."

"Good." Scar cracks her neck from side to side. "Everyone needs to leave the room. My gifts don't work as well with an audience. You'll throw off my focus. I could end up transforming into someone's dead grandmother, and that won't help Bryar Rose here."

Knox slowly walks over to stand before me. He towers above me, but even so, my mate has never seemed more frail. "You sure about this?"

"Positive. There's no question in my mind that the Void and Shadowvin are after the fountain of magic. We have to protect it. And the rest..." I don't need to say what the rest is. We both know that I'm talking about magic killing Knox for being near me. "We'll worry about that later."

Knox gently rests his palm against my cheek. "I'm not leaving you. I'm not losing you." All the intensity in the world shines in his ice-blue eyes.

What do I say here? *I'll allow you to stay by my side, even if it kills you? Or we need to stay apart, even if that destroys our souls?*

Az saves me from having to reply, though. "Let's go," announces Azizi. After that, the elder were wraps his arm about Knox's shoulder and guides my mate toward the door. It's a sign of how weak Knox is feeling that he leans against Az as he walks. My heart cracks. Knox is dying before my eyes. And I might be the one killing him.

I shake my head. I can't focus on that now. If I don't protect the fountain from the Void, many more people than Knox will be at risk. And maybe once we find the fountain, we can use it somehow to heal Knox and fix things. It's not much, but it's a plan.

Knox pauses by the door. "See you soon, Bry."

I nod and blow him a kiss, but what I really want to do is weep. Knox looks so pale and tired. *Please let me make the right decisions here.*

Within seconds, Knox and Az step into the main hallway, closing the door behind them. Now it's just Scar, Avianna, and me in the room.

"So how does this work, exactly?"

"Damned if I know for sure," says Scar. "Normally, soul shepherding takes days to transport. But Vi and I have been buds since were kids. We stumbled across this trick for speeding up the process when we were nine."

"Seven, as a matter of fact," corrects Avianna. She pulls a small vial from the folds of her robe. "Drink this, and within seconds, you will be transported in time to the point you most need to see."

For a moment, I hope I might see the day I was born. How amazing would it be to actually get a look at my parents? I shake the thought off, though. What I really need right now is information on how to find the fountain and save Knox.

I scoop the vial from Avianna's palm and down the contents in one gulp. It tastes like rotten apples. Crimson lights flash in my peripheral vision.

"Did you see that?" I ask.

"It's my magic," says Avianna. "The spell is starting to work."

Scar loops a bit of golden cord between our wrists. "Like I said before, we need to stay in touch for me to guide you." She turns to Avianna. "And you need to get out of here."

Avianna nods and scurries away just as everything in my vision turns a singular shade of red.

When Scar speaks again, her voice takes on a deep resonance. "This child seeks the answer to the riddle of the Shadowvin. Transport through time. Reveal wisdom. Bring joy."

An odd warmth fills my veins. The familiar sensation of riding a Ferris wheel takes over my stomach.

I'm transporting somewhere.

And I'm accompanied by a powerful soul shepherd that I barely know.

*Let's hope this works.*

# CHAPTER THIRTEEN

The next thing I know, I'm standing in an open plaza at night. The air is thick and humid. People are everywhere, all of them wrapped in the same long gray cloaks I had been wearing in my dreams. Most have the hoods pulled low over their faces. The full moon casts everything in a bluish glow. The air is thick with heat and moisture. In the distance, I see the forms of three massive pyramids backed by a wall of palm trees and jungle vines.

I try to focus on where we are in time, but my head feels like it's full of cotton. I turn to Scar. "Where are we, do you think?"

"The past, thank magic."

My eyes widen. "You weren't sure?"

Scar shrugs. "You never know with these kinds of spells. I've ended up in some crazy-weird places with six-armed aliens that claim to be someone's super-great grandkids. Crap like that keeps me from sleeping for days."

"Oh." It's all I can manage to say. Scar certainly lives an odd life, and I should know. I've quite the bizarre existence myself. "Back to my question. Any guesses as to timeframe?"

"I'd say we're in South America, about five thousand years ago," replies Scar. "Based on those pyramids, this is the time of the First Wardens." She eyes a group of cloaked people walking by. "We've probably hit one of their ceremonies for the fountain of magic."

"Five thousand years ago." The words rattle around in my head, but don't make sense. Maybe it's the six-armed alien story, but my brain feels like total mush. "Are you sure?"

"No doubt about it." Scar gestures toward the horizon line. "Nothing else looks like those three pyramids. I've seen them before during other trips to the past."

My heart lightens. Even though my head still seems foggy, I remember enough from the Colonel's story to know that we've come to the right place. "The First Wardens were the only ones who could use the fountain correctly. But something went wrong…" I rub my forehead as if the motion will help to stir my memories. "For some reason, I can't recall why, though."

"It's time travel. Messes with your head at first. Give yourself a few minutes, and you'll be good as new." She jiggles her left hand, which is still connected to my right via a thin golden cord. "Just don't let this break or get untied until you're ready to return to the present."

I nod. "Now that I can remember."

Scar inspects the scene. Her eyes hold the golden glow of shifter magic. "Everyone's wearing the same gray cloak. Based on the way they're glaring at us, we need to change as well. Time to blend in." Scar gestures across her face with her open palm. For a moment, the barest hint of gold-colored mist surrounds her skin. *Magic.*

When the haze disappears, Scar is wearing the same long gray cloak as everyone else. She looks like she belongs here, but everyone—and I do mean everyone—is still eyeing me from head to toe. All their faces are either scrunched with disapproval or frowning with menace. I blink hard, trying to think through what I can do to fix this. My head feels too messed up to focus.

Scar turns to me. "We need to get you a gray robe, too."

I rub by eyes, trying to think through this news. "How are we going to do that?"

"This is a bazaar. Someone's got to be selling robes."

I nod slowly, trying to soak everything in. With each passing moment, my thoughts become clearer. Scar is right. The place where we've appeared—it isn't just some random plaza. There are tables set in neat rows, with all of them backed by different vendors. A bazaar. All of a sudden, I feel on much more solid footing. I don't know much about traveling through time, but I've bought stuff from New York street vendors all my life. You can tell a lot about a city by who sells what. "Someone around here must sell robes, that's for sure. But how do pay for them, exactly?"

Scar winks. "Just watch me do my thing." She scans the nearby tables and nods toward the far-left side of the plaza. "That direction."

It isn't easy to walk while you're hand is tied to someone else's, especially when you're in a crowd where people are constantly pushing to get between you and the person you're tied to. In short order, Scar and I figure out that we need to stand shoulder to shoulder, and that takes care of the worst of the trouble.

As we step along, I take stock of the faces around me.

Young.

Old.

Every shade of skin.

Every nationality.

This place reminds me of being back outside West Lake Prep. I start guessing what someone's power is by how their body looks under a long hooded robe…instead of a glamoured-up school uniform. The big linebacker types are easy; those have to be shifters. The slim and graceful folks are probably fae. I figure everyone else is a witch or warlock.

We almost walk right into someone with orange skin and pointed ears. Definitely fae. I pause, waiting for my wolf to howl that she wants to come out and play.

But my inner animal is silent.

I turn to Scar. "I can't detect my wolf. It's not even like she's asleep." A pang of panic moves through my insides. "She's completely gone."

"No worries," says Scar. "It's the first question everyone asks when my powers are active. Whatever I do, it always puts your shifter animal on pause. She's fine. Don't sweat it."

I force myself to take in a few long breaths. My inner wolf is fine. I just need to focus on getting a gray robe to blend in. As we continue marching through the bazaar, I catch snippets of conversation.

"This is my fourth visit to the sacred celebration."

"Have the First Wardens arrived yet?"

"What power are you choosing?"

"Did your magic come from your parents or the fountain?"

"I join the celebration every year. Never miss it."

Each morsel of information is precious. I quickly piece together that you can gain magic either by inheriting it from your parents or having it granted to you from the fountain.

Scar pauses before one of the tables. A young man with a shock of red hair stands behind the stall. Based on how he's tall and lithe, the guy is probably fae. Piles of gray robes cover the tabletop before him.

"Greetings," says the guy. "Welcome to my table. Bramblethick-skin is my name."

I purse my lips. *The jury is back, ladies and gentlemen.* With a name like Bramblethickskin, he's definitely fae. He also has about a one hundred per cent chance of having Rumplestiltskin as his fairy tale life template. Just saying.

Bram gestures across the table before him. "You looking for a gray robe for this petitioner?" He hitches his thumb at me.

"That's right," I say.

"Forty pieces of gold," says Bram.

"You don't want to charge us anything," counters Scar. "This petitioner has traveled through the mists of time to reach this ceremony. You should give her the robe for free." Her eyes have taken on that golden glow. She's definitely planning another spell.

"How fascinating." Bram rolls his eyes. "Eighty pieces of gold."

Scar swipes her free hand across her face. A thin layer of golden mist surrounds her body. When the haze vanishes, Scar appears to be an elderly woman with a shock of red hair and tons of laugh lines. "You should be ashamed of yourself, Bramblethickskin. Did I raise you to be like every other fae in the forest? Selling goods at the sacred ceremony is an honor. Worthy petitioners should never be charged."

All the color seeps from Bram's face. "Mother?"

"Who else?" asks Scar/Bram's mother.

"But you passed away."

Scar/Bram's mother rolls her eyes. "What do I always tell you?"

"Good fae never truly die."

"That's right."

"I'm so sorry." Bram picks up one of the robes and shoves it in my direction. "Take it."

I scoop the garment from Bram's hands as Scar wags a bony finger at his face. "Remember your true path. Do not follow gold." With that, she turns and walks away. It's a dramatic exit, but I wasn't prepared for it. The tie between our wrists pulls taut and almost yanks my arms out of its socket. By the time I catch my balance and walk side by side with Scar, she's returned to her regular appearance.

Bram follows up behind us and grabs my hand. "Here, take this, too." He presses an amulet onto my palm. "You're clearly Trilorum."

I stop, which makes Scar pause as well. She no longer looks like Bram's mother, but our new fae friend doesn't seem to notice. "What do you mean?"

"You are Trilorum, aren't you?" Bram lowers his voice. "You're not the chosen one who can prance around the ceremony with the First Wardens. You might get picked up and chopped up for spells. Take the amulet. It will help."

I look down at my palm. A small amber stone hangs on a silver chain. "Thank you."

"Don't get too attached to it," mumbles Scar under her breath. "Anything you get here disappears in the present."

I nod once. "Got it."

"And you," Bram steps closer to Scar. "You're a soul shepherd, aren't you?"

Scar frowns. "Don't say that so loudly."

Bram presses something into her palm as well. "This is a ring of protection. It will hide you from the Shadowvin."

"Shadowvin?" asks Scar.

"Surely you've heard of them. Slythe and Tithe. They're supernatural creatures who have been killing off everyone, Magicorum and human alike. No one is safe. Well, not until the First Wardens fix things. They're going to make everything right tonight." He shakes his head. "I'm talking too much. I do that when I'm nervous. Just take the ring. I appreciate what you did for me." His overlarge eyes glisten with held-in tears. "I never thought I'd see my mother again."

Scar slips the ring onto her thumb. "Thank you."

"You're so welcome," says Bram quickly. "Now, I have to get back to my table. Farewell!" Turning on his heel, Bram runs off into the night.

"That was intense." Scar rounds on me. "You know anything about these Shadowvin?"

"Unfortunately, yes. They're as evil as Bram says, but they haven't been around for thousands of…" I stop in my tracks.

"What?" asks Scar.

"Colonel Mallory told me that the First Wardens wanted to destroy the fountain of magic, the Shadowvin, and the Void, but they failed. Everything blew up instead. The First Wardens injured magic and the Void, but they didn't destroy it." I rub my neck, thinking things through. "Do you think we've traveled to that ceremony?"

"Meaning the one where the First Wardens try to blow up both the fountain of magic and the Void?"

"That's what I mean."

Scar bobs her head from side to side. "It's likely."

I can't believe this girl. "We're about to witness magic and the Void almost be destroyed, and your reaction is 'it's likely?'"

"Just keep that in mind for the times I *do* lose it. Then you know we're in deep." We turn down a deserted aisle, and Scar holds out her hand. "The robe, if you don't mind."

"Wait a second," I say. "There's something else about Bram that sticks out to me. Did his fae mother want her child to actually be *kind* to humans?"

"That's right."

"It's just strange. The fae are unpredictable and evil."

Scar sniffs. "I've done this time travel thing for years. You never know what special circumstances are going around right now. Just go with it, that's my advice." She twiddles her fingers. "And hand over the robe."

"Sure." As I pass the garment over, I picture Scar's transformation into Bram's mother. "That was amazing, by the way. How did you do that?"

"What part?"

"All of it, I suppose."

"In that moment, magic wanted Bram to get his life on track. It's like a dance. Magic moves. I respond."

"It tells you what to do?"

"Hell, no. That would make me a seer. The things is, not everything you want to know guides your soul. Besides, why would magic make anything easy? I just get a vibe and run with it. That's my gift in a nutshell." Scar pulls a dagger from a holster on her leg and then cuts open one side of my robe, from wrist to hem. "There." She hands the garment back to me. "Now, you can just pull it over your head without having to break the tie between us."

I take the robe back. It's light fabric, the kind elves are known for. With careful movements, I pull it over my head. The robe covers me perfectly.

Scar resets the dagger into its holster. "Ready?"

Now, I'm tempted to ask for more detail about Scar's powers. After all, I rarely meet someone with unusual gifts like me. But at that moment, a cry echoes over the bazaar.

"The First Wardens have arrived!"

"Hurry, get to the pyramids!"

Scar and I share a look. There's no need to say anything else. We take off for the pyramids at a run.

It takes an hour of jostling through the crowd, but soon, Scar and I make our way to the edge of the pyramids. They're situated on a triangular plaza lined with more triangle-shaped stones. A low stone wall encircles the place, keeping all of us petitioners outside. At each corner of the plaza, there stands a small pyramid. The structures aren't as big as the ones from Egypt—maybe twelve feet tall—but what they lack in height they more than make up for in terms of the intricate carvings on their surface.

My eyes widen. The *Book of Isis* uses special glyphs that share some things with Ancient Egyptian hieroglyphs, but not a ton. These pyramids are covered in the exact same glyphs. Sure, they are carved in an Aztec style with lots of looping lines and intricate images. Still, it's the same set of glyphs.

"Can you read that?" asks Scar.

"Yes, can you?"

"Nope, I only understand the spoken word when I go back in time. What does it say?"

Thankfully, the moonlight is pretty bright here, so it's no trouble to translate. "The first pyramid talks about the fountain of magic and how it spouts magic into the air, just like a geyser."

Scar lifts her brows. "Does it actually say *geyser*?"

"The glyph is a little weird. It can mean geyser, fountain, or figure."

Scar purses her lips. "That's pretty broad."

I gesture to a spot in the center of the plaza. "One guess what that is."

Scar follows my point. Everyone is staying back behind the low wall—and the center of the plaza is deserted right now—so it's clear to see what sits in the middle of the grounds. There, a colorful mound of rock juts up from the tiled floor. In some ways, it looks just like the carving I found in the sandbox: a conical structure that has drips of red, silver, and gold along the sides. In other ways, the stone looks very different in real life. It's a bit wider, more like a basin than a cone. Even so, there's no mistaking what it is.

"That's the fountain of magic," I say.

"Sure looks like it," says Scar. Her tone is the definition of *unconvinced*.

Now it's my turn to raise my brows. "But?"

"It's like I said before. The past is unexpected. We come to it with assumptions that we don't even realize. Trust me, until that thing spouts multicolored power, we should call it a geyser."

"Fine," I counter. "Geyser it is." That's what I say, but I'm thinking *you're totally wrong about this*. I've spent countless hours studying fountains. That geyser is the exact same thing as the fountain of magic, no question.

A perfect hush rolls over the crowd. Four figures step onto the plaza. All of them wear long robes, just like the rest of us, only theirs are colored in red, silver, gold, and white.

*Wait a second. White?*

That's a color I associate with the Void. Then, I remember what Bram said. The First Wardens bring one member of the Trilorum into the ceremony with them. That seems strange.

The warden with the silver cloak raises her arms, exposing the blue hue of her skin. She's definitely fae. "Welcome, petitioners. I am the first warden of fae magic."

Behind me, the petitioners start to whisper among themselves.

"That's her…the great Quetzali."

"She's the one who created all this."

"She'll destroy the Shadowvin, I know it."

Quetzali raises her right arm and the crowd silences. "Tonight," she says. "I stand before you with the first warden of witches and warlocks." She gestures to the figure in a red cloak.

As Quetzali introduces the second warden, there's no chatter from the crowd. Clearly, Quetzali is the people's favorite.

"Also with me is the first warden of shifters." This time, Quetzali points to the figure in the golden cloak. Again, no commentary from the crowd. This is definitely the Quetzali show.

I can't help but smile. So far, all of this is going just as I'd expected. There are three wardens before me, one for each kind of magic. Sure, there's another figure there in white, but maybe they keep a Trilorum around as a guard or something. And we're on a plaza with three pyramids and a geyser-fountain. Excitement speeds my blood. This is happening. The answers are close.

And once I find the fountain and its magic, I'll discover some way to protect my friends and cure Knox. I know it.

Quetzali continues. "Tonight, I welcome you to our annual sacred ceremony. Whether you are Magicorum or regular human, this ceremony has helped countless others just like you. Even if you don't wish for magical powers, attending this ritual can bring back your youth and beauty."

I suck in a shocked breath. *Youth and beauty?* Like everything that has to do with magic, this place is aligned to its own fairy tale life template. In this case, it's the Fountain of Youth.

*Huh.* Ponce de Leon wasn't too far off when he hunted for it in Florida.

"Many thousands of years ago, I designed these first pyramids." Quetzali gestures across the plaza. "These structures harness the power of magic into three distinct forms: shifter, witch, and fairy. Ever since then, we have held our sacred ceremony every autumnal equinox. Tonight, all of that changes. And the reason for that change? The Shadowvin, Slythe and Tithe. At first, these evil creatures lurked in corners and caused no pain. But over the years, they've become more bold and cruel. Now they slaughter Magicorum and mortals alike. Everyone here has lost a loved one."

Behind me, the crowd starts to call out to Quetzali.

"My sister is gone."

"Our village was wiped out."

"My child! Slythe took my child!"

Quetzali lifts her arms, and the crowd falls silent. "Slythe and Tithe must be stopped. And to do that, I have created a new device." The sleeves fall away from Quetzali's raised arms. Although the silver hood still covers her face, there's no mistaking the blue of her skin. It's that distinct shade of azure that only happens with water fairies.

A heartbeat later, silver fairy dust appears between Quetzali's raised palms. The power glows more brightly, showing off the blue webbing between her long fingers. When the haze vanishes, Quetzali holds a small wooden box aloft.

"Behold," announced Quetzali. "The Codex Mechanica. It will always find the fountain of magic. And where the fountain of magic is, so we will find the Shadowvin and the Void."

My skin prickles over with awe. For so long, I've longed to see how to see the fountain of magic in action. And although I only recently discovered that the Codex Mechanica, I've been dying to figure out how it works. And now? I'm seeing it firsthand. I'm a very lucky girl.

Turning to Scar, I gently tap her shoulder. She looks to me with her brows lifted. I'm quickly learning that's Scar's way of saying, *What?*

I mouth two words: *thank you.*

Scar's mouth quirks with a smile. She speaks two silent words in reply: *you're welcome.*

Back on the plaza, Quetzali lowers the device. Since Scar and I are so close, I can see how the lid of the box is cut with three vertical slots. The sides of round disks show through each of these three openings. Glyphs are written onto the edge. The discs must spin to give messages. The Codex Mechanica reminds me of an ancient slot machine.

"I designed these pyramids. Do you trust me, my people?"

"Yes!" yells the crowd.

"I have created this Codex Mechanica to fight the Shadowvin. Do you wish to see them destroyed?"

"Yes!" comes another cry.

"Good," says Quetzali. "Then we must all gird ourselves for the sorry truth. To protect us all, both the fountain of magic and the Void must be destroyed. The Codex Mechanica is built to do this task."

My eyes glaze over in shock. Did she just say both the fountain of magic and the Void must be destroyed? The crowd starts grumbling again.

"Destroying magic means I'll lose my powers."

"My inner wolf will die."

"How will we cast spells without magic?"

"Silence!" calls Quetzali. "We must begin the ceremony. The fountain and magic and the Void will be no more. Be thankful to be alive at all, not questioning if your life will continue to have magic."

After that, everything starts happening so quickly, it's hard to keep track. Thick plumes of white smoke roll over the plaza grounds. Searingly bright light blares out from the geyser, congealing into a massive figure glowing white with all black eyes. The Void. He grips the geyser and tears it from the plaza floor. "I want the fountain!"

The crowd gasps, but doesn't move. Quetzali opens the Codex Mechanica and pulls out the discs inside. She gives a ruby disc to the first warden of witches and wizards. The golden disc does to the first warden of shifters. Quetzali keeps a close grip on the third silver disc. The white-cloaked figure stands nearby, silent and watching.

The Void's voice booms once more. "The fountain!" His voice is wild with rage. "The fountain!" A great boom sounds as he tosses the geyser-fountain onto the ground.

Now, the crowd decides to turn into a frenzied mob. Everyone starts running away from the plaza while screaming with terror. More white mist rolls over the plaza. Soon, everything is covered in such a thick haze I can't see a thing.

I can still hear the voices of the First Wardens, though. And although I'm new to this whole magic thing, I know a spell being cast when I hear it. Flashes of silver, gold, and red light pulse within the thick clouds around me.

Scar pulls me closer to her side. "We have to get out of here. I know my history. This whole place is about to explode."

The pyramids pulse with light, every one a different color. The white haze turns even thicker, but I can still make out each pyramid as it glows silver, gold, or red. A woman's scream cuts though the air.

I suck in a shaky breath. "That scream," I say to Scar. "It was Quetzali." I start to scale the low wall before me. "Hurry, we have to see what's happening."

Scar grips my wrist, and dang, that girl is strong. "I am not going anywhere near that mess."

Across the plaza, the pyramids pulse erratically with their different hues of the light. Great chunks of glowing rock tumble from the structures, slamming into the ground with such force, the earth shakes. I yank harder on Scar's arm. "I have to see what's happening. This might be the only way I can save Knox."

"No."

Her word strikes me like a fist. "No?" I point toward the plaza. "You can't mean that. You heard what she said. The Codex Mechanica is built to find and destroy all magic. This affects more than Knox. It could hurt everyone. We have to find out what we can."

Great cracks form along the edges of the silver pyramid. Spider webs of light peep out from between the breaks in the stone. For a long moment, the silver pyramid vibrates in place.

After that, it explodes.

Huge boulders fly through the air. Small stones cascade all around us. On reflex, Scar and I kneel down into a protective crouch.

"The two of us ending up dead?" Scar pulls on the cord between us. "That doesn't help anybody."

With that, she breaks the tie that was holding us in the past. A flash of golden light overtakes my consciousness. The scene at the plaza disappears.

I can only hope I learned enough in the past to help everyone in the present

# CHAPTER FOURTEEN

For a long minute, there is nothing but the golden brightness that can only come from shifter magic. The next thing I know, I'm back in Az's room at Lucky's. Scar and I are alone in the chamber. Our gray cloaks are gone. We're both back to wearing our leathers.

"Got anything to say to me?" Scar sets her fist on her hip. "I swear, if you give me crap about pulling your ass out of death's door, I'll shift into your worst nightmare." Her eyes glow with golden power.

A weight of guilt settles on to my shoulders. "No, I won't give you trouble about what happened. You saved our lives."

"Damn right."

I offer her my hand. "Are we still good?"

She pulls me into a quick hug. "Shut up and save us all from that Void thing, especially that hot man of yours."

I'm not really sure what just happened, but I know one thing. I'm really starting to like Scar.

Scar steps back; her face creases into a frown. "Why were we hugging again?"

I let out an exasperated breath. It's starting once more. The Curse of the Void. "Do you remember anything from our trip through time?"

"White mist and…that's it." She winces. "Why was I talking about your boyfriend?"

"You wanted to be sure I was taking good care of him. He's been sick lately."

Speaking of Knox, I catch the barest scent of sandalwood and musk, along with the now-familiar smell of pain. Inside my soul, my wolf awakens.

*"What happened?"* she asks. *"Where is our mate?"*

*"Long story,"* I explain in my head. *"I went back in time. You and Knox couldn't join me."*

*"Our mate has been ill,"* grumbles my wolf. *"We should check on him."*

*"I like that plan."*

Crossing the room, I open the door. Knox, Avianna, and Azizi come in. The moment Knox crosses into the chamber, the scent of pain grows stronger than ever before. Worry prickles through my soul.

"Where's the Codex Mechanica?" asks Knox. "Where can we get it?"

Scar frowns. "We traveled in time to some white mist, but… that was it."

Avianna shakes her head. "That happens sometimes. Something went wrong with my potion."

"No," I say quickly. "Your potion was fine."

Az moves to loom over me. "Was it fine?" He slowly folds his arms over his chest. "Really?" Az is one of those men who doesn't have to say things with words. I know what he means here.

*Do I really want to pull Knox in deeper to all of this?*

"Don't try to intimidate her, Az." Knox moves to stand by my side. Sadly, even moving three steps has him winded.

Pangs of anxiety move through my chest. "Are you all right?"

"I'm fine," pants Knox. "Tell me. Did you find out anything about the Codex Mechanica? Where can we find it?"

On reflex, my glance lands on Az. The old were's mouth thins to an angry line. I know what he's saying without speaking a word: *if you take Knox with you to find the Codex Mechanica, you'll kill him.*

A realization weighs on me. I need to find the Codex Mechanica. Alone. Knox, Elle, Alec… The Void and Shadowvin threaten them all. And now that I saw what happened with the First Wardens, I know the truth.

My mission is more than using the Codex Mechanica to find the fountain of magic. I must destroy it as well. My heart sinks. Destroying magic would also destroy our inner wolves. And a shifter without their animal? They turn into a lifeless husk. It's pretty much a death sentence. I shake my head.

*Worry about destroying the fountain later. For now, you just need to find the Codex Mechanica and protect the fountain of magic from the Void and the Shadowvin.*

Knox steps closer. "Did you hear what I said, Bry? Where's the device?"

There's no way I'm dragging Knox along on this mission. That will kill him for certain. I need to find a way of answering his questions without lying. Shifters can smell an untruth a mile away.

"Scar is the expert in going through time." I look to her. "Do you remember anything?"

"No," says Scar. "It happens sometimes, though. Don't worry. We can try again tomorrow."

"That's, uh, good." Knox takes in a wheezing breath. All the color has drained from his face. I'm not so sure he even heard what Scar said. My mate is barely hanging on here.

Az focuses on me. "Yes, come back tomorrow with Knox. You can all try this again." Once more, that's what he says, but I know what Az means. He doesn't want me anywhere near Knox.

I give him a small smile. "Agreed."

"Good." Az falls forward, only by the time he reaches the ground, he's shifted into the form of a huge gray wolf. Az rests his chin on his front paws. "And now, you must give an old man his rest." *Which is a big fat lie.* I've never seen Azizi look better. He just wants us out of here. As it happens, I can't wait to leave. There is no way I'm calling Az on his lie.

"Sure thing, Az." Knox takes my hand. "Where do you want to go?"

"Home. It's been a long day."

"I think we both could use a break."

With thoughts on home, my heart lightens. If nothing else, my trip through time has one benefit—I've seen the Codex Mechanica. Thanks to Elle's sideline of locating and selling jewelry, I know all sorts of websites where you can buy and sell rare, old, and valuable stuff. Someone will have seen or sold and ancient box that looks like the first slot machine ever.

If nothing else, it's worth a try.

# CHAPTER FIFTEEN

About an hour later, Knox walks me to my apartment. He still looks so pale, I hate to make him walk an extra yard, let alone all the way to my door.

"You don't have to walk me home," I say. "We're only two floors apart, you know."

Knox inhales deeply. "You're worried."

"Well, you know…" I grip the door handle behind my back and try to think of something totally honest—yet misleading—to say to Knox at this point. *You look at death's door* isn't what he needs to hear. "There's a lot to worry about. I must find the Codex Mechanica and protect the fountain of magic. It won't be easy."

Of course, I don't add in the part about destroying the fountain of magic. That will just have to wait.

Knox grips the upper ledge of the door. His body frames mine. Normally, the sensation of him looming so close makes me feel calm and safe. Right now, though? All I can notice is how his body trembles.

Inside my soul, my wolf whimpers in fear. *"Our mate is ill. Make him go rest."*

*"I'm working on it,"* I reply in my mind.

Knox leans in, brushing his nose along the length of mine. "I know I look like hell, but just because I look like crap doesn't mean I'm not on top of this. Believe me, Ty is up to something. If I lay low tonight, I'll be ready to plan our next move tomorrow."

Silent calculations flicker through my mind. Today, there's four days until the autumn equinox.

Four days until the fountain of magic rises again after five thousand years.

Tomorrow there will be three.

Time is running out.

*Think about something else, Bryar Rose.*

"So, no school for you tomorrow?" I ask.

"Taking a sick day," says Knox.

This piece of news is something my wolf likes very much. *"No school for Knox! Let's stay home and comfort him forever!"* She prances around in a happy circle. *"We can spend every day together, away from those nasty fairies that won't let me chew on them anyway."*

*"Ho, there,"* I say to my inner wolf. *"This is a sick day. Day."*

*"No school ever again,"* howls my wolf. *"No schoooooooooooooool!"*

I press on my temples. "Stay quiet or I can't think."

Knox's full mouth quirks with a smile. "Your wolf wants to skip school tomorrow, yeah?"

I hiss in an embarrassed breath. "I said that last thing out loud, didn't I?"

"Sure did." Knox chuckles. "Glad I'm not the only one who does stuff like that." He shakes his head. "But tell your wolf not to skip because of me. We're both going back."

I give him the side-eye. It's not like Knox to have a strong opinion about school. "And why's that, exactly?"

"Like I said, Az will kick my ass harder than ten West Lake Preps." Knox's face turns serious. "But if you wanted to, we could start our own classroom. You, me, and Az. That old were would love to kick your academic butt too, you know."

My wolf is now leaping with joy. *"No school. Let's be with our mate! Maaaaaaaate!"* She's having such a good time in my head I don't even bother to tell her to shut up.

"And how hard exactly would that ass-kicking be?" I ask, smirking. "Elle and I have been setting our own study schedule, you know."

Knox chuckles again, and it's a rumbling sound I like very much indeed. Maybe it's just in my head, but some of the color seems to be back in his cheeks. Perhaps being around me isn't what's making him sick, after all.

"Let me put it to you this way," says Knox. "This whole conversation? I can repeat it in Greek, Latin, and Persian."

I mock-frown. "Just those three?"

"Nah, a bunch more, too. But I thought the Persian might really impress you." He leans in close until our mouths almost touch. "Did it work?"

My wolf adds in some yipping with her prancing. *"It worked! It worked! Kiss him noooooooooow!"*

"Keep up the commentary, and you're going into a time-out," I reply. "There's no way I can enjoy a kiss with you yipping in my brain."

Knox leans back. The way he's pressing his lips together, I just know he's holding back the mother of all laughs.

I wince. "I said that last part out loud again, didn't I?"

Knox clears his throat. "Don't put your wolf in a time-out because of me." He steps away and scrubs his hands over his face. My mate certainly looks exhausted. "What are you gonna do now? See if you can find that Codex Mechanica?" He snaps his fingers. "Wait. There was something else I was going to ask you about that device, but I can't remember it right now."

I decide to skip over the whole *you can't see or remember anything concerning the Void right now because of a memory curse* conversation. Instead, I answer the first question. "Yes, I'm going to search online for evidence of the Codex Mechanica."

Knox nods slowly. "Long night of hacking ahead of you, yeah?"

"That's right." My heart lightens just thinking about it. Finding stuff on the internet is my special gift.

"You have trouble sleeping, you call me, yeah?"

"I promise." Maybe it's the terrible lighting in this hallway, but it seems like dark circles have formed underneath Knox's ice-blue eyes. A second ago, he seemed better. And now he's getting worse again.

But that can't be the case.

It's definitely the lighting.

Maybe.

"Go on," I say playfully. "Get some rest now."

Moving closer, Knox leans in and brushes a gentle kiss against my cheek. The scent of pain encircles him like a cloud. My heart cracks. This is so bad.

"We'll talk more at breakfast, yeah?" asks Knox. "Then, we can chat about that whole West Lake thing too." He heaves in a rattling breath.

My inner wolf goes back to whimpering. *"Our mate is very ill."*

*"I know,"* I reply.

Knox slogs down the hallway. It seems to take forever for him to step into the elevator and disappear. That's another thing that isn't like him. Usually, there's at least one smartass comment before he goes.

Sighing, I turn my attention to the master security panel in the wall by my door. All of a sudden, finding the Codex Mechanica never seemed more important. One way or another, that damned fountain is the source of all Knox's pain. I know it. And if destroying it at least gives him some peace, then maybe that's just what I have to do.

# CHAPTER SIXTEEN

I step into the apartment. There's no telltale clacking of keys and grumbling from the living room, so I figure Alec isn't here for once. The place seems strangely quiet without him.

Elle's voice echoes into our little reception hall. "I'm in the kitchen!" she calls. A delicious scent fills the air.

My wolf grumbles inside me. *"Elle ordered from City Lights of Beijing again."* Her tone says she is definitely not interested.

*"That's your favorite,"* I reply in my mind. *"Don't you want any?"*

*"Not hungry."*

I step into the kitchen and see the largest spread of white delivery boxes ever. "Dang." I start counting the containers. "Twenty?"

Elle spears a fried crab rangoon from the box in her hand. "And they are going quickly, my friend. I am one hungry girl."

I take my regular seat at our high top, sniff out some mu shu pork, and try to force in a few bites. My wolf isn't the only one without an appetite. "How was the rest of school?"

Elle talks through a mouth full of rangoon. "Weird. How was the basement?"

"Creepy."

"The workstation?"

"Decent." Not that I expected anything less. Alec's parents were footing the bill, and they wanted me to find the fountain and empower Alec to have an heir ASAP. You'd think the two of them were going to die any day now, the way they're obsessed about an heir.

"And the papyri?" asks Elle.

I freeze, my chopsticks halfway to my mouth. "I found something out."

"Go on." She motions her hand in circles, encouraging me to speed up.

"The workstation at school also had some new papyri on them. I found the fountain."

Elle's mouth falls open. "No. Way."

"Well, not exactly the fountain, but this thing that will find the fountain. It's called the Codex Mechanica." I could add in more about visiting Az and the Void—or needing to destroy all magic to stop the Shadowvin—but Elle wouldn't remember any of that anyway.

Stupid memory curse.

Elle straightens. A determined look gleams in her eyes. This is what I call her plotting mode. She's getting ready to act. "What can you tell me about the device?"

Now, I could tell Elle what the Codex Mechanica looks like and how we could search for it online, but the words seem stuck in my throat. If Elle knows all that stuff, she'll want to help me find the device and face down the Void.

I can't have her risking herself like that. As Az said, this is my task. Magic chose me. I can't risk anyone else's life against the Shadowvin and the Void. It's bad enough I have to face them. Plus, there's the whole "taking responsibility for destroying all magic" part. I don't want to load that on anyone else.

My wolf sits up straight and lifts her furry chin. This is her judgy pose. *"You know more about that Codex Mechanica. I was sleeping when you were with Scar. You learned things, I know it."*

*"We're not having this discussion,"* I reply in my mind.

*"You're holding out on both me and Elle."* She then curls up into a ball and pretends to go to sleep.

Elle's still looking at me. Waiting for an answer. "Um…"

"Okay, Miss Mysterious, don't tell me. I love a challenge." Elle scoops up a bunch of white food containers in her arms and marches off for the living room because that's where we keep our best computer system. "Finding the Codex Mechanica on the internet? How hard can it be?"

A twinge of guilt tightens across my rib cage. I searched on the term *Codex Mechanica* back at school. There's nothing on the web about it. Like zero. Without knowing what the device looks like, Elle won't get very far. Guilt weighs down my limbs. I should tell Elle she's about to waste her time, but that would open up a lot of questions. And once Elle starts asking questions, I crack like a boiled egg.

Nope, it's better to let her try, even if it is nearly impossible that she'll find anything.

I force on a smile. "Let's get hacking."

And by hacking, I mean breaking into a ton of different secured computer systems about illegal or magical devices. Elle and I have workstations in our bedrooms as well as the master system in the living room. I scoop up my own set of preferred Chinese food containers and follow Elle into the living room.

At least, I think it's our living room.

The place looks redecorated with a bunch of silvery stuff. I slowly step around the space. Normally, all of our furniture is what I'd call modern generic. Now there are small statues, big statues, and tons of canvases covered with silver images.

They are all about the same subject.

Elle.

Setting aside my takeout grub, I pause by a life-size statue of Elle by the window. She's wearing her school uniform and laughing. "Um, what's all this?"

Elle plunks on the couch. "Oh, some of the kids at school made me gifts."

I step over to a smaller statue by the couch. This time, it's an imagined version of Elle in a ballerina costume. "Gifts from who?"

"The other fae students." Elle fires up the main monitor and starts typing passwords into a keyboard. "I think they do it for all new kids."

I step over to a stack of canvases against the wall. "Is that what Alec told you? They didn't have anything like that for me or Knox."

Elle keeps pounding away at a furious pace. "These are the fae. They're weird."

She has a point; there's no knowing why the fae do anything. Only, it's not like them to do anything nice. I flip through the canvases. "Wow. And there's no sleeping dust on these paintings?"

"Nuh-uh."

"No booby-traps?" I ask.

"Nope."

"No magical dust that makes you break out in zits?"

"Definitely not."

"Huh."

I stop and hold one up. "You look really good in these. Like perfect hair and everything. Don't any of them show you with slobber on your chin or something?"

"Not that I've seen." Elle's gaze stays locked on the screen.

"That's so un-fae." I step over to another stack of canvases and look through them. The fact that fairies would do something so genuinely kind just floors me. I pause at one particular image: it shows Elle with long silver wings cascading down her back.

The moment I pick up that particular canvas, Elle stops typing. "It's weird to see a picture of me with wings, isn't it?"

"Not really." I quickly set the canvas down again. "I really don't care about fae wings, one way or another."

Elle leans back into the couch and sighs. "Well, that was before Principal Goldi started making a big deal about it. Now, it's only a matter of time before you ask me, so I might as well tell you." Her big blue eyes glisten with held-in tears. "I'm a freak. I think that's why all the fae are being so nice to me." Her voice shakes. "I lost my wings."

I move to sit beside Elle on the couch. My aunties rarely showed their wings. As in, I can remember seeing them like once or twice, tops. And they were dinky little things anyway, so nothing to show off. Even so, even faes with massive wings keep them hidden. It's all part of avoiding unwanted attention from humans. A flash of wing and—BOOM—you're surrounded by mortals trying to get a selfie with you.

All these years, I just figured Elle was the same way. In fact, I never really thought about the whole wing issue until today. When we were in in the principals' office, Goldi asked Elle where her wings were. It never occurred to me that Elle had lost them. I don't know much about fae culture, but I'd have to imagine losing your wings is a big deal.

I scooch closer to Elle on the couch and take her hand in mine. Her palm is cool and slick with sweat. This is really bothering her.

"You don't have to tell me anything if you don't want to," I say.

"No." Elle sniffles. "It's time to get this off my chest. I had to leave my stepfamily. They had me under a curse, Bry. It was the Cinderella life template. I was basically their slave."

I give her hand a gentle squeeze. "Go on."

"My fairy godmother, Blackaverre, figured out how to break the curse, but there was only one way. And the spell? Only a very strong fairy could do it. And I had to give up something special in order for it to work."

I nod slowly. "Your wings. You had to trade them for your freedom. I'm so sorry."

"I looked different before. Losing my wings made it possible to change my appearance, and that helped me hide." Elle sighs. "I don't even know if I'm really a Cinderella life template. This could all be a way to hide me. There are other fairy tales where someone's kept locked up."

"I'm so sorry this happened. Did Blackaverre explain all this before it happened?"

Elle nods. "She told me everything. It was my choice." She shivers. "I had to get away from them, Bry." She hangs her head. "My stepfamily. Or I should call them the people who kept me imprisoned, really. They made me do terrible things with my magic. That's why I have to be so careful about my powers now. My magic has a unique signature. My stepfamily thinks I'm dead. If they got wind of my magic, they'd know I'm alive."

"So that's why you developed, uh, other skills."

Elle's shoulders slump. "That's why I lived on the streets and became a master thief, hacker, and con artist, yes." She releases my hand and tosses her hair over one shoulder. That's Elle's way of saying she's done sharing and wants to change the subject. "Hey, you'll never guess who I saw today."

I shoot her a sad smile. I'd love to hear more about what happened to Elle, but it's amazing enough that she's shared as much as she has. "Let me think." I tap my chin. "Avianna and Scarlett?"

"So you saw them, too?"

"Yes, after I translated the papyri, Knox and I went over to visit Az. You know how that old were knows everything about everything. Well, Avianna and Scarlett were there, too."

"So two other people skipped school so you could get more use out of skipping school. Nice." She shakes her head. "Starting capers a little early, eh?"

I roll my eyes. "Well, Knox and I were stuck in the basement, so there wasn't much for us to skip. But yeah, it was an eventful first day, that's for sure."

Elle grins, and it makes her entire face light up. "So, what did Az have to say?"

"Oh, you know Az. Mister Doom and Gloom. He had Avianna and Scarlett use their powers to help me learn more about the Codex Mechanica."

Elle leans forward. "And?"

Once again, it's on the tip of my tongue to spill everything. The journey back through time to the pyramids. What the fountain really looked like in its prime. The First Wardens who figured out how to control magic. But that would lead to the whole "I have to go off, face the Void, and find the Codex Mechanica" thing. I'm just not ready to share that yet. So, I go with the other whammy discovery of the afternoon.

"Here's the big news," I say. "You know how Knox has been sick?"

Elle nods.

"Az thinks that magic is hurting Knox. It doesn't like the fact that Knox is a warden and he's my mate." I hate the wobble that's crept into my voice. "Being around me might be killing him." All of a sudden, my eyes sting. I wipe beneath them with my fingertips. "I need to find the fountain. Maybe then, magic will stop torturing Knox…or we'll figure out a way to heal him."

Again, I can't even get to the part about possibly having to destroying it because, dang, there's enough going on already.

"No time to lose then, right?" Elle turns back to face her computer screen. This is such an Elle move, by the way. She's not one to mope around. "Codex Mechanica, here we come."

I step back from the couch. "If it's okay with you, I'll search from my room. This Elle artwork is a little creepy."

All of which is a lie. I want to search on sites where people trade ancient stuff and then post about the specifics on the Codex Mechanica. I don't want Elle to know anything about it. If she knows I've found the device, she'll want to help me acquire it.

There's no way I'll put her at risk with the Void.

I'm finding the Codex Mechanica on my own.

A shiver rolls across my shoulders. The idea of going solo makes my insides squirm with fear.

*Don't get ahead of yourself, Bry. Find the Codex first. Everything else is second.*

"I hear you on the artwork," says Elle as she types away. "Alec transported it here, but we need to find something else to do with it." She leans back as fresh lines of code scroll across the screen. My bestie is deep into a hack now. "Give a yell if you find anything."

"Will do." A pang of guilt moves through my insides. I never hold things back from Elle. Or Knox either, for that matter. Now, all of a sudden, I'm holding out on both of them, big time.

It's just one more reason why everything about finding this Codex Mechanica feels way wrong. Part of me wants to go back to my room, pop in a good movie, and forget any of this ever happened. But then, I picture the dark circles under Knox's ice-blue eyes.

Hiding from this problem is not an option.

Instead, I return to my room, fire up my computer, and start to search for the one thing my soul tells me most to avoid. The Codex Mechanica.

# CHAPTER SEVENTEEN

Hours later, my eyes sting with the need for sleep. I've been hacking away all night, posting on hidden message boards to find someone who has the Codex Mechanica. Back around 3 a.m., Elle fell asleep on the couch. I didn't wake her. Now it's a little after 5 a.m. Considering how school starts at 8:30, it's good one of us had a decent night's sleep.

Pounding on my keyboard, I access another chat room on what's called the Magiweb, which is basically a secret internet for shifters, fairies, and witches/warlocks. Sure the name is cute and all, but the Magiweb is a place to find all sorts of illegal and nasty stuff. I've tried all the above-board places to locate the Codex Mechanica. Now, I'm going to the illegal side of the internet.

The chat board fills my screen. Every time I reach one of these rooms, I do the exact same thing. This board will be no exception. I start typing away under one of my dozens of aliases.

*Looking4Goods: Hello, I'm searching for a particular historical item for a client of mine. Specs: created about 2000 BC, wooden box with three discs inside. Any ideas or leads? Willing to share part of the buy price.*

I see the triple dots that mean someone is typing a response.

*Selling3000: Don't have anything like that in stock. Will keep an eye out for you. I take it this is a sensitive buy?*
*Looking4Goods: Yes. Keep me posted.*

I wait a few more minutes and get a few more replies just like the first one. This is the same routine I've been going through for hours. I post about the device. They say they've never heard about anything like it and will keep an eye out. It's super-disappointing. I'm about to log off and try another board when another user pops onto the screen.

*WaterGirl: Join me in private chat.*

My heart kicks at a faster pace. Private chat means that Water-Girl may have news for me and doesn't want any of the other sellers stealing her deal out from under her. I open up a secure and direct chat room. Before I can even invite WaterGirl, her name pops onto the screen. On reflex, I start running my latest tracer bots. These programs can always figure out where someone is really typing from. More small dots appear as WaterGirl types away. A moment later, her text appears on the screen.

*WaterGirl: I have the Codex Mechanica and am willing to sell.*

My breath catches. I didn't even say the name of the device and WaterGirl goes right to Codex Mechanica? This is looking good.

*Looking4Goods: How much?*
*WaterGirl: Free. To the right person.*

I roll my eyes. It's a total red flag when someone says they want to give you something for free. No one works for free, especially on the Magiweb.

*Looking4Goods: What's the catch?*

*WaterGirl: None at all. Why wouldn't I want to help you, Bryar Rose? After all, it's not everyone who can take down the undead version of Julius Caesar and live to tell the tale. Perhaps I merely wish to have someone as powerful as you who owes me a favor.*

My heart, which had already been going at double speed, charges right into palpitation territory. How does this WaterGirl know who I am? Even so, I know enough not to make things worse by confirming that she's blown my cover.

*Looking4Goods: I don't know what you're talking about. Are you willing to sell or not?*

*WaterGirl: Meet me at the Boucle-Roux. Tonight. Midnight.*

I open a new window on my computer and start searching like mad. Turns out, Boucle-Roux is a deserted farm outside Paris. While I'm searching, the three little dots appear on the screen. WaterGirl is typing away once more.

*WaterGirl: You can still catch the 6:20 a.m. out of JFK and be at Boucle-Roux well before midnight. I know you think this is a trap. It's not. I have the device and only want to help. It's in perfect condition, including the three discs inside that are made of silver, gold, and ruby. Can you really afford to ignore me?*

My fingers hover over the keyboard. I need to get WaterGirl typing some more about herself and what she's up to. If I find out enough, I can determine if this is really not-a-trap. Elle has taught me all sorts of techniques to keep folks talking. I'm about to type a question about the glyphs on the device when WaterGirl leaves the chat.

Damn.

I check my tracer program. Nothing there, either. All of which means that I have no clue who this person really is and what they're after.

Even worse, I have about half a minute to decide whether to hightail it to JFK and catch that plane to Paris.

The thirty seconds tick away slowly as my mind runs through all the reasons not to meet WaterGirl. This is dangerous. I could waste an entire day on a wild goose chase. After all, I met this girl on Magiweb, for crying out loud.

Then, I picture Knox's pale skin and how his frame trembles with pain. I grab a duffel from my closet and stuff a bunch of clothes inside.

Looks like I'm going to Paris.

# CHAPTER EIGHTEEN

I've fought the undead, so you'd think JFK wouldn't be an issue.

It is.

And there are four reasons behind this.

First, I've never been in airport before. I mean, in the past I barely left the penthouse. Going to the Adirondacks or to Brooklyn was a big journey. Now, I'm in an airport.

Second, there are people everywhere. They're all rushing around with their bags and their briefcases. Everyone seems to know exactly where to go and what to do. For my part, I needed to ask four people in uniforms before I figured out how to get my ticket and go through security.

Third, why do they hate my shoes? I was almost past the scanner gateway thing, but I had left my flats on. Not sure what that was all about, but I was basically dragged back and had to go through again. However, leaving my shoes on seemed to mark me as dangerous. They even had to bring over a lady guard to touch my junk. That was unexpected.

All of which brings me to the present moment and item number four. How do I find my gate? It's all very confusing to find signage, in my humble opinion.

If there's one benefit to this situation, it's that my wolf is still asleep. What she'd make of this entire situation, I don't even want to imagine. The words *freak* and *out* come to mind. My inner animal isn't fond of crowds.

Although I don't have to worry about my wolf, that doesn't mean I'm not carrying around another kind of anxiety. As I step along, a weight of guilt settles into my bones. I know what it's about: Elle and Knox. I left them a lame note saying that Colonel Mallory asked me to join him on a tour of Europe, so they shouldn't bother trying to text or call for a few days. It seems pretty believable and something the Colonel would do, but I still feel crappy about lying.

Finally, I find my gate and get in line to board.

And that's when a familiar face steps out of the crowd. All the blood seems to drain from my body.

Standing before me is Reggie, the undead dude who was imprisoned in Alec's basement but escaped last summer.

The guy who used to follow Jules.

And I know for a fact that Reggie's favorite meal is human.

Oh, no. If Reggie starts attacking people in JFK, thing could get ugly. Fast.

Reggie strides forward. Like before, he looks like he fell out of a toothpaste ad in 1950. He's dressed in a three-piece suit and fedora. His black hair is slicked back with way too much gel. And his skin is too smooth and perfect to be real.

He waves at me like we're old friends. "Bryar Rose!"

I freeze. "Don't eat my brains." There are smoother things I could say at this point, but it's been a long twenty-four hours.

Reggie steps closer. "Didn't the Colonel tell you? I'm your guardian angel now."

"Buzz off." There, that sounded much more like me.

A manic gleam returns to Reggie's blue eyes. "Haze, plays, means and ways. Ignore my words, he'll die in three days."

My heart sinks. Reggie loves to speak in singsong style. It's super-creepy. Every cell in my body wants to run onto the plane and forget this conversation ever happened. But I can't get past the last thing Reggie said.

*Ignore my words, he'll die in three days.*

"You're talking about Knox," I say in a low voice.

Reggie nods, his eyes still gleaming manically. How could Colonel Mallory think that having Reggie help me would be a good idea? I stare longingly at the jetway. I'd love to walk away right now. But if there's any chance Reggie knows something that will help Knox, I simply have to try.

I grip the straps of my duffle so tightly, my nails bite into my palms. "Tell me what you know."

"Fountain of magic, fountain of magic. Destroy it all and life turns tragic."

I frown. "No one's been talking about destroying the fountain, Reggie."

*Not yet, anyway.* But if I haven't confided the fact to my mate and best friend, I'm certainly not sharing it with an undead freak who's accosting me in JFK.

"Ties, tries, words and lies. Remember that and no one dies." Reggie then turns and stalks off into the crowd. I watch him leave, shaking my head in shock.

Well, that was a useless conversation.

With Reggie gone, I'm finally able to walk the jetway and find my seat on the plane. The flight no sooner lifts off than my eyelids feel like they're weighed down with boulders. Looks like staying up all night hacking is finally catching up with me. Within minutes, I fall asleep.

At first, my dreams are pretty cool. I have a vision of the plane's cabin filling with white mist. Child-Me runs up and down the aisle. I catch flashes of bright red hair. Her laughter is like the tinkling of bells.

"Come and find me!" she calls.

I unbuckle my belt to do just that when I notice the shadows creeping down the curved walls of the fuselage. The mist on the floor turns a thicker shade of white. The darkness on the walls congeals into the form of two Shadowvin. A knot of emotion tightens in my throat.

I'm in a plane.

Over an ocean.

And a mile into the air.

The Shadowvin showing up here can't be a good thing.

With halting steps, I force myself to move away from the Shadowvin. The mist by my feet turns even thicker. The air thickens. It becomes an effort to pull in a breath.

*This is a dream, Byrar Rose. Everything will be fine.*

Up front, the door protecting the pilots bursts open with a BANG. The plane rocks; I fall onto my butt. A wave of mist and white light pours into the main cabin. All the passengers start to lose their minds. Everyone screams and crawls over one another, moving in a mad rush to get away from the front of the plane. The aircraft lurches violently from side to side. My heart beats with such force, I worry it will break through my rib cage.

The Void appears at the far end of the aisle, right by the ruined pilot's door. I want to scream and run, but I'm rooted to the spot.

Stupid dream.

When the Void speaks, his voice booms through the air. "Bring me to the fountain! The fountain!"

Somehow, I'm able to croak out one word. "No."

The Shadowvin cackle with glee. "Whether you want to or not," they say in unison. "You're already helping us."

The plane starts to spiral downward. My body becomes squished against a nearby wall. Luggage falls out of the overhead bins and tosses through the air. The screams turn deafening.

I grip the top of a chair and yell with all my strength. "Never!"

The dream ends. I find myself wide-awake. My wolf is alert too and shivering with fear. A super-nervous fight attendant stands at the end of my aisle. "Are you all right, miss?" he asks.

I look at the two business folks in the seats beside mine. The way their eyes are bugging out of their heads, I was definitely just screaming *"never"* at the top of my lungs.

*Ugh.*

"I'm fine," I say quickly. "Bad dream, that's all."

The flight attendant narrows his eyes at me. He isn't buying my bad dream story and I don't blame him. But what do I say? *There's a supernatural big bad following me around?*

"Seriously." I force a grin. "I'm all right now."

The fight attendant nods. "You'll want to buckle your seatbelt. We're about to land in Charles de Gaulle."

After clicking my buckle, I let out a long sigh. We're almost about to land. That's good news.

I think.

# CHAPTER NINETEEN

Landing in Charles de Gaulle was a nightmare. Not the part about the plane actually touching down; that bit went pretty smoothly. No, I'm talking about how everyone was staring at me like I'm nuts for screaming NEVER at the top of my lungs.

Ugh.

After that, it took a while to get through customs, but that was my bad. The fake passport I grabbed was classic Elle—meaning it looked great—but I forgot my false name. In my defense, the name Brianna Rosacea doesn't exactly roll off the tongue. In the end, I got through fine. You can get away with a lot, as long as you smile afterward. *Did I misspeak? Silly me.* Elle taught me that trick. Works every time.

The real trouble came with finding a cab. Once I told them I wanted to go to Boucle-Roux, they'd speed-talk in French and motion toward the door until I left. Finally, I found a guy who would do it. Which brings me to the present moment.

Gustav has been driving me in circles for at least three hours. Boucle-Roux is right outside Paris. I checked the distance before I left for Europe. Doctor Google says I should have reached Boucle-Roux from the airport in about an hour.

So Gustav wants himself a big fare. Fine with me, so long as I arrive by midnight.

Which is about twenty minutes from now.

I lean forward and clear my throat. "Hello?"

"Eh?" Gustav is an old and balding dude who reminds me of a human-size troll doll. He's a lumpy dude with a large nose, bald head, and truly massive eyebrows.

Now, here's where it would be useful to show Gustav my cell phone, complete with a handy map to Boucle-Roux. However, if I turn my cell on, it's sure to blow up with calls from Elle and Knox. Leaving a fake note was hard enough. If I pick up the phone, I'll totally crack and tell them where I really am.

Instead, I use my newfound skills as a mime. "Boucle-Roux?" I pretend to be hoeing the ground, farmer style. "When?" I point to the nonexistent watch on my wrist because, really, who uses a watch when you can just check your cell?

Gustav grumbles something that sounds like *bleugh-bleugh-bleugh-stupide-bleugh-bleugh-bleugh-BLEUGH*. Over the past three hours, Gustav has been crystal clear that he think visiting Boucle-Roux is a bad idea. Amazing what can be conveyed despite the language barrier.

I point to my wrist again. "When?"

Gustav pulls over to the side of the road. We're in a deserted area of farms and a ton of sheep. The landscape around here changes in a heartbeat, by the way. One second, you're in the middle of a big city and then—ZOOM—just two minutes later, it's farmville.

Closing my eyes, I check in on my inner wolf. Sure, she slept for most of the plane ride. But that all ended when I flipped out. Charles de Gaulle wasn't her favorite either. Once the cab hit the countryside, she konked out again.

"Are you awake?" I ask my inner animal.

There's no response, unless you count snoring.

*So my wolf is still asleep. Good.*

I stare out the window at the darkened landscape. We're surrounded by rolling hills dotted with sheep. A dirt road leads from the street to a large wooden farmhouse. Other than the sheep, me, and Gustav, there's no one else around.

"Are we here?" I ask.

In response, Gustav points to a small wooden sign stuck into the ground nearby. The words *"Boucle-Roux"* are written in cockeyed letters.

I pretend to write on my hand, which is the universal signal for *how much do I pay you?* Gustav asks for a crazy amount of euros, which I hand over happily. Funny how when it comes to requesting money, Gustav is suddenly very familiar with English. Good thing Elle and I have deep bank accounts. As I hand over the cash, I check the digital clock on the dashboard.

Ten minutes before midnight.

I made it, just like WaterGirl asked.

Now I need to meet WaterGirl at the farmhouse, and the Codex Mechanica is mine. All in all, things are going pretty well. Scooching my way closer to the door, I wave to Gustav. "Merci."

Swinging about, Gustav wags his craggy pointer finger at me. This time, his French sounds a lot like "Bleugh-bleugh-bleugh-STUPIDE-bleugh. BLEUGH."

"Thank you, I got the stupide part."

I grip the door handle. Who cares if this seems like a dumb idea? In thirty minutes, my adventure will be that much closer to over. I'll have the Codex Mechanica, the location of the fountain, and a lot more control over the entire situation. Not so *stupide*, in my opinion.

I twist the handle just as a low rumble shakes the night air.

Crud.

*Thunder.*

Nothing more happens, so I figure maybe that's it, storm-wise. Hoisting up my duffle, I leave the cab and step onto the side of the road.

A torrent of fat raindrops pelts my head because, of course, it's going to rain.

Oh, well.

The faster I get to the farmhouse, the more quickly I'll be out of the storm. As Gustav peels away, I hustle up the dirt road and quickly discover a fun fact: Wearing leather pants in the rain is a terrible idea.

Talk about chafe.

In record speed, I reach the top of the hill and find a two story farmhouse. There are lights on inside, but all the windows are open. The front door is ajar as well. I step up onto the porch.

"Hello?" I ask. "Anyone here?"

The good news is that the porch is mostly covered. The whole place is built with weathered wood that is so warped, there are huge spaces between each slat. It's like whoever built this place never heard of insulation. Still, it's better than nothing. Even standing on the porch, I'm no longer getting pelted so badly by the rain. The air scents of green grass and sheep. It's the second smell that awakens my wolf.

My inner animal stretches. *"Where are we? Can I eat the sheep?"*

*"We've arrived at a place called Boucle-Roux,"* I reply in my mind. *"We need to meet WaterGirl here. Dinner can wait."* And we aren't eating random sheep, although I don't add in that part.

I set down my duffel and knock on the opened door. "Water-Girl? Are you in here?"

No reply.

I scan inside the house because, hey, if they didn't want anyone peeping around, they should have closed the door. The interior is French rustic. I'm talking rickety wooden furniture, faded drapes, and threadbare braided rugs. It's a look that could be cool if it were shabby chic. Only here, it's just shabby. Rain drips through holes in the floorboards and seeps through the walls. Great puddles form on the floor. No one's even bothered to put out a bucket to catch the fall.

The place looks deserted, only it isn't. A long wooden table sits against the far wall. Three bowls of stew have been laid out in a neat row. Wisps of steam curl up from the meals.

People definitely live here.

Cautiously, I step inside. "Hello? WaterGirl?"

My skin breaks out into gooseflesh. Nothing like being in the rain and then a drafty farmhouse to trigger your shiver reflex. My inner wolf perks up again. Rain always throws off her sense of smell.

*"There's something strange in this place,"* grumbles my wolf.

*"You're not kidding,"* I reply in my mind. *"WaterGirl should be here by now."*

*"That's not what I meant."* Inside my soul, my wolf hops up onto her four paws. Her eyes gleam with golden light. *"We must shift."*

*"I'm not changing into wolf form in some stranger's house."*

*"Shift!"* howls my wolf.

At that moment, the scent of foreign wolves becomes strong, along with the smell of burnt charcoal. Shifters are nearby. And whoever these wolves are, they are furious.

The wall to my right buckles. Windows shatter. Beams of wood snap apart like kindling. A wave of rain and wind pelt into the house. Tearing through the ruined wall, six massive werewolves leap into the room. Their eyes all shine with golden magic. Low growls reverberate through their chests. Since their ears are back and teeth bared, there's no question what these shifters are here to do.

Attack.

I make a quick assessment of the pack. Five of the weres have dark gray fur and lean bodies. All of these wolves hang back in a semicircle around the largest of their number, a massive wolf with pale gray fur and extra-long fangs.

That one's their alpha, no doubt.

Inside my soul, my wolf claws at the ground. *"Make the change,"* she urges. *"These are six male wolves. I smell burnt charcoal on them. You know what that means—rage."*

My wolf is right. Enraged shifters won't join a discussion about WaterGirl and ancient devices. They'll kill first and ask questions later.

I take my wolf's advice and shift.

Fast.

Energy and magic charge through my nervous system as my arms and legs transform into hefty limbs with massive claws. White fur erupts across my body. My fangs descend.

I become a wolf.

Moving in unison, the six weres leap at me. Finishing my shift, I lunge out of the way, sliding into the opposite wall. The weathered boards snap under my weight. The other wolves follow in a mad rush for the same wall.

I go low on my haunches, my back legs braced against the half-broken wall.

*Bring on another mass attack. I'm ready.*

The scent of rage grows stronger as the pack closes in. Once the alpha's front claws scrape against my muzzle, I leap into the air and over the pack. The group of wolves can't stop their momentum. All six of them slam into the same wall; it shatters.

We now have two busted walls and a very rickety farmhouse.

The sound of snapping wood fills the air. The corner posts on one side of the room buckle. The floorboards above my head sag.

Not long now before the whole place collapses. All around me, the weathered boards creak and shudder. Good. All I need is for the place to fall apart. It will be the perfect opportunity for me to counterattack.

"Fight with your heads, boys," growls the light gray wolf. "You watch sheep; you don't act like them. Stop following her around. Attack like a pack."

This shocks me for three reasons. First, it's a pretty rare shifter who can talk in their animal form. And second, this guy speaks English. Also unexpected. Third, he's asking them not to just chase me around and slam into the walls anymore. That really throws a monkey wrench into my number one plan for winning this battle.

Crud.

The wolves fan out to encircle me, which really gets my adrenaline pumping. Elle and I watch our share of Jackie Chan movies. We always love it when twenty ninjas go after the hero at once. Jackie takes them all down in like thirty seconds, flat.

But in reality? That's incredibly hard to do. I try to keep them all in my line of sight, but that just ends up with me twisting about in circles.

I'm panting now. This is really bad.

"Close in slowly, boys," says the alpha.

The wolves keep circling me in ever smaller loops. This isn't going to end well for me unless I do something quickly. Leaning back on my haunches, I prepare to try another leap over their heads.

And that's when the roof decides to fall in.

Ceiling beams snap. Floorboards collapse. Someone's massive sleigh bed falls right onto my back. Ouch. A ceiling beam slams onto the back of my head. White-hot hurt explodes behind my eyes. Dizzy with pain, I try to get up, but some of the wolves have jumped onto the massive piece of furniture that's across my back. Plus, that massive beam isn't giving an inch. With all my strength, I twist and writhe.

Nothing helps.

My wolf, who'd been pretty quiet through the battle, decides that now is a good time to give strategic advice.

"*Shift back into human form,*" urges my inner animal. "*They won't expect it.*"

"*Neither will my spine,*" I reply in my mind. "*Or the back of my skull.*"

The alpha strides into my line of sight. "Good thing we were warned about you." His eyes flare with golden light. "No one comes to steal our flock. You hear?"

I buck even harder, but it doesn't help. I'm pinned down tightly. Plus, twisting about only makes the ceiling beam press harder onto the back of my head. I can't even open my jaw enough to speak.

The alpha strides closer. "I hate to make an example of you, considering how you're a woman and all, but a deal's a deal." Leaping forward, he sinks his teeth into the tender flesh of my neck. The copper tang of blood fills my senses.

My inner wolf howls with agony and terror.

This is where I die. *No, please no.*

155

Outside the ruined farmhouse, the storm grows more fierce. Fresh bolts of lightning strike around the grounds, casting flickering shadows around the room. From the corner of my eye, I see what looks like a huge black wolf leap through the ruined wall, his massive form highlighted by a bolt of lightning.

Knox is here!

A sense of joy balloons through my soul. Somehow, when I needed him most, Knox found me. Inside my heart, my inner wolf howls with glee.

*"Mate!"* she cries. *"We love our maaaaaaaaate!"*

Fast as a heartbeat, Knox tears into the wolves that are pinning me down. One by one, he flings the shifters off my back. After that, my mate clamps down onto the alpha's neck, tearing him away from me as well.

My inner wolf howls with glee. *"Our mate is here! He saved us!!!"*

I'd howl as well, if I didn't have so much blood loss to worry about.

With the wolves off me, Knox kicks away the beam and mattress. He leans in and checks out my neck. "Bry, are you okay?"

Before I can answer, the other wolves race toward us, ready to counterattack.

In response, Knox's entire body shines with golden light and magic. "Enough!" he cries. Waves of alpha energy radiate off him, making the entire room tremble. Floorboards creak. Broken bits of glass jingle in their shattered frames. The air shimmers with waves of power. As Knox's alpha energy reaches the other wolves, they all freeze in place.

"I'll say this one last time," growls Knox. "Back off my mate or I will kill you." A final burst of alpha power shimmies through the air. After that, Knox releases his magic. My mate's fur returns to its regular shade of black.

For a long moment, there is only the rain, lightning, and no one moving. Then the other alpha tilts his head. "Knox, is that you? We haven't seen you since we all hunted Denarii together." The alpha shakes his head again. "That can't be you."

Knox scrapes at the floorboards with his front claws. "You know another huge black wolf who can kick all your asses in thirty seconds or less?"

"Damn," says the alpha. "And this shifter here... Is she really your mate?"

Knox growls out one more word: "Yes." He turns to me. "Are you all right?"

I force myself back onto my legs. "I'm feeling better. Good to see you."

An awkward moment follows where Knox and I stare at each other. The air becomes thick with emotion. Joy that we're together. Fear for our future. And in my case, a healthy dose of guilt.

"I'm sorry," I say in a low voice. All of a sudden, I can't help but stare at how my claws scrape against the floor. "I shouldn't have run off without you."

Knox steps closer. "No worries. Az can be very convincing with his all-knowing Gandalf routine. I get it." He nuzzles into my neck, sending warmth through my core. "But you're my mate, and no one, not even Azizi, can change that."

In the movie of my life, I'd have a great speech for this moment. But this is me, not a film, so I can only smile and lick his muzzle. "Okay."

"Good." Leaning in, Knox nuzzles my neck more deeply, and I sigh. Nearby, one of the weres clears his throat.

*Oops. I forgot about them.*

"Sorry about your neck," says Bo.

Knox steps back and checks my neck again. "It's almost healed. Bo here isn't a very efficient killer, thankfully." Knox shoots an angry look at the alpha.

Bo's tail goes under his legs. "She was coming here after our sheep."

"And who told you that?" snarls Knox.

Bo's ears go flat against his head. "That would be..."

"Let me guess," growls Knox. "Ty."

"That's right."

It's been a day for shocking news, but this one still floors me. I focus on Knox. "Do you mean *the* Ty?" *Is there anyone who doesn't know Knox's ex?*

Knox nods. "My guess? She engineered this whole thing so I'd have to pay attention to her. Ty called me in New York and said you were about to be attacked at Boucle-Roux."

"And I came here because she told me she has the Codex Mechanica," I say.

Knox's eyes narrow. "She probably does. Ty loves to collect rare stuff."

Bo crouches down onto the floor. I have to hand it to the guy, when he goes for a grovel, he's all in. "Look, Knox. We didn't know she was your mate. Ty called us and told us a fierce warrior was after our sheep. She even said the scents would be misleading. In exchange for the information, we promised Ty that we would kill the intruder."

"We need to talk about this, and not as wolves," says Knox. With that, he starts to change back into his human form. His bones realign and fur retracts. Within a few seconds, there's an awful lot of naked butt standing in front of my wolfy self right now. And I can't help but notice that Knox is looking totally recovered from the last time I saw him in New York. Back then, he'd lost all his muscle tone. In fact, my mate could hardly stand by himself.

But now? Knox seems fully recovered, judging by the quality of his glutes. And there's his ripped back too, let's not forget that part. Oh, and great legs. Plus, his arms look pretty buff again. Heck, even his toes look better.

The good news is that I love how Knox looks healthy.

But the bad news? Knox's recovery happened right after I left him.

And that's a point for the *Az is right* column. When I'm near Knox, I make him sick.

All of which is terrible, but at this point? I'm so happy to see my mate, I really can't muster too much sadness.

Knox glances over his shoulder. Grinning, he rakes his hand through his mop of wet black hair. "Like the view?"

I mock-pant a little. "Woof."

Knox strides over to a wooden chest by the wall. The thing is covered by fallen plans and debris, so Knox has to pull off all the heavy stuff. I won't lie. I do enjoy the show. Eventually, Knox opens up the box and pulls out a pair of jeans along with a black T. He pulls them on and looks to the other wolves. "Get changed, guys."

At this point, I realize that I should probably shift back as well. Within a few seconds, I'm back to my human form. Happily, my unshreddable outfit is once again in place. And somehow magically cleaned in the process as well. The fae may be crazy, but they make good clothing.

The moment my shift is over, Knox pulls me into a hug. "I've been so worried, Bry."

"I'm sorry. This was something I had to do." I lean into his embrace. "Besides, I was making you sick."

Knox leans back and cups my face in his hands. Even in the few minutes we've been together, it seems like the color is fading from his skin.

I frown. "You're already worse." I inhale deeply. The barest scent of pain lingers in the air.

"I won't lie to you. Now that we're together, I feel a change inside. Something's happening. Making me weaker. But it's not you, Bry. Never you."

Across the room, Bo clears his throat again. Knox and I look up to see six very buff guys in overalls standing around a ruined farmhouse. Knox slides his arm around my waist. "Bry, I'd like you meet Beauregard Roux and his people."

My eyes widen. "Oh, I get it. Your fairy tale template is Bo Peep."

Bo nods. "You know how it goes: 'little Bo Peep lost her sheep and doesn't know where to find them? That's not me. I never lose my sheep."

"What about the second part?" I ask. "Leave them alone, and they'll come home, wagging their tails behind them?"

Bo sniffs. "If you leave sheep alone, they don't come home. Other weres have them for dinner."

One of the other guys raises his hand. "We're vegetarians, by the way. After spending years going after the Denarii, you lose your taste for red meat."

Knox looks around the place. "I'd say sorry your house got ruined, but you attacked my mate."

"It's all right," says Bo. He even has curly blond hair like his namesake. "Been meaning to rebuild anyway. This place was always a dump."

"We live mostly in the wild with our flock," adds the guy who made the vegetarian comment before. I decide to call him Chatty Cathy since it goes with the Bo Peep theme somehow.

"Hey," says Bo. "Maybe your warlock friend can come over and conjure us up a house?" He scans the room like Alec is hiding under a floorboard. "Where is your buddy, anyway? Isn't he always with you?" Bo hitches his thumbs into the sides of his overalls. "Although, I guess if your mate travels alone, maybe Alec does too now."

For the record, I've been a very patient person about being attacked and having my neck chomped on. But getting critiqued for travelling alone? That is just one step too far. I round on Bo. "Look here, buddy. I came to Europe to save all of magic for *everybody*, you guys included. You don't even know what that means, but it's a big deal and an even bigger pain in my neck. Want to know why I came here alone? I'm not a big fan of people who drag those they care about into trouble just because they can. I could get this job done on my own and keep my mate safe, so that's what I did. Because unlike some people in this room, I don't think like a sheep and do things just because that's what someone told me to do." I toss my hair over my shoulder. "Plus, I hope your stupid crappy house burns down."

Not sure why I added that last part in, but it sure felt good.

Bo's mouth hangs open for at least twenty seconds. "I can see why she's your mate."

"She's also right about the magic stuff," says Knox. "We need to go see Ty. You got a bike or a car I can borrow?"

"Let's check out the old barn," says Bo. "There might be something in there."

In the end, Bo gives us his old Fiat to drive, which is more like a golf cart with doors, but it's still better than nothing. We get in and start up the engine. I'm surprised there's even an engine, really. I half expect us to peddle the thing forward, Flintstones-style.

I squirm in the frayed pleather seat. "Look, I can't imagine what you think about how I took off—"

"You don't have to say another word, Bry. Everything was explained back there with Bo. I understand why you tried to do this alone. I also get why you don't want to pull Elle and Alec into this, either. But I'm here now. There's no way I'm leaving your side, yeah?"

A weight I didn't know I was carrying seems to lift off my bones. "Yeah."

"Good." Knox puts the car in gear and takes off down the dirt road. "I know the way to Ty's. You get some sleep."

"I'm not sleepy." That's what I say, but the moment the words leave my lips, my eyelids instantly feel super-heavy. I fall asleep within five minutes flat.

At least, I don't have any nightmares of the Void.

# CHAPTER TWENTY

I stay konked out and comfortable until sunlight blazes onto my closed eyes. I flip my arm over my face, block out the brightness, and try to get comfy again. It isn't easy. I'm sprawled across the front seat of the Fiat with my legs jammed onto the dashboard and my head smooshed against the passenger-side door. Huh. My sleepy brain tries to process all this. How is Knox is driving, exactly? My left leg uses the steering wheel as a footrest.

My eyes flutter open. We definitely aren't driving anymore. Knox isn't even in the car. I scrub my hands over my face. Where am I again? The last thing I remember, Knox and I were driving away from the Boucle-Roux farm and into the night. I must have slept longer than I thought.

Craning my totally cramped-up neck, I see that Knox has parked us before a fancy iron gate somewhere in a countryside that positively screams France. The roads are lined with quaint houses that might have fallen out of a fairy tale. Everywhere, the buildings are made from heavy wooden frames filled in with white plaster and topped by overly pointy roofs. There's even an old man on a bicycle with a baguette strapped behind him. The town isn't what interests me, though.

Beyond the gate, a gravel road winds up the side of a cliff. Atop the mountain, there stands a castle. It's another fairy tale classic: a sprawling structure with a gray façade and skinny windows. Now what fairy tale life template would that fit in with? I frown, thinking through the options.

Unfortunately, most fairy tales have a castle or two in the mix. I scan the facade closer, looking for some kind of clue.

Everywhere you look, the castle is lined with stone turrets that end in tiny conical roofs. At the center of the ground floor, there's a seriously huge set of wooden doors, which are most definitely closed.

Around the castle itself, the cliff side has been crammed with dozens of fountains and small, perfectly manicured lawns. Topiaries are everywhere, and for some reason, they're all snipped into the shape of fish.

Wait a second. Fish? I've never of any story where there's a castle with an aquatic theme. Not that I'm an expert in fairy tales, but that seems odd. Knox stands with his back to me, gripping the bars of the main gate and staring up at the castle. I want to call out to him; but I'm sort of jammed in an odd position. Some conversations are best had when your leg isn't wound around a steering wheel, especially ones that cover topics like:

*Is this a sightseeing stop, or does Ty really live here?*

*And if Ty is here, since when does anyone have an ex-girlfriend who lives in a castle in France?*

Long story short, I need to get myself upright for this conversation. Since I'm stuck in an odd position, it takes some work to get unstuck. As I shift around, my foot gets caught in the steering wheel. The car horn gives out a friendly little toot-toot.

Hearing the noise, Knox turns around and smiles. The sight makes me both happy and miserable. Knox's health has certainly taken a nosedive since last night. All the color has drained from his skin. A pang of guilt tightens my stomach.

Knox was better last night.

He's sicker today.

Either Ty is casting a spell to make Knox sick…or Az is right that magic is somehow punishing Knox for finding a mate instead of the fountain.

*Whatever way I look at it, the situation isn't good.*

Plus another night has passed, so the equinox is only two days away.

*Correction. The situation is looking worse.*

Knox stalks over to the car, grips the roof, and leans into the side window. "How're you feeling?" He taps the window frame. "I left this open to give you some air."

"Thanks, it must have worked. I really slept hard." Narrowing my eyes, I scan his features. Now that Knox's face is only a few inches from mine, I don't like how the veins have popped out on his forehead and neck. The barest scent of pain lingers in the air. "How about *you?*"

"No worries."

I slip my palm against his bristled cheek. "I still do worry."

Knox kisses my palm. "Which is why you're my girl." He exhales a long breath. "I need to explain about this place, but there isn't a lot of time."

Blinking hard, I try to get the sleep out of my brain. My guess is that Knox wants to explain this place's fairy tale template, but I'm not sure I'm awake enough for story time yet. Even my wolf is still snoozing. Plus, my stomach is growling. I'm hoping there's a chance to get a croissant or something before we get into anything too intense.

"Not a lot of time?" I ask through a yawn. "What do you mean?"

"The horn. *They* definitely would have heard that."

"They?" It's still taking me longer than usual to catch on to things here. "Oh, you mean the people who live in the castle?"

"Yeah, them. I never told you my fairy tale life template." The edge of a growl creeps into his voice. I don't need to catch Knox's scent to know that whatever his fairy tale life template is, the idea saddens him.

Inside me, my wolf yawns awake as well. *"That terrible principal asked our mate the same question at school,"* she says. *"We don't care what Knox's template is."*

Knox tilts his head. "Does your wolf have something to say about that?"

"As a matter of fact, she does. And I believe the same thing, too. It doesn't matter what your fairy tale life template is. You're with me now. We make up our own story."

"That we do, Bry." Those are the words Knox says, but I can still scent the acidity of his worry. "When I fought the Denarii, I lived out my template. Hard. I was a different guy. A killing machine."

"You were avenging your parents."

"It wasn't what I was doing, it was what I became to get the job done." He closes his eyes. "Not a man. Not even a wolf."

I lock my gaze with his. "I'm with you today, not some version out of the past." My shifter hearing picks up a new sound: soft wooden creaks. The main doorway is opening in the castle above. Knox sucks in a sharp breath.

"What has you worried?" I ask. "The people who live in the castle?"

"Not all of them," says Knox slowly. "Just one."

My eyes widen as more of my thoughts come into focus. "So your ex *does* live here."

"Yeah." The slight growl in his voice is unmistakable.

My pulse flutters with this news, and not because it's a surprise. The whole reason we were driving here was to confront Ty. Knox's ex was supposed to hand over the Codex Mechanica last night at Boucle-Roux. Instead, she tricked some French weres into attacking me. Honestly, I'm more worried what my wolf will do when she meets Ty. My inner animal is rather protective.

All of a sudden, the castle seems to loom taller on its cliff top. Not sure where I pictured Ty living, but it definitely wasn't a castle.

Knox inhales. "You smell of anxiety. Does seeing Ty worry you?"

I hold my thumb and forefinger an inch apart. "Only a little bit, and that's because of my wolf."

Christina Bauer

As if on cue, my inner animal yips with glee. *"Ty is bad. She makes our mate angry. Now, we'll raid her stone den and bite her!"*

It's amazing how my wolf can go from *barely awake* to *ready to bite ex-girlfriends* in thirty seconds or less. Over the past months, I've learned to nip these ideas in the bud early. When I next speak to my wolf, I take care to use my no-nonsense voice. "Get that idea out of your head, fur girl."

A small smile rounds Knox's full lips. "Fur girl?"

I pop my hand over my mouth. "I said that out loud, didn't I?" *For the umpteenth time.*

"Yeah." Knox's smile broadens. "Don't worry. It's cute."

My inner wolf preens. *"Our mate is the best."*

*"Agreed,"* I reply in my mind.

Back in the outside world, I can't help but match Knox's grin. "Actually, it's my big bad inner werewolf. I'm trying to keep her in line."

"Even cuter. What's she want to do?"

"Ah. That would be…" I try to think of a subtle way of expressing this but come up empty. "She wants to bite Ty's face off."

Knox chuckles. "I'd like to see that."

With a loud thud, the main gates finally swing open. A small army of servants pours out from the castle and starts heading our way. Even from a distance, I can tell that they're a rather fancy crowd of servants. All the men sport dark suits with cravats, while the ladies wear gray dresses with poofy maid hats. I scan the group for someone who might look like ex-girlfriend material and come up empty. Knox told me that Ty was our age—all these servants have gray hair.

Inside my soul, my wolf growls her displeasure. *"Is the one who angers our mate drawing closer? Can I chomp her?"*

*"No and no,"* I reply in my head.

*"Please? I just want to bite off her ankle."*

*"The answer is still no. Besides, she isn't here yet anyway."*

*"Fine."* My inner animal huffs out a frustrated breath. *"I can wait."*

Knox eyes me carefully through the car window. "Your wolf still feeling chatty?"

I nod. "In case you're wondering, she'd be happy biting off Ty's ankle."

My inner animal chimes in again. *"What's wrong with that?"* asks my wolf. *"She's got two ankles. She doesn't need them both."*

This time, I decide to ignore my wolf. Engaging with her about whether Ty needs two ankles is not a conversation that will end well anyway.

"Ankles," says Knox. "Got it." He lowers his voice. "You still good? We can come back later if you need some time with your animal." He cracks his neck from side to side. "Tell the truth, we could both probably use a good run. Long car rides and wild animals don't mix, yeah?"

"Look, I'm fine," I assure him. "My wolf's definitely under control."

Inside my mind, my inner animal is not dropping the issue. *"What about a finger, then? She's got ten of those."*

Knox gives me the side-eye. "You sure?" he asks.

"Honestly, I'd rather get this over with." *And not just because we're running out of time before the equinox arrives.*

That results in more side-eye. "Not even one quick run?" My mate is always protective about giving our animals time in the wild.

"Both my wolf and I are fine. Absolutely."

Inside my mind, my wolf is definitely not giving up. *"If you won't let me have a finger, how about a toe?"*

Now, this has gone on long enough that I can't ignore it. *"If you keep talking about taking Ty's body parts, I'm going to have to put you in stasis."*

*"You wouldn't."*

*"Try me."*

Knox inhales. "Your scent mixes aggression and determination. That's good. Ty's tricky, you know."

I shrug. "Tricky goes along with being a sorceress, right?"

"Partly." Knox frowns. "Ty's a little nutty, too."

Unfortunately, my mate is the master of understatement. If Knox is saying Ty is a little nutty, then that can only mean one thing…

"In other words, Ty is bat-crap crazy."

"Oh, yeah." Knox glances over his shoulder. "Here they come."

The servants rush down the gravel driveway, a small cloud of dust puffing up behind them. For a bunch of older folks, this group is certainly spry. All the while, they chat away in rapid-fire French, so I try to catch some of their talk. Since I only speak English, I can recognize Knox's name and that's about it. It'll be great when I learn how to harness my witch power. Then, I'll be able to cast translation spells for situations like this one.

Within seconds, the servants congregate by a small iron door off to one side of the main gate. A super-tall guy stands up front, a loop of old-fashioned keys in his veiny fist. After some jangling and stuff, Tall Guy unlocks the side door. Everyone races out to surround Knox. Turning around, my mate faces the group and starts to converse. Of course, Knox speaks perfect French because, well, that's Knox.

I have no idea what's going on, apart from the fact that everyone's speaking French and seems incredibly happy to see my mate. Then I hear one thing I do recognize. A name.

"Reginald."

My skin prickles into gooseflesh. I must be hearing things. Then, it happens again.

"Reggie."

After that, I catch another word.

"Denarii."

Officially, this has become one conversation that I don't want to miss…And I can't have it in the car without some translation help. Gripping the handle, I start to open the door, but everyone is pressed up against that side of the Fiat in their efforts to encircle Knox.

The whole situation is anxiety-inducing to my inner wolf. *"Denarii mean danger! We must shift and run!"*

My wolf has a point. At this moment, I can easily use my shifter strength to burst through the car door, but that's overkill, especially with this particular group of servants.

*"Let me talk to them first,"* I reply. *"These servants don't smell like shifters. I could hurt them."*

*"But Ty could be nearby,"* counters my wolf. *"If we're in wolf form, we could get that toe."*

And here we go again. My wolf has a one-track mind. *"We are not biting anyone's anything. Last warning."*

I cup my hand by my mouth. "Hello, there."

No one replies. Instead, the servants all keep right on talking at once—at ever higher volumes—and always in French. Worse, Reggie and the Denarii are definitely the highlight of the conversation. My pulse speeds faster. Has Reggie been running around here trying to "help"?

Time to get some answers.

I set both pinkies in either side of my mouth and let out a long whistle. Everyone quiets.

Knox turns around. Laughter dances in his blue eyes. "You want something, Bry?"

"I heard the name Reggie."

"Sure thing; I'll fill you in." Knox turns to the group. "Stand back, everybody. Make some room." The way he talks to the servants is more conversational than bossy. Maybe Ty owns this castle, and Knox got to be buddies with the staff while they were dating? Seems reasonable.

The servants step back and form a long, neat row. It must be part of their staff routine because I've never seen a group line up so quickly. There are about twenty servants in all, evenly split between men and woman. All of them are staring at me, wide eyed. I sniff the air. Times like these, it's great to have a shifter sense of smell. I this case, I catch the lemon of anxiety mixed with the flowery bloom of happiness. Most likely, these servants are pleased to see Knox, along with a little worried about how their mistress will handle the new girlfriend in the Fiat.

Makes sense. If I were them, I'd worry about my boss freaking out, too.

Knox pulls on the car door; it swings open with a long creak. It's as if time slows down as I make my way out of the Fiat and into the morning air. A blush crawls over my skin.

For a moment, I wonder if I should get back in the car, but I shake the idea off. Knox knows these people. If he thinks it's okay for me to meet them, then it's fine.

I straighten the folds my black duster. I'm still in my unshreddable outfit from this morning. In fact, I even have my bracelet on in case I need to glamour myself into looking like I'm wearing a regular school uniform. I shake my head. Was my first day at West Lake only two days ago? Seems like a million years have passed since then. I clear my throat.

"Good morning," I say.

All the servants start talking at once.

In French.

Not helping.

Knox raises his arms, palms forward in the universal sign for *stop right there*. "Whoa, guys." They quiet instantly. "Bry here doesn't speak French, so you'll need to use English from here on out." Everyone nods, which I take as a good sign.

"Thank you," I say.

"First things first." Knox steps to my side and wraps his arm about my waist, pulling me close against him. "This is Bryar Rose. She's my mate."

That news changes things for the servants. The scent of anxiety, which was pretty faint before, now becomes overwhelmingly strong. Still, if these folks worry about how their mistress will handle meeting Knox's new mate, that's their problem. I need to find out if Reggie is running around the French countryside and causing trouble. And then there's the issue of finding the Codex Mechanica, but that will have to wait a minute.

I focus on Knox. "I heard the name Reggie before. Why?"

It might just be me, but it feels like the servants just reached an entirely new level of quiet. All eyes seem to be locked on me and Knox in a way that isn't entirely comfortable.

They know something I don't.

"To begin with," says Knox Slowly. "I used to hunt Denarii with Ty."

"You did?" Not sure why this surprises me, but it does. I guess I always pictured Ty as off somewhere casting spells over cell phones, not doing something useful like killing zombie-mummies.

"Sure," continues Knox. "Back then, I hired folks to help me out, depending on the job. Ty's one of the best mercenary sorceresses around. She was with me when I first captured Reggie, and the two of them got to be friendly."

I purse my lips. "Friendly? Reggie only talks in creepy songs that he makes up on the fly. He's not really friend material."

"Anyway, he and Ty still hit it off," explains Knox. "They're both…" He bobs his head, trying to find the right word.

"Off their rocker?" I ask.

"Yeah. That."

I rub my neck, thinking through the implications of that bit of news. "So when Reggie escaped last summer, you thought he might come here."

"Right," says Knox. "That's when I reached out to these guys." Knox gestures to the line of servants. "I asked them to give me a heads-up if they noticed anything suspicious. They just finished telling me how they haven't seen anything out of the ordinary."

The tallest servant—the guy who'd opened the side gate door with his keys—steps forward. He's a lanky dude whose lean face is topped by an artful swoosh of gray hair. When he speaks, it's with a serious French accent. "We've kept zee watch just as you requested, my Master."

Now, that's one really thick French accent, but I can still understand what he says. Surprisingly, I'm pretty sure Tall Guy just called Knox his "Master." I frown. Maybe I'm mishearing things. It has been a long twenty-four hours, after all.

171

Knox shakes his head. "You know I don't like that name, Louis." The way Knox says the name, it's with a little accent as well: LOO-eee.

"Apologies," replies Louis. "We've kept zee watch as you requested, *Sir*." He bows a little after he says that last bit, as if he needs to make up for not saying Master.

It's taken me a little while, but I'm finally catching on to what's happening here. I turn to Knox. "Is this *your* castle?"

"But ov course," answers Louis. He's a fairly chatty guy, now that he's broken the ice. "As I said, Knox eez our Master."

"Technically, this is Az's place," says Knox. "One of many. He left it to me."

I open my mouth, ready to correct Knox because actually, when you leave something to someone, it's not yours anymore. In other words, Knox is definitely the master of all these folks now, whatever that means. But I close my mouth instead. Knox is my mate and we need to provide a united front, at least in front of his team. I can bring up the *you're actually the Master here* discussion later.

Louis lifts his chin. "Whatever you say, *Sir*." Looks like Louis is also on Team Keep Your Mouth Shut For Now. "Shall we take you to see Mademoiselle Ty now? She is still in residence." The way he says *in residence*, it's clear that Ty didn't just stop by here on a whim. Knox's ex is living in his random French palace.

This is getting complex.

Inside my heart, my wolf paces in anger. That's not a good sign. "*Ty*," growls my wolf. "*We hates her.*"

And she's talking like Gollum again.

An even worse sign.

"One second." Knox turns to me and lowers his voice. "Sure you don't want to know my fairy tale life template?"

It's a good question. On the one hand, I'm super-curious about this whole Ty situation. However, the other hand, there are about twenty servants standing around, waiting to hear our personal business. Like the conversation about who owns what castle, it can wait.

"I stand behind what I said before." I lift my chin. "I don't need to know your fairy tale life template."

Knox leans in, brushing a gentle kiss across my lips. My knees turn wobbly. "Thanks for that."

"Any time." I wink.

"All right." Knox takes my hand, and together, we head toward the castle. "Get ready to meet my personal nightmare."

Inside my soul, my wolf prances about with her tail held high. *"Our mate thinks Ty is his personal nightmare. Good, good, goooooood! We'll get to chomp her face off soon. I know it!"*

*"No,"* I counter in my mind. *"Chances are, this will be bad, bad, bad. Ty is a sorceress and a nutjob. We need to be careful."*

*"You ruin all my fun,"* my wolf grumbles.

That does it. Tapping into my shifter power, I pull on the cords of golden energy inside me. My wolf instantly falls into a deep sleep. She's been warned to be careful; now she's going into the equivalent of a magical time-out.

*No wolf and Ty at the same time, thank you very much.*

After stepping through the gate's side door, Knox and I begin the long walk up to the castle. How did all those senior citizens speed down this driveway so quickly? Right now, every step feels like I'm treading through molasses.

I straighten my shoulders. Who cares about some ex-girlfriend? Why I should worry? I fought Jules, the undead Roman general and creepster extraordinaire. Plus, last night I battled werewolves with Knox at my side. And now, my mate and I are reunited and loving it.

We can face down one off-the-wall sorceress.

Who used to be Knox's ex-girlfriend.

And who still lives in his castle for some reason.

Personal nightmare, here I come.

# CHAPTER TWENTY-ONE

As Knox and I walk along the never-ending gravel road to his castle, I can't help but notice how he glares at all the fish-shaped topiaries and fountains.

"Something wrong with the gardens?" I ask.

"This is all Ty's doing. I told her not to change anything. And she knows I hate all this fish stuff."

"So." I try to process this bit of news. Nope, I can't do it. "Let me get this straight. Your ex-girlfriend is living in your castle and redecorating."

"We only dated for a few weeks. Before that, we were just friends, you know?"

I don't really know because Knox is my first kiss and boyfriend, not counting how I fake-dated Jules when he was pretending to be that loser Philpot. Even so, I nod. Knox is trying to share here, and it seems like the right thing to do.

Knox continues. "Most of the time, Ty and I just killed Denarii together. That went on for years. It all changed after we caught Reggie, though. Once Reggie was in custody, Ty thought there could be more to us." He sighs. "I gave it a try. From the get-go, it was clear things wouldn't work out. Ty could never move on from that fact."

Now, I have total faith in my relationship with Knox. But does it feel just a *little bit* awesome to know he only dated Ty for a sort time and didn't enjoy any of it?

Um, yes. Not sure what that says about me as a person.

Talking to Knox must help the time go faster, because before I know it, we're stepping through the main gate and entering the castle proper. Inside, the place is all huge rooms with lots of heavy wooden furniture. Some threadbare tapestries of wolves hang on the walls. And there are indoor fountains everywhere. There are even ones set into the walls where stone fish heads spit out water into a lower basin.

Knox is really a leather chair and modern furniture kind of guy. All these fountains don't match his style. They have to be Ty's handiwork.

WaterGirl.

Sure, we're here to get the Codex Mechanica and find the fountain, but I must admit, my curiosity is definitely piqued about Ty herself. She's got to be some piece of work.

As we walk along, there's no missing the tons of servants running around. All of them human and wide eyed. They hold the doors open for us as we make a lot of twists and turns inside the castle. At last, we pause in front of a heavy wooden door.

For the first time, this one is closed.

Louis—who'd been following behind us up until now— suddenly steps up to the door and clears his throat. "Presenting Mademoiselle Ty."

Louis pushes the door open. Inside, there's another long stone room with fountains set into the walls. Only here, there's also a hefty wooden dining room table and a lit fireplace.

And Knox's ex.

It's easy to pick her out. At the end of the table sits a beautiful young girl dressed in a yellow gown. She looks about eighteen with pale skin and brown eyes the same shade as her long hair. As we enter the room, she pretends to read a book. I know the pretending part because even from across the chamber, I can see that it's an upside-down encyclopedia.

"You must be Ty," I say.

Ty doesn't even glance in my direction. Instead, she slams the book onto the tabletop. "You interrupted my very important and intellectual book, Knox. You know how I love to read."

Something about this girl sets off my rebel-reflex. I point to my own face. "I'm still here, you know. And you had that book upside down."

Knox wraps his arm protectively around my waist. "Ty, this is Bryar Rose. She's my mate."

In response, Ty pounds her fist on the tabletop. "I want breakfast, people!" Her ability to ignore things and just start demanding stuff is actually impressive. Color floods her cheeks as Ty raises her voice. "I'm your guest, remember?"

And with that, I know exactly what Knox's fairy tale life template is.

He's a Beast.

And Ty thinks that she's his Beauty.

Ugh.

The servants rush in and out, their arms laden with silver platters. Within seconds, the entire table is covered with every kind of food imaginable, regardless of whether it's breakfasty or not. There's even one of those baked pigs with an apple stuck in its mouth. Gross.

Ty makes a great show of pushing every platter away. "I have no appetite. But what do you expect? I'm a prisoner. Trapped."

"No," says Knox. "You're trespassing."

Ty sets the back of her hand on her forehead in the universal move of drama queens everywhere. It has zero effect on Knox.

"This is horrible." Ty lets out an overlong sigh. "Release me from your castle."

"Great. Go already." Knox hitches his thumb toward the door. "I broke up with you. Leave. For the love of all that's sacred. TAKE. OFF."

If Ty hears what Knox is saying, she doesn't show it. Instead, she keeps right on with her own personal tirade. "And the servants all act strangely to me." Ty clasps her hands by her throat. "You know, I believe that they might be enchanted?"

"They're not under a spell," says Knox.

"Poppycock." Ty sniffs. "I tell you, the servants treat me strangely."

"No, the staff hates you because you treat them like crap. Not the same thing." Knox gestures across the table. "I mean, what's all this? You demand these huge meals and then you don't eat a thing." He points at the pig. "And that's just nasty."

I raise my hand. "Totally agree."

Ty's mouth hangs open for a second before she speaks again. "I have it. You're simply out of sorts today. I know just what will cheer you up. I'll sing a song to the tune of 'Oh My Darling Clementine.'" Ty stands.

I speak to Knox from the side of my mouth. "She's not really going to do this, is she?"

"Why do you think we broke up?"

Ty starts singing. "Oh your darling, oh your darling, oh your darling me-me-meeeeee!" She taps her chest when she says the "me" part. "I'm so lovely and your Beauty. You're my Beastie, Knox sweetieeeee."

Knox and I share a long look. I mouth two words: *Knox sweetie?* For a minute, I'm not sure if we'll both scream or burst out laughing.

It ends up being the second thing.

Knox breaks into a deep, rumbling guffaw that is everything awesome. Meanwhile, I chortle for so long, I might pee my pants a little bit.

Eventually, our giggle-fest ticks off Ty enough that she halts right in the middle of a *Knox sweetieeeee*. "Do you two mind? It's my moment here."

"Look." Knox exhales a long breath. "Much as I appreciate the crazy show, we came by for a reason."

I set my fist on my hip. "You have a certain device that you promised to give me. Instead of making good on your word, you tried to get me killed. Bad plan, by the way."

Ty slumps into her chair. All pretense of acting like the innocent Beauty is gone. "Screw you," she says with a sneer. "I knew them French weres wouldn't make a dent in your precious hide. I just wanted to get Knox to haul his shapely ass to my side of the pond."

Now, there are two things that really bother me about that little speech. First, Ty has stopped acting like a pretty princess and has instantly transformed into a streetwise potty mouth. Second, I'm the only one who gets to appreciate Knox's butt.

"You called and told me she was at risk, and it was all a trick to get me closer." Knox's voice lowers to a growl. "That's low, even for you."

"That's what you say now," retorts Ty. "But wait until we all have a little chat and clear things up."

"Not happening," I say. "I'm not doing anything until you hand over the Codex Mechanica."

Ty gestures to the chairs nearby. "Have a seat, answer three questions, and then I'll give you the device, just as I promised."

I frown. "Really? Three little questions and we get the device?"

"I'll cast a spell to ensure it happens," says Ty.

I'm still not sure about this. "What kind of spell?"

"One that will hold me to my word. Watch." Ty raises her hands, palms upward. A pair of rubies gleams on her outstretched palms. I've seen Alec with those kinds of stones before. Classic tools for any witch or wizard. For a moment, the gemstones flare with unearthly light. After that, a line of water arcs from her left hand to her right. Inside the water there gleams tiny red spots of brightness.

I hate to admit this, but it's a pretty cool spell.

"This spell is unbreakable," says Ty. "It will hold me to the following promise. I will give you the Codex Mechanica if you answer my three questions honestly." The crimson lights inside the water gleam more strongly. After that, they disappear. With it, the water vanishes as well. "And the spell is cast."

I look to Knox. "You know her better than I do. Can we trust that spell? Will Ty keep her word?"

"We can trust it." Knox stalks over to the table and pulls out a chair for me. "Have a seat, Bry."

I plunk down and drag out the chair beside me for Knox. He slides in as well.

"We'll answer your damned questions," says Knox. "After that, I want you out of my house."

Ty picks something out of her molar with her pinky. "Oh, I'll go all right." The way she says the words, though? It's clear that she'll be right back. What an operator.

Knox waves to the servants. "Give us a little privacy, yeah?"

None of them need to be told twice. The servants all exit in record time. Soon it's just me, Ty, and Knox.

A nasty smile rounds Ty's perfect smile. "Shall we begin?"

I match her smarmy grin with one of my own. "Please."

Outside, I think that I'm looking pretty calm. But inside? My soul is churning with worry. Ty lured me and Knox to this very spot for a reason. And my mate is right. Ty is unhinged.

Whatever questions she's about to ask, I don't think I'll like them.

Not one bit.

# CHAPTER TWENTY-TWO

The world seems to pause as I soak in everything around me. The fresh wood lets off a musky scent as it burns in the fireplace. Lights flicker from the candelabras above me. The low gurgle of water echoes in from all the wall fountains. And finally, there's Ty. Knox's ex has transformed from a hyper-gentle dream girl into a hard-boiled nightmare. Ty lounges at the table's head, her right leg slung over the arm of her chair. Behind her, the massive fireplace outlines her in red flame. Talk about drama.

Ty sneezes. "Damn. This place is murder on my allergies."

"You could always leave," offers Knox.

"You'd like that, wouldn't you?" she asks.

Knox levels her with a glare. That would be *yeah*.

Ty shakes her head. "Whatever. I'm staying, and it's for your own good, Knox. You'll see."

With a pointed motion, Knox reaches across the armrests between us and links his hand with mine. "Let's get this over with," he says. "What's your first question?"

"It's for your little mate here." Ty narrows her brown eyes in my direction. "Suppose I give you the Codex Mechanica. What is the device designed to do?"

My gaze flicks over to Knox. He doesn't know that the First Wardens tried to use the Codex Mechanica to kill all magic—which in turn would've destroyed our inner animals. *Good thing they failed.* Trouble is, every time I introduce the topic, Knox can't remember it two seconds later. Stupid curse from the Void.

"I could explain everything, but there's a curse that goes along with the topic. You'll forget everything I tell you in two seconds."

"Just answer the question," counters Ty.

"Fine." I take in a deep breath. "The First Wardens designed a device to destroy both the Void and the fountain. It didn't work."

A small smile rounds Ty's mouth. "So if you use the Codex Mechanica as intended, what will it do?"

"I don't have to use it as intended."

"That wasn't the question."

Inside my soul, my wolf growls with frustration. *"She's trying to trap you,"* grumbles my wolf. *"Don't answer the question."*

*"I have to answer,"* I reply in my mind.

Leaning back, Ty laces her fingers behind her head. "I'm waiting."

"If I used it as intended, I'd destroy both magic and the Void."

Ty hops up to stand, bracing her arms on the tabletop. "If the Void had to be destroyed, you'd consider wiping out all magic, wouldn't you?"

And with those words, I feel like a mouse who'd been nibbling some cheese and now, found herself with her tail caught in a trap. I stare at Ty, openmouthed. Unlike Elle, I'm not a good reflex liar. Unless I've had time to practice a response, I take way too long to reply.

Finally, I manage to say something. "Is that your second question?"

Ty plunks back down into her seat. "It doesn't need to be. You just answered it anyway." She turns to Knox. "See? She'd kill off all magic."

Knox's forehead lines with confusion. "What? But that would destroy our wolves."

"I've tried to explain this before," I say lamely.

As if on cue, Knox's eyes glaze over. A strange and electric charge fills the air. It's that damned spell from the Void again, wiping out all Knox's memory.

For a moment, Knox keeps staring out into space. After that, the mist vanishes along with the strange charge in the atmosphere. The spell is definitely over. Knox shakes his head. "What were we talking about? I can't remember."

Sadly, I've gotten really good at redirecting Knox after one of these magical memory episodes. When I speak again, I make sure to use a very calming tone.

"We tried to talk about some things," I explain. "But there's this curse from the Void. You never remember." I arc my thumb over the back of his hand. "It must be so frustrating to get halfway through this topic, over and over." I turn to Ty, expecting her to be just as overwhelmed and confused.

She's not.

Instead, Ty sits upright and slaps on her innocent girl face. "Oh, my. He seems to have forgotten all abut the Void."

"But you haven't." Anger starts to heat up my bloodstream. Ty is hiding things again. "That's a little strange, don't you think?"

"Strange?" Ty blinks dramatically. "Why, no, it isn't."

Knox levels Ty with another glare. "I may not know everything that's going on, but I do know this." He points straight at his ex. "You're putting on an act again. Drop it."

Ty slumps back into her chair once more. "Something's screwing up your memory, Knox. Give me a mo'. I'll fix it."

This whole situation is so stunning I can only repeat her words. "Fix it?" For the record, I would have had Alec or Avianna fix everyone's memories a long time ago. Trouble is, witch spells are all about intent. You can't cast to fix something when you don't even remember what that *something* is.

But Ty remembers.

My anger burns into outright fury. This whole thing is some kind of a test or a trap, and Ty keeps pulling us deeper into it.

"Ty." Knox lowers his voice to a growl, and it's one of those growls that makes lesser beings run for the exit. Honestly? If I weren't dating him, I'd take off as well. "What's really going on here?"

"Calm down. I'll show you." Once more, Ty raises her arms with her palms facing toward the ceiling. Fresh rubies are gripped in her fists. The gemstones flare with light while a familiar crackle of energy fills the air. Instantly, crimson-colored raindrops pour from the ceiling, covering the entire dining room in what looks like blood. On reflex, I start to wipe the liquid from my arms. Meanwhile, Knox sits transfixed, just like he did when his memory was being erased by magic.

Ty lowers her hands. "Enough." The magical rain instantly stops falling.

"Wow," I say. "The room looks like a cow exploded in here. I'm not sure how that helps."

"Give it a moment," says Ty.

For a few seconds, Knox rubs his neck in a slow rhythm. Then he turns to me. "That's right. You were talking about the Void. And to get rid of the Void…" He frowns. "Did you say that you're going to destroy all magic, too?" His features slump with shock. "That'll kill our animals."

"It's what the First Wardens built the device to do," I explain. "That said, I don't know that it really has to happen."

Which is a little bit of a lie. The Void and Shadowvin are nasty. The First Wardens look pretty accomplished. If they thought destroying magic was the only way to get rid of those big bads, then I'm about ninety-nine percent sure it has to happen. That said, there are other things to worry about for now.

Like getting my hands on the Codex Mechanica.

"The thing is," I say. "Whatever the ultimate plan is, we definitely need to find the fountain first. The Void is after it, and if he claims the power inside, he'll be able to destroy everything. After we get the fountain secured, we can figure out something."

*Come on, one percent chance.*

Ty claps her hands, grabbing our attention. "Eyes on the prize, people. Let's get to my second question, *officially*." She focuses on me. "Bryar Rose, what do you think magic is doing to Knox?"

I scrub my hands over my face. "There's no way I'm going to answer that."

"Then I won't give you the device."

*Gah. Okay, maybe that is the one way I'll reply.*

I squirm a little in my chair and turn toward Knox. "Here's the thing. I think magic is hurting you, and it's because of me."

"Yeah, I know." Knox glares at Ty. "But that's not the truth. My ex cast a spell to make me sick when I'm around you."

"Please." Ty rolls her eyes. "I didn't even know you were sick until Az called me with the news. He's the one who figured out that magic is punishing you for finding true love instead of the fountain."

"Az said the same thing to me." I shake my head. "He's never been wrong before."

"Well, Az doesn't know Ty the way I do," snarls Knox.

The very core of my soul aches to admit this, but there's no avoiding it. "The reason that you're in pain is because you're with me."

Knox's mouth thins to a determined line. "I don't believe that." His ice-blue gaze locks on me. "No, we're just missing something. The Curse of the Void is over now. I can remember everything you tell me. So let's start at the beginning."

Knox's intensity gives me hope. Closing my eyes, I picture my trip back in time with Scar. "The Shadowvin and the Void were out of control. The First Wardens created a device to destroy both magic and the Void. They failed. This was thousands of years ago. Ever since then, magic has been slowly fading from our world. The Void has been MIA."

"That should be a good thing," says Knox.

"For a while, it was great. But both magic and the Void were only injured. They weren't destroyed. Since that day, they've both slowly gained strength. Now, magic is returning, so the Void has come back as well."

"I still don't believe that the Codex Mechanica can only destroy both magic and the Void," says Knox. "Can't we monkey with this device? Make it focus on just the Void?"

"Not according to what I've learned." I shake my head. "With Scar's help, I traveled back in time and saw the whole thing. The First Wardens wanted to destroy the Void, but there's only one way kill it."

"Destroy all magic," says Ty with a smile.

"Come on." Knox shakes his head. "I was talking to my mate." He focuses on me. "Is that what you've learned, too? We have to kill all magic to get rid of the Void?"

"Yes, unfortunately," I reply. "The First Wardens built the Codex Mechanica to do two things." I raise two fingers. "First, the device finds the fountain. Second, it destroys all the magic inside."

Ty sneers. "And I hope the damned thing works, too. The Codex Mechanica somehow works with the pyramids of Egypt, right? You take the device there and—BAM—no more magic."

My jaw falls open with shock. "Whoa, there. The plan is to just find the fountain with this device. No one is going to Egypt and destroying anything." At least, not if I can't find any other way out of this mess with the Void. I'll never say never at this point… Not that I'm sharing that insight with Ty around.

Ty sniffs. "If you knew magic the way I do, then you'd know the truth. Magic isn't good, it's evil. The First Wardens were right. Magic deserves to go buh-bye."

I can't believe what I'm hearing. "You can't mean that."

"Think about it," continues Ty. "If you want to be with Knox, you have to kill magic before it kills him. If that's not evil, I don't know what is. And suppose you do find a way to destroy magic. You'll be killing Knox's animal in order to be with him. Do you think he'll ever forgive you? Do you think you can ever forgive *yourself* for murdering your own wolf, even if it's for a good reason? Face it. The two of you are doomed."

I open my mouth, ready to come back with a quick retort. Nothing comes to mind. Knox sits beside me, quietly glaring at Ty. This was supposed to be the triumphant moment we got the Codex Mechanica. Instead, it's turning into a relationship meltdown for me and Knox.

"Don't shoot the messenger." Ty holds up her hands with her palms facing us. "I didn't create this situation. I'm just trying to make the best of it. Have you seen what happens to shifters who lose their animals? They become a shell of who they once were—quiet, listless, and staring off into space. When you turn Knox into that, who will take care of him? Not you. You'll be just as useless as he is."

Knox grips the free armrest so hard the wood creaks. "Watch it, Ty."

"I'm trying to be the good guy here." Ty focuses on Knox, and for the first time, there's actual sincerity in her face. "You're going to end up with me. Once your animal is gone, I'm the only one who'll take care of you."

"Thanks," snarls Knox. "You're a real romantic."

Ty's eyes glisten with held-in tears. "All my life, I've only wanted what's best for you."

In this moment, I come to a big realization. Much as I want to, I can't totally hate Knox's ex. We share something in common. We both care about Knox.

"Now, here's my third question." Ty focuses on Knox. "Be honest, now. Wouldn't you be better off with me?"

Knox rises. "Absolutely not. We've been over this."

The sincere version of Ty evaporates into the hard-boiled *witch with a B*. Ty stands up as well, steps over to Knox, and starts poking him in the chest. "Don't you see where this all leads? Where it's always led?" She points in my direction. "This one is going to break your heart and destroy your wolf. I can erase all memories of her right now. You can have a fresh start. You and me. We're supposed to be together."

All that poking and demanding sends anger spinning up my spine. My wolf may still be in an enchanted time-out, but that doesn't mean I don't want to bite Ty anyway.

I rise as well. "So, Knox is supposed to be with you."

"Duh." Ty rolls her eyes "Knox is a Beast. I'm obviously his Beauty."

"Really?" I ask. "Because the last time I checked, Beauty wasn't a sorceress who specialized in water magic."

Knox hitches his thumb in my direction. "My mate makes a good point."

"That is so not true," says Ty. "The story doesn't say she is without magic, only that she doesn't cast any spells."

"Ah, no." I raise my pointer finger. "I'm pretty sure Beauty is non-magical, or she would have water magicked herself out of that castle because, you know, she *really was* trapped. You're something else." I snap my fingers. "The right fairy tale template for you is almost at the tip of my tongue."

"Stop changing the subject," says Ty. "You're totally bad for him." She turns to Knox. "Answer my third question. Do you choose me or not?"

Knox replies without hesitation. "What part of *no* was unclear to you before?"

"Fine," snaps Ty. "When you're ready, I'm here."

Ty reaches into the pocket of her yellow dress and pulls out a handful of rubies. Gripping them tightly, Ty whispers a few words of a spell. Red light streams out from between her fingertips. The electric sense of magic fills the air. A moment later, Ty's body fades until she looks like a ghost made from red mist. The transparent version of Ty glares at Knox for a few long seconds.

After that, Knox's ex disappears.

On the floor where Ty just stood, there now sits a small wooden box with slots in the top. *The Codex Mechanica.* This is definitely the device I saw when I went back in time with Scar. The First Wardens had placed the three discs inside this very box. We actually did it.

The Codex Mechanica is ours at last.

# CHAPTER TWENTY-THREE

My hands tremble as I pick up the Codex Mechanica. Memories from my journey through time with Scar appear in my mind. Back then, the First Wardens had placed three discs onto spindles and set them inside the box. Once you closed the lid, the slits in the box top showed the edges of the discs, which were all covered in glyphs. In turn, the discs spun and stopped, showing different glyphs through the holes in the box's lid.

Basically, the Codex Mechanica is an ancient slot machine on steroids.

I gingerly set the device onto the tabletop. The wooden case is warped and cracked. The colorful paints that once decorated the exterior are now faded beyond recognition. Two bronze clasps still hold the lid in place. I carefully undo the fasteners and open the box's lid. With each passing second, my heart thuds harder against my rib cage.

This moment is really here.

We've found the Codex Mechanica.

Now we'll find the fountain as well.

It doesn't seem real.

Inside the box, I find the discs, each one about the size of my palm. The first one is made from gold, the second is made from a single ruby, and…that's it.

The silver disc is missing.

I carefully lay everything out onto the tabletop. Maybe I missed something. Nope. The silver disc is definitely missing. I stifle a groan. I'd be angry, but this is Ty, after all. I'm amazed she actually handed over anything at all.

Knox has been watching my actions the entire time. "Something wrong?" he asks.

"There should be three discs." I keep counting the items, like the third disc will appear if I just review the numbers enough. A chill creeps up my back.

*Tell me I didn't get this far only to find a busted device.*

Knox brushes his fingers over the pieces. "It's amazing that the thing has lasted thousands of years and is still in such good shape." He picks up the golden disc. "I bet it's like any machine. Assemble it with most of its parts, and it will mostly work."

Now, I know for a fact that Knox can put together a carburetor at a rate to boggle the mind. He basically built his own Harley from scratch. If anyone can figure out how to make this device function, it's my mate. I step back. "Want to give it a try?"

Knox doesn't reply. He just starts putting things together. The expression on his face is the definition of ease and confidence.

I wish I could be so calm, but nothing about finding this fountain has been easy. First, I spent years trying to decipher the papyri. Second, there was no small amount of drama to find the Codex Mechanica. And third, now that the device is in our hands, it might even be busted.

"I got the two discs in place." Knox carefully closes the box's lid and reseals the hook and eye clasps.

"Nice work." The interior is a mess of brass brackets. It would have taken me hours to figure out.

"Thanks." Knox taps the top with his pointer finger. "Now, let's see what you can do."

Immediately, the two working discs spin. After that, they pause. Through the slots in the box top, a pair of glyphs appears. Along with Alec, Knox spent years trying to translate papyri, so it's no problem for my mate to read what the box says.

"Seek the lost disc," reads Knox.

The discs rotate once more before pausing once more again. Knox translates again. "It's in the geyser." He frowns. "Geyser?"

"When I went to the past, there was definitely a geyser. There was no question that it was the fountain." I bob my head. "Well, not to me anyway."

"But Scar didn't agree."

"The geyser was covered in streaks of gold, silver, and red. It had to be the remnants of magic. And the glyph for fountain can also mean geyser."

"It's a tricky symbol," says Knox. "It can also mean form or something, right?"

"True."

"So it might not be the fountain."

"I suppose."

That's what I say, but I still think the geyser is the fountain.

The discs spin once more. "Location," reads Knox. The tiny wheels spin again. More glyphs appear. "Caesar's villa." The discs shift until there are no more glyphs visible through the box top. The device stops moving.

"Guess that's the end of the message," I say.

"Julius Caesar's villa," Knox murmurs. "I visited that place when I was hunting for Denarii."

Now, I know Knox spent years hunting down evil Denarii in general, and Jules in particular. Somehow, it's different knowing that my mate was roaming around Jules' house. My voice lowers to a hush. "What was it like?"

Knox tilts his head. "The villa?"

"Yes." I'm still whispering for some reason. "Was it filled with zombie brains or secret plans to take over the world?"

"Nah," says Knox. "It was just a bunch of old rundown buildings. There was a ruined Roman temple and some modern houses, but those looked abandoned years ago. There were no people or interesting-looking stuff, either. That said, I was looking for Denarii, not fountains. What did you say it would look like again?"

"Based on my trip back in time, the fountain of magic should look like the chopped-off top of a geyser. Are you sure you didn't see anything like that?"

"Unless it was undead, I didn't notice anything in those days."

"Okay." Taking in a deep breath, I resolve to start the next phase of our adventure. "Next stop, Italy."

"Not just yet. We need to chat first."

Maybe it's because we're mates, but I instantly know what Knox is talking about. "About Elle and Alec."

Knox holds up his phone. "I turned it off after the fight at Boucle-Roux. No one's been able to call, thanks to the new spell Alec put on my phone. You know Elle and Alec must be losing their minds now. We can't expect them to hold off searching for us forever. In fact, I'm surprised Alec hasn't already used a tracker spell to starting yelling nastygrams at me through space. It's not like the guy is Mister Patient."

A pouf of red smoke hovers in the air before us. Warlock magic. Within a few seconds, the haze takes the shake of a transparent version of Alec's head. Only, it's about four feet tall. In fact, if the wizard's head from Oz were transparent, red, and a surfer guy? That's what's in the room right now.

"Did someone mention my name?" asks Head-Alec. "I may have sent a spell out to detect if a certain person starts to think about *other* people beside himself."

"Yeah," says Knox. "I did mention you, and surprise, surprise… Your spell worked."

"Good. That means you're done hiding under whatever rock you've crawled under. Now turn on your damn phone, Claw Boy."

I stare at Alec's floating head. This is so strange. I go on tiptoe to whisper in Knox's ear. "Can he hear me?"

"Nah," answers Knox. "Only me. We have an agreement that we don't bug each other when our cell phones are off." Knox says that last part extra loud. "That's bro code and a total douchebag move to cast a spell and track me anyway."

"What?" asks Head-Alec.

"Two words," says Knox. "Bro. Code."

"That it is," replies Floating Head Alec. "Unless you have a douchebag bro and an awesome bro. In such cases, the douchebag bro disappears, which then freaks out the awesome bro. After which point, the code clearly allows the amazing good bro to track the douchebag bro just in case he starts talking about someone other than himself. After that, the awesome bro can send a magical version of their floating head to chat with the douchebag bro."

Knox chuckles. "Oh, I didn't know about that part of the code."

"Well." Alec gives another from his collection of eye rolls. "Now you know."

"Give me a sec with Bry," says Knox. Turning away from Head-Alec, Knox focuses his attention on me. "What's wrong? I can smell the worry."

Head-Alec's eyes get large. "What's up with Bry? Should I transport over?"

"I asked for a minute," says Knox. "And some privacy."

"Fine. Sixty seconds." After closing his eyes, Head-Alec covers his ears with his palms.

"Guess he's not really going anywhere," I say.

"Don't mind him." Knox rubs his palms up and down my arms. "What's wrong?"

"Look," I begin. "I still feel the same way I did back at Boucle-Roux. There's no reason to get Alec in on this. Elle, either. It's too dangerous."

Knox tilts his head. "You really think we can keep them out?"

"Time's up." Head-Alec lowers his hands, opens his eyes, and pretends to look around the room. "What shall I do when I'm being ignored and using up incredible amounts of magic to try to communicate?" He makes an exaggerated *a-ha* face. "I've got it. How about I count down until you decide to acknowledge me? Nah nah nah nah, nah nah nah…"

Yes, Floating Head Alec is now singing the Jeopardy theme song. My life is beyond bizarre.

"Nah nah nah nah NAH nanananana. Nah nah nah nah, nah nah nah. NAH nah nah nah. Nah. Nah. Nah. Boom, boom. I can do this all day, and I know you find it totally annoying." He clears his throat. "Second verse, same as the first. Nah nah nah nah…"

While Alec keeps singing, Knox pulls his phone out from his jacket pocket. The device is glowing red with magic. Holding it between his thumb and forefinger, my mate jiggles his cell from side to side. The question is there but unspoken: *Should I turn it on?*

"Do it," I sigh. When Alec sets his mind on something, there really is no way to stop him. Plus, he has a terrible singing voice.

Knox turns on his phone, and the floating Alec head disappears. Within seconds, the cell blares out "Darth Vader's March," which is Alec's special ringtone. Knox takes the call. "Hey."

Through the tinny speaker, Alec complains in rapid-fire style. Knox's best friend talks so quickly, it's hard to make out what he says, but I do catch a few choice words, like *dickhead* and *stubborn*.

Knox raises his voice. "You want to come here?"

This time, I can hear Alec's voice clearly. "What do *you* think, Fur Bunny?"

"Then stop your bellyaching and transport over already. We both know you have enough of my personal crap so you can find me anytime."

Alec's tinny voice sounds again. "I was trying to be sensitive. We have a deal about this stuff. And you went out of town to find Bry. I knew you'd track her down. There was no way I'd just transport over and interrupt. You and Bry could have been having a moment."

"You guessed it, genius," says Knox. "We were having a BIG moment. And with that little song of yours, you just interrupted us."

"Like romaaaaantic?" Head-Alec makes kissy faces.

Knox shakes his head. "Oh, grow up."

My face blazes red. *Earth, please open up because I need somewhere to hide.*

When I speak again, my voice comes out as a chirp. "There was no moment." I know Knox is just busting on Alec, but it still feels important to clarify the moment-thing. It's not like we were getting naked in Knox's fancy dining room.

In his castle.

Which his ex-girlfriend just decorated in red slime that looks a lot like blood.

Did I mention my life is weird?

Knox hangs up. "Alec will be here any second." He eyes me carefully. "I scent concern. What worries you? Is it how I told Alec we were having a moment? I forget you weren't raised with shifters. We're really open about stuff like that."

Once again, my mouth starts moving on its own. "No, I'm totally fine. I get that you and Knox just bust on each other. And if you wanted to, you can tell our friends how we kiss and stuff. So totally good. I don't care. Not me. At all."

*Wow. Terrible speech, Bry.*

I clear my throat. "You know what? It might be time to change the subject."

Knox's blue eyes glisten with mischief. "If you say so, but you're really cute when you're embarrassed."

"Okay. So. Well. Since Alec is on his way, I'll just revive my inner wolf now."

Knox's brows lift. "You've had her in stasis all this time?"

"What can I say? My wolf really wanted to bite your ex's face off. Or her ankle, finger, or toe."

Knox cracks out another one of his thinking-faces. In this one, he acts like he's contemplating something super-serious, but he's mostly kidding. "Sounds like you made the right choice."

"Thank you." I wink. "I'll just wake her up now."

Closing my eyes, I concentrate on picturing the strands of golden power that interlace through my soul. Sure enough, I picture them as they weave and dance in space. I send them a command.

*Awaken my wolf.*

Inside my heart, my inner animal stirs. After smacking her lips, my wolf does one of those animal yawns that make you wonder how anyone's tongue could possibly be that long.

*"You put me to sleep,"* she grumbles.

*"You were in stasis,"* I say in my mind. *"There's a difference. And then, I only did it because you were losing your cool and wouldn't listen to reason. Ty just gave us the Codex Mechanica, by the way. That couldn't have happened if you'd attacked her."*

My wolf lifts her chin. *"She doesn't need a face to hand over some box."* After that, my inner animal plunks her head back onto her forepaws and pretends to be asleep. I've seen this move before. This is my wolf's version of the silent treatment. I decide to give her some space.

All of a sudden, a whirl of red smoke appears on the floor nearby. The twisting mist winds and lengthens until it's about as tall as Knox. An electric sense of magic fills the air. That crimson mist is most definitely a transport spell. No question who's casting, either.

Alec.

The mists disappear with a flash of red light. Where the haze once appeared, there now stand both Alec and Elle. The pair of them are dressed in jeans and T-shirts. Of course, Alec is also wearing his ever-present sport coat (Alec believes that real wizards don't tote around enchanted gems in man bags). Elle looks like she always does: tall and slim with long blonde hair and wide blue eyes. I'm so happy to see her, I could do a cartwheel or something equally embarrassing. Instead, I race over and give her a big hug.

"I missed you," I say.

She pats my back. "Of course, you did. I'm awesome." We step apart. "So, are you done being noble and ready to accept my help?"

I can't help but smile. "Yes, I am."

Meanwhile, Alec scans Knox from head to toe. "You look like hell," he announces.

Knox quirks his right brow. "Stuff it."

When I first started hanging out with Knox and Alec, I'd worry how they'd greet each other with insults. Now, I know it's a Knox-Alec thing. Those two have been friends since they were kids.

"Fine, I take it back," says Alec. "You looked like hell back in New York. Now you look like whatever is *below* hell. Maybe some kind of deep sub-hellacious space, like a basement type-area where Satan stores his old records and stuff."

Knox shoots Alec a rude hand gesture.

"I'd be angry about your crude and immature display," says Alec. "But like I said, you look near death, so I can't be upset with you." Alec constantly looks like he's posing for a menswear catalog. Right now, he's taken on a pose where he sets his pointer finger on his chin. After a moment, Alec snaps his fingers. "Oh wait, I take it back. I should totally be pissed because HOW COULD YOU TURN YOUR PHONE OFF?"

Knox shrugs. "Because you put that silencer spell on it. That way, I can shut it off and no one bugs me."

Alec rolls his eyes. This guy has a collection of eye rolls, by the way. The one he's using now is his sarcastic half-roll maneuver. "I only did that because your crazy ex-girlfriend kept calling you. You weren't supposed to use that spell on me. Elle and I have been wor—" Alec stops midsentence. For the first time, he scans the room. "Whoa, we're in your castle in Aix en Provence."

Inside my soul, my wolf perks right up. All her anger about going into stasis vanishes under this news about Knox. *"Our mate has castles! Yay! So many dens for our cubs."*

I decide to ignore the *cubs* comment. *"Don't get too excited,"* I reply in my head. *"We don't know what Alec meant."*

Turning to my outside voice, I address Alec directly. "Wait a second. Do you mean to say that Knox has more than one castle?"

"Sure," says Alec. "He's got dozens."

"It's not dozens." Knox looks to the ceiling, his mouth making silent calculations. "Only eight."

Within my heart, my wolf prances about with her tail held high. *"Dens for cubs! Dens for cubs!"* I keep right on ignoring her.

"My bad," says Alec, this time with a three-sixty eye roll. "You only have eight castles."

"I don't have anything," counters Knox. "Az had a ton of castles, and he left them all to me."

Elle shoots me a look. "Interesting distinction."

"I know," I say. "That's what *I* was thinking, too."

*Fact:* this is why life's so much better with Elle around. Estrogen-laden mind reading.

Alec moves into another one of his catalog poses. This time, he leans back on his left leg while shoving his hands into the front pockets of his jeans. "So let me get this straight. You brought your new mate here to meet your old ex?"

"Long story," growls Knox.

Alec turns to me. "Is that why there's blood everywhere?" His smile widens. "Tell me you killed her." Alec bobs his brows. "I simply can't stand Ty."

"All this red isn't blood," I say quickly. "It's left over from a crimson rain spell that Ty cast." After that, I have a slow moment to think through what Alec said. "Although, what kind of friendship do you and Knox have where transporting into a bloody room doesn't surprise you?"

Alec shrugs. "I know how your mate likes to kill stuff. And I like to transport him out of danger before that stuff kills him back. Speaking of which…" Alec turns to Knox. "Did you maybe…" Alec mimes a stabbing motion. "Tell me that you at least got Ty a little bit."

My inner animal takes his words as total validation. *"See?"* she says in my heart. *"I could definitely have gotten a toe."*

"Ty isn't dead," says Knox. "She just evaporated away for a while."

Alec mock-frowns. "How disappointing."

Elle points at a streak of crimson on the oak wall. "So what is that red stuff, anyway?"

"It's the residue of a memory spell," I explain. "Ty cast it to help Knox recall information about the Void. Otherwise, there's this curse that wipes everything out like that." I snap my fingers.

"The Vo—" Alec pauses midsentence. *Here we go again.* A long moment passes while Alec looks around the room, confused. At last, he speaks once more. "What were we talking about again?"

Knox hands him a glass of red-tinted water. "Drink this, and we'll tell you everything."

I do the same for Elle. "You, too."

Elle and Alec both take in big swigs of water. A red haze appears around their skin while that familiar something-something fills the air. The spell ends. The crimson mist disappears. With that, our friends now have tons of questions about the Void.

It takes a few minutes, but Knox and I explain all about the Codex Mechanica and the Void. Elle seems excited to learn that magic could be wiped away. Not that I blame her. It was Elle's magic that made her a target to her stepfamily. For his part, Alec doesn't seem too upset about losing his abilities as a wizard. In fact, Alec only appears worried about Knox.

"So what does that mean for my furry friend here?" asks Alec. "Will Knox lose his animal?"

Inside my soul, my wolf whimpers. Whenever this topic comes up, my animal never worries about herself, strangely enough. All she cares about is that she doesn't want anything to happen to Knox. Wolf mate bonds are intense.

For the record, I'm slowly coming to terms with the fact that magic and the Void need to be destroyed. It sucks, but it's less awful than the universe being devoured by a crazy ghost man. Even so, it's too early for us to get wrapped around that particular axle.

"Look," I say. "It's true that the First Wardens tried to use the Codex Mechanica for a two-step process." Putting it in official terms seems to make this easier to discuss, somehow. "Step one, the device finds the fountain and step two…" My voice wobbles as I say this next part. "The Codex Mechanica destroys all magic."

Alec shakes his head in a movement that means *say what?* "As in inner shifter animals and everything?"

Knox nods.

Alec folds his arms over his chest. "I really don't like this."

I hold my hands palms up in the universal motion for *don't worry*. "The destruction part was a big fail." I bob my head, thinking. "Actually it was more like a medium fail."

"Not helping," huffs Alec.

"All I'm saying is that right now, we only want to focus on step one, finding the fountain. The part about killing magic is a distant step two."

"So, says Elle. "Step one is to just find the fountain and protect it from the Void."

"Exactly," I point at her. "If the Void gets the fountain's power, he'll devour the world."

Elle taps her lips with her pointer finger. "And the Codex Mechanica says that the fountain's hidden in Julius Caesar's villa."

"Technically," says Knox. "It said to find the third disc in the geyser."

Alec folds his arms over his chest, lifts his right hand, and touches his cheek with his pointer finger. It's another in his collection of menswear catalog poses. "You don't believe these wardens, do you?"

"I don't trust anyone but you and Bry," says Knox. My mate turns to Elle. "I don't know what to make about you yet."

Elle shrugs. "I'm a con artist. Good call."

Alec taps his pointer finger against his cheek. "And your lack of trust for these past wardens… Does it have anything to do with the fact that magic is making you sick for being around Bry?"

The veins pop out in Knox's neck. "Magic isn't making me sick for being near Bry. There is another explanation and she just left a few minutes ago."

I know what he means. *Ty.*

My heart sinks. Don't get me wrong, I wish this were all Ty's doing, but I just don't buy that yet.

Inside my soul, my wolf whimpers. *"If we're making Knox sick, then we have to destroy magic. He's our mate."*

*"Let's just find the fountain first, okay?"*

*"If I have to die so Knox can live, then you have to take my life."*

My eyes widen. Elle and Knox both catch the movement. Knox is the first to speak. "What's wrong, Bry?"

"It's my wolf," I explain. "She's not happy about this."

Elle steps closer, her face all smiles. "How about we all get back to finding the fountain?" She focuses on Knox. "The Codex Mechanica said it was at Caesar's villa?"

"Yeah," grumbles Knox.

"So." Elle scoops some kind of puff pastry from the tabletop. "Looks like we're off to Italy, then." She eyes the now-pink treat.

Focusing on food is a lot easier than dealing with destroying all magic and our inner animals to boot. For a long moment, I stare at the once-white pastry. It's now dotted with red from Ty's spell.

"Are you sure you want to eat that?" I ask. "It's probably all soggy from the rain."

Elle looks at me like I'm crazy. "It's *pastry*, Bry." My best friend loves food. After that, Elle pops the thing in her mouth anyway because, hey, she's Elle. "It's goooood." After that, she talks to Alec through her mouthful of pastry. "So when are you transporting us?" She ends her question with a grin and a wink.

Some pink colors Alec's cheeks. "I could start right now, I guess." For the record, Elle's the only one who transforms Alec from Mister Smooth to a red-faced babbler. It's really sweet.

"Wait, before you cast that spell, can you...?" Knox gestures around his head, which is still matted down with red stuff.

Alec cracks out another classic from his collection of eye rolls. In this one, Alec shakes his head while staring at the ceiling. "I suppose."

"Thanks, man." Knox gestures around the room. "Oh, and one more thing. Can you clean up this place, too? That way, Louis isn't scrubbing walls for days."

Through the door, I hear a familiar French voice. "Merci, my master. *Sir.*"

Knox cups his hand by his mouth. "No worries, Louis. And remember, call me if Ty gets to be too much. She promised to go away forever, so she'll be back in two weeks or so."

"I promise," says Louis.

"And stop listening at doors," adds Knox.

"I only do it to keep ze Master safe. But zen, I will leave as requested."

After that, an exaggerated set of footsteps sound from the outer hall. Clearly, Louis is trying to make it obvious that he's walking away. That said, I know Knox well enough to realize that he must trust Louis a lot. Otherwise, Knox would have had Alec cast some ward and silencer spells around the dining room so all our conversations would have been private.

Alec's gaze flickers between Knox and the red mess that is the dining room. "Wait just a minute here." Alec wags his finger at Knox. "Did you finally turn on your cell because I sang the Jeopardy song...or was it because you hate being sticky and you didn't have time to clean up?"

If Alec has an eye-roll collection, then Knox has one for thinking-faces. This time, Knox bobs his head while puffing out his lower lip. "Could be the sticky thing."

Alec gasps. "You're such an ass. I am doing zero for you. Do you hear me? No spells. No cleaning. No transport. You can haul your own ass to Italy."

"I get that you're pissed at me," says Knox. "But what about Bry and poor Louis here?"

I give Alec my best puppy dog impression. "Please?" Sure, I'm begging, but I'm also in a big hurry. Plus, there's no way I want to go back into that Fiat. Talk about uncomfortable.

Elle points to her shirt. "Hey, I dribbled some red goop on my shirt, too, so...help?"

It's the *help* that does it. The moment Elle asks anything, Alec gets all gooey-eyed. We're totally getting all the spells.

"Fine," says Alec. "I'll cast some cleaning and transporter spells. But that's it." He pulls some gemstones from his pocket. "Now get ready to witness my awesomeness."

As Alec fiddles with his gemstones, I remember something Az once told me.

*We all have our family of chance and our family of choice.*

All my life, I've had no idea who my real parents were. But in this moment, I know with certainty that my true family consists of Elle, Alec, and Knox. Just having them here makes a terrible situation almost fun.

A fine choice, indeed.

# CHAPTER TWENTY-FOUR

A few minutes later, Alec finishes his transport spell. Knox, Alec, Elle, and I all stand at the end of a winding dirt road. A bright yellow sun burns down from an impossibly blue sky. Around us, a landscape of rolling hills is sliced into neat rows of grapevines. The scent of earth and green leaves fills the air. I scan the area. No one else is around. I clutch the Codex Mechanica under my right arm. No way am I letting this thing out of my sight.

Before us, the road ends with a low hilltop that's crowned by a small cluster of dingy buildings. At one time, I'd imagine these structures were all gleaming white walls and neat peaked roofs of red ceramic tile. Now, the place is rundown, gray, and moldy. Large holes gape in the tile rooftops. Gnats buzz about the scene. Other than the insects, the place sure looks deserted.

"Is this the place?" I ask Knox. After all, Knox came here before to hunt Denarii. If anyone would know if we'd reached Julius Caesar's old villa, it would be my mate.

My inner wolf stands at attention. *"I hope we see our mate kill something,"* she coos.

*"I've seen it."* I shudder, remembering how Knox had to take down Madame Grimoire, my old therapy group leader who was actually a Denarii zombie-mummy. Head removal was involved. *"It's not as pleasant as you might think."*

Knox scans the landscape carefully. "Nothing's changed since the last time I came by. Still looks abandoned." He gestures toward the villas. "This is all one compound for Jules. He had servants and visitors. There were no locals or anything. But like I said, all that was long over by the time I got here."

"It's pretty modern," I say. "Somehow I expected more Ancient Rome."

Instead of pointing, Knox chin-nods toward a particular spot on the horizon. "There's a building on the back of the property that is a classic Roman ruin. You know, a small round temple with smashed-in walls and busted columns."

Not sure what I expected from Caesar's personal estate. Maybe a big statue of Brutus with the words *original backstabber* written on it in Latin? A bunch of rundown modern villas wasn't exactly what I'd had in mind.

Still, if it's where the fountain of magic is hidden, it'll always be a gorgeous spot in my book.

Alec mock-bows and offers Elle his arm. "Shall we?"

I take a half step forward and pause. Something nags at the back of my brain. My inner wolf perks up again. All her fur stands on end.

*"I don't like this,"* she growls.

*"Yes,"* I say slowly. A chill of unease creeps up my spine.

Knox steps up beside me. "What's wrong?"

"My human intuition is telling me to wait. So is my wolf."

Alec slings his sport coat over his shoulder, male model style. "Intuition? What? We're here. There's some old ruin nearby and some new-ish McVillas right in front of us. The fountain of all magic is here somewhere. We have to look for it."

Knox hitches his thumbs into the back pockets of his leathers. It's another one of his thinking poses. He keeps his attention riveted on me. "What's got you worried?"

I sort through everything that's happened. The Void. The papyri. Boucle-Roux. At last, the wrong piece stands out in the puzzle of my thoughts. "It's Ty. She's holding out something and we don't know what it is."

"Let me guess." Alec sighs dramatically. "You want me to cast more spells so you can see her?"

Knox gives him the side-eye. "Like it would be that hard. All you need is a piece of her clothing, and you could track her down easy."

Alec wags his finger at Knox. "And do you have something of hers handy?"

Knox rolls his eyes. "Like I keep Ty's crap around. It's all back at the castle."

"And that's exactly what I was saying," groans Alec. "I am not transporting any of your big asses around again."

Knox chuckles. "Come on, you big baby."

Alec narrows his eyes. "It's Sir Big Baby to you."

"Seriously," says Knox. "Don't dismiss the idea just because it means another spell. We've got questions here."

"Think about it," I say. "We need to question Ty. Everything that's happened is one sketchy thing after another. I came to Europe to get the Codex Mechanica, and only because Ty found me online. But one I got here, she actually sent me to Boucle-Roux to get my butt kicked."

Knox steps forward. "After that, I'm lured along in a step two of her plan when Ty calls me to say that Bry's about to be attacked. My ex knows I won't stay away from my mate. This whole thing reeks of a setup."

Elle raises her hand. "Speaking as someone who sets up people all the time, I have to agree with Knox."

"Not seeing the master plan here." Alec folds his arms over his chest. "Ty wanted to prove she could scare your girlfriend while luring you to the castle to pay attention to her. No big deal." He hitches his thumb toward the villas. "Let's find ourselves one fountain of magic."

"There's more." I start counting off the items on my fingers. "First, Ty had the Codex Mechanica. I get that she collects ancient stuff, but what are the odds of finding that thing? Second, Ty knew I wanted that particular device. Very sketchy. Third, Ty knew exactly who the Void is. That memory curse that affected all of us? It did zero to her. And there's only one other person I know who was immune to that curse. Az. He got that way because he had a run-in with the Shadowvin."

"Hmmm." Alec kicks at the dirt road. "Those are the shadow monsters who sucked out your powers, right?"

"Yup." I gesture toward the nearest stucco condo. "And now, Ty wants me to go in there. This is like Boucle-Roux all over again. I don't trust her. And I totally think she knows more than she's telling us. We need to find her and make her share what's really going on."

Alex pauses and thinks for a moment. Then he tosses up his hands while shooting an angry look at Knox. "I hate it when you're right."

Knox shrugs. "Bry's the one who's right. I just get to tell you about it."

"Fine, fine." Alec lets out a long puff of breath. "I'll track Ty down. I just need something of hers for a locator spell."

"You could go back to castle and grab something."

"No." Alec's eyes narrow as he scans the horizon. "This place is definitely bad news. I don't want to leave you here alone. I'll transport all of us back to the castle. Once we're there, I can cast a locator spell there and force Ty to return." Alec reaches into his pocket and pulls out a handful of rubies.

He's about to cast a spell.

My breath catches with anxiety. I can only hope Alec's casting will work, considering how the equinox is messing up magic and everything.

White mist rolls in over the countryside, snapping me out of my thoughts. Dark clouds descend over the sky. A pair of long shadows creeps along the dirt road, reminding me of a shifting pool of black paint. The breeze dies down. My pulse skyrockets. Even the insects stop their buzzing. This is such bad news.

*The Shadowvin are coming.*

Knox pulls me against his side. "Do you see that?" he asks.

I nod. "We need to get out of here."

Alec lifts a fistful of rubies. "Exactly what we're about to do."

As Alec murmurs spell, the stones gleam, sending beams of light through his clenched fingers. A moment later, a small red cloud appears in the air by his fist. The haze flares with crimson light before congealing into a physical shape.

A rabbit.

I blink hard, trying to clear my head.

A rabbit?

No matter how much I blink, the bunny doesn't vanish. Alec is actually holding a red rabbit by the scruff of its neck. The critter is all twitchy and wide-eyed with fear.

I point at the bunny. "Let me guess. Your magic is still wonky."

"Yeah, it's been getting worse as the equinox gets closer." Alec releases the rabbit, which then scampers off into the mist.

Elle smacks her lips. "A bunny?"

Alec shrugs. "I first learned magic by doing human tricks—you know, *pulling a rabbit out of the hat* type of stuff. Only in my case, I tried to make it real. Sometimes when my powers go off the rails, they go back to the beginning, if that makes sense."

"Don't worry," says Knox. My mate moves in slow circles, scanning the mist with every step. He's moved into Knox the Denarii Killer mode. "Your powers will come back online in a few minutes. They always have before. Then we're out of here."

Alec stares down at the gems cupped on his palm. Now that he's finished casting the rabbit, the magic in this particular set of rubies is all used up. Alec repockets the now-darkened stones.

I grip the Codex Mechanica more tightly against my chest. "Maybe this isn't so bad."

"Are you going to give a pep talk?" asks Knox. There's no mistaking the smile in his voice.

"You know it." I force myself to grin. "Sure, there's some mysterious white mist here, and that isn't a good sign." I nod toward the sky. "And the way that everything turned dark? That's another red flag."

Elle shakes her head. "When do you bring on the pep?"

"I'm getting there. All I'm saying is that a bunch of mist isn't necessarily a bad thing. And we can't get out of here right now anyway."

"I'll cast again in a little bit," huffs Alec.

"Absolutely," I say. "But until then, we should hang out."

"No, we should check things out," counters Alec.

"That's a last resort," snarls Knox.

"Running off into the mist?" I ask. "That's what all the soon to be dead dum-dums do in every horror movie ever." I turn to Elle. "Am I right?"

"Truth," she says.

"Now, get ready for the pep. We're stuck here. So what... We can't handle a little funky weather? We're way tougher than that. Let's just hang out. No one goes running off into the mist. No one casts a spell for two whole minutes. We'll just be together until the mist burns off or whatever."

Elle nods. "That was a good pep talk. I like how you slipped a plan in there as well."

"You're welcome." At this point, I'm feeling really solid about my speech when it happens.

An electric charge fills the air.

The temperature drops, turning my skin into gooseflesh.

Every hair on the back of my neck stands on end.

*Not good.*

"Something else is here," whispers Alec.

"Or some*one*," adds Elle.

Little by little, two humanoid shadows rise up from the misty ground. I'd know that pair anywhere. Slythe and Tithe. Their eyes flare with white light.

My mouth starts moving on its own. "Or this could be a total catastrophe where we're stuck in the middle of misty nowhere with no spell casting ability or safe place to run."

"No need to panic," says Knox.

"Are those the Shadowvin?" asks Elle.

"That they are," I say.

Alec steps in front of Elle, placing himself between her and the figures. "What do they want?"

Another form rises up from the mist. This one is eight feet tall and glows with white light. His eyes are fathomless holes of darkness. The Void. Tilting back his head, he roars to the clouds. "Take me to the fountain!"

Slythe and Tithe float closer. If that wasn't creepy enough, they begin talking in unison. "Accept the inevitable. The Void will devour the world. No one will have the strength to destroy the fountain. Give us the device, Bryar Rose."

I grip the Codex Mechanica so hard against my chest, the wood starts to creak. "I'll never help you."

"But you will and soon," they say together. Moving in unison once more, the Shadowvin face a single target.

*Knox.*

Adrenaline pumps through my system. I know what these two ghostly scumbags are planning. Once before, the Shadowvin threatened Knox and Elle, showing me how they could possess someone's body.

Not happening.

On reflex, I stand between Knox and the Shadowvin. "If you want to get to my mate, you have to go through me first."

My inner wolf roars to life. *"Through us both,"* she growls.

*"You got it."*

For a long moment, the Shadowvin pause. No one else moves, either. In fact, I'm not sure anyone even breathes. As time ticks by, hope sparks in my chest. Maybe the Shadowvin are done being supernatural creeps. They could just mist their way out of here and take the Void with them. Weirder things have happened.

Fast as lightning, the Shadowvin slide right past me and into Knox's body.

Or not.

Panic zooms through my limbs. "NO!"

Just like they showed me in my dreams, the Shadowvin start to possess Knox. My mind races with fear. When it comes to possession, the more spirits you have inside you, the harder it is to fight back. And fighting possession? That hurts like hell. Most people don't even bother to try, and that's when they only have one spirit inside them. My heart sinks.

Knox has two.

Even so, my mate fights back. Hard.

Crumpling onto his knees, Knox screams with pain. His veins run black. My inner wolf starts to lose her mind. Her eyes turn wild as she paces a frantic line.

*"We have to help him,"* she moans inside my soul.

*"I don't know what to do,"* I reply.

I kneel before Knox. "How can I help?"

When Knox looks up at me, his eyes swirl with black. "Run." His voice sounds like a hundred ancient men and women, all speaking at once.

"No," I say solemnly. "You know I won't do that."

Elle and Alec rush to stand beside us. Both of them look wide-eyed with worry.

"There's been enough time," says Alec. "I can cast a dispossession." After reaching into the pocket of his sport coat, Alec pulls out a handful of fresh rubies. Gripping the gems in his fist, Alec raises his arm high. Crimson light shines through his fingers. "With my magic, I call on thee, Shadowvin! Leave this place!" A small cloud of red mist hovers in the air before Knox. With a flash of crimson light, the haze hardens into a pair of red doves.

Doves. My stomach falls. Another magician's trick. For their part, the birds coo and fly away.

Alec's shoulders slump. "I'm so sorry. Just give me another minute. I'll try again."

"No," says Knox through gritted teeth. "Run… They want me… to hurt you."

"I know you won't hurt me," I say.

The Void's deep voice booms across the countryside. "Bring me the fountain." He floats closer. "Fountain!"

*Crud. This is not going well.*

I focus on Alec and Elle. "You guys should run."

Elle kneels at my side. "We aren't going anywhere."

211

Knox grips my hands. "Remember when…I used shifter power…your wolf…"

Images appear in my mind. When I was first learning how to control my wolf, Knox used his alpha power to help me focus. Whatever Knox is doing, he's barely keeping control. Maybe some shifter magic will help. "I understand."

Reaching forward, I rest my hands on Knox's shoulders. Within my heart, I pull on the threads of golden shifter power inside me. In my mind's eye, I picture them winding down my arms and into Knox's soul. His skin shimmers with a golden hue.

"It's working," says Elle.

"Try the spell again now," I tell Alec.

Alec jams his hand into his pocket once more, pulls out more stones. Again, he raises the gems high. The magical rocks shine so brightly in his hand, they're like a second sun. "Shadowvin, you must go!"

Waves of red light shimmer around Knox, reflecting off the golden hue of his skin. A pack of red playing cards bursts out of his chest, flying through the air in a long arc. I suck in a shaky breath. It's another magician trick gone wrong. Only, the cards keep flying out, and with them, I see misty forms separate from Knox as well.

"It's working!" I cry.

My mate lets out the mother of all roars and falls backward. The Shadowvin tumble out of his body. They both round on Elle.

"How about you?" they ask in unison. "Perhaps you'll be easier to control."

Elle and I share a shocked look. There's no need to review our options again. Alec's magic is still on the fritz, and when transport spells go wrong, you end up dead. Turning to the guys, we yell out the same word: "Run!"

Knox slings his right arm over Alec's shoulder. My mate braces his left arm on me. Together, the three of us race toward the villa at the top of the road. Elle keeps pace at our side, checking back every few yards. "They're following us," she reports.

"Make for the first villa," says Knox. "Last time I was here, all the houses had serious protection wards against spirits. Jules was nuts about that stuff."

Which makes sense. Jules killed a ton of people, both as a mortal and then later, when he became a zombie-mummy. If angry ghosts were going to attack someone, Jules would be target number one.

"Once we get there," adds Knox, "we'll be fine, but the Shadowvin shouldn't get through."

Alec and I push ourselves harder. Sweat lines my forehead and drips down my back. Elle runs on a few yards ahead, scoping out the ground for us as we go. Every so often, she yells out stuff like, *Watch out for a rock on your right.* Normally, our shifter senses keep us from tripping over anything, but when you're co-dragging along a very large Knox? Every bit of advice helps.

With all of us working together, it's a short run to the first villa, but it feels like a marathon, especially since I'm helping carry Knox. Plus, it's hard to see the ground under all this mist, not to mention our pursuers. I don't see the Shadowvin, but I'm not stopping to scan for them, either.

Finally, we reach the front door. The thing is half off its hinges, but that won't affect the warding spells that Jules put in place. Those castings will work whether the doors are open or closed.

Elle rushes in first. "It's clear!" she calls.

Alec and I haul Knox inside. Once we cross the threshold, my mate collapses onto the floor, panting. The motion sends puffs of white dust rolling away from him in every direction.

"Well," says Knox flatly. "That hurt like fuck." He looks to Elle, who's taken to standing vigil in the doorway. "Any news?"

"You were right about the wards," says Elle. "The Shadowvin have stopped about twenty yards away. They're pounding on some invisible barrier." She exhales. "And they aren't breaking through. Looks like Jules put on some decent spells on this place."

I kneel beside Knox. "Do you need some healing magic?"

"Nah." Knox shakes his head. "Let Alec save his stones for when we really need them." My mate does look a lot better. His veins are no longer black, and the swirling shadows are gone from his eyes. "You still got the Codex Mechanica?"

I hold it up from where I'd kept it jammed under my arm. "Still here."

"Good."

Elle turns around and smiles. "They've gone."

Little by little, the clouds roll away. The mist completely disappears from the countryside. Beams of sunlight shine through the broken door and cracked windows.

Knox glares at the doorway. "I don't like this. It's—"

"Another setup," finishes Elle.

Alec shakes some of the bits of plaster off his head. "Did you see how fast the Shadowvin can move when they want to? They flew into Knox. But when it came to chasing us, they always stayed a few yards behind. That wasn't a hunt. The Shadowvin were herding us onto the property. At this point, all we need are cow costumes, and the look would be complete."

A half-smile curls on Knox's mouth. "I don't know, Alec. You've got a little paunch going already. You might already be rocking the cow look."

"Remind me," says Alec. "Why do I transport my ass all over the world to save yours?"

Knox shrugs. "I've got a nice ass."

I shake my head and smile. "Do you guys ever take anything seriously?"

Alec winks. "Not if we can help it."

"We should check out the property," I say. "Look for the fountain systematically."

Elle winces. "Do you think the Shadowvin will come back?"

"I don't know," I reply. "But Alec is right. They herded us here for a reason."

Alec pulls more gemstones from his pocket. "Give me an hour. After that, maybe we can try to transport away again."

Knox and I exchange a long and determined look. We don't exchange a word, but I know we're on the same page here. Rising, I address the room. "Here's the thing. For thousands of years, people like us have searched for the fountain of magic. Now, the fountain is right here. Maybe we were herded to this spot, but I'm not going to sit around. It's time to stop running from the Shadowvin. Once we find the fountain, then we'll have the power in this situation." I scan Elle and Alec's faces. "What do you guys think?"

Elle lifts her chin. "Bry is right. I say we go for the fountain."

Alec mock-sighs. "I still wish cable were an option, but I'm in, too."

I look to Knox. "You know this place best. What's the fastest way to check everything out?"

Knox stands up and wipes some dust off his jeans. "There are four villas in this area." He rubs his neck. "They're all warded, but you never know how those spells have held up over time."

"Meaning?" asks Alec.

"We shouldn't split up. Let's all start by looking around this villa. If memory serves, it's got about a dozen rooms." He turns to me. "Any place in particular where you want to start?"

I shift my weight from foot to foot. All of a sudden, there's no question which place I want to check out. "The bathroom?"

"Sure." He hitches his thumb over his shoulder. "Down the hall on the right."

Elle and Alec tear open a half-collapsed wooden chest. Alec lifts up a sheet of paper. "Check this out," calls Alec. "Your parents disappeared in the Yukon, didn't they?"

Knox pauses. "Yeah. Why?"

"There are some old plans in here from Jules. Yukon is all over them. What are the chances?"

"I'll take a look." Knox turns to me. "You good, yeah?"

"I've been going the bathroom for a long time, Knox. I'll be fine."

Knox rushes over to kneel beside Elle and Alec. Together, the three of them begin poring over piles of documents. I find the nastiest bathroom in the history of ever, but at least the toilet has some greenish water in it. I do my business, glad that at least there's a little toilet paper left for some reason.

I'm heading down the hallway to the main room when I hear it.

A little girl's laughter.

I stop by a rickety door that swings open on its single hinge. Outside there stands a little girl covered in a pale gray cloak.

Child-Me. And I'm awake.

"I found you!" she cries. "Now follow me to the temple."

With that, Child-Me takes off for the tree line. The forest flexes, like it's inhaling in time with my own breathing.

But is this a dream…or am I awake?

The girl disappears into the forest, and suddenly, I know one thing for certain. This time, I simply can't let her get away.

I take off after her at a run.

# CHAPTER TWENTY-FIVE

It's a short run through the forest. Every time I get within a few yards of Child-Me, she rushes off ahead, always out of reach. Within seconds, she rushes out from a cluster of trees and into a clearing. I follow and pause, my breath coming in rough gasps. I've got shifter strength and stamina, but after today, I'm wondering if I need to get back into Pilates.

Before me, there stands a small temple nestled the clearing's center. It's a round structure, about twenty feet high and just as wide. All the columns are cracked. At one time, the temple's roof must have been a white dome. It's smashed in now, like an egg that got hit with a spoon. Low scrub grass surrounds the ruin on all sides. A few spindly olive trees stand around it, reminding me of lonely sentinels.

More laughter sounds. This time, it's definitely coming from inside the temple.

Child-Me. She's here.

With slow steps, I march down the hill and into the temple itself. The moment I move inside, I notice the smooth stone walls appear to be breathing. It's just like when I saw the forest. This typically happens before I have a night vision.

Am I dreaming while I'm awake now?

No matter. I've gotten this close, and Child-Me is inside the temple. No matter what the question, I know one thing.

She has all the answers.

I step inside the ruined structure. Once inside, I find that the place is almost bare. At one time, there were markings on the walls. Quite possibly, these were paintings at some point, but they're now all faded beyond recognition. Or rather, I might be able to figure them out if I really looked closely, but I can only focus on the center of the temple floor.

The girl is standing there.

The child is a mess of knobby knees and bony arms that are all wrapped up in a Roman toga. She appears to be about six years old. But that's not what's most remarkable about her.

No, that would be her golden skin, silver wings, and long red hair that glistens like rubies.

Within my soul, my inner wolf pauses, tilting her head. She's as curious as I am. *"How can that be you?"*

*"I don't know."* For some reason, I can only stare at the girl.

*"Ask her,"* urges my wolf. *"Go on."*

I take a half step closer. "Who are you?"

"A memory," says the child. Her voice is like tiny bells ringing. "I'm a wish that never was." She gestures to the box under my arm. "And it's all because of that bad thing."

I lift the Codex Mechanica. "Do you mean this?"

"That's horrible." Looking up, she starts clapping wildly. "Oh, look! He's here, too!"

The interior of the temple darkens. For a moment, I worry that the Shadowvin have returned, but I dismiss the idea. Those creatures drip darkness down the walls in a way that reminds me of paint. Whatever is causing this shadow, it's big enough to block out the sun. What could do that? A moment later, I have my answer.

A black-scaled dragon dips its head through the break in the roof.

I run forward. On reflex, I want to protect the little girl from the dragon. However, the child's reaction is the exact opposite. She bobs on her tiptoes and reaches for the dragon's head as if the creature were a long-lost friend. Once the dragon is close enough, the girl wraps her arms around its muzzle. Since the dragon is so huge, the child can only grasp a small part of its chin.

"Colonel Mallory?" I ask. The dragon version of the Colonel doesn't seem to hear me. Instead, his focus is on the child.

"What did I tell you, sugar?" asks the dragon. "You can't go running off from me like that."

All the air seems to get sucked from my lungs. The walls of the temple start bowing out and in at a faster pace. It's like the very chamber is breathing more quickly. There's no mistaking that dragon.

It's Colonel Mallory.

The girl pats the massive dragon scales with her tiny hand. "I just wanted to go outside and play."

"But you can't, now can you, honey? Do you remember why?"

The child shivers. "The man in the mask. He can't find me."

The room rattles on its foundation. Bits of stone tumble from the open ceiling. The girl and dragon disappear. A familiar voice echoes around me.

"Bry, wake up!"

That's Knox.

It's takes an effort, but somehow I open my eyes. Knox kneels beside me. I'm inside the temple, curled up on the floor. The Codex Mechanica rests on the ground beside me. "What happened?" I ask.

"You weren't answering your cell," says Knox. His skin looks extra pale. A thin sheen of sweat covers his features. "I got worried."

"I ran in here." Blinking hard, I check out the room. It looks just as it did a moment ago—all round walls and faded paint. My body feels different, though. Every muscle aches as if I ran a marathon.

*Huh. Maybe I did.*

"Yeah," says Knox. "I found you here, passed out on the floor."

"Did you see anyone else along the way?" Some small part of me hopes Knox saw the little girl, or at least Colonel Mallory in dragon form.

"There was just Alec and Elle behind me," answers Knox. "What's this all about, Bry?"

It takes some doing, but I force myself to sit up. "I walked in here and thought I saw…something. Someone, actually. But maybe it's the stress of everything. It's those strange dreams I get again."

Knox eyes me carefully. "The ones you told me about? Those dreams with the little girl?"

"They always start off with the little girl, but they end with the Shadowvin and the Void. This time, it was a little different. When I walked into the temple, I saw—"

At that moment, Elle and Alec step inside the temple, panting for breath. Evidently, they ran here, too. All of a sudden, the pair starts cheering their heads off.

"You did it!" cries Elle. "I knew you would."

I squint at her. "What do you mean?"

Alec points behind me. "The fountain," he says. "You found it."

My eyes stretch so wide, I'm surprised they don't fall out of my head. "I did?"

Knox nods. "When I came in, I saw you passed out and rushed over to you. I didn't really care about anything else." He glances behind me. "But yeah, Elle and Alec are right. That sure looks like part of a geyser."

Little by little, I crane my neck to look at whatever is hidden behind my back. Sure enough, I find a large cone-shaped rock waiting in the center of the temple floor, right at the spot where the girl had just stood. I rise to stand on shaky legs. It looks just like the geyser from my trip to the past. The sides are streaked in red, gold, and silver.

Every cell in my body seems to freeze.

This is it.

At last.

The fountain.

"You're right," I say slowly. "It's here."

This is everything I've been looking for. I run my hand over the mottled stone. Layers of magic have colored its surface. This is definitely the fountain. I should be cheering for joy, same as Elle and Alec. In the end, I can only muster one sensation.

This feels wrong.

All of it.

And to top it off, Knox is looking sicker than ever. His muscle tone is fading by the second. Now, his shirt hangs loose on his newly bony frame. The ice-blue of his eyes has faded to an almost gray. No question about it.

This is killing him. My throat closes with held-in sobs. Inside my soul, my wolf whimpers in mourning. Back in New York, Knox said he only has a few days left. Am I playing with his life by being close to him?

It's not just that he's dying, it's that I'm what's killing him.

# CHAPTER TWENTY-SIX

Something is wrong. I've found the fountain of magic, but it's off somehow. Perhaps Jules made a copy just to screw with people? It seems like something he would do. I pull the partly assembled Codex Mechanica out from under my arm and hold it before me.

"Is this truly the fountain of magic?" I ask.

The innards of the machine whir as the discs spin and spell out a reply. Knox leans in for a better look. Every time the discs pause, Knox reads the glyphs that appear on the box's lid. "The fountain of magic... in Julius Caesar's home... inside the ruined temple." His ice-blue gaze locks with mine. "Why did you ask that, Bry?"

I shiver. "Something about this feels off. I thought this might be a decoy."

Knox gives me one of his chin-nods. "I get you. This whole thing is wrong."

Alec throws up his hands in frustration. "I can't believe this! The two of you faced down Ty, got here, faced down the Shadowvin, and found the fountain of magic...and not without a ton of expert help from me and Elle, I might add." He focuses on Knox. "This is everything we've always wanted. You and I..." Alec motions between himself and Knox. "We can't get married without this."

Elle steps forward. Her blue eyes never looked wider with wonder. "I thought you didn't want to settle down."

Alec shoots her the quickest of glances. "Not today, but..." A blush colors his cheeks.

My inner wolf snaps to attention. *"Alec would like to make Elle his mate,"* she says in my head. *"They should have a ceremony and cubs."*

I'd roll my eyes, but that would look pretty out of place to everyone else in the temple. My wolf and cubs. It's her favorite topic lately.

"Most guys don't want to settle down at eighteen," explains Knox. "But Alec and I? Wardens like us live for hundreds of years. That's a long time to be without a home and family. We want the choice to have a future with someone." He gives Alec a sideways look. "Even so, that doesn't mean we should jump into trouble."

"Tell that to my parents," says Alec. "I wouldn't be surprised if they cast some kind of spell that alerted them if I got within two yards of the fountain of magic. They'll freak if they know I found it and walked away. They want an heir yesterday." He gives Elle another nanosecond long glance. "Not that I have to get married today or anything. People might have complex issues that need to get worked out first."

Knox and I share a look. We've talked about how obvious it is that Elle and Alec like each other. We've also discussed the total bummer about Elle's stepfamily. Love is a kind of magic. The way Elle was magically hidden has certain limits. Elle can't cast too many spells or it will send out a magical signature to her stepfamily. Plus, there's no greater magic than love. If Elle kisses someone she cares about—especially that first kiss—then that'll send out the mother of all magical signatures. Elle might as well show up at her stepfamily's doorstep and say, *I'm still alive! Imprison me now!*

Long story short, it's better for her to avoid a relationship with Alec at all costs, at least for now.

Even so, the whole train of thought barrels into a realization. Alec and Knox have spent years searching for the very thing in this room. The least I can do is make sure we explore it thoroughly. Any piece of information could be critical someday. I hold up the Codex Mechanica again and speak directly to it.

"How do we activate the fountain?" I ask.

The discs whir once more. Again, Knox reads the glyphs as they appear on the box's top. "Find the last disc. Inside the fountain. Fully reassemble the device."

Alec leans over the geyser top and peers inside. "The machine is right. The red disc is right inside here."

I carefully set down the Codex Mechanica. Although my legs suddenly feel boneless, I'm still somehow able to stand up and peer inside the geyser top as well. Sure enough, there's the red disc, resting on one of the natural small ledges on the inner channel. The realization appears in my mind.

*Someone set this thing here.*

*Why?*

I glance over to Knox. "This is more of a setup."

"Yeah," he says. "We've been herded along for a while now." He rubs his neck in a worried rhythm. "Honestly? I don't know if we should take off or see it through."

The red disc pulses with the faintest crimson light. "I don't know, either."

A voice echoes in from across the temple. "Plop, slop, boil and chop! I'm just in time to make you stop."

A shiver of awareness moves up my limbs. I'd know that particular kind of singsong crazy anywhere. Turning around, I find exactly who I'd expected.

"Reggie?" I ask.

"Reggie!" Alec snarls.

Knox sighs. "Great, Reggie."

For his part, our zombie-mummy visitor skip-walks toward us. Reggie looks exactly as he did in the airport: three-piece suit, fedora, and that manic gleam in his eyes that says, *Hello, I'm magically unhinged.*

Reggie pauses beside the fountain and waves in turn to me, Knox, Alec, and Elle. "Mend, bend, toil and wend. I'm here today as your best friend!"

Elle takes a half step backward. "What?" The last time my bestie saw any Denarii, she was shooting them with a magical seed gun. Long story. All in all, my best friend is clearly not pleased that Reggie has decided to show up.

"Don't worry," I explain. "Colonel Mallory asked Reggie to keep an eye on me. So it's okay that he dropped by. Maybe."

Elle raises her hand. "I'm still worried."

"Whisk, frisk, death and risk. Whatever you do, don't touch that disc." Reggie smiles broadly.

*Ugh.* He really thinks he's helping here.

"You know," says Alec. "When the Shadowvin were herding us to this very point, I might have thought twice about grabbing that disc. But if Reggie is saying we shouldn't touch it? We definitely need to grab this thing." Alec leans over the edge of the geyser's mouth and scoops up the disc.

Reggie frowns. "Show, go, halt and flow. Listen now when I say no!"

Alec turns to me and offers the disc. "I want to go back to my life," he says. "So do all of us. What do you say, Bry? Assemble that thing and find out what we have to do to protect the fountain? I'm not even saying activate the thing. Just keep it away from the Void."

For a long moment, I stare at the disc in Alec's hand. "You make a good point." Turning, I focus on Reggie. "Sorry, bud. No matter what the Colonel says, I don't really trust you." My gaze shifts between Knox and Elle. "What do you guys think?"

"Pop the thing into the thing," says Elle.

Knox gives me a chin-nod. "I'm with them."

After flipping the latches on the sides, I open up the box. Knox swipes the red disc from Alec and fits it into the device's inner workings. I snap the lid closed.

"Now you've done it!" cries Reggie. He must be really upset because he's stopped speaking in rhymes. "You leave me no choice!" Turning on his heel, Reggie pointedly stomps his way out of the temple. For a long moment, I try to brainstorm what Reggie is *really* up to. He can't be giving up on magic. The undead dude's life depends on it.

Then again, this is Reggie here. Who know why he does anything?

Alec gives him a sarcastic wave. "Goodbye, buddy! Thanks for escaping from prison and giving us all a heart attack for a month."

I rub my shin. "What do you think he meant by, *You leave me no choice?*"

"Who knows?" Alec rolls his eyes a full 360. "Reggie is certifiable. Any time spent trying to interpret his singsong nonsense is a waste."

My inner animal perks up inside my heart. *"He didn't smell of lies,"* says my wolf. *"Maybe the crazy mummy man was right. We shouldn't use the wooden box."*

*"Where was this opinion when we were deciding all this?"*

My wolf sniffs. *"I was busy grooming."* She's used this line before. Honestly, I don't know what grooming entails, especially when you're trapped in a magical state inside my soul. Plus, I'm not sure that I want to know, either. Some mysteries are better left alone.

Well, it's done now. Time to see what a fully reassembled Codex Mechanica can do.

I speak directly to the device. I'm not sure if this is part of a spell or something, but it's always seemed to work before. "How do we protect the fountain?" I ask.

Knox translates. "Activate the fountain. Release its bounty. Defend the fountain. The only way to protect the fountain is to..." He winces. "This glyph order is unusual." He looks to me. "Any ideas?"

I look more closely at the images on the top of the device. "The only way to protect the fountain is to use the fountain."

A weight of worry settles into my bones. I was really hoping we could find a way to just hide the fountain away from the Void. Using it is basically asking for trouble. The Shadowvin have been perfectly clear that they want to consume the power of the fountain. Activating it is the equivalent of sounding off the world's largest supernatural dinner bell.

"Can we disguise the fountain?" I ask.

The reply is clear: NO.

I rattle off a series of rapid-fire questions. "Can we kill the Shadowvin?

The device whirs. NO.

"Destroy the Void without destroying magic?"

Whir. NO.

"Guard the fountain in some way?"

Whir. NO.

Knox gently sets his hand on my shoulder. "Ask the real question, Bry."

How I hate doing this. "How do we activate the fountain?"

The machine whirs out new answers. Knox translates once more. "Bring the fountain to the new pyramids."

"New pyramids?" asks Alec.

"The old ones were in South America," I explain. "If the machine is talking about new pyramids, it means the ones in Egypt."

The codex whirs away until the discs stop on a new message. "Use the discs," translates Knox. He looks to me. "Any ideas what that means?"

"When I traveled back in time with Scar, I saw the ceremony of the fountain. There were three wardens there, along with someone else."

"A fourth person?" asks Alec.

"The three wardens were wearing cloaks in the color of their magic—red, gold, and silver. But there was a fourth person there who was wearing a white cloak. This guy Bram told us that a Trilorum always accompanied the wardens to the ceremony. I thought it was maybe a guard or something."

An image appears in my mind. The child version of me with my golden skin, ruby hair, and silver wings. Do all Trilorum look that way when we're young? That might explain a lot. Perhaps one of the Trilorum always gets mixed up with the fountain.

The discs begin to rotate once more. "Let no wardens follow," Knox translates.

My breath catches. The very thought of doing this alone makes my throat tighten with worry. "That can't be right." I look at the device once more. "The fountain must be activated with the wardens nearby. That's what I saw when I went back in time."

The discs spin again, but land on the same glyphs. "Let no wardens follow," repeats Knox. The device changes the glyphs once more. "That is all," reads Knox.

After that, the machine turns the discs to a blank spot. It's what happened before when the machine was done giving information. My thoughts keep churning over the news.

I'll take the fountain to the pyramids.

Alone.

And most likely, the Shadowvin and Void will be there.

Dread weighs down my shoulders. My aunties always told me I was doomed. Weak. Jules told me the same thing as well: I'd never be able to succeed without him.

I force my stance to straighten. If this is my doom, then I'll face it with everything I've got.

Knox gently brushes his fingertip along my jawline. "What are you thinking?"

I lift my chin. "This is my task. I must do it alone." My gaze shifts to Alec. "Can you transport me and the fountain to the pyramids?"

Elle grabs the box out of my hands. "Like hell you're going there alone."

"Agreed." Alec moves to stand by Elle's side. "I don't care what some ancient box says. I'm a warden, and it's my job to protect this…" He gestures at the geyser. "Big rock fountain thing. I'm not leaving it and I'm not abandoning you."

Knox gives me a crooked smile. Normally, that makes my stomach get all woozy but now? I can only notice how pale his skin has become and the scent of pain that wafts from him. "Going alone is not an option," says Knox slowly. "And it's not just because I'm the warden of all shifters. You're my mate. There's no way you're facing the Shadowvin and Void alone."

"But you'll be in danger," I say. "And the Codex Mechanica said I have to leave you behind."

"You know how I feel about fairy tale life templates," say Knox. He gestures at the device in Elle's hands. "That thing just spouted off another story to us, that's all. In my heart, I know we're meant to be together. Like I said, we write our own futures."

My inner wolf sits up at attention. *"Our mate is wise. We should never leave him."*

I'm still not convinced this is the right move, though. "So, do you think it was wrong about other things?" I ask. "Do you think we can hide the fountain?"

"What do you think, Bry?"

I rub my temples with my fingertips. It's a good question. Thoughts and facts race through my mind. Ty. Boucle-Roux. The Shadowvin chasing us here. The fountain. Reggie. My Child-Self. All of these facts should come together into a new story. I can only see parts, though. "I think the Shadowvin want me to take the fountain to Egypt and activate it. Somehow, they convinced Ty to help them."

"Go on," urges Knox. His voice and manner are all things calm and encouraging.

"Reggie is against activating the fountain because if the Void consumes all the magic, Reggie is a dead man and for real this time." I look around the room. "The Shadowvin have never been far from me. If I refuse to activate the fountain, they'll reappear and try to push me toward that again. My best bet is to help activate the fountain and get the magic out into the world. That's what the fountain is meant to do. Once that task is done, then there won't be any supernatural meal for the Void to consume. Not easily, anyway." I take in a long breath. "The best thing to do is to activate the fountain on our terms."

"Right." Knox all-out grins. "*Our* terms."

"But what if things go wrong?" I ask. "All the device said is that we need to activate the fountain. We could end up destroying all magic or getting it out in the world in the wrong way."

"Not sure I see another option," says Elle. "It's like you said, we're being herded into a direction. Either we take charge of the situation, or it keeps taking charge of us." We share a fist-bump.

I look to Alec. "Is that how you feel as well? If you decide to go along with this, it could cost your life."

"I'm with you," says Alec. And those three words are spoken with such conviction I know they're the truth.

"Then it's agreed," I announce. "All four of us will go to the pyramids along with this geyser thing."

With those words, the temple changes. White mist rolls out across the floor. Dark shadows drip down the walls. The air takes on a deathly chill. Three Shadowvin rise up from the mist-covered ground. There are Slythe and Tithe, who I've seen before. The third one is new and definitely different from the others. For Slythe and Tithe, their bodies are relatively the same proportions. There's something about the new Shadowvin's arms that seem off somehow.

"Greetings," says the new Shadowvin. "I won't say this twice, so listen carefully." She has the same feminine silhouette as Tithe and her voice is similar, like many old women speaking all at once. Except, with this new Shadowvin, her multi-voice carries the weight of authority, like she's used to bossing the other two Shadowvin around. I can't shake the feeling I've heard her before.

"This Trilorum." The new Shadowvin points to me. Something in the motion looks odd and familiar, all at the same time. "She must go with us to the pyramids. Alone. And you." Now she points to Alec. "Your role is to transport her there. The Shadowvin will rise. That is inevitable. Accept this and do as I say."

All of a sudden, I remember where I saw this Shadowvin. It was when I went back in time.

"I know you," I say. "You're Quetzali, First Warden of fae magic." Knox tilts his head. "You sure?"

"I can tell because of her hands—they're extra long with webbing, even as a Shadowvin." I focus back on Quetzali. "But mostly, I know who you are by the way you act. You did the same thing in the past. You just showed up at a ceremony, announced to everyone you were about to destroy magic, and then were surprised when people didn't just bow down and do as they were told."

Quetzali's eyes flare more brightly. Menace rolls off her in waves. I get the idea she isn't used to being critiqued.

Tough.

"I don't get it," says Elle. "You said Quetzali wanted to destroy magic to protect the people from the Shadowvin and Void."

More of the story falls into place. I round on Quetzali. "That was all a lie, wasn't it? Back in time, there were no Shadowvin. Not yet, anyway." The moment, I say the words, I know that they are the truth. "You just pretended that the Shadowvin existed. It was a way to scare everyone."

"And why would I do that?" asks Quetzali.

The answer appears in a flash of realization. "Because you never really were going to destroy magic at all. You wanted all the power for yourself. Three Shadowvin. The three First Wardens."

"Many things come in three," offers Quetzali.

I turn to Elle. "To answer your question, the First Wardens might not have been the good guys. Maybe their motives had nothing to do with keeping people safe. This all could have been a power grab." With every word, my soul feels more certain I'm speaking the truth. "I've never seen the Void do anything but say he wants the fountain. The Shadowvin are the only ones who've stolen magic from me. Magic has strange ways of punishing people. It turned you into the very monsters you pretended existed, didn't it?"

Quetzali floats closer. "I said I would only tell you once to go to the pyramids. That chance is over." She raises her arms. "Slythe! Tithe! Now!"

Moving as one, all three Shadowvin fly across the temple.

And they zoom straight into Knox's body.

Knox fights the possession harder than ever. His entire body vibrates with agony. When my mate turns to me, his eyes swirl with grey mist. "Run…Three this time…Too many…"

"No, I won't leave."

My mate hunches over in pain. With every cell in my body, I want to ease his agony. When Knox stands again, all signs of struggle have vanished. He seems his old self again.

*Please, let this be good.*

When Knox speaks again, his voice sounds like dozens of old men and women talking at once. "Time to go visit the pyramids. Shall we?"

*Nope. Not good.*

Inside my soul, my wolf shivers in terror. "*What have they done to our mate?*" she cries.

"*He's possessed,*" I reply in my head.

"*How do we help him?*" she asks.

Tears well in my eyes. "*If only I knew.*"

But I don't. And Knox is stalking toward me with three evil Shadowvin possessing his soul. Hard to imagine how things could get worse.

# CHAPTER TWENTY-SEVEN

Knox's upper body expands. Fur erupts across his skin. His face elongates into a muzzle. His fingers lengthen into claws. I pop my hands over my mouth.

He said his life template was Beauty and The Beast. Knox said that when he fought Denarii, he became a half-human killing machine.

The Beast.

It's one thing to realize that your boyfriend turns into an eight-foot-tall humanoid wolfman. It's quite another to see it happen before your eyes. Normally, weres are either human and wolf. This halfway state makes my pulse skyrocket. I've never seen anything like it before. Add to that how his soulless eyes are staring at me like I'm lunch? It takes all my mental strength not to run.

Knox reaches for me. "Come with us to the pyramids or else." I step backward. My inner wolf whines in confusion.

*"Why is our mate threatening us?"* she whimpers.

*"He doesn't want to do this,"* I say. *"Not really."*

Grey mist has overtaken Knox's eyes. Now, that haze swirls even faster. "Follow us or die."

"Leave Bry alone!" cries Elle. My best friend lunges for Knox. With one swipe of his mighty arm, my mate bats Elle away, sending her flying across the room. My best friend slides across the temple floor until her head rams into the far wall. A loud CRACK echoes through the stone chamber. I gasp.

*Now, that's a concussion. Or worse.*

I race toward her. "Elle!" Kneeling beside my best friend, I set my fingers on her throat. My hand shakes with anxiety as I test her pulse. Still there. I gingerly pull back her eyelid. Elle's pupils contract. I exhale.

Nearby, Alec's features tighten with rage as he rounds on Knox. "What have you done?"

"She'll be fine, Alec." I explain. "Keep your cool."

"You. Hurt. Her." Curling his hands into fists, Alec races toward Knox. I've never seen Alec go for physical battle before—he's always reached for some gemstones. That said, I've never seen Alec this furious before, either.

Alec only gets within a few feet of Knox when my mate strikes. Grabbing Alec around the waist, Knox flips the wizard over through the air. Alec ends up slammed backfirst onto the temple floor. He doesn't move afterward.

*No, no, no.*

If the possessed version of Knox kills Alec, my true mate will never forgive himself. I stare at Alec's prone form, searching for any sign of life. For a long second, nothing is visible.

Alec's chest shifts ever so slightly. Is that his last breath or the first of many more?

With Alec out of the picture, Knox focuses on me. "You have two choices. Go with us on your own. Or get dragged along because you're in too much pain to fight." He stalks closer. "What will it be?"

Every muscle in my body freezes with shock. If seeing Knox transform into a half-human monster was bad, but threatening me and beating up our friends? It's so much worse.

*"Our mate,"* my inner wolf whimpers. *"He'll tear us apart."*

*"That's not true,"* I counter in my mind. *"Knox is strong enough to fight this."*

*Hopefully.*

I keep my gaze level with Knox's. It's important to shifters not to look away or cower when you're trying to be badass. In my case, emphasis on the word *trying*.

"You won't hurt me, Knox." I'm happy with how level my words sound because inside? I'm a shivering mess. "You're my mate."

When Knox speaks again, his voice takes on the tone of a hundred people speaking at once "Knox is gone."

Inside my heart, my inner wolf yips with fear. *"What did I tell you? Our mate will hurt us. We must run for our lives."*

This time, I don't disagree.

*"Right,"* I reply in my mind. *"Let's go."*

Angling my head, I shoot a quick glance at the main archway. It's the only way in or out. I have shifter speed, same as Knox. Of course, I'm not possessed by Shadowvin, but with any luck, that extra supernatural luggage will only slow my mate down.

Knox stalks closer. "Are you ready to listen to reason? Will you come with us to Egypt?"

I don't reply with words. Instead, I race toward the exit arch with all my strength. In my peripheral vision, I can see Knox take off after me. My mate's movements are so fast, he's little more than a blur.

The next thing I know, Knox crashes into me from behind. I slam face-first onto the stone floor. WHACK! The right side of my head takes most of the impact. Instantly, my head feels woozy. I'm barely aware of Knox's teeth clamping onto my neck. With sluggish movements, I try to fight back, but it's no use.

A thin rivulet of warm blood flows down my neck.

Knox is trying to kill me.

This can't be happening.

As I keep up my struggle, I hear a familiar voice echo through the temple: "Hover, lover, seek and discover. I've come back, better run for cover."

It takes a moment for my muddled brain to realize the truth. *Reggie has returned.* My rib cage swells with a combination of elation and relief. *Reggie has returned…*Who would have thought those three words would bring me pure joy?

Knox leaps to his feet. "You."

"Bend, fend, try and mend. I've come back and brought a friend."

Another voice gets added into the mix. "Yes, me." I'd know that southern lilt anywhere. "Hello there, sugar. Sorry I'm late."

Whatever sense of relief I felt before? It's now doubled. The Colonel is here. Like always, he looks unflappable in his white suit and matching hat. However, I know the old fae well enough to notice the way his eyes gleam with silver light. He's enraged. Now, certain supernatural dickheads are going to get what's coming to them.

It's a supreme effort, but I force myself to twist my head toward the Colonel. What I'm about to say is important; I simply must be understood.

"Knox is possessed by the Shadowvin," I whisper. "Don't hurt him. Please."

"Would never hurt your mate, sweet pea." The Colonel raises his arms. Instantly, a thick haze of silver fairy dust encircles his hands. The Colonel lowers his arms, and the silver cloud whips toward Knox. As the fairy dust flies through the air, it takes the shape of eight long spears.

I gasp. I've seen fairy dust turn into massive fists and knives. Every time, they've punched and cut their way into flesh, just like a real weapon would do. Panic zings through my bloodstream. "Don't hurt him!" I cry.

The Colonel says one word. "Never."

The silver spears slice right through Knox and come out the other side. When the weapons leave Knox's back, they have impaled the three Shadowvin on them. The spears keep flying across the room until they stab into the far wall. The three Shadowvin are stuck onto the wall as well, like insects on a pin.

I try to sit up and get a better look at Knox, but it's no use. I have shifter healing, and even so, I'm still taking some time to recover from whatever whack possessed-Knox gave to my head. I croak out one word. "Knox?"

He races to kneel by my side. "Bry, are you all right? What happened?"

The Colonel strides over. "You did, my boy." He gestures to the wall. "You were possessed, and I took care of the problem. You're welcome."

Knox turns to stare at the far wall. The three Shadowvin remain stuck there for a long moment. After that, they slowly vanish.

"The Shadowvin." Knox clutches his stomach. "I remember them coming at me but after that, nothing." Even though Knox is kneeling, he sways a bit from side to side. Being possessed by the Shadowvin can't be good for your health.

The Colonel raises his arms once again. New silver mist forms in his palms. Within a few seconds, the haze takes the form of a crystal ball. The Colonel stares into its depths. "According to this here crystal ball, you're under some bad mojo, my boy. Seems that the longer you're with my Bryar Rose, the worse you feel."

Knox's eyes narrow. "Yeah. That a problem?"

"As a matter of fact, it is," says the Colonel. "I want to have a discussion with Bryar Rose, but the topic is a bit disturbing. I think you'd better come along to help. And to do that, you need a little healing magic." The Colonel scans the room. "You all could use some, as a matter of fact."

Reggie, who'd been standing by the exit arch this whole time, now steps deeper into the chamber. "New, you, flew, ah-choo. I'm a little sick, so heal me, too?"

"Reggie, you're more than sick," says the Colonel. "You're dead as a doornail. I'm not wasting my good magic on such foolishness." The Colonel lowers his arms. The crystal ball that has been cupped in his palms keeps hovering in space for a moment or two. Then it splits into four smaller orbs. Now, each one of those spheres no longer appears to be made of crystal. Instead, the hovering orbs look like balls of silver fairy dust. The Colonel snaps his fingers, and the tiny spheres go flying across the chamber. Knox, Alec, Elle, and me... One orb slams into each of our chests.

The moment the ball of fairy dust touches my rib cage, a pleasant warmth enters my body. The sphere seeps into my bones and blood. Energy and life flow through me, healing my wounds. I hop to my feet and grin. "Thank you, Colonel."

Knox rubs his chest. "Same here," he says.

"You're both most welcome." The Colonel tips his hat before turning to me. "And Bryar Rose, you'll notice soon that I put your wolf in stasis as well. Trust me, she needs some rest. And she'll wake up soon enough."

Closing my eyes, I reach out to my inner animal. Sure enough, I find her deep within my soul, curled up in an O shape and snoring. I eye the Colonel warily. "My wolf is safe and everything, but it's downright rude to go around putting other people's inner animals in stasis without permission."

"You're quite right. Exceptionally rude. I'll owe you a boon. How's that?"

A boon is a Get Out of Jail Free card from a fairy. They can't take it back or refuse, no matter what you ask them to do. In fact, I've never heard of Colonel Mallory awarding one, ever. "I'll take it," I say.

Across the room, Elle and Alec awaken. They've been knocked out for a little while, so they're rubbing their eyes and looking mighty confused.

"What happened?" asks Elle.

Alec points to Knox. This time, the gleam of rubies shines through his clenched fist. "You're possessed." Keeping his gaze locked on Knox, Alec starts to murmur a spell. The gems in his hand flare with light.

*This is not good.*

"Whoa, there." Knox raises his arms and shows Alec his palms. "I'm not possessed any more, thanks to our new visitor."

The Colonel bows slightly. "Greetings, Mister LeCharme."

Alec takes a half step backward. "When did you get here?"

"Reggie brought me," explains the Colonel. "I asked our undead friend here to keep an eye on y'all, and it's a good thing I did. The Shadowvin can get rather peevish. I sent them away, but those three are worse than jackrabbits in a carrot patch. You scare them away one minute, they run right back two minutes later."

"Jackrabbits," says Elle slowly. "Got it." In Elle-speak, that means she's actually having a hard time adjusting to the new reality here. Not that I blame her. It's been one crazy day, and her world just went from fighting a possessed Knox to chatting up an extremely courteous Colonel Mallory.

"Look," says the Colonel. "Why don't y'all stay here with Reggie and set a spell? He can explain everything. In the meantime, I'll just take Knox and Bryar Rose on a quick walk. There are a few things we need to discuss. Then we'll be right back."

"Talking with Reggie," says Alec. "We can do that." Those may be the words that come out of his mouth, but Alec is staring at Reggie like he's an extra-large cockroach that crawled into the room. Not that I blame Alec for being cautious. Reggie is a nutcase.

"Good news," says the Colonel. "Oh, just don't let Reggie run off."

"We won't." Elle shoots him a thumbs-up, which is sign that my best friend is feeling far more in control of the situation.

The Colonel starts for the exit archway, pauses, and then turns around again. "And scream the bejeezus out of your lungs if those Shadowvin show up again."

"Not a problem," says Alec. "We don't want the Shadowvin to get the fountain."

"Fountain?" asks the Colonel slowly.

Elle gestures to the geyser top. "Sure, this thing right here. The Codex Mechanica confirmed it's the real fountain of magic, not a replica or anything."

"Ah, I see," says the Colonel. "Yes, you guard that thing real well for us all. We'll be back soon." With that, the Colonel saunters out the exit archway. Knox and I follow behind, but not before I scoop up the Codex Mechanica from where I'd placed it on the floor. After so much hassle, I am not letting that device out of my sight.

Once we're outside, the Colonel heads off into a different stretch of forest. "This way, please." he calls.

"Where are we off to?" I ask.

"My old villa," replied the Colonel.

I stop in my tracks. "You have a bungalow on Jules' old estate?"

The Colonel pauses as well. "That I do, sugar. What did you expect?"

"Honestly?" I ask. "I thought you were imprisoned here some time ago. And then, maybe you saw me somehow and cast the curse on me to keep my powers locked up."

Knox steps closer to my side. "Bry thought you were locked in a dungeon somewhere."

The Colonel exhales a long sigh. "I've done a lot of things I'm not proud of. It's beyond time I told you some of them." He glances around at the trees. "But not here." Without saying another word, the Colonel marches off into the forest.

As we follow along behind the Colonel, Knox links his fingers with mine. His touch is firm and centering. Considering how I'm holding Knox's hand on one side and gripping the Codex Mechanica on the other, you'd think I'd feel a little better. I don't, though.

Every few yards, Colonel Mallory glances over his shoulder to me. His face is the definition of the word guilty. His words reverberate through my soul.

> *I've done a lot of things I'm not proud of, sugar.*
> *It's beyond time I told you some of them.*

As conversation starters go, that isn't very promising. Plus, the Colonel has done some pretty scary things. Point of fact: I watched him transform into a dragon, breathe fire, and fry a whole forest full of Denarii. I know for a fact that charbroiling all those Denarii wouldn't even register on his "guilt radar." So what would a guy like that actually feel badly about?

For better or worse, I'm about to find out.

# CHAPTER TWENTY-EIGHT

The Colonel, Knox, and I walk through the woods that surround the small temple. As we step along, spindly trees loom over us, the thin branches covered in tiny green leaves. The air smells of fresh soil combined with the bitter tang of salt water. In Italy, the ocean is never far away. We step out of the forest and onto another clearing. This one holds a single villa.

I pause. The sense of déjà vu is strong here. Throughout my soul, there's this all-encompassing sense of knowing this place. Belonging here. A little girl's laugher sounds. I tilt my head. The child version of me is near.

Colonel Mallory steps closer. "I can see this spot is affecting you."

"It is," I say. "Why?"

"I magically sealed your memories up to age six, sugar. It was for your own good, but nothing works perfectly especially over time. Lately, my spell has been leaking on you, allowing you to see people from the past as if they were here today." He sighs. "Wasn't my best spell, but it did the trick at the time." He gestures to the villa. "Shall we?"

I look to Knox. "Is it me, or does that guy talk in riddles and half truths?"

Knox slants his gaze toward the Colonel. "All the time. But he's fae. Goes with the territory."

Across the clearing, the Colonel holds open the door to the villa. In this case, using the word *door* is being generous. The Colonel's holding what's little more than a screen that's held on by a single hinge. Knox and I follow him across the threshold.

Inside, the place looks a lot like the other villa I saw. There are threadbare rugs on the floor. Odd patterns of black mold cover the walls. A few sticks of warped furniture are piled in a corner. All of the stuff looks like it was the height of design in 1950. In other words, there are lots of sleek black wooden tables and uncomfortable-looking chairs.

The place is familiar and not, all at once.

The Colonel pulls back a frayed oriental carpet, revealing a cutout rectangle of wood set into the floor. My eyes widen.

"That's a door to the basement." Bands of anxiety constrict my rib cage. "I've seen that before."

"Yes, darlin'. You have." The Colonel picks up one edge of the wooden slat and pulls it aside, revealing a staircase leading downward. "Let's go."

The Colonel marches down the darkened steps. My legs feel boneless beneath me. Every muscle in my body starts trembling as I walk down the rickety wooden stairs. There aren't many steps. Even so, it seems to take forever to reach the bottom. Once I'm there, what I see takes all the air from my lungs.

This is the room from my dreams. It's all here. The dirt floor. The small bed in a corner. The great wooden chest against one wall. And a small sandbox in the opposite edge of the room. When I speak, my voice has a dreamy tone. "I've seen this place."

"Like I said, I had to lock down your memories, sugar. It was only to protect you."

"Today, I saw the child version of me. It was outside the temple. She had gold skin, silver wings, and red hair. Do all Trilorum look that way when we're children?"

"No, sugar." The Colonel's silver eyes soften. I can't place the look; it's somewhere between sadness and grief. "Trilorum are indeed rare. But even in that select group, you're even more unusual."

Knox pulls me close against his side. "What are you saying?"

The Colonel walks over to the wooden chest and sits down upon it. "Most of my life, I haven't been a good man, even by fae standards. Over the centuries, I made some fine enemies, all of them in the Faerie Lands. I escaped to this realm, but assassins got sent my way on a regular basis. Then, on one of my escapes, I ran across Jules. Sure, he was a zombie and mummy, but he was also a power to be reckoned with. He promised to hide me from my enemies. In return, I was to bring him meals of humans that I thought worthy of death. So I did. I hid here and did Jules' bidding. Mind you, that was before Jules refined his tastes to Magicorum."

The words make my stomach churn. *I was to bring him regular meals of humans.* "You didn't."

"I'm not proud of it, sugar. If it makes any difference, I did take care to find only the most disgusting specimens. But find them, I did. And I liked living here. I won't deny that either. As a matter of fact, everything was going along fine until I found something in the temple one day, laying smack dab at the foot of that geyser."

I can't help but notice how the Colonel uses the word *geyser* instead of *fountain of magic*. Something in the back of my mind says I know what he really means, but I can't quite find the words yet.

The Colonel rises, opens the wooden chest, and pulls out a drawing. "I drew this of you, right on the day I found you."

With trembling fingers, I pull the sheet of paper from the Colonel's hands. On it, there's an image of a baby with golden skin, a shock of red hair, and tiny silver wings. And in that moment, I know one thing for certain. "That's me."

The Colonel nods. "You were such a little thing. Here I was, living in the lap of luxury. Jules was still hiding me from my enemies in the Faerie Lands."

My forehead crumples as I think through this news. "But I knew Jules for years under an alias. Why wouldn't I have recognized him?"

"I can explain that," says the Colonel. "Right before your sweet baby self appeared, Jules got in a big fight with another one of my fae enemies. My foe lost, but Jules got half his face ripped off in the process. It took that man years to consume enough organs to rebuild his look. Until then, Jules wore a—"

"A mask," I finish for him. "He wore a golden mask."

*I had seen him, after all.*

"That's right. Jules wore a mask, but he still needed meals. And I needed a place to hide. Only with you, I wasn't the only one hiding anymore. I used my magic to make a hidden nursery, and I became something I never thought I'd be. A father."

The thought that had been nagging at the back of my mind becomes clear. I know what the fountain is. Lifting the Codex Mechanica, I speak once more into the device. "Tell me where the fountain of magic is."

The gears whir.

My heart beats at double speed.

Knox translates once more. "The fountain of magic is in the basement of the dragon fairy's villa." His brows droop with confusion. "Bry, I don't understand. It should say the fountain is in the temple."

"No, the device is right," I say. "It's me. I'm the fountain. Magic created me; I have no parents."

Knox rounds on the Colonel. "Is this true?"

"I'm afraid so."

Knox turns to me. "Are you sure about this?"

I nod. "Remember how the hieroglyph for *fountain* could also mean *form* or *figure*? That meant a person. And back in the temple? The Shadowvin didn't ask for the geyser to be transported to Egypt, only me. In fact, this whole scam has been in order to trick me into visiting the pyramids willingly."

"That's right." The Colonel opens up the chest once more. "Once I figured out who you really were, I spent years looking up everything I could find on the Shadowvin, First Wardens, and the fountain of magic." He pulls out a heavy leather-bound book and offers it to me. "This book tells the story of the first recorded fountain, meaning the first person we know of who was made of magic like you. It was a boy named Calibur."

"Calibur." I turn the name over in my thoughts. It seems fitting somehow.

"The records show they tried to drain Calibur when he wasn't willing," adds the Colonel. "Only got a trickle. That was before the First Wardens came along. Those three built the Codex Mechanica, which channels power to the pyramids, where the energy is stored. The records are vague, but something about the First Wardens made Calibur change his mind."

"I saw them in the past," I say. "They were pretty convincing."

"Whatever the First Wardens did," continues the Colonel, "Calibur became a willing part of the ceremony. The First Wardens were able to drain the full force of his magic. So you're right, sugar. Magic is most easily extracted when you agree to the process. That's why the Shadowvin have been trying to lure you to Egypt."

Knox rubs his neck in a slow rhythm before focusing on me again. "What about your trip to the past?" he asks. "You saw a Trilorum in a white cloak. Was that Calibur?"

"I didn't see the person's face." Lines of fear snake their way up my back. Something about this next question sets off my fight-or-flight reflex in a big way. I focus all my attention on the Colonel. "The person I saw in the past, was it Calibur?"

"No, sugar. I'm afraid not."

A chill runs up my back. "Why not?" I have a sneaking suspicion Calibur wasn't available.

*Most likely, Calibur met bad end.* Is that what will happen to me?

"I can see you focusing on Calibur, sugar. He's not important right now." The Colonel offers me the leather book again. "This lists every Trilorum who attended the annual ceremonies."

I hug my elbows. "I don't need to read it now. Just answer my question, please. Tell me what happened to Calibur."

"The person you saw was a Trilorum. He or she attended the ceremony in order to symbolize Calibur."

My eyes widen as I think through the Colonel's words. "What do you mean *symbolize* Calibur?"

The Colonel's silver eyes fill with pity. "According to the records, after Calibur gave his bounty—meaning that after he was willingly drained of his magic—then he died."

The walls of the room seem to press in around me. I can only repeat the Colonel's last word. "Died."

Knox steps before me and cups my face in his hands. "That won't be you, Bry. Never you."

Nodding, I swallow past the lump of terror in my throat. If there's any chance for me to survive, it will because I learn how this whole ceremony thing works. "And what happened to Calibur's magic?"

"According to the records, Calibur's magic was stored in the pyramids. Every year, a little magic was released during the ceremony. In the ritual you saw, the First Wardens tried to let all the remaining magic out and consume it. Instead, the magic made them into the Shadowvin."

For the first time in my life, I can truly guess what was my real fairy tale life template. "The fountain of magic is born once every five thousand years. On the autumn equinox, I give my bounty. And then, I die. That's my real fairy tale life template."

Before me, Knox leans in, pressing his forehead against mine. "No, Bry."

The Colonel resets the book into the wooden chest and slams it shut. "I read everything I could on this subject. As long as the Void and the Shadowvin didn't rise again, I thought you would be safe. That's why I tried to hide you. No one needed to know who you really were. But the Shadowvin *did* rise again. And the equinox takes place tomorrow night. I'm so sorry. Magic created you for a purpose." Heaving out a sigh, the Colonel sits upon the closed chest. "I've done all I could. You're going to have to live out that story now, sugar."

My lower lip quivers with sadness. "I have to die for you all."

Knox pulls me against his chest. "I don't believe that. My wolf doesn't believe that, either. There's something we're missing." Knox looks to the Colonel. "Tell us more about what happened with Bry."

The Colonel gives me a sad smile. "You were my little golden-skinned girl, toddling around down here. The ruby strands of your hair glistened so brightly. And let's not forget your lovely silver wings. They rippled behind you as you ran. I wanted to keep you here with me, but I couldn't hide you forever. Soon, you figured out how to escape this place and roam the grounds." He chuckles. "We had a few close calls, and that's when I realized the sad truth. I had to give you away. If Jules so much as saw you, he'd have figured out what you were: the reincarnation of the fountain."

"And he'd have killed me on the spot."

The Colonel nods. "I couldn't let it happen. I had to change the way you look."

Another realization appears. "You took my wings to change my appearance. It was the same thing that happened to Elle."

The Colonel stares at the floor. "It burned my soul to take your wings. But it had to be done. Changing how you looked required a sacrifice."

"Then you locked up my magic inside my soul with the curse."

"Now that part was easier to do. Once you were disguised and your magic was locked up tight, I told Jules that I'd found a human orphan with magical potential. Jules did the rest. It was his usual thing. He blackmailed your aunties into raising you until you were old enough to be a decent feast. Once you were gone, I couldn't stay here anymore, not alone. I had to go back and face my troubles in the Faerie Lands. I didn't think I was away for long, but you know how time goes in Faerie."

"Hours there can pass, while decades go by here on Earth," I say.

"That's right. It was too late by the time I figured out what had happened. You were almost seventeen years of age, and Jules had started taking notice of you. He'd figured out how powerful you were and wanted to make you one of his special wives." The Colonel shakes his head. "If Jules had realized who you really were, you wouldn't have lasted a day." He scrubs his hands over his face. "Sorry for taking your wings. I couldn't find any other way to hide who you were."

"I understand. You had to change the way I looked."

"Then I chose your life template and named you Bryar Rose."

My gaze lands on the sandbox in the corner. Just like in my dreams, it has wooden versions of the pyramids in it. I gesture toward it. "What was that for?"

"You asked me to conjure it up for you. Every day, you'd tinker with the placement of those silly wooden pyramids. It was like you were trying to figure out how they worked. You wanted me to make a little model of you, but you kept calling yourself the fountain." He nods toward the chest. "I'd found some records about the old geyser, so I made that for you. That way, if you ever called it the fountain in front of a stranger, no one would be the wiser."

"And I drew pictures of pyramids in the sand, all with eyes above them."

"That you did," says the Colonel. "Never could figure out what those meant, either."

Knox rubs his neck. "Eyes and pyramids. I've seen them before, too." He shakes his head, then focuses on me. "What about your trip through time with Scar...any clues there?"

I think back to my trip through time. "There were pyramids in South America as well. They all exploded. Do you have any idea how they work with the fountain?" I shake my head. "I mean, with me?"

"I don't. And I asked you as well. You said you didn't know, and I believed you. My girl never lied to her Poppa." His voice breaks as he speaks those last words.

This man was my Poppa, and I hardly remember a moment of it all. None of this seems real.

"So I have to go to the pyramids tomorrow night. Alone."

Knox pulls me closer against his chest. "No. I'll be with you."

The Colonel nods. "As will I."

This has been a day of terrible realizations, and this next one is the worst. "This is why magic has been killing you," I say to Knox. "It knows I have to die, and the power's trying to protect you."

"No way, Bry." Knox's voice turns rough and fierce. "Our connection is real because I'm a warden and you're my fountain. I've been protecting you all along."

"Then why am I making you sick? How can I be the one who's placing your animal at risk...and mine as well?" All of a sudden, I realize why Colonel Mallory went ahead and put my inner wolf on a time-out. She wouldn't be handling this very well. It was wrong of him to do that without my permission, but he was doing it for the right reasons. Leaning back, I gaze up into Knox's ice-blue eyes. "If magic is protecting you, isn't that what I should do, too? After all, I am magic."

"It's like I've said, Bry. We have to trust in what we feel for each other." He kisses the top of my head. "Think, Bry. You've figured out so much. I know it's in your mind somewhere."

Closing my eyes, I sift through everything I know. My mind keeps returning to images of the Void. "The Void never said he wanted to destroy anything. He just wants to find the fountain. Find me. Maybe he doesn't want to consume my power. Maybe he's here to help me somehow. The Codex Mechanica interacts somehow with the pyramids to drain my power. Meanwhile, my three wardens watch over everything while it happens."

"So we all go to the pyramids tomorrow night," says Knox. "We just need to get the three wardens together."

"Trouble is, we only have two," I say.

A small smile rounds the Colonel's mouth. "Now, I think I can give you some good news at last. You've got the warden of fae magic waiting back in the temple."

For a long moment, I can only stare at the Colonel. Then, the answer appears in my mind's eye. "It's Elle. She's the warden of fairy magic. No wonder all the fae kids at school follow her around."

"Does she know?" asks Knox.

"Heavens no," replies the Colonel. "If that girl knew the full extent of her powers, she'd flatten all of us while just trying to cast even a basic spell." He points at me. "Except you, darlin'."

Knox links his fingers with mine. "We can't wait around here, Bry. We need to get our friends together and leave before the Shadowvin return."

"Agreed," I say. Now that I know who I am and what I need to do, my heart fills with a kind of steely resolve. "We have a day to plan our trip to the pyramids. Let's get started."

Knox brushes a gentle kiss across my lips. "We'll make our own story."

I can't help but smile. "Yeah."

But even as I say that word, part of me counters with another term.

*Maybe.*

# CHAPTER TWENTY-NINE

A few minutes later, Knox and I step back into the temple. The Colonel follows along behind us. Once inside, we find Elle and Alec standing by the geyser and decidedly far away from Reggie, who's grinning manically from ear to ear. Everyone looks up as we enter.

"You okay?" asks Elle.

"Fine," I reply. "We have a lot to talk about."

Alec gestures toward Knox. "And you look like death warmed over."

Unfortunately, Alec is right. Whatever healing magic the Colonel had given all of us, it's already failing my mate. Not that it's polite of Alec to point that out, but that's Alec and Knox for you. If they hugged and said *love you, man* when greeting each other, I wouldn't know what to do.

Alec frowns. "Although technically, Reggie here actually *is* death warmed over, and you look way worse than him. So there's that."

Knox barely lifts his right brow. "Great story, Alec. Thanks for sharing."

I brace myself, waiting for my inner wolf to start up her commentary. She doesn't. Apparently, the stasis spell from the Colonel is still in effect. On the way over here, I'd asked the Colonel when my wolf would awaken. He said the spell is set to protect my animal until I'm ready to explain my status as the fountain to her.

Guess I'm still reeling from the news, because my wolf is most decidedly still in stasis.

Everyone stands around, staring at me with expectant looks on their faces. I realize they're waiting for me to say something here.

*That's right. I went to talk to the Colonel.*

I clear my throat. "Well, everyone. The Colonel spoke with me and Knox." I pause. There's so much to say here; I'm not sure where I can even begin. I decide it's best to start small and lead up to the big stuff. "Elle, I have good news for you."

Reggie moves to lurk over Elle's shoulder. She takes a pointed step away from him. "Tell me we're sending Reggie away."

"Not that. So." I rub my palms together, waiting for the best speech in the world to appear in my mind's eye. It doesn't. "You're the warden of fae magic. How about that?"

Elle's normally animated features fall slack. "I'm *what*?"

"The warden of all fae magic, sugar." The Colonel tips his hat. "Congratulations."

"Don't con a con artist." Elle flips her hair over her shoulder. "How would you know that I'm the warden of fae magic?"

"Did you know Blackaverre and I are good friends?"

Color drains from Elle's face. "No, I didn't."

"We are. In fact, Blackaverre did me a great service. She helped me escape the Faerie Lands when I was entrapped by my enemies. In response, I promised her a boon—one request and no matter what it was, I couldn't say no."

"What boon did she ask for?" Elle's face crumples with confusion, but she rubs her shoulder blade, right where her wings would be attached.

"I think you know, sugar. Blackaverre had a charge who needed to escape from a terrible situation." The Colonel lets out a long breath. "I didn't want to take your wings, but it was the only way you could change the way you look and escape. Just like what happened with Bryar Rose, the spell required a sacrifice to work. I had to take your wings. But there was no other way to hide what you truly were. The whole reason your captors imprisoned you was because they knew you were warden of fae magic. I'm so sorry."

Elle's hands ball into fists. "Why didn't you ever tell me I was the warden? Or Blackaverre, for that matter?"

"Now, that one's on me," says the Colonel. "I made one condition after taking your wings. Magic usually chooses close friends for wardens, or folks that magic knows will become close friends. I forbade Blackaverre from telling you because, well, you might have figured things out with Bry here."

Elle rounds on me. "Figured out what?"

Worry, fear, and excitement battle it out in my nervous system. Once again, I wish I had a great speech at the ready. I don't. I steel my shoulders and meet Elle's gaze straight on. "I'm the fountain."

Elle glances between me and the geyser top. "You don't look like a fountain."

"The fountain isn't a thing," I explain. "It never was."

Knox steps closer to Elle. "The glyph for fountain can also be translated as *geyser* or *form*. That means it can be a person."

Reggie's huge smile grows even larger. "Cheers, tears, hopes and fears. A fountain is born once every five thousand years."

I stare at Reggie in disbelief. "You knew I was the fountain? How long has this been going on?"

"The Colonel told me," says Reggie, for once weirdly lucid. "Ever since, I've been trying to tell you over and over."

"Next time," I say, "you might want to stop with all the cryptic sing-songs and just say stuff."

Reggie lifts his chin. "That's what I get for helping the living."

"When it comes to Reggie," drawls the Colonel, "I needed his help to protect you, so I explained things a little. Plus, I knew he'd never be able to explain what he knew, even if he wanted to." He focuses on Reggie. "Your communication skills are thankfully limited."

Alec goes into one of his men's catalog poses. This is the classic one where he sets his hands in his pockets and looks up. "Wait a mo'. I remember Knox talking about the autumn equinox. That's tomorrow night, isn't it?"

Elle narrows her eyes. "Why do I think I'll hate whatever comes next after that little equinox comment?"

"The fountain—that's me—is supposed to give its bounty on this autumn equinox. And yes, that's tomorrow night." The way I say the words, it's like I'm reading my own obituary.

Elle's voice takes on a dangerous edge. "What happens when all this bounty-giving is over?"

"Red, thread, trials and bread." Reggie goes back to his usual singsong self. "After the ceremony, Bryar Rose will be dead."

*Nice.* Of course, Reggie shares that little piece of information, no trouble.

"Now, now." The Colonel raises his hands so his palms face outward. It's his motion for *calm down.* "Knox here thinks we can try to change that. Maybe there's some way to keep Bryar alive."

Reggie starts singing again. "Red, thread, trials and bread—"

"Can it, Reggie," snarls Knox.

In reply, Reggie closes his mouth with a popping sound.

Elle focuses on me. "What do *you* think happens after the ceremony?"

"I don't know, but…" I swallow hard past the knot of fear in my throat. "I hope I can write my own story. Get a happy ending for all of us." I sneak a glance at Knox. A look of pain flashes in his ice-blue eyes. For once, I know it has nothing to do with whatever magical spell is draining his energy.

It's me.

All this time, Knox has been so patient and solid. He didn't believe magic was punishing him for choosing me. Later, he refused to believe that I had to share the same fate as Calibur, the last fountain.

*We can write our own story.*

With all my heart, I wish I could believe that was the truth. But this isn't like anything else I've ever encountered. Before, my worst challenge was fighting Jules. Sure, the guy was an evil mummy-zombie and had an army, but he was still a person. And the rules of what it meant to be Denarii were pretty clear. Now, I'm facing down all the power of magic—and it's inside me. No one knows how any of this works. I just can't pretend everything will work out right.

Stepping over to Knox's side, I rest my hand on his lower arm. He gives me a small smile and whispers three words: "Our own story."

I force a smile in return. "We'll give it everything we've got." Turning, I focus on Elle and Alec. "Knox and I are going to the pyramids. We'd like your help, but we totally understand if you don't want to."

Alec rolls his eyes. "Like I'd be anywhere else."

"I'm in, too," adds Elle.

"Try, fly, pretty little cry," says Reggie. "This is where I say good-bye." With that, he skips out the door. Nutjob.

One by one, my gaze moves across everyone in the temple. There's Knox, Elle, Alec, and the Colonel. Here, in this place stands everyone in the world that I truly care about. And they're all risking everything to help me. And if we screw up? The totality of magic may get drained from the world, I'll end up dead, and so will everyone's shifter animals. No pressure.

Knox inhales. "I smell your fear." His gaze locks with mine. "Whenever you get afraid, just look for me. I'll always be here."

Stepping closer to Knox, I wrap my arms around his waist and lean into his embrace. This man is everything solid and strong in my life. "Thank you."

Across the room, Alec reaches into his pocket and pulls out a handful of gems. "Let me guess. Now, you need me to transfer everyone over to Egypt and the pyramids."

"Actually," says the Colonel. "I was hoping I might be of service in that regard."

"You'll magically transport us?" asks Alec.

"No, I was more thinking that I'd loan y'all my personal jet and pilot," says the Colonel. "We need to keep up our magical strength up for whatever comes next. Transport spells are a drain."

For some reason, my brain stays stuck on one fact only. "You have a personal jet?" I ask.

The Colonel shrugs. "Why wouldn't I? The pilot is a troll, so be polite. Don't stare."

I'm not a hundred percent clear here. "Do you mean a troll as in ugly?" I ask.

Sure, I'd heard the stories about trolls, but I'd always put those tales in the same category as soul shepherds: super-cool stuff, but until I see one with my own eyes, I wasn't going to believe anything.

"No," says the Colonel slowly. "A troll as in…a troll."

"Right." Elle purses her lips. "So we're flying to Egypt, human style, and our pilot is a troll. I've got time to make a few calls. Maybe I can find us some weapons." She rubs her palms together. Elle loves magical weapons. "There must something that'd be useful in fighting the Void."

"Look, I'm not so sure the Void is a big bad," I say. "All the guy's ever said is that he wants the fountain. The jury is out on that one, in my opinion. He might want to help me."

"What about the Shadowvin?" asks Alec. "Nothing's changed there, right?"

"The Shadowvin are not too big," I reply. "But they're definitely bad." I shiver, remembering how they possessed Knox.

The Colonel waves his hand. "Y'all don't need weapons. Once the ceremony starts, you'll only be dealing with magic."

Elle narrows her eyes. "So we need protection spells."

"With that much magic around," says the Colonel. "No ordinary spells would work." He nods toward Alec and Knox. "That's why the Luxalta wardens gave you two those glyphs of protection on your backs." The Colonel's gaze locks on Elle, and the old fae's silver eyes glisten with regret. "Or in your case, the glyphs were on your wings."

All Elle's excitement about weaponry evaporates. She takes a half step backward. "Oh."

My inner wolf takes this moment to awaken. Within my heart, she yawns and stretches. *"What happened?"* she asks. *"What did I miss?"*

*"The Colonel had some big news. He thought it best to explain it to me first, so he put you in stasis."*

My wolf lowers her head and growls. *"How dare the Colonel put me in stasis?"*

*"I'll explain more on the plane ride."*

*"But I hates planes!"*

*"I get that you're upset, but please don't go Gollum on me now."* When my wolf starts talking like that evil creature from *The Lord of the Rings*, she's so loud, I can hardly think. *"I need to focus on Elle right now."*

My best friend shifts her weight from foot to foot. "No protection glyphs and no other way to guard myself. Thanks for clarifying."

"You won't be without protection." I shoot a pointed stare in the Colonel's direction. "That's why the Colonel is coming along with us, to guard you."

"Sorry, sugar." The Colonel shakes his head. "I've studied the Shadowvin for years. Even with my powers, I only have enough energy to protect one person." The old fae stares pointedly in my direction.

Now, it's sweet that the Colonel wants to guard me, but there are limits to this fatherly-protection situation. Elle is my best friend, and she's risking her life with no one to watch her back. Not acceptable.

"I'm calling in my boon, Colonel."

My inner wolf perks up at this news. *"Boon? What boon?"* she asks.

*"The Colonel gave me a boon,"* I explain in my mind. *"It was his way of apologizing for putting you into stasis without asking permission."*

Across the temple, the Colonel blinks innocently. "Fine. You call in your boon, and I'll play guard."

I haven't been around fae all my life to miss those verbal acrobatics. The Colonel said he could guard one person, but he didn't specify a particular name. "Colonel." I lower my voice to a level that says, *I mean business.* "You're guarding Elle."

"I disagree," says the Colonel. His skin glows with silver light, and he looks more like a supernatural being than ever before.

"When the fountain gives its bounty, no one can be there except the wardens. No one. I refused to accept that for my little one. Do you know how many years I searched for information about the fountain? I made so many sacrifices, cast so many spells, and all so I could protect just one person at the ceremony. No matter what, I wanted to be at your side when the time came. *Your side,* sugar. No one else's."

Elle steps forward. "Look, Bry—"

"Forget it," I say to the Colonel. "I appreciate all you've done, but you're guarding Elle, first and foremost. That is the only way to satisfy the boon."

The Colonel bows slightly and tips his hat. "Agreed at last." He straightens his stance. The frightening fae disappears, and the Colonel becomes all smooth human-like charm once again. "Now, if y'all don't mind, I'll call my pilot and get the flight set. I expect everyone to sleep and eat on the plane. Y'all need to be prepared for what's to come."

Those last three words reverberate through my soul.

*What's to come.*

That's the core of the problem, really. We've no idea what's about to happen. Whatever it is, it might kill me along with everyone I care about. Worry presses in around me, tight as a vise. I force my spine to straighten.

*Remember, you can write our own story.*

The trouble is, I can't even picture a happy ending, let alone make it come to pass.

# CHAPTER THIRTY

Hours later, we're all being driven through Cairo in a stretch Escalade that's the definition of *obnoxiously large*. The vehicle is all black with tinted windows and a license plate that says FAE ONE in Sanskrit. The Colonel's driver is a lanky troll named Idjit. Our chauffeur has an overly large head, beady black eyes, and warts. Lots of warts. His charcoal-colored suit blends in perfectly with his leathery gray skin. Tufts of white hair peep out from under Idjit's black cap.

When it comes to doing his job, Idjit seems to believe that traffic laws apply to everyone but him. He loves to honk at other drivers while blowing past stop signs. Idjit also flew us here in the Colonel's jet. Happily, he's a much more careful pilot than chauffeur.

The divider between the front and back seats rolls down. Idjit keeps driving wildly while simultaneously turning around to address us all. "Welcome to Cairo, ladies and germs." For some reason, Idjit also talks like a bad game show host.

The Colonel waves him off. "Pay attention to the road."

Idjit sniffs through his exceptionally large nose and rolls the divider back up. As we tool through Cairo's narrow streets, I grip the Codex Mechanica tightly in my lap. After so many hours of clinging to this thing, it's like my baby binkie or something. No way am I letting go.

Idjit takes yet another high-speed turn. This time, it's so fast that we tilt onto one set of side wheels. My stomach lurches. The Colonel knocks on the divider.

"Watch it, Idjit," he says. "There's only so much my protection spells can do."

A ceiling speaker crackles to life. "Yes, Colonel. That idea is a winner!" The way Idjit speaks, I keep expecting him to start talking about our lifetime supply of candy bars or something.

Glancing out the car window, I watch the sun dip toward the horizon. It's late afternoon now. Since we didn't use magic to transport, it took us a while to reach Egypt. Soon, the fountain—that would be me—needs to be activated.

But at what time, exactly?

When it came to my wolf, I needed to shift before the sun set on my seventeenth birthday, or I'd lose my inner animal forever. Today is the autumn solstice. Technically, the exact moment of the solstice is a few hours from now. Even so, does the ceremony need to start at that precise moment? The Colonel says the records are rather sketchy on this point, which is frustrating. Every cell in my body is keyed up for this nightmare to be over, one way or another. I don't want to stand around for hours, waiting for the inevitable.

The back of the Escalade is filled with a C-shaped leather couch. The open part of the C is where the door opens. Knox sits beside me. On the rest of the couch lounges Elle, Alec, and the Colonel. Reggie made good on his promise to disappear. We haven't seen him since Italy. *No problems there.* Once or twice, I thought I saw Ty in the crowded Cairo streets, but that could just be my mind playing tricks on me.

Knox rubs my shoulder in a soothing motion. "What are you thinking?"

At these words, my inner wolf prances with delight. On the flight here, I explained everything that happened to her. For some reason, she's completely skipped over the whole *possible death* side of the situation. Instead, she's decided that Knox and I are about to battle side by side, and that will be fun.

Call it wolfy denial.

I can't seem to get her to understand the true danger here, and I'm not sure I want to. In this situation, having my wolf in fight-ready form is much better than her sulking around in Gollum mode.

*"Knox is so wonderful,"* says my wolf. *"Tell him that when the Shadowvin show up, we'll team up and bite them in two."*

*"Sure, I'll tell him. Eventually."*

This is a very fae style of answering, by the way. *Eventually* can mean anything. It's a handy verbal trick that I learned from Elle.

Knox gives my shoulder a gentle squeeze. "Talking to your wolf again?"

I shift in my seat. Getting caught having silent conversations with my wolf? It continues to make me squirm. I hate the thought that I'm staring off into space or something without knowing it. "Yes, we're chatting."

"When you're done, I'd still like to know what's on your mind." He nuzzles my ear, which sends all kinds of warmth and happiness through me. That gets my focus and how.

"I was wondering about the autumn equinox," I say. "When do you think the whole *activating the fountain* stuff will start?"

"Don't forget," adds Elle. "There's also the part about your *giving your bounty*. Do you think they mean handing over paper towels or what?"

Knox and I share a sad look. *No, they mean giving up my powers and possibly my life.*

Elle sucks in a shaky breath. "Oh, I'm so sorry, Bry. I was just trying to make a joke, but that was a bad choice. You're formed from magic, and well…" She scrubs her hands over her face. "I'm making it worse, aren't I?"

Thankfully, Idjit's voice blares over the internal speakers, interrupting the rest of this awkward conversation. "Our estimated time of arrival is…NOW!" With a mechanical whir, our driver rolls down the tinted partition between the front and back seats. Twisting around, Idjit turns to face us, his leathery face creasing into a big smile. "We have arrived and guess what? YOU get a pyramid! And YOU get a pyramid! And YOU get a pyramid!"

"Thank you so much, Idjit," says the Colonel smoothly. "No need to get the door." That's a strategic move on the Colonel's part. If Idjit stepped outside, we'd be swamped with humans taking selfies. And it would be a big crowd, too. If humans get excited about seeing a fae, a troll would send them positively over the moon. Trolls aren't even supposed to exist.

The Colonel opens the car door and steps outside. From where I'm sitting, the false arctic chill of air conditioning is immediately wiped away by the dry heat of Egypt.

"By the way," says the Colonel with a grin. "I figured something out about the ceremony."

My breath catches. "You did? Tell me." The Colonel spent years studying the fountain. If anyone could uncover the ceremony's secrets, it would be man I once called Poppa.

Reaching into his pocket, the Colonel pulls out something, leans forward, and slips the object into my hand. "Keep this close, sugar. It'll help when the time comes."

My skin prickles over with excitement. Can this be the secret I need to survive today's ceremony? Looking down, I scan what the Colonel has given me.

A single American dollar.

I frown. "Why give me this?"

The Colonel sets the stub of a cigar into his teeth. "You'll figure it out when the time's right." With that, he slips out the door.

Elle nudges me gently with her elbow. "Mind if I take a look?"

"No problem." I hand her the dollar. Elle sniffs it, holds it up to the light, and generally checks the thing over. At length, she gives it back.

"It's just a regular old dollar." Elle winces. "Sorry, thought I might have been able to detect something magical on it for you."

I shrug. "It's okay. We both know how the fae are."

"Cryptic at best." Elle slides over to the door, grips the handle, and pauses. "I'd hang onto it, though. You never know."

"That's the truth." I slip the dollar into my pocket and wait for Elle to leave. A long silence follows. Guess no one wants to go yet. Not that I blame them. The air becomes heavy with worry. A sad thought occurs to me.

Knox, Alec, Elle, and me… This may be the last time we all sit together.

All of a sudden, Elle leans over and pulls me into a huge hug. "Love you, girl," she whispers.

"Same to you," I say. All the while, I try to focus on Elle's sweet gesture. Even so, I can't help but notice how her arms tremble with fear. My unflappable friend is totally scared. My heart sinks. I hate that everyone is here—and in serious danger, no less—and it's all because of me. My eyes sting with held-in tears.

"You'll be fine," adds Elle.

"We'll *all* be fine." In my heart, I hope that's the truth.

"See you outside." Elle breaks the hug and slips out of the car. Watching her leave is like watching part of my soul break away. After today, will we ever return to Manhattan? Go to school? Eat too much Ben & Jerry's on a Friday night?

Alec turns to me next. For a guy who's so put together, it's hard to see him all fidgety with worry. "I…um…" He rakes his hand through his golden hair. "Good luck, Bry."

With that, he speeds out the door, and my flight-or-fight response kicks up another notch.

It's just me and Knox.

My mate and I share a gaze that pulls at my heart. I want us to be riding Harleys up to the Adirondacks…running in wolf form under a canopy of trees…or even fighting the principals at West Lake together. Anything but this.

A warm tear rolls down my cheek. "You better leave," I say, my voice husky. "Or I'll never have the strength to get my butt out of this limo."

"I understand." Knox starts to go but waits. "Remember, trust your instincts."

A fresh weight of worry settles into my bones. I know exactly what Knox means here. After all, we've been talking about this nonstop—ever since the Colonel showed me my underground room. I'm about to start a ceremony that somehow drains my magic into the pyramids. There's only one other human fountain who went through this process.

Calibur.

And the ceremony killed him.

Ever since we left Italy, Knox and I have been pressing the Colonel for tidbits he might remember from his research. You never know—any scrap of information might reveal how I could survive this ceremony. In the end, there was nothing new for him to share. That's why the Colonel went through so much trouble to make sure he could be here in the first place. There's no way of knowing what happens next.

In the end, Knox and I just decided that we'd trust our intuition and when the time came, we'd figure something out. After all, why be a shifter if you can't rely on your instincts? Admittedly, this isn't the best plan. It's all we're getting, though. There's no time left to figure out something else.

Knox leans in closer, his ice-blue gaze turning intense. "Let me hear you say it."

I force my voice to stay calm. "I'll trust my instincts. We'll figure something out."

At these words, my inner wolf shivers with fear. *"This is too dangerous. Let's run away with our mate."*

*"No, the safest path is forward,"* I say in my mind. *"That's what the Codex Mechanica told us."*

That final thought seems to calm my wolf a little. Knox already moved nearer to the door. Now, I scooch across the seat to close the distance between us. Knox's hard expression softens as I come near. Reaching forward, I set my palm against his bristled cheek. "We can do this."

"Yeah." Leaning in, Knox brushes the barest kiss across my lips. "You're my mate, Bry. My life. My soul. I love you."

*Whoa.* That's a pretty amazing speech. I wish I could find something as stunning to stay back, but it's been a crazy, emotional day. In the end, it's all I can do to manage a half-smile while I say three words. "Love you, too."

After that, Knox leaves as well.

A sad thought runs through my mind. Was that our last kiss? I shake my head, as if the motion will break loose all these dark imaginings. Straightening my back, I grab the handle, push open the door, and peep outside.

Idjit has driven us to the parking spot near the Pyramid of Menkaure, the smallest of the three main pyramids. Although calling this a *parking spot* is being generous. Technically, Idjit has left the parking area behind and pulled our Escalade up onto the desert itself. The Menkaure Pyramid stands about a quarter-mile away, outlined against a bright blue sky. Human tourists march around, snapping pictures and chatting. The other two pyramids loom farther toward the horizon.

"I wonder if we have to wait for the exact moment of the equinox," I say while slipping out of the Escalade.

Knox opens his mouth, but doesn't get a chance to answer.

The moment my feet reach the desert floor, a giant bubble forms around me. That's sure an attention grabber. The huge orb stands twelve feet tall and just as wide. Red, gold, and silver hues shimmer along the bubble's surface. *Magic.*

The sphere encompasses Knox, Elle, Alec, and the Colonel as well. We all share shocked glances.

"Is this what's supposed to happen?" I ask the Colonel.

"You got me, sugar."

For a moment, the bubble trembles; the colors on its surface start swirling around each other in an intricate dance.

Then it grows.

The bubble swells high into the atmosphere while surging across the Giza Plateau. As it rolls outward, all signs of modern life vanish. Humans disappear. Old trash and new tents melt away to nothing. Scrub brush and paved roads are replaced with rolling desert. Soon, the bubble expands so far, I can't even see its boundaries anymore.

I spin about, taking in my new surroundings. There are no people—only a sheet of desert that's broken by three pyramids. Alec once told me about spells like this one. *Illusion zones.* In reality, no one here was actually magicked out of existence. The spell merely creates the illusion of a separate little world until a certain task is completed. Which gets me thinking.

*This might be how Giza looked thousands of years ago, back when Calibur was the fountain.*

All of a sudden, the ground beneath my feet vibrates madly, throwing me off balance. Knox steps to my side and wraps his arm around me.

"Earthquake," he says.

I scan the horizon and gasp. "It's not an earthquake." I point at the pyramids. "Look."

The three pyramids of Egypt, some of the largest structures ever built, do something I never thought would happen.

They move.

The ground trembles as these huge stone structures shift closer. Dirt, sticks, and rocks kick up around their base as the pyramids slide across the sands, reminding me of massive ships breaking through a strange kind of ocean.

The sight is beautiful.

Magical.

And absolutely terrifying.

The pyramids are moving. *What the WHAT?*

Within seconds, all three pyramids tower around our little group. The structures have altered in other ways as well—they're now all the same height. I turn around in slow circles, taking in the changes around me.

"Do you guys see this, too?" I ask. "Or have I finally lost it?"

"Oh, I see it," says Knox.

Alec steps up. "The glyphs on my back feel like they're on fire." He looks to Knox. "Is that the same with you?"

"Yeah." Knox pulls up his T. Sure enough, the markings on his back are in bright colors. The glyphs have changed as well.

I read the new text on Knox's skin. *"Activate the fountain. Share its bounty."*

Inside my soul, my wolf whines with excitement. *"Why don't the glyphs say to go fight the bad people?"* she asks.

*"Because,"* I reply in my head, *"if we're lucky, the Shadowvin won't show up."*

*"You're no fun,"* huffs my wolf.

I rub my neck and read the glyphs again. "As instructions go, that's not very specific." I focus on Alec. "What about you? What do your glyphs say?"

Alec peels off his sport coat and white button-down. I don't ever think about Alec in a romantic way, but facts are facts. This guy is ripped. For her part, Elle is doing her best not to stare.

And failing miserably.

My best friend will drool soon if she isn't careful.

Alec turns so his back faces me and Knox. "What does it say?" he asks.

"Same thing," replies Knox. *"Activate the fountain. Share its bounty."* Alec pulls on his shirt and jacket. The guy's sport coat is loaded with gemstones, and he rarely takes the thing off for long.

"Well," drawls the Colonel, "that's still not very helpful, is it?"

"Let's try the Codex Mechanica." I look down at the device in my hands. "What do we do next?" The discs whir and spell out the same answer.

*"Activate the fountain. Share its bounty."*

Knox, Alec, Elle, and I all try asking the question dozens of different ways. The Colonel watches, looking very fae as he moves his cigar from one side of his mouth to the other.

He's up to something, that tricky old guy.

Even so, prying secrets out of the Colonel can wait. Instead, we all focus on finding novel ways to ask the Codex Mechanica the same old question: What do we do now? Unfortunately, the answer never changes.

*"Activate the fountain. Share its bounty."*

Eventually, the Codex goes back to what I think of as its resting state: all the discs are set to showing no glyphs at all. In other words, it's saying: *I'm done answering the same question for you people.*

*Time to try something new.*

Elle pats the sweat from her forehead with the back of her hand. "What do we do now? We can't wait here forever."

I stare down at the device in my hands. "The answer has to be in this box, one way or another." I don't say what I'm really thinking, though.

*We simply must find a solution before the Shadowvin arrive. Otherwise, things could get ugly and fast.*

# CHAPTER THIRTY-ONE

I run my fingers across the chipped wood of the Codex Mechanica. There must be a way to use this device to start the ceremony.

*Come on, inspiration. Any time now.*

Knox moves to stand at my side. His body heat and strength envelop me, calming my heart. Inside my soul, my inner wolf beams with delight.

*"Our mate is here,"* she croons. *"He'll help us, you'll see."*

I give Knox the side-eye. "Got anything for me?" Just now, Knox was a total ideas machine, thinking up new ways to ask the same old question to the Codex Mechanica.

"Yeah." Knox wraps his arm over my shoulder. "Close your eyes and clear your mind."

I take in a shaky breath. "Okay." I shut my eyes. Memories appear. There's West Lake, the Denarii League, and finally, my papyri translations. Specific glyphs stand out in my mind. They overlap in a dance of connections.

I open my eyes.

Suddenly, parts of the fountain's story come together for the first time. Time periods align. Tiny scraps become part of a bigger whole. Words pour out of me in a rush. "When magic first came into the world, all the power was undifferentiated. A mess. The First Wardens figured out how to divide it into shifter, fairy, and witch. There were three types of magic. And now? There are three pyramids." I tap the top of the Codex Mechanica. "Plus, three discs are kept inside here. I think all of them work together somehow."

"Three discs, pyramids, and wardens." Alec takes on one of his catalog poses where he sets his fist under his chin and stares at the horizon. "You're on to something."

Knox leans in to kiss my cheek. "My brilliant mate."

"Thank you." My face heats, and it's not from the weather. Meanwhile, my inner wolf prances with joy.

Elle eyes the Codex Mechanica. "So what do we do with it? Asking more questions is out."

"I think I know." Opening up the Codex Mechanica, I pull out the silver disc and turn to Elle. "This is for you."

"Okay." My best friend scoops up the round object from my palm.

After that, I hand the ruby disc to Alec and the golden one to Knox. All the while, the Colonel stands nearby, silent. The nub of his cigar is now lit; a winding trail of smoke curls up from the tip. His expression is the definition of *intense interest*. He's still up to something.

*Oh, well. A mystery for another day. That is, if we live through this one.*

My wardens all hold their respective discs. For a long moment, nothing happens.

A deep voice booms across the desert. "You have given out the discs. Now, the ceremony officially begins." I don't see the speaker yet, but I'd know that basso tone anywhere.

It's the Void.

I exhale. The Void is here. This is a good thing.

The disembodied voice booms again. "Soon, the high sacrifice shall be made."

My insides twist with worry. I liked the whole *starting the ceremony* part, but the *high sacrifice* stuff? We could skip that bit, thank you very much. I look to Knox and wince. "High sacrifice?" I ask.

But before my mate can answer, the world changes once more.

A few minutes ago, the pyramids shifted across the ground. Now, my three wardens move across the sands. This time, they don't walk so much as get magically swooped across the earth while still standing upright. Magic places Elle, Alec, and Knox each before a different pyramid.

After that, I'm moved as well. It's like an invisible rope is tied around my waist, pulling me across the desert until I stand in the center of the three pyramids and wardens, the vortex of it all.

The Void speaks once more. "I call upon the powers of your wardens."

At the Void's words, the device vibrates in my hands. Looking down, I examine the now-empty wooden box in my grasp. Red smoke envelops the device.

*Magic.*

All of a sudden, the edges of the Codex Mechanica snap. Seams crack. Red smoke winds up from the side panels. *Magic.* With a great whoosh, the device disintegrates into dust. Tiny particles cascade through my fingertips.

I suck in a shocked breath. *Who's casting spells on the Codex Mechanica?* I took to the Colonel. "Did you do that?"

"No, sugar. But I've seen castings like that one. Someone preset a spell to destroy the device once the Void said he was calling on your wardens."

Elle frowns. "But we need the Codex Mechanica, right?"

"I don't think so," I say slowly. "The Void said *he* was going to start the ceremony. Maybe we don't need the Codex Mechanica after all."

Even so, a sinking feeling crawls into my bones. If the Codex Mechanica was somehow the key to calling then Void, then destroying it means this will be the last time this particular ceremony ever takes place. There's one group who'd love to make sure that happens. They're same people who have no intention of harvesting magic for anyone but themselves.

The Shadowvin.

I scan my surroundings, looking for any telltale signs of darkness. Nothing but daylight stretches off in every direction. The Shadowvin aren't here. Sadly, the Codex Mechanica isn't around, either. Would be nice to ask it a few questions, actually.

"Don't worry your head, darlin'." The Colonel rolls up his sleeves. "I'm on the watch for them Shadowvin."

"Wardens!" The Void still hasn't physically appeared, but his voice is louder than ever before. The force of his call vibrates through my chest. "Transform!"

Before me, my three wardens now change. Knox's body turns all gold, just like it did back in the principals' office when I thought he looked like an Oscar statue. At the same time, Elle changes so she looks like she's formed entirely of silver. For his part, Alec appears as if he were carved from a single massive ruby. Beams of late afternoon light reflect through his semi-transparent body. I blink hard, not believing what I'm seeing.

*Nope, they're still there...and made entirely of gold, silver, and ruby.*

My wolf finds these changes wonderful. Inside my soul, she romps about in a happy circle. *"Our mate is solid as metal,"* she declares. *"Even better for fighting."*

*"I hope you're right,"* I reply in my mind. This is yet another fae-style answer, though. In all honesty, I have no idea what will happen next. Will any of us be able to move or think, let alone fight?

I turn around in a slow circle. Knox, Alec, and Elle now stand in front of their respective pyramids, a disc gripped in their hands. There's no transfer of magic happening, so even though the Void made his announcement, the ceremony hasn't really kicked into high gear. Handing out the discs helped, but there is something missing.

That's when I remember it.

The dollar the Colonel gave me.

Reaching inside my pocket, I pull out the crumpled bill. On the front, there's the familiar image of George Washington's face. But on the back?

There's a pyramid with an all-seeing eye above its peak. And that's my clue from the Colonel. He handed me this dollar in the limo, saying it would help when the time came.

*Crafty old fae dragon.*

I examine the bill more closely. The image is similar to what Child-Me drew in her sandbox—an all-seeing eye above a pyramid. An idea sparks. What if the discs from the Codex Mechanica aren't just cogs in a machine; they're irises for cosmic eyes?

*Only one way to find out.*

I cup my hand by my mouth. "Your discs from the Codex," I call to my wardens. "Lift them up." To demonstrate, I raise my arms, cupping my hands together as if cradling an invisible disc. A heartbeat later, Alec, Elle, and Knox all hold their respective discs above their heads.

Nothing happens.

Then, all three discs flicker with the barest light. A crimson brightness shines from Alec's orb.

Silver for Elle.

Golden for Knox.

Elle's grip on her disc tightens. "It wants to fly away," she calls. "I can't hold it for much longer."

"That's fine," I say. "You can let go."

Knox glares at the disc in his grasp, then shoots a worried glance in my direction. "You sure it's safe?"

The honest answer here is *no, I have no idea.* Saying that won't help any, though. Instead, I opt for a true but somewhat misleading answer. "The discs need to rise up above the pyramids."

*I think.*

"Here goes," calls Knox. After opening his hands, he lowers his arms. Little by little, Knox's disc—which just began to glow with golden light—rises a few feet into the air.

Excitement pulses through my limbs. *This is really happening.*

After that, Elle and Alec release their discs and lower their arms as well. Just as with Knox, their discs keep glowing while rising a few feet into the air. Elle's disc shines silver; Alec flares red.

Inside my soul, my inner wolf yips in delight. *"We're doing it,"* she croons. *"The ceremony will be over any moment, and then we can leave with our mate."*

*"Not so fast,"* I reply in my mind. *"I'm pretty sure there's a high sacrifice part coming up."*

*"You've been sacrificing all along. Your time, your focus…those things matter, right? This is the ceremony and sacrifice all in one, mark my words."*

In all honesty, I have no idea where my wolf is getting this. There's no way we're skipping the sacrifice stuff. That said, I don't want to rain on my inner's wolf's parade, so I opt for a noncommittal answer.

*"I hope you're right."*

After that, the discs move even higher up their respective pyramids. As the glowing orbs ascend, their brightness intensifies. At the same time, the sides of each pyramid become awash in either red, silver, or golden light. A sense of awe chills my skin. I'm not sure if the ceremony is in full swing yet, but it certainly seems like we're getting closer.

Knox, Elle, and Alec all stand in their places, their bodies stock-still as they watch the discs rise. Only the Colonel moves as he takes the occasional puff from his cigar.

Soon the glowing discs reach the tops of their pyramids. Once there, they hover above the structures' peaks.

I grin from ear to ear. This isn't only working, it's going pretty smoothly. There are no Shadowvin to be seen. Everyone's safe and comfortable. It's taking a little while, but we're working together and figuring things out.

My mind captures an internal image of this moment. How the discs glow above the peaks of the three pyramids. The way each disc shines with a different shade of brightness—red, silver, or gold. *No mistake about it.* Those definitely look like supernatural eyes, just like the back of a dollar bill.

And beneath those glowing discs, my three wardens stand at the base of their pyramids, their bodies seemingly made of crimson, silver, and gold. All around, the desert stretches off in every direction, a sheet of sand under a bright blue sky.

The scene is unexpected.

Overwhelming.

Perfect.

Hope lightens my soul. Maybe there's no connection between the ceremony and Calibur's death. My wolf might even be right about the whole *high sacrifice* thing, too. Come to think of it, this could all have been a big misunderstanding. Perhaps what's happening right now is the entire ceremony, end of story. After all, magic is shining out here from supernatural eyes. Those discs could also be sending power and energy out across the world. My role as fountain could be as simple as standing at this spot, watching it all happen.

Yeah, that's it. *The sacrifice is made.*

Some small part of me warns that this theory's too good to be true. More of me decides that it's about time I had something go easy.

*This could really be it. The whole ceremony-sacrifice might almost be over.*

All of a sudden, the ground vibrates beneath my feet. Great rumbles echo through the air. The pyramids vibrate on their foundations. I blink hard, not believing what I'm seeing.

*Then again, this may not be over* just yet.

The desert floor trembles more violently, kicking sand and dust up into a low cloud that reaches ankle-height. The rumbling turns so loud, it's as if I'm trapped inside a thunderclap. The pyramids shudder on their foundations. I stare in disbelief. These are three massive structures. I never expected them to shift across the desert, let alone move again.

But that's just what they do.

The pyramids rise, their bases lengthening as they soar toward the heavens. Within seconds, the truth becomes clear. These aren't pyramids.

They're obelisks.

Turns out, these famous pyramids are actually just the pointed tops of long spear-like structures that had been buried deep underground. As the three obelisks rise, the eyes above them shine out even more brightly. A zing of shock moves through my nervous system.

*It's official. This is definitely* very far *from over.*

Dark clouds churn head, blotting out any trace of blue sky. Heavy white mist rolls out across the ground. From atop the pyramids—I mean, the obelisks—the colored discs keep radiating their respective shades of red, gold, and silver. As the sky darkens, those colors shine out more brightly.

A massive figure rises up from the white haze that now covers the ground. It's a man made of pale mist, standing over eight feet tall, and with eyes as black as midnight.

*The Void.*

His deep voice echoes across the desert. "Fountain!" he cries. "Where are you? Will you make the high sacrifice?"

My stomach lurches. On reflex, my gaze locks with Knox's. We'd talked about this moment on the plane ride over. What would I do when the Void arrived? In the end, we decided to trust our instincts. And right now, my intuition is saying the Void isn't here to hurt me. All the guy's ever done is stand around and ask for his fountain. Maybe starting the high sacrifice part will be a good thing. You know, the kind of thing that's all happy-joy and no owie-Bry.

Maybe.

A small voice in my head says that's a big *maybe.* The Void could also be here for an all-you-can-eat fountain buffet.

"Fountain!" he cries again. This time, the Void looks genuinely sad. No question about it. I'm trusting my instincts and answering.

I only hope it's the right choice.

Lifting my chin, I face the supernatural creature before me. "You want the fountain and a high sacrifice? Here I am."

Inside my soul, my wolf comes to life. *"Wait a second!"* she cries. *"We should fight this monster, not talk to it."*

*"No, the Void isn't evil. He's here to help us."* But even as I speak the words in my mind, they come out as more of a question than a statement. What do I know about any of this, really?

Inch by inch, the Void floats closer. My heart beats so quickly I'm surprised it doesn't burst. The Void pauses before me, all eight feet of white mist and unclear intent. For a long moment, I wonder if I've just made a huge mistake. Then the Void's dark eyes crinkle with a smile. "Fountain."

I answer his grin with one of my own. "Yes, that's me."

"Dark to light. Day to night. Magic to Void. Make the high sacrifice. Give your bounty." The Void stares at me with his all-black eyes. "Will you do this?"

*In other words, will I sacrifice myself? Tough question, really.*

It's my choice, but I certainly didn't come all this way *not* to finish the ceremony. Still, it's the *give your bounty* part that holds me up. I've heard this phrase before. It's another way of saying: *let us drain the magic from your soul.* A chill of fear runs up my neck.

Calibur gave up his bounty. After that, he died.

The world takes on a dream-like quality. Around the obelisks, the colored beams of light seem to dim. The air smells dry and filled with spices. A realization hits me to the bottom of my soul.

*I want to live.*

My gaze locks with Knox's once more. He looks like some kind of god as he stands before an obelisk, his body seemingly made of gold. Every ounce of my mate's focus stays trained on me while his voice echoes across the desert.

"Trust your instincts, Bry."

I take in a shaky breath. Trust my instincts. *I know what Knox means.* We can figure this out; Knox has my back. Taking in a deep breath, I return my attention once more to the Void. When I speak, my voice is calm and low.

"Yes, I will do this."

The Void nods slowly. "Now you shall all raise your arms. None shall move until the ceremony is over, unless..." He scans the landscape.

Unfortunately, I have a pretty good idea who the Void's looking for. I swallow past the bands of fear constricting my throat. "Unless the Shadowvin arrive," I finish for him.

"Yes." The Void lowers his voice to a growl. "They are evil. They kept me from you."

I open my mouth, ready to say, *hey, that would have been really helpful to share before now,* but I close my mouth instead. Now isn't the time for that particular discussion.

"I do not see them," says the Void. "For now."

An idea sparks. If the Void can be some kind of Shadowvin-detector, that could come in handy. "Can you—" I begin.

"The time for speech is over. We must begin the ceremony proper." The Void raises his own arms into a V shape. I don't will this to happen, but my own arms rise into the same form. The same thing happens with my wardens as well.

"Can't move over here," says Elle.

"Same here," adds Alec.

"Me too," says Knox. "What about you, Bry?"

"I'm stuck too," I reply. "The Void says this has to happen for the ceremony to fully begin."

The Colonel takes another puff from his cigar. "Don't worry, y'all. I got you."

Now that everyone's arms are up, the Void turns back to me. "You will give up your bounty. I will guide you through the ceremony."

A smidgeon of tension eases from my body. "Guidance would be great. How will this work?"

Tendrils of white smoke curl up from the cloud-covered ground. These cords of white mist curl in on themselves, transforming into a familiar shape.

Hieroglyphs.

The symbols read: *"Speak my words to begin. Then I shall focus your power and count down to the end. That is all I can do."* Once I finish reading them, the glyphs vanish.

I scan the faces of my wardens, wondering if anyone else caught the Void's smoky message.

"Did you guys see that?" I ask.

"What?" asks Knox.

"The Void—he spoke to me through smoke glyphs. Says he'll help me through the ceremony."

"Help." Knox narrows his eyes. "Yeah."

Warmth and hope spread through my chest. I could almost hug the Void. That is, if he weren't an eight-foot-tall all-white smoke monster looming right in front of me. Did I mention he's really frightening looking? Well, he is. It's an effort, but I give the Void another shaky smile.

"Thank you," I say.

The Void doesn't reply. Instead, his body melts into a whirlpool of white mist that slowly spins around my feet.

And the magic inside my body goes berserk.

My pulse speeds. Red, gold, and silver…All the strands of power within my soul now come to life. In my mind's eye, these tiny cords dance, whirl, and expand. The rhythm reminds me of the drumroll before an execution. My nerves fray with worry. Those magical threads are preparing to do something.

Trouble is, I have no idea *what.*

Within me, my wolf paces an anxious line. *"What's happening? Is our mate all right?"*

*"Knox is fine,"* I reply. *"Our magic's going a little haywire, that's all."*

With an electric crackle, my inner lines of magic suddenly turn visible, shooting out from me in every direction. My fingertips, chest, and toes—even the strands of my hair—every inch of me erupts with threads of power. Pain tears across my skin. The tiny cords burn me as they move in their wild rush to free. It's agonizing, and more than that, it's wrong. There's too much power and no control. A question echoes through every corner of my soul.

How am I ever going to survive this?

# CHAPTER THIRTY-TWO

More cords of magic burst out from my body: red, silver, and gold. Soon, I'm surrounded in a haze of power and light. As each colored line leaves my skin, it's like I'm being torn apart from the inside out. My inner wolf whimpers in pain. *Poor thing feels the hurt, too.* Although my mind is hazy with agony, I remember the Void's instructions.

*"Speak my words to begin. Then I shall focus your power and count down to the end. That is all I can do."*

At least, the instructions here are clear. *Speak his words.* Thankfully, the Void isn't a big talker, so there's no question what to say here.

Focusing past the tearing pain, I talk in a loud, clear voice. "Dark to light. Day to night. Magic to Void. I give my bounty."

Moments ago, the Void had melted into a swirl of smoke around my feet. Now that cloud rises up until the Void becomes a white column that churns around my entire body, forcing my wild magic to take the same shape. Within seconds, my undifferentiated power becomes a rod of multicolored energy that streams toward the dark clouds. Red, silver, and gold...all of the lines of magic are there and winding together. The hurt slowly vanishes.

Inside my soul, my wolf howls in delight. *"We're so beautiful! Our magic colors the night sky!"* For my part, I'm just glad the pain has vanished. Whatever else the Void does, he focused my power and took the hurt away.

The mists of the Void then lower. Within seconds, he returns to his state as a whirlpool surrounding my feet. Although he Void has receded, my power stays focused in a column. *Good.* The intertwined threads of magic weave through the storm clouds, reminding me of random bright threads in a sheet of dark fabric.

My mind clears. A sense of rightness overtakes me. This is what's supposed to happen. The magic inside me is flowing into the world. Only trouble is, it's still an undifferentiated mess. Worry bunches up my shoulders. *I said the words; isn't the ceremony supposed to start?*

That's when the pyramids change.

The colored eye at the top of each obelisk glows more brightly. Instantly, the mixed-up power inside my column of magic breaks apart, forming three distinct channels: red, silver, and gold. Each channel recedes from the clouds and reenters my body. Closing my eyes, I picture the threads within me. They're no longer a jumble of lines. Instead, the powers are clustered together by type and color.

Three sets of Magicorum.

Three lines of power organized inside me.

My mouth falls open with surprise. I knew that the pyramids would somehow change undifferentiated power into each of the three types of Magicorum. Somehow, I didn't expect that would happen inside my soul.

Deep rumbles fill the air, the noise as strong as the beating of a thousand kettle drums. The ground vibrates. Something's happening under the earth once more. Little by little, the obelisk behind Alec moves once more.

It spins.

Alec tries to turn his head but can't. "Guys, what's going on behind me?" he asks.

"Your obelisk is turning around," answers Elle.

Alec's features turn slack with shock. "Because of course it is."

"The power must move out of me in stages," I explain. "I'm guessing you're first."

Alec frowns. "Is it going to hurt, you think?"

"I don't—" Before I get a chance to answer, lines of red power burst out of my rib cage, wind down my arm, and then zoom off my fingertips.

After that, they go straight toward Alec.

More and more tiny threads of my crimson power whip off my hand, cross the desert, and then connect with Alec's fingers. From there, the red threads wind across his arm and chest.

Inside my soul, my wolf growls. *"Is our friend safe?"*

This time, I'm not so sure of the answer. "Alec," I call. "Are you all right?"

"Surprisingly fine," he replies.

Then, line after line of crimson power leaves Alec's free hand and slams into the obelisk behind him. Now, there's a clear arc of power that starts with me, crosses Alec's arm and chest, and then zooms into the structure behind him. Great bolts of lightning-style magic then wind around the length of the obelisk, covering it entirely in cords of red light.

*Wow. Just wow.*

A memory appears. My aunties once took me on a tour of a power plant in New Jersey. I suppose it was their way of trying to act parental, considering how they rarely allowed me to leave the penthouse. When I was there, I saw rows of metal rods lined up inside the power plant. The bars gleamed with sparks as electric energy coiled up and down their lengths.

That's what these obelisks remind me of now: supernatural rods that conduct not electricity, but magic. Taking in the scene, my sense of rightness deepens.

*Now, this is what's supposed to happen.*

This obelisk will store the power of witch and warlock magic. It's draining the red power from me. I remember the glyphs I translated from the *Book of Isis*. They'd always list witch-warlock power, then fairy, and then shifter. That wasn't a coincidence. The chain of events becomes even clearer in my mind.

First, my red power will drain.

Then fairy energy will leave me.

And finally shifter magic will go.

I shiver, trying not to think about what that will mean.

My death.

Definitely.

Maybe.

I shake my head.

*No dark thoughts now, Bry. You'll trust your instincts and figure it out.*

I force myself to focus on what this ceremony will deliver. Once today is done, the annual ceremony of the wardens will release a little more Magicorum energy from the obelisks into the world. This very place will become the new Fountain of Youth, driving magic and power for a new age.

*What a legacy.*

Tendrils of smoke rise up from the swirling haze by my feet. It's the Void, trying to communicate again. The misty cords take the shape of a single hieroglyph.

*"Ten."*

Understanding fills my mind. The Void said he would count-down to the end of the ceremony. That's exactly what he's doing now. Like before, the ceremony will drain each warden in turn, and now the clock is officially ticking. My heart lurches in my chest.

*Please, let this be a countdown to my future legacy, not just the end of my current life.*

Power continues to flow into Alec and his obelisk. At the same time, thinner lines of colored magic connect me to Elle and Knox, keeping them in place and ready for their turn. Together, my wardens are guarding the fountain's power.

No, not guarding.

Now that the ceremony is in action, I see what the phrase *guarding the fountain* really means. My wardens are here to channel my energy into the safety of the correct pyramid. All the while, the Colonel watches from the sidelines, grinning from ear to ear.

A sense of peace and calm infuses my soul. This is what I was born to do—bring magic back into the world. As every stand of energy leaves my body, it's as if another burden lifts from my soul. Alec's pyramid glows more brightly as more arcs of red power zoom around and inside it.

A name appears in my mind's eye: Calibur. He was the first recorded fountain, and going through this ceremony was enough to kill him. Would it kill me as well? It doesn't feel like it; at least, not at this moment.

The next hieroglyph appears before me.

*"Nine."*

Fresh waves of red power stream up the obelisk behind Alec. Only eight more numbers and this ceremony is over. My body feels so light and joyful, it's as if I could float off the ground. Things are going so smoothly, it all seems too good to be true.

And then, it is.

Suddenly, lines of darkness drip down Alec's obelisk. The flow of crimson power and magic slows. My energy needs to go into my wardens and then into the obelisks. Now, it's stuck. The power is entering my wardens, but it isn't leaving to get stored in the obelisk behind them. A chill of terror seeps into my bones. My wardens lose their look of calm. Like me, they all gaze about in terror.

The Shadowvin are coming.

Even worse, Elle isn't protected by glyphs, not like Alec and Knox. Sure, the Colonel has agreed to defend her, but suddenly, that seems like a thin plan. These are three Shadowvin we're talking about here. Plus, the Colonel's magic hasn't been working perfectly these days. Back in New York, he needed my help to just fight some pixies in our kitchen. Why did I think he could singlehandedly fight a trio of super-ghosts on demand? Every nerve ending in my body goes on alert.

This is such as bad idea.

Inside my soul, my wolf howls with fear. *"Elle is our friend. We must defend her!"*

On reflex, I try to race over to my best friend. Still, I can't do more than flinch. Magic keeps my body locked in place. Panic zings through my nervous system. I scan Alec, Knox, and Elle. All three of them are straining to move as well. None of them are able to do more than twitch.

*Oh, no.*

Colonel Mallory steps closer to Elle, his arms raised. Silver clouds of fae magic swirl around his hands.

"Hang on," he calls to Elle. "I got you, sugar."

My inner wolf flattens her ears and growls. *"Our dear friend,"* she whispers. *"We must fight for her."*

*"Trying."* I wrench my muscles with more force, but I still can't move.

Darkness seeps down each of the obelisks. A moment later, the three Shadowvin materialize, one at the base of each structure. Moving in unison, the tall, transparent figures swoop across the sands, pausing to stand in a small cluster right before my best friend. Fresh adrenaline pumps through me. I twist and writhe harder, but it's no use. Moving simply isn't possible.

The Shadowvin close in on Elle. Terror lights up my dear friend's eyes. I focus on the Colonel, who's been building up his magic all this time.

"Do it, now!" I cry. "Help Elle!"

The Colonel releases the fairy dust from his arms. A haze of silver power flies off his hands. As the magic speeds through the air, the dust takes the form of long rods. These misty bolts slam into the desert around the Shadowvin, forming a makeshift prison. More bars cross the top, boxing them in. I scan Alec's obelisk. Even though the Shadowvin are locked up, his obelisk is still dark.

The power transfer is stalled out.

So is the ceremony.

Not good.

The Colonel turns to me, his face contorted with strain. "My magic isn't working too well for me today, sugar. I can't hold this for very long. Y'all better hurry."

"On it," I say.

The Shadowvin slam against the bars of their prison, but they can't escape. Not yet, anyway. Unfortunately, the Colonel is already looking pale and wobbly. He won't last much longer. Unlike the situation with the pixies back home, I can't help the Colonel with extra power. That said, there is still something I can do.

Get this ceremony over as quickly as possible.

The ceremony began by moving power from me into Alec's obelisk. That's the best place to start. Closing my eyes, I reach into my soul, picturing the many stands of red magic inside me. With all my focus, I will the witch and warlock power to flow out of my deepest being. A burst of crimson light shines as fresh magic zooms off my fingertips, moving into Alec and then his pyramid.

Sweat lines the Colonel's brow. His entire body trembles with effort. I've seen this before. Even though the containment spell has left the Colonel's hands, he still needs to send in fresh energy in order to keep it going.

That won't be easy.

I inspect the flow of energy from Alec to his obelisk. It's not the steady flow that happened a minute ago, though. A sickly thread of power winds from Alec's fingertips into the structure behind him. Thanks to the Shadowvin, all the obelisks are dark; none of them can accept my power and light. At this rate, the first phase of the ceremony won't finish anytime soon.

We're running out of time.

With a moan, the Colonel crumples onto his knees. The bars of the supernatural prison start to fade. My heart tumbles.

The Shadowvin won't be confined much longer.

The three dark spirits stare at Elle with hungry eyes. There's no question in my mind what they wish to do: possess her like they did Knox. And since she doesn't have glyphs? That possession might very well be permanent.

I redouble my efforts, pulling on more strands of witch and warlock magic inside me. We simply have to finish the ceremony before the Colonel's containment spell collapses. Although I pull more power, the Shadowvin are still somehow dampening the connection from Alec to his darkened obelisk. I can't drain my other kinds of magic until witch-warlock is gone. Plus, the Void hasn't called out another number. Every cell in my body feels weighed down with lead.

The ceremony still isn't going fast enough.

Moving in unison, the Shadowvin attack the prison around them. Their misty forms howl with rage. The air turns thick with the force of their counter-spells. It's too much. Groaning, the Colonel crumples onto his side. From this far away, I can't even tell if he's still breathing.

"Colonel!" I cry. "Are you all right?"

No response.

The silver prison surrounding the Shadowvin disappears entirely. A jolt of worry moves up my spine. There's no time to worry about the Colonel now.

The Shadowvin are free.

I try to move. Again, all I can manage is to twitch my limbs. I call down to the power that swirls about my feet.

"Void, can you help us?"

The answer appears in smoke hieroglyphs. *"Speak my words to begin. Then I shall focus your power and count down to the end. That is all I can do."*

*In other words, I'm on my own.*

With three Shadowvin.

And Elle stands unprotected.

Things just went from bad to terrible.

# CHAPTER THIRTY-THREE

Moving fast as a heartbeat, all three Shadowvin fly at Elle. With a burst of dark mist, the trio of dark forms zooms straight into her chest. Bands of fear tighten around my throat. I watch in horror as Elle, in her all-silver figure form, twists against the overlapping outlines of three gray ghosts.

*No, no, no.*

I saw this happen once before with Knox. Back then, the Shadowvin possessed my mate. Now these evil creatures are trying to do the same thing to my best friend. Like Knox, she's fighting back. But for how long? Elle doesn't have the protection glyphs Knox does.

"You can do this!" I cry. "Keep fighting!"

Elle's face contorts in pain and terror. A scream tears from her mouth, the sound ripping through my soul.

*Please. Somehow, let Elle fight this possession.*

After that, Elle stills. Every cell in my body goes on alert. In some ways, things have returned to how the ceremony should be. Elle still has her arms raised, so they keep making the proper V shape as before.

But something has changed as well.

Elle's eyes have transformed into a swirling shade of gray. No irises. No whites. My heart cracks. This is what happened before to Knox.

Swirling gray eyes.

Unnatural stillness.

Possession.

When Elle next speaks, her voice sounds like dozens of old crones combined into one. "You should have agreed willingly, Bryar Rose."

I can only manage one word. "No."

The lines of Alec's ruby face tighten with worry. "Elle!"

Knox's all-golden gaze stays locked in my direction. His mouth pulls down into a scowl. My mate doesn't say a word, but I know what he's thinking. This is really bad.

Inside my soul, my inner animal whimpers with fear. *"We need to help our friend."*

I try to move. I still can't even so much as twitch, let alone race off anywhere. When I answer my wolf, all the sadness in the world echoes through my soul. *"It's too late for that now."*

But if there's one good thing about this situation, it's that the Void said he'd help me though the ceremony. Maybe he needed a more serious threat to rally. I speak to the swirling mists around my feet.

"Need some ideas, here." I say to the Void. "I've got a possessed warden on my hands."

Glyphs rise up from the mist: *"Speak my words to begin. I shall focus your power and count down to the end. That is all I can do."*

"All you can do? Really?" I can't help the note of desperation in my voice.

The same response appears.

*Thanks for nothing.*

Instead, I scan my wardens, looking for ideas. Knox appears grim as he tries to break free and move. Alec keeps staring at Elle, his eyes wide with desperation. And my best friend?

Shadowvin-Elle gives me an inhumanly large grin.

*Whoa.*

Even when Elle became all silver, she was still my best friend. Her inner energy stayed joyful. Familiar. Heartening. Now, every movement from this possessed figure seems calculated, chilly, and downright terrifying.

"I designed the Codex Mechanica," says Shadowvin-Elle in her many voices. "And these pyramids, too."

"You did?" I ask. "I thought the First Wardens did that…and I believe there were three of you."

"Three?" asks Shadowvin-Elle. "No, there's only ever really been one of us with any plan or power. Me."

With that, I know one thing for certain. The other Shadowvin may be part of possessing my best friend, but only one is in charge.

Quetzali is running the show. Or I should say, Quetzali-Elle.

"You found my Codex Mechanica," says Quetzali-Elle. Her gaze flicks to the beaming spheres atop the obelisks. "After I became a Shadowvin, I loaded those discs with special spells that engage once you start the ceremony. I was the one who loaded the spell to make the Codex Mechanica self-destruct. I didn't want you asking questions and discovering my schemes."

My heart sinks. I remember how the Codex Mechanica fell apart. It sure seemed suspicious at the time. Guess that was right.

"Do you have any idea how many centuries it took to cast all the spells for today?" asks Quetzali-Elle. "Or how hard it is to speak an effective incantation without a physical form?" She sighs. Evidently, it isn't necessary for me to answer any of these questions. Quetzali-Elle keeps right on talking. "I had to find women who looked as I did when I was alive and then possess them. It was the best way to fool their magic into working for me. Such an exhausting process."

My skin prickles over with gooseflesh as I realize what her words mean. "The many voices inside you…" I shake my head, not believing anyone could be so horrible. "When you possessed those women, you took on their souls somehow. They're imprisoned within you."

Quetzali-Elle lifts her chin. "It wasn't only me. All three of the First Wardens did the same. Now all of us speak with many voices." She sighs once more. "I made so many sacrifices for this day. I couldn't take any chances. Why do you think I led you all here, step by step?"

Her words ring through my mind. *I led you all here.* Translating the papyri…Finding the Codex Mechanica…And discovering the truth of my identity in Italy. Quetzali planned all this from the start, and I played right into her schemes.

A realization settles into my bones, heavy as granite. Everyone I love is in this dangerous spot, and it's all because of me. The Colonel lies collapsed nearby, unmoving and possibly dead. My mate groans with pain as he tries to break free and fight. Alec stands stock-still as he watches Elle, his gemstone face frozen in a look of torment.

"Yes," says Quetzali-Elle slowly. "I was the one who led you all here, and now I can finally cast the final part of the spell set. At last, I will link the magic I placed on the discs with the ones that I so painstakingly loaded in the pyramids." She looks to the top of the obelisks. Lowering her head, Quetzali-Elle murmurs a low string of words.

Another incantation.

My breath catches. New magic from Quetzali-Elle? *Talk about your red flags.* Atop the pyramids, the trio of discs shines more brightly. Fast as lightning, the three discs lower until they hover chest-height, forming a direct line between me and Quetzali-Elle.

What happens next takes place so quickly, there isn't time to react, even for those of us with shifter reflexes. The cords of power between me and Alec vanish. I'm now a lone figure in the center of this little scene, no magic pouring out of me at all.

In other words, I'm a sitting duck.

Magic comes alive inside my soul, rattling and ready to be released. Meanwhile, the discs stay hovering at shoulder-height, about ten feet apart. It strikes me that they are forming a crazy sort of *connect the dots* between me and Quetzali-Elle.

In a single burst of light, my magic breaks free. Lines of silver, golden, and red power zoom off my body, move across the line of discs, and rocket straight into Quetzali-Elle. Her grin becomes wider, which I didn't think was possible.

Quetzali-Elle smiles as she realizes her dream: stealing all my power.

And she's making my life into a new kind of nightmare.

When I chose to be drained of magic, it didn't hurt at all. But having power dragged out of me? It's as if I'm being torn apart, cell by cell. A memory flashes through my mind's eye. I'm back in my dreams from New York with the Shadowvin. Before, they had been pressuring me to vow that I'd help them. To convince me, they'd pulled some wispy lines of magic from my soul.

That hurt like hell.

This is so much worse.

My only consolation? Knox and Alec are now free. Even better, they look like regular humans again. No more all-gold or gemstone bodies.

Inside my soul, my wolf whimpers. *"Our mate can escape now. He must run, even if we can't."*

*"Agreed,"* I reply in my mind.

Knox races across the desert, grips my hand, and tries to pull me out of my connection with the discs and Quetzali-Elle. Lines of power snap free from our mainline link and zap right into my mate. Long fingers of silver, gold, and red power knife into Knox. The power of those magical strands sends my mate flying across the desert. Fear constricts in my throat while my body trembles with pain.

"You need to run," I grit out through the hurt. "Take the Colonel and Alec with you."

"Not happening," says Knox.

Instead, my mate races back up to me. His T-shirt now has burn holes in it, the magic was so fierce. He paces a line nearby, his face drawn into a scowl. Alec waits behind him. Quetzali-Elle watches the scene with a look of pure delight.

"I got a way to fix this," says Knox. My mate turns to Alec. "Remember that time I killed forty Denarii in Tel Aviv?"

Alec's gaze stays locked with Quetzali-Elle. "What?" he says absently.

"The Denarii. Tel Aviv. They'd gotten some spell where they'd turned into ghosts," says Knox. "You healed me. We took them down. Remember?"

"Ghosts?"

Knox stalks closer to Alec. "Get your head in the game, Mister Wizard. Here's this plan." Knox whispers something to Alec. I can't hear what he's saying, but I'm hoping it's a plan for how to run for the hills. This situation's too risky for heroics. *They have to run!*

"Simple Bryar Rose," says Quetzali-Elle in her many voices. "I can tell what you're thinking. It won't work, though. It doesn't matter if your little friends scurry away; I won't let them get far." She shakes her head slowly. "Ah, if only you'd listened to me. You could have died like Calibur. His end was swift and pleasant. Yours will be extremely painful. Of course, Calibur died when I was young and foolish. I loaded his power into obelisks instead of trying to keep it for myself."

For a moment, Quetzali-Elle trembles. I see the other Shadowvin flicker inside her. There's an old lady with yellow skin the color of dried-out cornhusks and a large man with muscles on top of his muscles. Those are the same wardens I saw with her from my trip through time.

"Having trouble with your friends?" I ask.

"No," snarls Quetzali-Elle. She taps the center of her chest; it's as if she's poking the other Shadowvin inside her. "Of course, I'm gathering power for you two as well. Now be quiet and let me cast." Lowering her head, Quetzali-Elle murmurs another spell. More strands of magic are torn from my soul. Red, silver, and golden— all kinds of lines of power zoom along the connection between me and Quetzali-Elle. Agony burns through my limbs.

My knees buckle, but I don't fall over. The line of energy between me and Quetzali-Elle keeps me pinned to the spot, like an insect on a pin.

"Not much longer. I've almost drained you." Quetzali-Elle focuses at the spinning clouds around my feet. "Did you hear that, Void? I'm draining your precious fountain." She cups her hand at her ear in a motion of mock-listening. "What?" She laughs too loudly. "You can't even count down the ceremony? Poor little monster. My spell locks you up as well. How brilliant of me."

My eyes widen with surprise. *She trapped the Void, too?* It's not like the guy was super-useful after the ceremony started, but locking him up now? That's just cruel.

Quetzali-Elle focuses on me again. "Once I have all your power, I can take human form again." She slowly licks her lips, like the thought is a delicious one. "Soon, I'll break this cursed existence as a shadow creature."

White spots dance in my vision as I try to process her words. Quetzali and all the wardens lost their bodies when they tried to drain magic for themselves. That was the ceremony I saw in the past. At the time, magic punished them by blowing up the pyramids and turning the three wardens into Shadowvin. Now Quetzali wants her body back, as well as control over massive amounts of magic.

Sadly, it looks like she'll get it.

More lines of power are ripped from my soul. It's like I'm being shredded from the inside out. My eyelids flutter closed. A single thought overtakes my mind.

*This is what it's like to die.*

Across the desert, the Colonel stands up once more. I'd be excited for that fact, but the old fae shouldn't be helping me now. I'd rather the Colonel ran for his life.

"Hello, sugar plum," says the Colonel to Quetzali-Elle. He even adds in a little wave. "Guess who cast a healing spell on me? My good friend, the little wizard." The Colonel gives Alec an approving nod before turning to Quetzali-Elle. "We've got business, you and me."

"I've taken the body of a friend of yours," says Quetzali-Elle. "You won't hurt me."

"Don't worry your ugly little head about Elle. I can take care of you and keep her safe." The Colonel chuckles. "I'm so not done with you." He hitches his thumb at Knox and Alec. "Neither are they."

I force myself to focus through the hurt. Alec, Knox, and the Colonel have teamed up; now they're trying to save me and Elle. This is a terrible idea. When I speak again, my voice is a hoarse whisper. "Please. Go."

The Colonel shakes his head. "Not this time, darlin'." The old fae lifts his arms. Lines of silver magic curl around his hands. A heartbeat later, the Colonel sends power shooting into Quetzali-Elle. At the same time, Alec raises a massive ruby in his fist. Crimson light peeps out through his fingers. No question what that means.

Alec is about to cast a spell, too.

This is too much. I try to warn them all one last time, but the words get stuck in my throat.

Across the desert, Alec rounds on Quetzali-Elle. "You want physical form?" he asks. "You got it!"

Lines of power and magic shoot out from both the Colonel and Alec. The energy winds around Quetzali-Elle. A moment later, there's no longer one figure standing across from me.

There are four.

Elle, Quetzali, and the other two wardens.

Emotions battle it out inside my nervous system. However, I'm also shivering with worry. A big battle is coming. All of them are passed out, stunned by the spell.

My lines of magic vanish. No more power rushes out from my soul to Quetzali-Elle. For a moment, the three discs hover in the air, only there is no mainline of energy to keep them in place. After that, they drop to the desert floor, all signs of light and power gone from their circular forms. Around my feet, the mists of the Void disappear.

With that, it's official.

All signs of the ceremony have stopped.

I feel like a marionette whose strings have been cut. Without magic to hold me up, I collapse onto my knees.

I'm proud of my mate for coming up with a plan to fight ghosts who want physical form. Knox had Alec give them exactly what they want: a body. Only, they forgot how vulnerable you are in a physical form. Even so, these are powerful wardens, no matter what shape they take. I doubt those Shadowvin will stay passed out for long. Are any of us ready for this?

Alec's obelisk stops spinning. Silence falls over the desert. The air crackles with magic. The faint scent of ozone reaches me, like the calm before lightning. Me, my wardens, and the Colonel... none of us move.

"My wolf," says Knox. "He's going crazy. Something's coming."

The Colonel turns to me. "That Quetzali pulled out some of your magic. What happened to it all?"

I hug my elbows. "I'm not sure, there—"

All of a sudden, colored lights burst around me: red, gold, and silver. Crackling sounds fill the air. The scent of ozone turns intense. Lines of power materialize around me. Thousands of threads of magic wind into my body, appearing in the nearby air and then zigzagging into my skin like reverse bolts of lightning. Pain bursts through my limbs—it's like countless knives are cutting into me at once.

Then it ends.

I close my eyes, seeing the magic once again inside me soul. "My powers are all back."

Alec nods. "When we knocked her out, we must have ruined her spell."

"Couldn't happen to a nicer creep," says Elle.

Speaking of that creep, I scan Quetzali. She's lying on her back, still passed out on the desert floor. Her body seems to vibrate, and I quickly realize why—she's not one person.

While she was a Shadowvin, Quetzali spoke with many voices. Now, her physical form is morphing through a dozen fae women at once. Sadness weighs down my bones.

Those are all the spirits of the women Quetzali possessed in order to cast her spells.

Beside Quetzali, there lie her two other wardens: the old woman and the hulking shifter. None of them look like a single entity. Instead, they're a blur of faces and bodies. *Wow.*

Alec leans over Elle, who's passed out on the desert floor, another gemstone is gripped in his palm. My bet? Alec is about to casting a healing spell on my best friend. He starts to murmur something, but there's no time to find out what.

Quetzali has risen to stand.

"You have ruined nothing!" screams Quetzali. "I'll destroy your power, and then I'll destroy you!" She turns to Alec and raises her arms. Dozens of rubies fly out of his pockets and right into Quetzali's hands. They burn up on impact, crimson light flickering to the desert floor like burning embers.

"Hey," cries, Alec. "Those were mine." He checks his pocket. "Only one left now."

"Alec?" Elle blinks her eyes open. "What happened?" Alec goes back to helping my best friend, which leaves Quetzali with me and the Colonel, considering how the other wardens are still passed out.

We can take her.

Hopefully.

Quetzali lifts her arms, calling on her fae power. Silver tendrils of energy gather around her hands.

But my mate is ready for her. Knox leaps into the air. When he lands again, he's in his full wolf form: a massive black beast with paws as large as saucers and canines longer than my forearm. He tears across the desert, making right for Quetzali.

Good choice.

Before Quetzali can finish her spell, Knox bulldozes right into her. The silver tendrils shoot across the desert floor and wink out one by one. Quetzali lies on her side, immobile.

*One evil warden down, two more to go.*

Inside my soul, my wolf stirs. *"Go after the other evil wardens,"* she growls. *"Fight!"*

Sometimes, I really love my inner wolf.

"*On it,*" I reply.

Across the desert, Quetzali's shifter warden morphs into a massive bear. Or, to be accurate, a conglomerate of bears, all of them overlapping. Yow, does that ever look strange. With a great growl, the bear races off in my direction.

*No time to lose.*

I try to shift into my wolf form, but it isn't easy. I'm tired, thirsty, and stuck in a hot-as-hell desert. Every muscle in my body feels limp as a wet noodle.

My inner wolf pants with effort. "*I need a little time,*" she says. "*The shift isn't easy.*"

"*No worries,*" I reply in my mind. "*I have a plan.*" Once again, that's definitely a fae-style answer on my part. My only plan right now is to come up with a plan.

Still, there's no way I'm giving up. I refocus my thoughts on starting to shift just as the massive black bear lands in front of me.

Gasping, I fall backward. The bear rears on its hind legs, towering over me. Tilting back its head, the animal lets out the mother of all roars.

Honestly? I might pee my pants just a little bit. That is one terrifying bear.

The bear lowers itself onto its front legs. I may not be able to shift, but my shifter reflexes kick in, which is a good start. Just before the bear swats my skull, I roll out of the way. Instead, the bear's massive front claws land beside my head with a mighty scrape. I slowly crawl backward, trying to get out of its line of vision without triggering the animal's predator reflex.

"*I think I can do it,*" says my wolf. Her voice wobbles with strain. "*Is it working?*"

My skin ripples with fur. "*A little.*"

The bear lumbers forward, swiping at me with each step. Every one of its claws stretches as long as my finger, and they all seem to move in slow motion toward my face. Although I try to move out of its path, I can't seem to go fast enough.

*Ugh. Having my nose torn off by a massive bear during today's ceremony...I have to admit, I did not see this coming.*

The claws are a breath away from my cheek when Wolf-Knox bites into the bear's limb, tearing the animal away from me. At the same time, the Colonel and Elle stand nearby, their arms raised. Mists of silver power wind around their hands.

"Now!" cries the Colonel.

Both fae release their power. A mist of silver magic hurtles toward the bear, who's now fighting Wolf-Knox. My mate leaps onto the bear's back and chomps down hard on its neck. The Colonel and Elle's spell combines in the air to take the shape of what looks like a silver missile. The torpedo slams into the bear's chest.

BOOM! The missile explodes.

The bear bursts into a silvery mist. From the center of the haze, there appears the tall form of the Shadowvin. A long screech echoes through the air as the shifter ghost fades from view.

The Colonel straightens his hat. "And that is how you kill yourself a Shadowvin."

Wolf-Knox prances up to my side, the silver disc held firmly in his teeth. I pull it from his jaws and lean in to his muzzle. "That was amazing," I say.

"We can celebrate later," replies Wolf-Knox with a wink. "The evil witch warden is waking up."

Scanning the nearby sands, my heart sinks. "Actually," I say. "She's wide awake."

The witch warden stands nearby. Like the Quetzali and the bear shifter, this warden isn't so much one person as an amalgam of many old witches who are overlapping each other.

More innocents that she possessed and killed.

And more of a reason to fight her now.

"I got this," cries Alec. He raises his fist. His last gemstone glows inside his hand. Lowering his arm, Alec releases a fireball that hurtles at the evil witch. Red mist surrounds Quetzali's last warden. The haze vanishes, and a red shield appears in its place. Alec's fireball hits its mark, but the evil witch crouches behind the shield, protected.

Alec reaches into his pocket. "Damn, that Quetzali destroyed the rest of my gems. I'm out."

The witch lifts her arm out from behind her shield, revealing a ball of crimson power in her hand.

"Watch out, Alec," I call. "She's about to cast a spell."

"No!" cries Elle. My best friend instantly conjures a much larger ball of silver power and sends it hurtling toward the evil warden. "Leave him alone!" she cries.

Like what happened with the bear, Elle's silver sphere lands squarely in the witch's chest, where it also explodes.

BOOM!

Yellow goop and cornhusks go flying everywhere.

But mostly on Alec.

Like with the bear, the witch may be gone, but her Shadowvin form remains to screech its undead head off as it finally disappears.

Good riddance.

Alec turns to us, his neat khaki pants and sport coat now dripping with goo and cornhusks. "How come I got the sloppy spell? You evaporated that bear guy."

Elle stares at her feet. "I got nervous. You were in danger."

The Colonel sets his hand on Elle's shoulder. "That's why I suggest the missile shape. Less mess, even when you're in a hurry." He gives her shoulder a little squeeze. "I'll teach you, sugar."

Fact: the Colonel may be cryptic and terrible with showing up on time, but he's a really great dad figure.

I scan the pile of slop that was once the witch warden. A little part of me feels bad that I just thought of a living being as *slop*, but not too bad. Those Shadowvin tried to kill me and possess people I love. They also possessed a ton of innocent folks who should never have gotten caught up in all this.

So, *sorry not sorry.*

Alec strides over to where I stand beside Elle, Knox, and the Colonel. "Before we do any more crazy stuff, I have one request." Alec rakes his hand through his gloppy hair. "I need to cast me a cleaning spell."

"Not so fast," says Knox. "The sooner this is over, the safer things are for Bryar Rose. Your cleaning spells take forever." I'm happy to report that Knox is now shifted back into his human form and wearing black leather pants and a dark T-shirt. On the plane ride over, the Colonel figured out how to make Knox an unshreddable outfit like mine.

Yet another benefit of having that old dragon shifter in my life.

Speaking of the Colonel, he folds his arms over his chest. "I concur with the wolf boy. Let's get on with things."

Alec lets out a dramatic sigh. "Fine." He looks to me. "How do we do this?"

I shrug. "I'm thinking I say the words I used before and hope for the best."

Elle shoots me a thumbs-up. "I like this plan."

Closing my eyes, I try to picture the words from the Void that started this whole thing. They appear in a flash. "Dark to light. Day to night. Magic to Void. I give my…" The hairs on the back of my neck tingle like it's nobody's business, making me pause. I open my eyes.

"What's wrong, Bry?" asks Knox.

I frown. "Whatever happened to Quetzali?" I ask. "We knocked her down, but she didn't go poof like the—"

At that moment, a great explosion of silver fae power rumbles across the desert, sending out a massive shockwave. The force makes me tumble backward, landing flat on my back. I glance over. That same shockwave knocked everyone over. I'm the only one who seems to be awake, though. Even worse, the Colonel isn't moving at all.

Another wave of silver power rolls over me, slamming my head against the desert floor. Pain radiates around my skull. I squeeze my eyes shut against the hurt. High-pitched ringing echoes in my ears. With a force of will, I'm somehow able to open my eyes again.

She's standing over me.

Grey robes.

Many blue fae overlapping into one person.

Evil grin.

Quetzali.

And in this moment, I have never loathed anyone more, not even Jules.

My inner animal howls with rage. *"Let's get her!"* she cries. And I agree.

Within seconds, I transform into a massive, enraged wolf with white fur and murderous intent. Leaping into the air, I land right on Quetzali, slamming her back-first onto the desert floor. My long claws sink deeply into her rib cage.

"Leave me and my loved ones alone," I say in a low growl.

"Never," says Quetzali in her many voices. She's panting, though, and looks pale. All the fighting with me and my wardens must have tired her out. Only one thing to do now.

"I'll give you a quick death," I growl. "Which is more than you would have offered me."

So I press my claws deeper into her chest, piercing her heart. Quetzali shivers for a moment, then exhales. Like the evil witch and bear shifter before her, her Shadowvin form rises up, exiting her body with a screech. Quetzali's ghostly self takes longer than the others to disappear. But at last, it vanishes as well. Quetzali is finally dead. Bile crawls up my throat. It's terrible to take any life, even someone as evil as Quetzali. Even so, it had to be done.

In my mind, my wolf speaks to me. *"We had no choice,"* she whispers. *"We had to protect those we love."*

*"I know, it's just not something I enjoy,"* I reply.

Focusing my magic, I shift forms once more. Bones pop and fur recedes as I retake my human shape. Knox, Alec, and Elle all stand nearby.

"You okay, yeah?" asks Knox.

"I am." I scan the desert. "Where's the Colonel?"

"He's still knocked out from that blast by Quetzali," says Elle. "But he's fine."

My gaze locks on Colonel Mallory. He lies on his side, breathing but unconscious. A realization appears. The Colonel's been with me through everything, especially this ceremony. He truly is my Poppa. I only hope I get the chance to tell him that, face to face.

I lift my chin. "We'll be okay." I look to Alec. "You still have your gemstones, right? You can heal the Colonel."

"Funny you should say that." Alec frowns. "Actually, I'm out of gemstones. I can't cast anything right now."

My stomach lurches. I was really hoping we'd have the Colonel's help through this last part. Or at least, Alec's gemstones.

Looks like we're on our own, though.

Knox gently touches my elbow. "Do you still want to do this?"

My mate's question echoes through every corner of my being. Without question, I know how my answer.

"Where are those discs?" I ask. "Let's finish this ceremony. Now."

*I came here to do a job and I'm not giving up. No matter what.*

# CHAPTER THIRTY-FOUR

With Quetzali and her friends out of the way, I can hand out all three discs again. The ruby one goes Alec, the silver to Elle, and finally, the golden to Knox.

Once my mate grips the last disc, a funny feeling settles into my chest. It's as if an invisible rope's tied around my waist. Around me, my wardens transform into figures of ruby, silver, and gold. That *rope feeling* grows stronger as I'm dragged across the desert, landing smack-dab in the middle of space separating the three obelisks. In the same way, my wardens get magically dragged back to their places before those tall structures.

My heartbeat goes into overdrive. *This is it.*

After everyone's in their spot, the discs transform into glowing orbs as they slowly rise up the obelisks, stopping only when the bright spheres reach the pyramids' peaks. Fresh clouds of white mist appear by my feet and start moving in a slow and clockwise whirl. Some of the tension loosens in my neck and shoulders.

The Void is back. That's good.

I scan the scene. Even better, this looks like what happened the first time we tried this ceremony, except for the poor Colonel who's still passed out nearby. The big difference? Now there are no Shad-owvin to block things.

Ending the ceremony will be good.

But it also means losing all my power.

And that might be bad.

My inner wolf lets out a sad yip. *"Will we live through this?"* she asks.

*"I'm not sure,"* I reply in my mind. *"But we'll trust our instincts and our mate. That should keep us alive."*

*Hopefully.*

Taking in a deep breath, I take a closer look at my wardens. They all appear as fidgety and worried as I feel.

"Hey, everyone," I say. "I thought I'd break the silence and give a little pep talk."

Elle's brows lift. "Are you sure?"

There's no question what my best friend means here. When it comes to pep talks, mine are always epic. And by that I mean either extremely awful or super awesome. It's about fifty-fifty split.

"Definitely," I say. "Mostly."

"Go on, Bry," says Knox. His face is so open and trusting, I can't help but continue.

I straighten my spine and prepare myself for the best speech ever. "Right here. This little patch of desert now holds everyone I truly love in the world." My voice breaks with both sadness and joy. "No matter what happens next, I want you all to know something…I'd never trade a second of my time with any of you." I focus on Elle and Alec. "You're my family." My gaze locks with Knox's ice-blue eyes. "You're my heart." I look to the Colonel. The old fae now lies on his side, eyes closed. "And you're my Poppa." I blink back tears. "I just wanted you all to know that."

There are no words, but I feel a sense of peace wash over and around us. No one gives any instructions, but at this point, we all know what position we should take. Little by little, we all raise our arms into a V shape. Soon my wardens all stand in their rightful poses, a trio of sentinels whose bodies are colored in silver, red, and gold.

We're ready.

Alec's advice replays in my mind. *Magic is about intent. To reverse Quetzali's spell, I must want that to happen.* So I picture all the magic Quetzali stole from me—that great mainline of power channeling past three hovering discs. That energy wasn't hers. It isn't even mine. It's energy that belongs to everyone. With that thought in my heart, I speak the Void's words.

"Dark to light. Day to night. Magic to Void. I give up my bounty."

Closing my eyes, I picture the final threads of magic residing within my soul. Red, silver, and gold cords dance inside the deepest parts of me. What happens next feels as natural as breathing. As I open my eyes, those threads wind out of my skin. The colored, glowing threads weave through the air until they reach my wardens.

Red for Alec.

Silver for Elle.

Golden for Knox.

Lines of power now connect me to my wardens. Like before, these many threads of magic hold us all in place. No one can move. Even so, the power stays stuck between me and my wardens. No energy connects my wardens and their obelisks.

*Yet.*

The desert turns oddly silent. Black storm clouds glower overhead. Stifling heat presses all around. We all stand in place, waiting. After taking in a deep breath, I speak the words to restart the ceremony.

"Dark to light. Day to night. Magic to Void. I give up my bounty."

All of a sudden, the cords of red power shift from my soul. With a burst of red light, fresh lines of crimson magic pour out of my skin. The connection between me and Alec flares brighter than ever before. Alec's entire body seems to shine as more red magic pours into him. Moments tick by.

Magic is moving into Alec, but that's not enough.

This ceremony won't end unless the energy goes into the obelisk as well. That's the only way the power will be stored for future ceremonies and generations.

With another flash of light, crimson power zooms off Alec's fingertips and into the obelisk behind him. I exhale. Once more, the obelisk flares with light as bolts of crimson magic wind around the tall structure.

Below me, smoke winds up from the swirling clouds around my feet. It's the Void. Three glyphs appear in quick succession.

*"Ten, nine, eight..."*

My eyes widen with shock. The first time this ceremony happened, it seemed to take forever for the countdown to reach nine. This time, things are moving at lightning speed. A small voice in the back of my head warns that it's hard to understand your instincts when events go so quickly, let alone trust them. That said, there's nothing I can do about it now.

Another glyph appears from the Void.

*"Seven."*

The power between me and Alec slows to a trickle. My heart beats at double speed. No question what this means. All my witch-warlock power is almost drained.

That's good because it's why I'm here.

It's also not-so-good because getting fully drained killed Calibur.

I really want to live.

My inner wolf whimpers in fear. *"What will happen to me?"* she asks. *"First witch-warlock power, then fairy. Once you lose all your shifter power, do I die as well?"*

*"Not if I can help it,"* I reply in my mind.

Alec wobbles from foot to foot. When he speaks, his words are slurred. "I can move now," he says slowly.

"Can't move." Knox strains against the magic holding him in place. "I'm still stuck like I was last time."

Between me and Alec, the stream of magic thins to a whisper. Then it dies out entirely. A moment later, the line between Alec and his obelisk vanishes as well. I search my soul, looking for the familiar lines of red magic within me. They're all gone. My warlock and witch powers have vanished. What happens when my shifter magic is gone? Is that the end?

"I can" —Alec's eyes roll back into his head— "move." He crumples to his knees and then falls over.

"Alec!" cries Elle. "Talk to me!"

No response.

"It's all right," says Knox. "He's breathing, just knocked out."

With a burst of light, silver threads now twist off my skin, arc across the desert, and land straight onto Elle's hand. There's no waiting this time. Right away, the magic zooms off Elle's fingertips and into the monument behind her. Within seconds, Elle's obelisk is surrounded in shifting cords of silver light.

More smoky glyphs appear.

*"Five, four."*

"We don't have much longer," I call to Knox. "I'm almost out of fae power. Shifter energy is next." With all my will, I try to move. Magic keeps me locked in place. "I can't get out of this."

"Let me try," calls Knox. His entire body trembles as he fights to move. "I can't. The magic is too strong."

The channel of power between me and Elle dies out. "I can move, guys." Her head lolls from side to side. "Let me help."

The bright lines of magic between Elle and her obelisk disappear. The structure turns dark once more. Elle crumples onto the ground, passed out. My pulse beats so fast, I can feel it in my throat.

The Void sends up another smoke-glyph.

*"Three."*

Nausea rolls through me. *I'm almost out of time.* There has to be something I can do here. Some way to stop myself from losing all magic.

*Think, Bry.*

My wolf whimpers in terror. Fear overtakes every cell in my body.

I don't have much longer.

"Trust your instincts, Bry." Knox's deep voice rumbles across the desert. "Think through the problem."

Knox's obelisk looms behind him, dark and waiting. Shifter magic dances inside me, ready to finish off the ceremony. With a flare of golden light, fresh lines of power wind between me and Knox.

"*Two.*"

And in this moment, I learn something. There's a sort of calmness and clarity to the end of your life. For so long, I've hedged and waited. I've thought that maybe Knox and I could write our own fairy tale life template, but I didn't believe that could happen. I thought magic wanted us to be apart. Everything was a matter of fate or someone else's power. I didn't believe in myself.

No, I didn't believe in us.

That changes now. I'm going after this with all my faith and heart. After all, love is the greatest magic there is. Knox is right. With love, we can create any story we want.

With everything inside me, I focus on the problem. A solution appears.

"Alec and Elle could move right before they collapsed," I say. "If we try to reach each other at the same time, maybe we can break the connection with the obelisk before…" I can't make myself say the words *before I die.*

"Let's do it. On my mark. Ready, set, now!"

A final glyph appears before me.

"*One.*"

Howling with rage, fear, and faith, I twist against the magic that holds me. I struggle.

Writhe.

Fight with everything inside me.

And I break free.

Across the desert, Knox snaps free from the cords of golden magic around him. He races toward me across the sands. I'm not sure when it happened, but I started running to him as well. We meet halfway in an embrace.

I'm alive.

A blast of golden light surrounds us, then everything goes dark.

# CHAPTER THIRTY-FIVE

When my eyes open, I'm lying on my back. The sky is clear blue again. Heat from the desert sand burns along my limbs. A figure in white looms above me.

The Void.

"Where am I?" Every inch of me feels drained. I can't remember ever being this thirsty. "Am I dead?"

"Far from it," says the Void in his booming voice.

My inner wolf perks up. "I'm alive, too!" She prances about in a happy circle. Seeing her so well makes me think of everyone else I love. Worry zings through my nervous system. I look to the Void. "What about my family?"

"Your wardens and father are all fine."

The Void leans in closer. "By the way, you and your mate took back a lot of shifter magic. No one has ever done that before. You'll be the most powerful mated pair of your kind."

"Is that a bad thing?" I shake my head. "Because I don't think I could handle more magical bad stuff right now."

"I'm unsure." The Void stands upright again and stares out to the horizon. "We shall wait and see."

*Wait and see? Really?*

"Please don't take this the wrong way, but as a magical ally, you aren't all that helpful sometimes."

His all-black eyes narrow at me. "It goes with being immortal and not being able to reincarnate, unlike some people."

My mouth falls open. "Hey, did you just make a joke?"

"Why, yes. I think I did." The Void bows slightly at the waist. "Until the next time you are reborn."

"Until then."

"I officially declare the ceremony over." With that, the Void disappears.

For a moment, I can only stare at the spot where the Void once stood. "You really need to work on your interpersonal skills, my friend."

Low groans sound nearby. Worry ricochets through my nervous system. My family! I rise, finding the Colonel standing a few yards away, hands on his hips, a cigar clenched in his teeth. Elle, Alec, and Knox all lay nearby, knocked out but breathing.

"You." I point at the Colonel's nose. "You were passed out."

"I'm a quick healer. All of us dragon shifters are." He flips the cigar to the other side of his mouth with his tongue and grins. "And guess what? Since you called me Poppa and all, I'll now heal our little family for you, too."

I set my fists on my hips in a pose of mock-annoyance. "You were eavesdropping?"

"Absolutely."

"Good. Let's heal our family, Poppa."

"We should help Elle first. I think she's worse off than the rest."

"If you think—"

But there isn't time to finish my thought. With a great rumble, the pyramids lower back into the ground. Shifting across the sands, they retake their former spots on the Giza Plateau. Next, the bubble of magic reappears as it starts to constrict around us. As the shimmering sphere speeds closer, it leaves behind modern Egypt in its wake. Tourists return to the darkened sands. Tents reappear. The noises of human voices and dance music fill the air. A red haze of magic fills the air once again. This time, it's accompanied by the unmistakable gurgle of water, as well as the outline of someone I hadn't expected.

Knox's ex-girlfriend, Ty.

I'd thought I'd seen her in the Cairo crowds, but I wasn't one hundred percent certain. Now, there's no question about it. Ty appears in all her yellow-gowned glory. She leans over Knox's body. I round on her, ready to confront her at last.

At that moment, the bubble disappears entirely. A burst of blindingly bright red light surrounds us all. The gurgle of flowing water fills the air once more.

Ty is casting another spell.

The next thing I know, we're all sitting in the back of the Escalade, awake and refreshed.

All of us, that is, except Knox.

My inner wolf growls with rage. *"Ty took him,"* she howls. *"Can we bite her face off now?"*

*"No, you can't. But I love you for wanting to."* What can I say? Almost losing my wolf has made me learn to appreciate her, even when she does want to bite someone's face off.

Alec is the first to speak. "What the hell happened?"

"I'll give you the quick summary." I count off the news on my fingers. "We recharged magic, I'm alive, and Knox's ex-girlfriend showed up. The good news is that it looks like she cast healing spells on you both. The bad news is that she took Knox with her and poofed out of here."

"That witch?" asks Elle. "I'll kill her."

"No, she healed you and Alec, remember?" I lean against the leather seats. Air conditioning never felt so good. "I don't think she means to hurt us or Knox. In fact, I think she's trying to help him."

"If she wanted to help him," says Alec, "Ty could have set Knox down in this car with the rest of us."

"No, Bryar Rose is right." The Colonel gives me a sly look. "I'll transport you to wherever *Knox* may be."

I smile, noticing how the Colonel had finally called Knox by his right name. "That's perfect."

"Besides, I think we both know what Ty is really up to." He bobs his eyebrows. "When do you want to go?"

And maybe I am becoming more like my crafty fae poppa, but yes, I think we are in agreement on what's truly going with Ty.

"How about now?"

"Whatever you wish, sugar."

"Thank you, Poppa," I say.

And I mean it.

# CHAPTER THIRTY-SIX

A few moments later, I've got a weird sinking feeling. Why? The Colonel's magic is transporting me to see Knox. Alec and Elle aren't along for the ride, though. Not that they didn't want to come along. Even so, I insisted on visiting my mate alone.

I have a theory about Ty, and to see if I'm right, I need to talk to her alone.

Soon, the Colonel's transport spell drops me off at the very spot where Knox is. In this case, it's his castle, the one where Ty is living. I can tell because I find myself standing inside a bedroom made of gray rock. Threadbare tapestries of wolves hang on the walls. A random fountain sits in one corner. And Ty is here as well. She sits on the edge of a large four-poster bed, wearing the same yellow gown she did a few moments ago in Egypt.

But Ty isn't what holds my attention. Atop the mattress, there lies Knox, passed out and pale.

I stand by the doorway, waiting. "I'm here, Ty."

Ty is across the room. She doesn't look up when she hears me speak. "I'd expect nothing else," she says. "I'm not going to hurt him."

"I got that part. You brought him here to heal him, didn't you?"

"That's right."

"So go on. I'll wait." Closing my eyes, I search for my inner animal. She's pacing an angry line inside my soul.

*"Our mate is sick,"* she growls. *"And you're letting that witch tend to him? There are other healers around, you know."*

*"But she's here and doing a fine job, isn't she?"* I ask. My wolf doesn't reply to that, which I take to mean that she agrees. Whatever else you can say about Ty, she's a very talented witch.

And I have my suspicions about why Knox is really sick in the first place.

Across the room, Ty raises her fist. Even from a distance, there's no missing the giant ruby that gleams through her fingers. Ty lifts her arm and speaks in a loud voice. "With this spell, I release you from my curse. From now on, you may stand beside your mate without pain."

Inside my soul, my wolf growls with rage. *"She cursed our mate? Let's tear her face off!"*

"*No*," I say in my mind. *"She cured our mate. That's what important."*

My wolf pauses and narrows her eyes. *"Our mate always suspected it was Ty who cast the spell on him to make him ill. He was right all along."*

*"Yes,"* I reply. *"He absolutely was."*

As Ty keeps her hand held high, the gemstone in her fist brightens. Beams of crimson peek out through Ty's fingers. *Magic.* For a moment, the red light becomes blindingly bright. After that, it disappears. Instead of the stone, Ty now holds a vial of red fluid in her hand. Miniscule points of brightness appear inside the liquid.

"Is the spell cast?" I ask.

"That's right."

"Now you need him to drink that, don't you?" I ask.

Ty shoots me a quick glance over her shoulder. She opens her mouth as if to speak, but closes it just as quickly. In the end, she only nods and offers me the small vial.

I step over, take the vial, and kneel by Knox's side. He's still unconscious, so it takes a while for him to drink the vial. I can only pour a few drops on his lips at a time. He swallows them slowly. Perhaps an hour goes by this way. Once the last sip is down Knox's throat, a thin layer of red mist encompasses his body. Tiny beams of crimson light leak out from his pores. The curse is disappearing. The red light dies out and Knox sighs with relief. Still kneeling beside him, I run my fingers through his silky black hair.

"Your curse made Knox sick when I was around," I say to Ty. "You took his energy."

Ty steps away. "You've every reason to hate me."

"That depends." I glance at her over my shoulder. "Why did you do it?"

Ty stares down at her hands for a long moment. "Reggie told me who you were. Magic reborn. You were going to die on the autumn equinox. I didn't want Knox to get hurt, so I tried to help. I thought if he saw that being around you made him sick, then he'd break up with you."

"And the fact that you wanted him to date you?" I ask.

"That was just me wishing that my life was different, that's all. It was all wrong of me. I'm sorry."

I keep brushing my fingers through Knox's hair. We're shifters; touch is always important. I shoot Ty a knowing look. "So, what was all this really about? What have you been hiding from in here?"

Ty exhales a long breath. "I hate my fairy tale life template." She stares longingly at the fish fountain set into the wall.

The one she conjured.

Because this is one sorceress who's obsessed with the ocean.

And with that, I know exactly who Ty really is.

"All this fish stuff. You're the sea witch from *The Little Mermaid*, aren't you?"

"You guessed it." Ty shakes her head. "That's my nightmare."

"How did Knox get mixed up in all this?"

Ty huffs out a long breath. "It doesn't matter."

I stand up and look her straight on. "I think it does."

Ty paces a line across the bedroom floor before pausing. "Knox and I used to hunt Denarii. For me, it was a good way to make money. Plus Knox was a great client. He always paid on time, and Denarii are easy to kill once you know how. Knox and I were pals, you know? Like work buddies."

"I understand."

"So, we went on this one gig, and that's where I met two men that changed my life. One was Reggie. The other was Triton."

"Like King Triton?"

"The same. Lives in the Red Sea. He's a merman and a ruler of his people. Smoking hot." Ty fans herself at the memory. "Like on fire. We met when I was swimming one night. The guy is a total player, but I thought to myself: *Ty, all you do is work. Why not have some fun and kiss a fish guy?* So I did. Triton invited me to see him again, and when I did? He was there with another woman already." She rolls her eyes. "So dumb of me."

"You didn't know you were a Little Mermaid life template?"

"I didn't think about it much, one way or another. Fairy tale life templates are for Magicorum who take part in society, not rogues like me and Knox. But after Triton? I'll be honest. I freaked the hell out. This is like the worst life template to be stuck in." She taps her chest with her fingers. "I'll spend my life sulking at the bottom of the ocean with eels for friends."

There's a rickety wooden bench on the other side of the room. Crossing the chamber, I sit down on one end and motion for Ty to sit on the other. This isn't the kind of conversation to have standing up. Or while sitting on your boyfriend's mattress, for that matter.

Ty worries her thumbnail with her teeth for a moment. Then she sits down beside me. "After I caught Triton with the *other mermaid*." Ty makes little quotation marks with her fingers when she says *other mermaid*. "That's when I met Reggie. Or rather, that's when Knox and I caught Reggie. Now, most people can't understand most of what Reggie says, but I get him. He said I was Beauty, not a Sea Witch." She taps her forehead with her fingers. "That's when the crazy idea started that I was Knox's Beauty and he was my Beast. It just got worse from there. Then Reggie told me you were doomed, I put Knox under a curse, and here we are."

"Look, Ty—"

"You don't need to lecture me. I know I acted like a total ass."

I slide closer to her on the bench. "That wasn't what I was about to say at all. I almost lost Knox because I didn't have enough faith in us." I set my hand above my heart. "Love is the greatest fairy tale. With it, you can make anything come true. I know it sounds sappy, but it's true."

Ty tilts her head. "Why are you being so nice to me?"

"Because I've been where you are now. Make your own fairy tale life template, Ty. Find Triton. See where it goes."

Ty looks away, her eyes glistening with tears. "I'll think about it." She stands up, walks across the room, and pauses by the door. "You can have Knox back now," she says. "He's always been yours."

With that, she steps out of the room.

Ty doesn't need to say another word. I know what she'll do next—pack up and move on. For a long minute, I stare at the empty doorway, wondering if I'll ever see her again. It may be strange to feel this way, but I certainly hope I do.

In fact, I'm so wound up in my thoughts that I don't even notice that Knox has awoken. When I become aware of him again, I find Knox lying on his side, looking over at me, and smiling. "How's your wolf?" he asks.

I know the reason for his question, too. It wasn't guaranteed that my wolf would make it through everything that happened at the pyramids. "She's fine, thanks to you."

Inside my soul, my wolf yips with glee. *"Our mate is so wonderful to ask about me!"*

*"That he is,"* I reply in my mind.

Knox narrows his eyes. "And what about the other magic that was inside you?"

"My witch and fae powers are gone. Somehow, when we broke the connection with the obelisk, we got ourselves a ton of shifter power. So there's that."

My inner wolf perks up at this statement. *"I never liked the other magic in here anyway,"* she sniffs. *"All those red and silver strings of power taking up space and getting in the way. Shifter magic, that's the best."*

*"You were always the strongest of my powers,"* I say to her in my mind. *"You fought that lockbox of Colonel Mallory's like nobody's business."*

Inside my soul, my wolf prances in a happy circle. *"Yes, that's right. Shifter power is supreme."*

"A ton of shifter power?" asks Knox. His smile widens. "Why do I think there's more to this story?"

"The Void says that when we become formal mates, we'll have more shifter power than anyone before."

"I like the sound of that." Knox pats the space on the bed beside him. "Come over here. I want to hold you and talk about where our story goes next."

My heart lightens. "You're pretty amazing, you know that?"

"Yeah." He winks. "I am."

And it's the wink that pushes me over the edge. I race over to the bed and slip under the covers. Knox quickly wraps me up in his arms, warmth, and love.

After all, I am one lucky werewolf.

# CHAPTER THIRTY-SEVEN
## ONE WEEK LATER

8 a.m.

I wait in the reception room of West Lake Prep. Students stream around me, heading into one of the three doors to the schools. No one really notices Knox and me as we hang out in a corner. Not that they should, really. Everything that happened at the pyramids was hidden by magic. The Colonel was the only outsider who saw, and he says we should keep everything a big secret until the fae wars are over. Which is fine with me. I'm in no rush to be known as the first fountain of magic in five thousand years.

Nope, I've got other priorities. Like going back to school. Today is my first day back after all our adventures. I can't wait.

Inside my soul, my wolf yips and prances with joy. "*School! School! We'll be with our mate in the Wolf's Den.*" Now that I'm officially part of the shifter school, my wolf has become a major supporter of West Lake Prep. Plus, I'm happy to report she hasn't commented on biting a single fae today. I take that as serious progress.

Knox stands behind me, his arms encircling my waist. Elle and Alec have yet to arrive, and we've decided to meet up before going into our respective doors. To kill some time, I whip out my cell and send a quick text.

*MyOwnBry: You up?*
*WaterGirl: It's late afternoon in Norway, so yes.*
*MyOwnBry: Norway? Not the Red Sea?*
*WaterGirl: Drop it. I am never seeing Triton again. I'm in Norway on a job. Troll trouble.*
*MyOwnBry: Europe. Figures they'd have troll trouble there.*
*WaterGirl: You'd be surprised. You've got a major infestation in Central New York. But those guys have kept to themselves lately, so no one calls me in. What's up?*
*MyOwnBry: I'm back at school today and I was wondering… were you the one who blocked me from passing through any of the doors at West Lake Prep?*
*WaterGirl: Just believe in yourself, Bry.*

With that, Ty switches her app status to "not available." If I didn't know better, I'd take that annoying non-answer as downright rude. But with Ty? This is actually her way of trying to be helpful.

That said, it's still an annoying non-answer. Worry corkscrews up my spine. I've been trying to sneak into West Lake Prep again to test out the doors, but it hasn't happened yet. Last time I tried to walk through, it was a total disaster. Now, I'm about to try it again in front of the whole student body.

*Please, let me walk through the doors this time.* I slip the cell into my pocket. Behind me, Knox nuzzles my ear. "How's Ty?"

Point of fact: two weeks ago, if anyone said that I'd be texting Ty as an actual buddy of mine, I'd have said they were nutso. But Ty and I have been in pretty close contact ever since she healed Knox. Funny how things work out.

"Hey," I say slowly. "Were you snooping?"

"You whisper the words while you type, Bry." *Which is true.*

I chuckle. "I need to stop doing that."

"Nah. It's cute."

"And Ty is fine. I was asking her about the doors being blocked here. She said to believe in myself. Any idea what that means?"

Knox shrugs. "It's her version of a pep talk." He warily eyes the door to the Wolf's Den. "But does it mean you can walk through the door today? No idea."

"That's what I thought, too."

Knox is quiet for a moment. "Did Ty go see Triton?"

"Nope."

"She's so stubborn."

More students stream through the main door from the outside. I notice a familiar pair of blonde heads in the mix. My heart lightens. "Elle and Alec are here," I say.

"Good," says Knox. "Let's do this."

Elle spots us right away and waves. Trouble is, she's surrounded by a pack of fae *fans*. There really is no other word for it. Now that I know my best friend is the warden of shifter magic, I get why all the other fairies are so drawn to her—Elle carries an extra level of power no one else can match, and power is attractive. My best friend tries to push her way through the crowd, but her fans just close in more tightly around her.

I cup my hand by my mouth. "Don't worry about it, Elle." Lifting my arm, I mime my fingers walking toward the fae door. "Go in now. We'll talk later." Since I'm only a shifter these days, it's not an option for me to pass through to Elle's school. Even so, I don't worry about her studying with the fae anymore. If anything, she's safer in the Silver Galleries than anywhere else in the city.

"See you!" Elle nods, grins, and makes a beeline for the fae door. Her fairy fanboys and girls stay close by the entire time, including her biggest fan, Alec.

I shake my head. "That's a gift."

"What?" asks Knox.

"Check out how Alec follows Elle through the crowd. If LeCharme goes out of business for some reason, Alec could make a good bodyguard."

"Yeah, that guy is full of surprises."

Once Elle has passed through the fae door, Alec makes his way over to us. "Morning, Bry." He then turns to Knox. "And to you, Fur Boy."

"Morning, Preppy McLoser," says Knox. "Elle get in all right?"

"Just fine," answers Alec. "I better get going myself, too. You two okay on your own?"

Knox sniffs. "I've been walking through doors all by myself for a long time."

Alec pinches Knox's cheek. "My little ray of sunshine, as always."

Knox swats Alec's hand away. "Take off already." Alec winks, sashays across the reception chamber, and passes through the door into the Crimson Keep.

With Elle and Alec gone, Knox links his fingers with mine. Hand in hand, Knox and I cross the main hall and step up to the open door to the Wolf's Den. There, we pause. My heart decides that now is a great time to pound so hard, it might break free from my chest. Knox gives my palm a gentle squeeze. "You ready for this, Bry?"

"As I'll ever be."

Walking in sync, we step toward the threshold…

And then pass right through the doors to the Wolf's Den. It's a moment that's all things wonderful. The true fulfillment of my lifelong dream to be a real teenager at a real high school. I could cheer, I'm so happy. Knox wraps me in a big hug. "I'm so proud of you, Bry."

"I'm proud of us." I quickly slip my cell phone out of my pocket and check my messaging app. Sure enough, Ty now shows as "available to chat."

*MyOwnBry: I believed in myself and walked through.*

*WaterGirl: Good for you! Anything is possible when you believe in yourself.*

*MyOwnBry: I get that, but I still want to know…Were you behind the original spell?*

*WaterGirl: Yeah, that was totally me. I blocked you from getting through the three doors. I'd already cast that curse on Knox to make*

*him sick when he was around you. I figured that when you couldn't
go to the same school, then he'd really come running back to me. Not
my best plan. Sorry.*

*MyOwnBry: Hey, we've moved past that. Just wondering.*

*WaterGirl: I've got some heads to bash in. Give Knox my best.*

*MyOwnBry: Will do.*

After slipping my cell back into my pocket, I check out the
Wolf's Den for the first time. Inside, the space is all leather chairs,
oak walls, and funky modern art. About sixty wolves are hanging
out and chatting, waiting for first bell. We'll have homeroom here
and then go off to classes. No sooner do we step inside, than Abe
and Hollywood spot us.

"My queen!" cries Abe. He rushes over with a big grin on his
face. "You made it."

"That I did." A memory appears. Abe and Hollywood protested
when I couldn't pass through the doors before. "Thanks for the sit-
in, by the way. Knox and I appreciate the support."

"No problem," says Abe. "We've got each other's backs."

Hollywood saunters up as well. "Hey, guys. I can't believe you're
both really here. We're so excited to have you around."

"Thanks," says Knox. "Means a lot." At those words, both Abe
and Hollywood almost visibly swell with pride and delight. It's
amazing to be part of a larger group. I can almost see the lines of
connection forming between us.

Hollywood tosses his amazing mane of golden hair. "See you at
lunch?"

"Yeah," says Knox.

After that, Abe and Hollywood take off. Knox watches them go
with one of his classic thinking looks on his face. In this one, Knox
tilts his head slightly and nods. "So," says Knox at length. "What
do you think?"

The words tumble from my lips before I can stop them. "I'm
ready to be part of a pack." The moment that statement leaves my
mouth, I want to rewind time and take it all back.

My inner animal hops to attention. *"Our mate isn't ready to be part of a pack. You'll scare him."*

*"You're right,"* I counter in my head. *"I need to do some damage control."*

"Look," I say quickly. "I didn't mean that—"

"Yeah, you did. And you know what?" Knox scans the room slowly. "I'm ready, too. Nothing like facing death to make you appreciate pack life. It'll be a great adventure, yeah?"

I go up on tiptoe and press a kiss to Knox's cheek. "Yeah." And this time, I mean that word to the bottom of my soul. In my heart, I know another chapter of our story is about to be written, and I can't wait to see how it turns out.

*The End*

*The Adventure Continues in SLIPPERS AND THIEVES,*
*Book 3 in the Fairy Tales of the Magicorum Series*

# ACKNOWLEDGEMENTS

I have a shit-ton of people to thank for helping me on the adventure of writing this book. First, there is the amazing team at Inscribe Digital. Thank you, Kelly Peterson, Katy Beehler, Ana Szaky, Larry Norton, Kimberly Lane, and Allison Davis. You are nothing less than stellar.

Next, there's the wonderful team at Monster House Books. Arely Zimmermann, where would I be without you? It makes me nauseous to even think about it. And GIE, thank you so much for your insight, gentle prodding, and teamwork. I'm so thankful to have you as Editor In Chief at MHB.

And I can never forget my readers and bloggers. You guys are the best, end of story. Thank you for every high five, sweet idea, and suggested change. I value each and every one!

Most importantly, heartfelt thanks to my husband and son. Your patience and support mean everything. I love you both with all my heart and soul.

# Collected Works
# Christina Bauer

ANGELBOUND ORIGINS SERIES
  .5 Duty Bound
  1. Angelbound
  1.5 Betrothed
  2. Scala
  3. Acca
  4. Thrax
  5. The Dark Lands
  6. Armageddon

ANGELBOUND OFFSPRING SERIES
  1. Maxon
  2. Portia
  3. Zinnia
  4. Kaps
  5. Huntress

ANGELBOUND WORLDS
  1. Walker

DIMENSION DRIFT WORLDS
  1. Dimension Drift
  2. Umbra

DIMENSION DRIFT
  1. Alien Minds
  2. ECHO Academy
  3. Drift Warrior

*Christina Bauer*

FAIRY TALES OF THE MAGICORUM SERIES
- 1. Wolves And Roses
  - 1.5 Moonlight And Midtown
- 2. Shifters And Glyphs
  - 2.5 Fairies And Frosting
- 3. Slippers And Thieves

**Christina Bauer** thinks that fantasy books are like bacon: they just make life better. All of which is why she writes romance novels that feature demons, dragons, wizards, witches, elves, elementals, and a bunch of random stuff that she brainstorms while riding the Boston T. Oh, and she includes lots of humor and kick-ass chicks, too. Christina lives in Newton, Massachusetts, with her husband, son, and semi-insane golden retriever, Ruby.